Praise for *The Institute Revie*

"Really good stories, really well made. You don't get better than that."
Ali Smith

"The short-story form is alive and kicking in here; so many distinctive new voices . . ."
Tessa Hadley

"There's breathtaking energy in these stories, and skilful pulling of the rug from beneath your feet."
Adam Marek

"These stories are vivid, sharp and surprising, which is why I will not be sharing them with my publisher. There's enough competition already."
Joe Dunthorne

"Once again, *MIR* proves itself as a hotbed of fresh and original talent, laden with intriguing voices that urge you to turn the page. An annual treat for short-story lovers."
Courttia Newland

"The short-story form is in safe hands. These writers — unafraid to take risks, to experiment, to push at structure — will go some way towards ensuring the future of the short work of fiction. This is a reason to celebrate."
Niall Griffiths

"Brilliant new writing, real, intimate and gripping."
Maggie Gee

About the Title

The first Mechanics' Institute in London was founded in 1823 by George Birkbeck. "Mechanics" then meant skilled artisans, and the purpose of the Institute was to instruct them in the principles behind their craft. The Institute became Birkbeck College, part of London University, in 1920 but still maintains one foot in the academy and one in the outside world.

THE MECHANICS' INSTITUTE REVIEW
ISSUE 14 AUTUMN 2017

Short Stories

The
Mechanics'
Institute Review

The Mechanics' Institute Review
Issue 14 Autumn 2017

The Mechanics' Institute Review is published by MA Creative
Writing, Department of English and Humanities, School of Arts,
Birkbeck, Malet Street, Bloomsbury, London WC1E 7HX

ISBN 978-0-9575833-8-2

Contents © the individual Authors, 2017
"Mrs Mackie Waits", by Jenn Ashworth, was developed from a much
shorter, first-person piece commissioned by New Writing North for
the BBC Radio 3 Free Thinking Festival 2017.

Project Director: Julia Bell

Editorial Team: Sarah Alexander, Kate Ellis, Caroline Macaulay,
Paola Moretti, Tamara Pollock, Miranda Roszkowski, Rebecca
Rouillard and Katherine Vik

The Editorial Team would like to thank Julia Bell and Sue Tyley
for making this project possible. Also Shaniqua Harris, Seema
Jamil-O'Neill and Tom Norton, for their editorial support, and
our readers: SJ Bradley, Charlotte Forfieh, Judy Hepburn, Seema
Jamil-O'Neill, Xavier Leret, Fran Lock, Tom Norton, Penelope
Overton, Clive Parish, Amy St Johnston and Laura Windley.

This project is supported using public funding by Arts Council
England.

For further copies or information, please contact Amy Flaye,
MA Creative Writing, Department of English and Humanities, School
of Arts, Birkbeck, Malet Street, Bloomsbury, London, WC1E 7HX.
Tel: 020 3073 8372. Email: a.flaye@bbk.ac.uk

Website: http://mironline.org/

Printed and bound by TJ International, Trecerus Industrial
Estate, Padstow, Cornwall PL28 8RW

Cover design and typesetting by Raffaele Teo

The Mechanics' Institute Review is typeset in Book Antiqua

Supported using public funding by
ARTS COUNCIL
ENGLAND

Table of Contents

Foreword: The Mechanics
JULIA BELL

Teaching creative writing is a pain in the ass. You bust a gut all year to put on thoughtful classes, to challenge, coax, and inspire the best work, you read reams and reams and reams of work in progress and then a few flinty, original pieces which give you hope, only to be met by student feedback that goes something like: *While I enjoyed the professors' knowledge of the subject and PowerPoint skills and their enthusiasm for the work of Virginia Woolf, I would still like the step-by-step guide to the mechanics of writing a novel.*

Patiently, you explain that the step-by-step guide to writing a novel doesn't exist. That every single book on the market shilling advice on how to write the best thriller/erotica/YA/whatever will be sharing with you some common advice repackaged for the genre but it won't transform the pile of pages in front of you into a successful novel. Nor will a creative writing course.

Of course there are means of gaming the system a little. If you really do have your eye on commerce, some basic bits of advice about plotting and character development are worth heeding, but this is no substitute for fluent prose, the original concept, for the adventure of the imagination. These gifts are unteachable, like the voice of the individual writer – essentially it's the writer against the page trying to communicate something. For hours, days, a lifetime. If you don't have that appetite for the work, chances are the pages will stay just that, the half a novel in the bottom drawer.

I say loudly and often that I can't teach boring people to be interesting but I can teach interesting people how to think and therefore how to write better. Teaching writing at MA level is Socratic – dialogic – a discursive process, a push pull between student and tutor, between reader and writer, where the story is always a negotiation – a creation – between the words on the page and what the reader brings to the story. The reader is not a passive actor in the process. Readers bring lives, language, prejudice, experience to the page; reading is an active process. This is where the teaching really happens, when the writers learn to read themselves, and the work of others, with close attention. A good writer and a good reader are two sides of the same coin.

This is a lesson that the short-story writer understands from the get-go. Because short stories rarely make bestsellers, the corruption of commerce is removed from the equation, meaning that short-story writers, much like poets, are creating for the sake of the art. For the adventure of prose, to see what can be made. To push an idea, a thought, a character, a voice.

The reader is presented with a series of knotty snapshots, pieces which can read your day, to be pondered on the commute, or as you take the dog for a walk. Good short stories are little problems, as Chekhov, the early master of the form, knew. He said in a letter to a friend that the job of a good story was not to try and answer a problem because that created didactic prose, but to "present the problem correctly".

Short stories shine a focused light in a way that the novel, full of words and characters, cannot. Brevity concentrates the attention. We know that the time to read one will be maybe fifteen, twenty minutes; the time to write one might have been, draft by draft, more than twenty years. In a culture with increasingly short attention spans the practice of writing a story, like a poem, can mean a deep engagement with language, but also with character – small gestures take on epic significance when under the pressure of the temporal.

Perhaps there is one mechanical piece of advice that applies here: show, don't tell. A good story is a showing – much like any other art form; a presentation of an idea shaped through language which should leave both the reader and writer with an experience. For the time-pressed reader stories offer a small window through which to think differently about the world; they take you out of the room of your mind. They focus attention away from all the distraction. In short – words matter and everything counts.

We have a long commitment to publishing short fiction at Birkbeck. *The Mechanics' Institute Review* has been in print since 2004 – every year a group of volunteer editors selects about twenty of the best stories to emerge from students who have done our courses. This volume, our fourteenth, marks a big change and is the first to be open to submissions from across the country and funded by Arts Council England.

What has emerged over the long process of reading the submissions is a unique snapshot of new writing in the UK, with subjects ranging from Iranian immigrants in London, coming out in Carmarthenshire and reunions in Gloucester, to celebrity culture, trial by social media, child sexual abuse, MGM and the refugee crisis.

Our pool of editors reflects the diverse profile of the student body: because we teach in the evenings, to allow people to remain at work while they study, we attract applications to our writing programmes from students not just from London, but from the Midlands and across the South-East and from all social backgrounds and ethnicities.

Stories have a way of tapping into collective narratives much more deftly than novels. A state-of-the-nation novel is a matter of luck and timing; a story, thanks to its brevity, can be dispatched quickly after the event. And short-story writers, because of their attention to nuance and language, can give us rich and pithy insights into the state we're in.

We hold a torch for the form, seeing it not just as a proving ground for new voices, but as a literary achievement in and of itself. This year's anthology is stuffed full of these small, but perfectly formed achievements. They are offered to you, reader, carefully edited and considered, and we hope that whatever you make of them, you will, as Raymond Carver said, be moved a little from the place you were in before you started reading.

Julia Bell
Course Director, MA Creative Writing
Birkbeck

Zoo Quest to Aberystwyth

ANNA POOK

I n the summer of 1964, we begin our search for a rare and sought-after specimen: the Gwilym Girl, a creature commonly known in this part of the world as the biggest troublemaker in Ceredigion. Her home is the seaside resort of Aberystwyth, a town Victorians branded "the Biarritz of Wales". Locals are somewhat baffled by the comparison as they are unfamiliar with the Basque city – the furthest most of them have been is the fifty-mile trip to Carmarthen. Indeed, the inhabitants of Ceredigion believe the untamed beauty of their county is impossible to beat. The same could be said of their wildlife, for the Gwilym Girl can be found here in Aberystwyth and nowhere else in the world.

Wales is often mistaken for a region of England but is very much its own nation and, as you can see here, has the distinctive shape of a discarded apple core.

The people are of Celtic origin and their native language, known here as Cymraeg, *differs enormously from English. The Welsh for "country", for example, is* gwlad.

The name of our house is misleading. Above the front door, written in curved letters of black paint flecked with gold, is the word *Tangnefedd*. It means "serenity" in our mother tongue. If my sisters and I are playing up, Mam's tongue is as sharp as the tapered prong of a pitchfork.

We live in one of the tall red-brick town houses strung along the Buarth. Our neighbour to the right is Father Geraint from Our Lady of the Angels and Saint Augustine. Mam says it's good the Father's got his eye on us because with three girls between the ages of twelve and fifteen, God knows she could do with a hand. Bethan says Father Geraint should keep his hands where we can see them.

Titch and I share the back bedroom, Bethan occupies the attic – a whole floor to herself. It's unfair but she's the eldest. If her hormones swing in our favour, she lets Titch and me climb onto the dressing table in the corner of her room so we can share a packet of Player's she pinched off Dad and blow smoke rings out the window. If we squint, we can just make out a glistening strip of the Irish Sea in the distance.

Aber, *of course, means "mouth" – as in "mouth of the river" – and the town itself is located a few miles north of where the River Rheidol and River Ystwyth converge. Not content with two rivers, Aberystwyth also features two bays that meet at the foot of the castle, the ruins of which are all that remain of a structure built to protect the town from invasion.*

In the summer we receive a mass influx from the Midlands – fat Brummies pulling their kids along the beach on the backs of ponies whose bellies hang so low they almost scrape the sand. They're not the only ones sweating out the weekend to keep the tourists happy. Each one of us girls has got a job. Bethan is a caddie on the golf course up on the cliffs, I man the ice-cream hut, and Titch works on the pier wiping seagull shit off the amusements for one and six an hour.

By the time we get home, our skin is tight from the sea salt and our legs are swollen and heavy with heat. We tip ourselves upside down on the sofa, the backs of our legs pressed flat against the wall, waiting for our knees to tingle with the glorious first rush of blood.

Like many Welsh towns on the country's periphery, Aberystwyth is poorly served by public transport and connections to major cities, such as Swansea or Cardiff, are few and far between. The funicular railway, however, which operates daily from the north end of the promenade, runs perfectly well but can only carry its passengers 237 metres up the cliff to the top of Constitution Hill.

At the peak of lambing season, Dad caves in to our pleas and takes us up to the farm. At 5 a.m. the town is silent, the sky awash with stars – perforations made by saints when they ascended to heaven. At least that's what Mam believes. Dad doesn't comment. The farm is his church, the sheep his disciples. They follow him around, feeding from the sack of cake he drags backwards through the fields.

We squat down in the straw and survey the ewes in labour. When the lambs have been licked clean by their mothers and left out in the sun, we grab them by their tails so Dad can brand each one with raddle. The red pigment slashed across their backs in inch-thick strips will help protect them from predators.

The chores done, we like to sprint down to the footpath that runs along the cliff, stand above the town with our arms stretched out wide and scream into the wind.

With over fifty public houses and almost as many churches, it isn't hard to see what occupies the inhabitants of Aberystwyth. The community is a God-fearing one that spends Saturday nights out drinking, and the following mornings at Mass.

We have to sit through the entire service: the psalms, the prayers, the sermons and the hymns. Dad gets off lightly and escapes to his flock at the farm.

If Auntie Iris gets up to the front, we know it's time for Psalm 23: *The Lord Is My Shepherd*. Part of the six-strong choir, she stands at the altar in her Sunday best, waiting for her solo. Her voice is as smooth as gravel and out of tune. When she belts out "He makes me lie down in green pastures", we bite the inside of our cheeks to stop ourselves from laughing.

Bethan has lain down in green pastures, on the far end of the beach, underneath the pier, and the shady side of the prom. There was a rumour going round school that she slept with Dai Jones behind the bike sheds.

"Give me some credit," she says. "It wasn't Dai. It was his cousin, Rhodri."

Mass over, Mam abandons us in the front pew to go and lead the Sunday school. She enjoys teaching other people's kids how to abide by the rules of the Bible. We can hear the swish of her over-starched suit as she marches up the aisle.

At confession, Titch owns up to Bethan's sins in the hope she will be forgiven by proxy.

The men here belong to one of two distinct tribes: the Towns or the Gowns – those who work with their hands, and those who work with their minds.

Bethan's not one to discriminate. She's courted boys from all walks of life, much as it pains our mother. The Towns have got "strong arms and soft lips", but the Gowns are more sophisticated. They drink brandy on the rocks, and earn enough money to treat Bethan to bottles of Babycham that she likes sipping through a straw.

The two tribes live side by side in relative harmony but rarely interact. Typical of indigenous tribes the world over, they tend to find safety in numbers and keep to their own kind.

Bethan tries her hardest to get expelled from school by the Sisters of the Holy Ghost. One day they find a tattered copy of *Lady Chatterley's Lover* tucked in the crook of her arm. But instead of sending her home with a note and a hundred Hail Marys, they phone Mam and ask her to pick up the book in person.

Me and Titch can hear Mam screaming from halfway down the Buarth as we're walking home from school.

"You are far too young to be reading such filth," says Mam. "I've a good mind to throw D. H. Lawrence on the fire."

"I'd much rather live like Constance," says Bethan, holding back tears, "than be stuck in a convent in Llanbadarn bloody Fawr!"

And with that she storms up to her room.

"Don't you dare come back down," Mam shouts after her, "till you can learn to behave like a proper young lady. For the life of me, I don't know why you turned out the way you did. Anyone would think you'd been brought up by heathens."

The Gwilym Girl is somewhat of an exception. Despite her reputation as a decidedly social animal, she often withdraws from her immediate community in moments of crisis.

Bethan stays in her room for what seems like days. We find Lady Chatterley stuffed between H and K in Mam's volumes of the *Encyclopaedia Britannica*.

With a little persuasion, however, she can still be tempted to come out of hiding.

Since he bought the TV we've been begging Dad to install it in the front room. Mam won't hear a word of it, says the room must be kept "for best" – funerals, visits from the bank manager, occasions that require Dad to wear a well-pressed suit and pull Auntie Den's crystal out from the depths of the cupboard.

So we congregate in the dining room. Dad sits in his usual place at the head of the table and has to turn one hundred and eighty degrees to get a good look at the TV looming large behind him. We sit and wait for the tiny white dot at its centre to spread to the corners of the screen.

"Bethan! Come on, *cariad*, or you'll miss it!"

Dad's wasting his breath. Bethan couldn't care less about *Zoo Quest*. She feels sorry for the animals dragged back to London Zoo in wooden crates from places with exotic names like Paraguay, Java or Borneo. She thinks it's cruel. Although she'd happily travel in a wooden crate for months if it meant a one-way trip to London.

It's not the capture that excites me and Titch, though, it's the expedition. Last week, David Attenborough was searching for life in the dusty plains of the Chaco.

"Meg, go and get her will you," says Mam. "I need a hand with the supper."

"But it's about to start!"

Mam juts her chin forward and inhales through her nose. She's not in the mood to negotiate.

As I sprint up the stairs two at a time, I hear the discordant notes of the *Zoo Quest* theme tune. I could murder Bethan.

Not one to miss out, Titch follows me up to the attic. We find Bethan lying on her back, struggling to fasten the top button of her jeans.

"Well, don't just stand there goggling. Get over here and help me."

We take a hand each and pull Bethan to her feet. She breathes in until the bars of her ribcage poke out beneath her bra, which is new and trimmed with black lace.

"God," she says, pinching her waist, "I'm getting fat. These fitted me perfectly before."

Titch shoots me a look. I know what she's thinking. There's only one reason girls get fat round here and Bethan told us exactly what happens to them. They get sent away till their bellies have stopped swelling and their newborn has been snatched from their arms and swaddled in a blanket, an empty name tag wrapped around its wrist.

"Whatever it is you've got planned, could you forget about it just this once and come downstairs instead?" I ask.

"No chance. I'm meeting Dai on the prom in half an hour."

"But Mam's cooking fish," says Titch. "At least stay for supper."

It's a long shot. As Mam says, Bethan's been breaching Christian tradition since birth. It would take a miracle for her to give up the warm-blooded fun of a Friday night to stay at home with us and wait for the wet slap of a cod fillet hitting her plate.

"Where's your sense of adventure?" says Bethan as she climbs out her window and onto the roof. We hold our breath while she shimmies down the drainpipe. She doesn't realise she's got enough adventure for the lot of us.

Dragging our feet downstairs, we pray our parents won't notice Bethan's gone till the credits of *Zoo Quest* start rolling. We don't want to miss the moment the animal's brought home from the wilderness, when it's spoon-fed condensed milk by a stranger.

"So," says Dad, as soon as we return to the dining room. "Where is she?"

If he weren't prematurely bald, never knowing the whereabouts of his firstborn child would have made all his hair fall out. Dad can divine water with nothing but a twig but even within the small confines of Tangnefedd, he can't keep track of his eldest daughter.

"She's not in her room," says Titch, staring at the floor.

"I swear that girl will be the end of me," Dad says to himself. "Gwen! She's only gone and done a runner."

Mam serves the fish cold, the greens overcooked, the potatoes pounded into submission. We hear her curse when she burns the tips of her fingers with the matches as she leans down to light the fire. "*Diafol.*"

The devil has entered the room.

When dinner is over, we clear up the plates in silence and daren't ask Mam for the bottle of pop that sits abandoned on the cold stone floor of the pantry. It'll be stowed away and forgotten about till next week, the bubbles flat, the lime syrup so sweet it's sour.

Dad paces the corridor, muttering under his breath. We've seen him do the same thing when one of his flock goes missing. He is forever counting his animals, logging how many have survived the night when the foxes are on the prowl.

"Well I can't just stand here and wait till she turns up," he says, grabbing his coat. "Come on, girls, we're going to look for her."

In order to observe the Gwilym Girl in her natural habitat, it is preferable to wait until nightfall. She is, after all, a nocturnal creature. This means making do with the most reliable mode of transport Aberystwyth has to offer.

The Hillman Minx is ancient and smells like the inside of the sheep pen. Dad doesn't bother with the ignition – he lifts the handbrake and lets gravity work its magic till we're halfway down the hill. We're grateful as it means we can coast past our neighbours unnoticed. Father Geraint's curtains twitch but it might just be the wind.

Dad slows at every corner to scan the side streets, searching for Bethan amongst the shadows. As we drive past the park at Plascrug, we recognise some of the boys sitting on the swings and slump further down in our seats.

"Dad, don't you think it'd be better to split up and look for her?" I ask, as we park at the far end of the prom. Some of Bethan's friends are skulking round the bandstand. If they see Dad, they'll scarper for sure and then we'll never find her.

"What and lose all three of you?"

"I'll keep an eye on Titch, I promise. This way we can look round the prom and you could drive over to Penparcau. She hangs around there sometimes with Liz Edwards and her brothers."

Dad rubs the length of his nose with his index finger. He's thinking.

"On one condition," he says. "You have to promise to meet me back by the bandstand at half past ten. And girls, not one word of this to your mother."

Soon after we arrive at the promenade, we are fortunate enough to encounter Dai Jones, a local Town, huddled on a bench with two other members of his tribe. As is the custom in many corners of the world, we introduce ourselves by way of the cigarette.

"Dai Edwyn Jones, I swear to God, if you don't tell me where Bethan is, I'm going straight round to your mam's house to tell her what you got up to with Kathryn Davies on the top of Penglais Hill."

Dai is sitting with Fuzzy and Merv on the bench by the bandstand, throwing pebbles at a lone seagull and taking swigs from a glass bottle of cider foaming with shared spit.

"Do you believe everything you're told?" he says, wiping his slick mouth with the back of his hand. "That was nothing but a stupid rumour. And I thought you were supposed to be the intelligent one. We only went dancing at the King's Hall."

I kick the bench, scuffing my white plimsoll. "You bloody liar. I saw Kathryn's knees the next day at school. You don't get burns like that from doing the twist. Right, come on, Titch. You remember Mrs Jones, don't you? Lives at Number 57. It's the white door I believe."

"All right, Meg," he says. "You win."

After a few minutes of fervent negotiation, Dai reluctantly agrees to be our guide. Turning a blind eye to the dilapidated state of his motorbike, we accept his invitation to climb on board. His driving is hazardous to say the least, so it's with a considerable amount of relief that we arrive at our destination.

"For crying out loud, Titch, don't be such a chicken. Just sneak in behind me. No one cares about kids being in there anyway. Bethan's been coming here for years. And Dai's sister? She's not even into double figures. I promise you, you've got absolutely nothing to worry about."

"Well are you coming in or not?" asks Dai. "By the time you two make your minds up, she'll have already left."

Once safely inside the public house, we are astonished to discover that it is packed to the rafters with revellers. The room in which we are standing is one of two used for entertaining. The second, larger room at the back of the building is filled with live music, young men with guitars strapped over their shoulders singing American hits imported to these shores on the long waves of the wireless. It is easy to determine their identity as they are dressed in the traditional attire of the Gown tribe: loon jeans, worn high on the hip, that come in a spectacular array of colours.

This must be what Bethan means when she talks about the "in-crowd". Everyone's kissed Dai Jones, but this lot are a different breed: older, the top buttons of their shirts undone. Who wants boys from the grammar school when there are college men in town?

"Aren't we supposed to be looking for Bethan?" says Titch, pulling on the hem of my dress.

"One dance," I say. "Just one."

In keeping with local tradition, males and females interact with the commencement of a "slow", or in other words, a popular low-tempo song – the male protectively wrapping his arms around the female, who in response rests her head upon his shoulder.

Two rounds of Babycham later, we're anybody's and never want to leave. But Bethan is still missing and we can't face meeting Dad at the bandstand empty-handed.

Despite enjoying the spectacle of this mating ritual, we begin to suspect that we have been led on something of a wild-goose chase. Dai and his friends have long since disappeared and we are no closer to finding the Gwilym Girl. Feeling somewhat disheartened, we resume our search and head to another Aberystwyth attraction.

"Missed a bit," I say to Titch. A white smear of seagull mess is splattered on the mini Ferris wheel.

"Give over," she says, not taking her eyes off the blot on her landscape. She loathes her job but it's taking all of her willpower not to grab a damp cloth from the staff room and clean that machine till it shines.

I drag Titch into the dark cavern of the amusement arcade, hoping Bethan will be hiding in the back, draped across the jukebox singing her heart out to Billy J. Kramer like she does at home when he comes on the radio. She turns it up the loudest it will go and parades around the house in her undies. Poor Dad doesn't know where to look.

But the pier is dead. Even the old ladies who sit unblinking by the fruit machines have gone home for the night.

"Yes!" says Titch, picking up sixpence from the dirty carpet. "Free go."

She rushes over to the penny arcades, presses her face against the glass cabinet that houses her favourite exhibit: a small ceramic elephant whose paint has started to chip. The instant Titch drops her sixpence into the slot, the elephant shudders to life and rattles along the miniature track anti-clockwise, a pink cardboard box strapped to its back. When the elephant finally comes to a halt, the tiny gift slides down the delivery chute and into Titch's hands.

"Should have kept the sixpence," I say when we see what she got for her money.

"I think it's pretty," she says, fingering the red plastic beads of the bracelet.

"Come on," I say. "She's not here."

Back outside, it takes a minute for our eyes to adjust to the lights, the string of bulbs burning above our heads, guiding us along the boardwalk and back up towards the prom.

And it is here, a mere fifty yards in front of us, that we see a makeshift camp: items of clothing lying damp on the rocks, a few empty bottles of cider, and the embers of a dying fire. As we edge closer, we can see what looks like a pair of jeans that are coming apart at the seams. Rather like a snake shedding its skin, it appears the Gwilym Girl has removed her outermost layer.

Titch spots her first, fanny-high in the sea, thrusting her arms into the water, trying to catch mackerel with her hands the way Dad showed us. My first thought is how happy Mam would be that her daughter's finally taken a leaf out of God's book and is trying to feed the five thousand. But at the rate Bethan's going she'll be lucky to feed the three boys cheering her on from the shoreline. Finally she grasps one between her fingers and tosses it, still flipping, onto the beach.

"See," she shouts, holding her arms up in triumph. "I bloody told you I could do it!"

Approaching the Gwilym Girl is not as easy as one might expect, surrounded as she is by a group of young Towns. Their presence serves not only for her own amusement, but also as a deterrent for unwanted company. We undoubtedly fit into the latter category so decide the most desirable option is to wait for her to come to us. Backing slowly away from the incoming tide, we take cover under a wooden jetty and lie belly down on the sand.

As Bethan wades out of the water, we realise she's wearing nothing but her knickers.

"As God is my witness," says Titch, "I'm glad Dad's not here to see this."

A few seconds after this sighting takes place, we hear a high-pitched sound coming from directly behind us.

We'd recognise PC Montgomery's voice anywhere. He must be at least forty but he sounds like Dai before his voice broke and he was forced to pull out of the Eisteddfod. Montgomery stands on the sea-wall steps with a whistle in his hand, a street lamp picking out the new stripe sewn onto his uniform. He's cautioned Bethan so many times, he's been promoted to sergeant.

"If I were you, Miss Gwilym," he says, "I'd get dressed this instant and come with me. Your only alternative is to run home to your mother. And to be honest with you, by the look on her face an hour ago, I think you'd be better off at the station."

The official designation for this intruder is Officer of the Ceredigion Constabulary – a rather archaic tribe known locally for their dogged pursuit of parking misdemeanours. To us, however, he is really nothing more than a poacher.

Bethan and her friends don't hear him at first, too busy falling about laughing as she fails to pull her jeans up over wet skin.

"Go and find Dad," I whisper to Titch.

"Why me?" she hisses. "None of this was my idea."

"You're small."

"So?"

"No one will notice you."

"And do what exactly?" she says, pushing her hair away from her face with her forearm. "I'm sick and tired of cleaning up other people's mess."

"This isn't a bloody summer job, Titch. This is Bethan we're talking about. She'd do it for you."

"No, she wouldn't. Because unlike her, I wouldn't be half naked on the beach at night with nothing to show for it but an epileptic fish!"

Titch is right. The closest she's ever come to rebellion is adding a teaspoon of sugar to her bowl of Special K behind Mam's back.

"We've got to do something," I say. "Mam will never let us out the house if Bethan ends up behind bars."

"At least we'd be allowed in the attic."

Before we can agree upon a satisfactory plan of action, the shrill pitch of the policeman's whistle awakens the seagulls roosting under the pier and finally arrests the Gwilym Girl's attention. In what can only be described as a deplorable lack of gallantry, the Towns leave her to fend for herself.

Bethan struggles to her feet. Her shoulders are pushed back but she's hugging her body because, despite her bravado, she's embarrassed by the small size of her breasts.

Montgomery gains on her but the tide's coming in. With each step his boots get swallowed by the sand. Titch uses her bracelet as a replacement rosary, muttering to herself, praying either for deliverance or a lift home from Dad.

"Admit it, Bethan," says Montgomery, taking off his helmet and attempting to get his breath back. "You've got nowhere to go but the water. Come with me now and I'll tell your mam you've finally learnt to cooperate."

It is in moments like these that we wonder if the expedition will ever reach a successful conclusion. Capturing her now feels almost cruel and it is evident from her behaviour that the Gwilym Girl never had any intention of being apprehended. Unable to advance, she retreats rapidly into the sea until her entire body is submerged. To our dismay, it is a long time before she resurfaces. When she does so, we realise she has swum a remarkable distance under water. Having reached the end of the jetty, she uses her forearms to haul herself up and onto the wooden structure. It is yet another astonishing display of the Gwilym Girl's determination to survive.

We should have known. Bethan would never go quietly. It's not her style. Not unless she's sneaking into the Red Lion for a lock-in. By the time we've scrambled out from under the jetty, it's too late. All we can do is watch as our sister streaks along the seafront, in and out the spotlights of the street lamps.

Now we see her.

Now we don't.

"I didn't mean what I said," says Titch, unable to tear her eyes away from the prom. "You know, about the attic."

"I know," I say. "I know."

At Gloucester Docks

ALAN BEARD

There was Bill, Bob, Marble, Mary, Mandy, twat, Gran and Bill2. There was Susan, Sam's mum, alternately quiet – drifting – and gabbling. Mary2 and Hannah in matching wigs. Different colours, same cut and style. Babies, toddlers, children. An adolescent girl in fawn jumper and frown – Sam's sister, I learnt later. But most of all there was Janice, Julie and Ted. With me.

They arrived in fleets of cars – well a minibus, motorbike and sidecar, back of a van. Converging from round about, within a twenty-mile radius, but some, like me and Janice, from further.

We stayed with Julie and Ted, my step-parents, and walked down the following day. I said the place had changed. It all looked smaller, grimy. They'd built on every available bit of green, sawn down an oak, closed the Youth Club. "Site of my first conquest." I pointed it out to Janice. "Did you have to fight her?" my current girlfriend said back.

"Nothing for the kids," said Ted and I nodded him on, my job this weekend. Nodding everyone on, like Ned Flanders in my green jumper.

We walked down under Gloucester skies through the what now seemed crap shopping centre which I remember new – real Mum took me to see it being opened by Leslie Crowther. It was now chipped and disfigured, empty shops and all but empty pedestrianised roads down to the docks, our destination. Ted pointed in the general direction of where Fred West had lived, like he always did. Claimed to know him vaguely, or at least men who worked with him. It was great to see them, both in their mid-seventies, walk at a clip, Julie in her black flat shoes, black flat hat. I told her she'd stepped out of the fifties and she was pleased with that. Her era.

We all met in the yards outside the tall, many-windowed warehouses converted into cafés and museums, offices and residences. I thought they looked like early attempts at brick tower blocks, but with sloping roofs. Boats bobbed at our side, ropes sagged and tightened. We filled a seating area, and each way down the wide towpath. There was greeting and patting of shoulders and cheek kissing and bowing down to see children and babies in pushchairs, and remarking on the blustery weather and the wellness of people. A swaddled, squalling baby was passed around; I didn't pass it on to Janice. Mary2 and Julie reached into large bags and brought out Marmite crisps, liquorice allsorts, chocolate brazils and handed them round. Favourites were fought over. I saved the last blue speckled jelly for Janice; I knew she liked them.

I wasn't sure she'd come. We'd only been together about six months, and she wasn't used to big family gatherings. "Treat it like a parents' evening," I'd said. We'd bonded over an imminent Ofsted inspection, shared our limited ideas, stayed late, later. Between lesson planning we noted how the school gates had become a rendezvous for single parents, and agreed the latest couple, a tall black widower, and white, dreadlocked single mum, were made for each other. I stopped at hers that night.

"Why are the Gas losing?" Ted was perplexed, but answered himself. "Down to the manager farting about with selection." Lack of consistency is Ted's number one complaint. About football, politics, weather.

In front of the bow of a ship, rigging clacking against masts, our crowd compared babies to their parents. "Looks like her father, with your nose." How children had grown, as if they'd expected them to remain the same height; the school day, the arrangements for sitters, the looking for jobs. Julie pointed to jumper girl. "She's looking for work, isn't she, Susan." "Yes," Susan said, "but she's too idle. Like it at school." Now I saw the resemblance to Sam. "I tricked her once. She asked for a note for PE and I wrote – sealed in an envelope to give to him – 'Nothing wrong with her, except bone-idle-itis.'"

"You got to watch them."

"You've got to keep your eye out."

"Don't be too harsh on her, though, Sue. What she's been through. All of you have."

A rich mesh of Gloucester accents was around me, not heard for a while. People wanted to talk about Sam, but waited for Susan to say it, his name.

We – some of us – filed into a building, others went for a boat trip, or to the military museum; the waterways museum was shut for refurbishment. Ted said we'd missed the Tall Ships festival. One or two went off to the Mariners Chapel. Apparently Ivor Gurney was the organist there. I should read him, always meant to. I learned from a plaque inside the building that rats were not the main cause of the Black Death. I read about the Sharpness canal, the import of raw materials, timber and cocoa beans, and wines, spirits and corn. Salt from Worcestershire going the other way. The match factory, England's Glory, had been nearby, and there were Union Jacks on all the souvenirs.

We looked around the advertisement collection, those of us who made it that far, the posters and tin signs, and had tea and scones in front of a TV that relayed old ads, that some remembered, including me. Gran, Bill2, Mum – Julie – sang *Now Hands That Do Dishes*. Gibbs SR. Player's Please.

Finally talk of Sam, dead too soon, as we waited for his mum to arrive. Not cancer either, something strange and twisty took him in the night. He just didn't wake up. Almost a year ago. Nobody's over it, can't get him summarised in our heads. We all had an adulthood for him imagined. He sang, he was sure to have conquered the charts, or got to *X Factor* at least. I knew him only a little, so I wasn't sure.

Susan did respond when Julie expressed sympathy when she arrived, put her gloved hand on her arm, got her to sit next to her.

"The ambulance ride went on and on, like it was more than just two miles. Just held his hand, sure he would wake up. They were pumping him, machines were bleeping." She put out her hand and looked at it. "Affected all of us. Bastard Rob couldn't take it and left me and Phoebe to cope. And she's eating obsessively, practising ballet moves and stuffing her mouth. Then vomiting in the toilet." Phoebe – the one in the jumper – for some reason I thought of falling leaves. The colour of her hair. She was outside somewhere among the boats.

"I know, I know, Susan, life's so short and no one knows what it all means."

"She should appreciate it, 'specially now her brother's gone."

"Whatever you do, don't take up religion." Ted turned to me. Though he married my stepmother, and therefore is not my dad, he likes to play the part. "Nothing worse."

Susan was speaking again and everyone leaned in to hear. "When he was a kid he was little for his age, and he used to hide under the table from his dad, scuttle about behind furniture, dive down entries, with that dead straight hair of his."

"Like a helmet."

"Like a helmet."

"But he was always singing."

"Knew the latest stuff. Could have joined a boy band."

Julie held Susan's shoulder. "He was beautiful. Eyes like Dean Martin."

"In another life he would have been Dean Martin." Ted tried to help.

"In another life I'd like to have been Elizabeth the First – you know, from history," said Gran to Mary2 and Julie who weren't listening, still giving Susan their attention. "She was marvellous. A woman in a man's world."

There's cancer – breast, prostate, bone, lung – dementia, blood clotting, sticky valves and fingers missing. There's deafness and strokes and people bent flat, or nearly, their spines curling. But Sam was too fresh, too young, too unknown yet.

In came Hugh – twat – late to the party as usual, to interrupt the talk of illness and condolence. Late because of deals that had to be set up. Late because of the future. With Hugh everything's in the future. He was a semi-professional footballer, had one good run in the league and used the money he hadn't wasted on a burglar alarm business. Talks in Mockney, comes from Birmingham. Married Denise, the beauty of the family (Phoebe is lined up next for that role), who later left him. Left us with him, too. Never see Denise any more, but this one though keeps turning up. Been everywhere, done everything. Scored in cup finals (actually third division play-offs). Survived car crashes. Designed kitchens. He kissed Julie, pinched her arm, threw his arm round me. "And is this teacherly beauty yours?" he asked of Janice.

"Who's that?" she asked later, and I tried to explain.

"He feeds off everyone," I said. "You've got to watch him."

We met up again outside at the prearranged time, the afternoon growing long, the whole bunch of us out in the eddying breeze which rippled the water and the sails about. I caught a glimpse of the cathedral tower, the four intricate turrets pointing up to heaven. We settled at the slatted wood tables in cagoules and coats or collars turned up. Snapping of Tupperware for those who'd brought their own, releasing hammy air or else moony cheese. We ate more too, some biscuits and leftovers, getting set up for the last of the day and night ahead.

"Went with her on holiday. Never again – didn't like the heat, the sand, the pebbles, the sea, walking, sitting or eating out. 'Get some eggs and bacon and let's have a fry-up,' she used to say."

"She got married in the Dominican Republic, got blessed in Merthyr Tydfil."

"Got that misunderstood face on 'er again, 'er has." Pointing at Phoebe, going down towards the Severn, appearing between the bows and sterns of yachts and longboats.

Hugh promised to have a word, and went off, wiping his hands down the back of his trousers as he went.

We chucked the remains of our sandwiches and cakes and the stale bread we'd brought for the purpose to ducks that came up. I'm cajoled to take a kid or three to see the model boats. My job made me a suitable candidate apparently. So I marshalled them, half the age of the kids I teach, and went to where the pot-bellied and mostly bearded members of the club stood staring down at their boxy controls. They controlled little liners, speedboats cornering, yachts listing, galleons with detailed masts and even a submarine out on – or under – the water.

Coming back a kid I didn't recognise tried to clamber up the side of a boat towering above him. Was he one of ours? I didn't know who'd left me in charge. I looked around for help. There was Phoebe, emerging from steps up to the dock. "Help," I asked her. "Can you keep an eye on those three? I'll just rescue him."

"Sure, Uncle Dave." She remembered me. She didn't seem so surly close up. I wasn't her uncle, was nobody's uncle; could never quite work out the connection to her side of the family. Will have to ask Ted.

Later we headed for the 'Spoons pub for a grand finish. Some had to go, to liberate dogs from kitchens, to relieve babysitters – and we hugged and shouted across roads at the departing. A boy suffered his grandmother's embrace, her stick in the air behind his head; he helped her into the car.

Even though we didn't always talk of him, Sam was there in the beat of the music, in the swallows of beer and the swirling movement as one went to the bar, one to the toilet, and people swapped seats to gain the ear of one or present an ear to another.

There was cancer, dementia, blood clotting, toes and eyes missing. There were dentures and deafness and people bent flat, but here in the docks, in the taken-over pub, things seemed to join up as our voices intertwined. Others in the pub fell silent, listened in, moved off. We were the kings of the show, slopping pints back and forth, interrupting pool games to get by. Sons and daughters of cousins calling me "Uncle". Ted filled me in on names and ages and connections. Even though he only married into the family, in fact not even that, he had become its keeper, its archivist. One older kid, pushed forward, asked for advice on becoming a teacher, where to apply, what to study.

"Don't," I said. "You'd be daft to."

Younger ones to my right, sat away from me, discussed best-looking men: George Clooney, no, David Tennant, although one stuck out for Kanye West. What they might do with them.

A man I didn't know who knew me bent to my face. He said he was going back to work soon. His breath was tight in him, he creaked, his face had patches of brown.

"The last doctor said there was no chance of it."

"I suppose they know best."

"Do they?" He nodded once. "Well I'm going to ask. What's the good of staying home?"

His face looked like it expected rebuff. Julie on my left, ash-grey hair like trapped smoke, wanted my attention so I turned to her.

"Jan-ice. Janice. Old name really." She nodded over at my girlfriend. "No chance of grandkids."

It wasn't a question, we'd already had this conversation last night at hers. We're both nearly fifty.

"Is she – finally – the one?"

"Maybe."

Julie from the fifties, glove wearer. We – me and Dad – called her posh. She's just finicky. Sharp with it. Her eyes are metal/iron-coloured, always focused. Photos showed she was a bit like my real mum. Now if I imagine Mum older, it would be like this. Like Julie.

Dad, on the other hand, was nothing like Ted. Had hair for a start, wavy and full. He was a mellow, quiet man. Kept to the sidelines, didn't like to interfere. A slide guitar sound when I think of him, real Dad, some warm slide guitar.

Sam's mum circled the day again and again. "No one knows why. He just didn't get up. Some thought meningitis, some heart attack, some some brain thing, but it seems he just stopped wanting to breathe. Or knowing how."

I was trapped for a long while halfway along a banquette, three or four people either side of me, table in my gut, and couldn't really disturb them too soon, so I sat there twenty minutes or more bursting for a pee.

"Hardly see the son, in a submarine somewhere, occasionally in some Scottish loch."

"Half of Minchinhampton have seen my boobs."

"No chocolate, no fags, no drink, what's the point?"

"It was the night we usually had sausages."

There were sticking points, places where the years and the deeds in those years didn't mesh for everyone. Those going to vote Brexit, those not. Voices were raised. Not much, but a row was in the air. Ted would usually interject, completely off subject: last night's X Factor, birds in his garden. On a walk once he'd seen a tree full of goldfinches.

This time it was, "He's different from most cocker spaniels you know, in general they have terrible temperaments, but not Max."

He said when the kids grow up and leave you, the dogs remain and still want you. I wondered if he was talking about me, or generally.

Now was the time to move, a further distraction, by making them shift their legs, knees all pointing one way to let me by.

There was some crying when I caught them out the back. Beyond a wall where I'd gone to smoke (I'd told Julie and Ted I'd quit, and I all but had). Phoebe with Hugh, his hands all over her, pushing up that autumn jumper. How he disappeared when he saw me, like a stage magician he was gone, leaving her in disarray. Adjusting jumper, bra. Above her the cathedral tower was softly lit.

I said, "Stupid girl, out in the open like that." The abandonment I'd witnessed quickened me, a feeling I thought I'd lost. She came over, shaky, and clutched me. Sobbed in, on my chest. I could feel her tremble, and put my arm around.

"I'm sorry, Uncle Dave. Don't tell anyone. Not Mum, not now." She wasn't the defiant teenager, she was small and defenceless. Puzzled. Her brother had died.

I looked down at her ear, cheek, hair, swirls of dark I wanted to touch, could legitimately kiss her head, feeling her body lean into mine.

I moved back. "Don't worry. Nothing's going to happen," I said. "Forget it. Come back in."

We took a slow walk down the wide grey-brick towpath. She dried her eyes on the back of her hands. The rigging went mad in a sudden wind, water chopped like a miniature sea in the basin, and her hair was flung back from her face. I wanted to ask about Sam, seeing the similarity, whether she missed him, but my mouth dried.

I sat her with Marble and other young mothers, cut free from children, sat around a ring of laid-down mobiles, and a litter of glasses. I went off to stand with Janice for a while.

She'd been hearing about my growing up from Gran she said. "Not your gran though?"

"No, my aunt really, Mum's sister, but a lot older. Usual tearaway stuff?"

"No, reading Enid Blyton and playing with pegs."

"The pegs were soldiers," I protested, "army of them crossing the kitchen, matchboxes tanks, table legs trees and pillars to hide behind."

"Yes," Janice said. "You have mentioned it before."

She was keeping sober to drive us and others in a borrowed car home. I asked her how she found us, watching us get drunk.

"Turn left, and straight on till morning."

Would she come again – it's an annual thing – I try to make it every year. Not always Gloucester docks though. That was Ted's idea, the outsider we trust. Got a thing about ships and rigging.

"And slavery?"

"You haven't read the guide," I said. "All this was well after slavery."

Someone had put a load of sixties tunes on the jukebox and the gang pushed back chairs to create space in which to shimmy. Julie clapped along from her seat, but Ted got up and got his thumbs moving. I wondered about asking Susan to get up with me, but I'm not a dancer. Neither is Janice. We watched the women kick legs high, and grab at blokes going by. Marble and Hannah got Phoebe up to dance between them, and shouted the songs into each other's faces – "My one and only baby" – and mirrored moves back and forth. The cancer wig was passed around and posed with, snaps taken, and ended up slightly skewed on Ted's bald head, blond strands curled beneath each cheekbone. "Up the Gas," he said in order to smile for another mobile phone photo.

The Cut
CHARLIE FISH

Feda admired his father. Gurion was a woodworker and joiner of a skill unmatched this side of Ngoro. He could make a plank straight and level enough to satisfy the gods themselves – the elder women demanded it to show their dominion over nature – but he was happiest, as now, making peasant furniture that respected the grain of the wood.

The backrest of the chair he was working on now was a single slice from the base of a red sapele tree, its concentric age lines drawing the eye hypnotically into its centre. Gurion had sheltered and smoked the piece for over a month to dry without cracking. In the humidity of the jungle, it was said, the driest things were Gurion's wood and Mother mRoto's humour.

Gurion knelt, bracing the slice of wood between his legs, cutting precise notches into one edge with a chisel and hammer, being careful to apply force in just the right direction. Feda had learned his father's trade and hoped one day to be as skilled a craftsman as he, but for now his job was to gather the shavings for kindling.

This was to be Feda's ritual chair. It would be complete by sundown, but it would not really be finished until it had been splashed with Feda's blood. Gurion shifted his weight into a squat. Feda knew that his father found it uncomfortable to kneel for too long since having undergone the ritual of manhood himself, many monsoons ago.

Once, he had asked his father exactly what the ritual involved. Gurion had slipped with his plane and ruined a fine headboard. In all the cursing and scolding, Feda's question had been lost, but he knew better than to ask again. Feda knew only that the ritual involved a cut, a cut in his most private and sensitive part, and it was bound up in his head with desire, pain, fear, belonging, becoming.

Having completed the joint, Gurion mixed a paste of sap and crushed leaves until it had the texture of semen. Feda filled his head with the carnal smell. He became self-conscious of his crotch.

Feda asked his father, "Does it hurt for long?"

A gobbet of the paste Gurion was using to glue the joint fell to the ground. "The pain is the price of manhood. You'll be given to a wife. You'll make a home. You'll have a profession."

Feda wondered what it felt like to be a man. He knew there were secrets between grown men and women, and he was curious to see how this cut would help him discover them.

At that moment Mother mPene appeared. "Gurion!" she reprimanded. "Why are you still working on the ritual chair? Tromo is coming tomorrow."

"I know, I know. I'll make eight more chairs."

"Make them now!"

"Tromo's chairs will not be sat in tomorrow. Feda's will. The glue needs as long as possible to set."

Tromo with his big-city clothes, his computers, his smell like a carrion flower.

"Make ten more chairs!"

"I've only planed the wood for eight."

"Make twelve more chairs!"

Gurion looked at his feet. "Yes, Mother."

mPene gave a curt nod. "Feda, walk with me."

"But I need his help," Gurion protested.

"Gurion, come to bed tonight when you're done. Don't wake me. Feda, walk."

Feda obeyed, head down. mPene held Feda's hand and led

him through the vines, past the children playing with hoops and sticks, around the big cooking pit and into her hut.

She sat Feda down and fixed him with a disquietingly benign gaze. She was silent for a long while. Feda kept his back straight and tried not to fidget.

"Tomorrow you'll become a man. Prior Lami will administer the cut."

"But why?" Feda asked, and immediately regretted it. He knew that women had their own blood rite bestowed upon them by nature, and to challenge the necessary act of balancing was churlish. But mPene was not angry.

"Your penis is a disgusting thing, young Feda, and as you age it becomes far worse. The most evil sins in your soul become concentrated upon it and manifest as scurf beneath your foreskin. Lust, anger, greed, envy, pride. By cutting these free your soul is released to allow you to take your proper place in the community, as a man serving his Mothers and his wife."

"Who will be my wife?"

"Mother mRoto's eldest granddaughter, mFana, has chosen you."

Feda's ears burned red. Mother mFana! Surely the most desirable young woman in the village. Certainly beautiful. He felt his crotch stir with excitement and was immediately ashamed.

"I feel . . . fearful."

mPene became stern. "Don't let me down, Feda, my child."

She stood and Feda took his cue to leave.

That night as Feda lay on his bed, he pressed his nails into his foreskin, trying to persuade himself that the pain would pass quickly. Then he thought of mFana's silken skin and felt himself becoming aroused. He turned to lie on his stomach, pressing his growing shame against the rattan, willing it to recede again.

The ritual the next day was performed with little ceremony. Gurion, his eyes swollen, presented Feda with his chair; the chair was carried into Prior Lami's medical tent and Feda followed feeling numb to his fate.

Lami was a skinny man with hollow eyes, skin like

biltong, and a permanently amused expression. He had been administering the ritual cuts for this village and the next for two decades. He smelled faintly of iron.

"You must be completely naked," he said, facing away from Feda and laying out his tools. He turned a moment later. "Come on, come on."

Feda took his clothes off and sat. He took comfort in the chair, knowing that his father had expended much effort and love making it for him. He looked down at his genitals. A sorry-looking slug hiding in straggly moss. At that moment he hated them and they did not feel part of him.

Lami pushed Feda's knees apart and knelt between his legs. Deftly, he tied a string tightly around the middle of Feda's penis. Feda gasped at the sudden constriction. Sweat pricked at his brow. Lami produced a tool that looked like Tromo's cigar cutter, a miniature guillotine.

Feda's penis was threaded through the device, which pushed his foreskin back so that the tip of his penis was fully visible, looking like a closed cup mushroom. There was a smart clicking sound like a hammer tapping the end of a chisel, and Feda had the sudden sensation that he had wet himself. Dismayed, he moved his hands to cover himself, but Lami batted him away.

"You're bleeding," said Lami flatly, preparing a hasty poultice. "Be still."

Feda focused and saw that where the end of his penis had once been, there was now a river of blood. He jumped out of his seat, tugging at the severed stump between his legs.

"You cut off too much! You cut off too much!"

"Idiot child!" scolded Lami. "Sit on your hands and let me stem the bleeding. You're aggravating it. Sit down!"

Feda sat, not out of obedience but because his balance felt suddenly compromised and his vision became dim – or rather, white, as if the sun shone directly in his eyes. His legs squirmed beneath him as he struggled to bear the agony in his groin, which sucked up his whole being like a black hole.

Feda was vaguely aware of Lami talking as he pulled and

pinched at the terrible wound. He forced himself to hear the words.

"Crazy child," Lami muttered, shaking his head and half grinning. "You think I'd cut too much? I've been doing this since before you were born. I cut every man in this tribe. I cut your father, just the same amount. Now, hold still."

Lami might have said more, but just then a stab of pain more severe than Feda could have imagined possible consumed his very soul. He threw his head back and uttered a soundless howl. He felt his consciousness falter, but it stubbornly remained.

"OK, all done," said Lami. "Now get up."

Feda jerked his head forward and, sweating and grinding his teeth, he glared wide-eyed at Lami's face. Had he heard correctly?

"Come on, up, up. Go to your father. I will bring the chair so you can rest a while." Lami hoisted Feda to his feet, helped him into a robe and escorted him out of the tent.

As he crossed to his father's hut, Lami at his side dragging his ritual chair, Feda cast his eyes about like a wounded dog. Could it be that all these men, casually going about their business, had each been so violently trimmed? It seemed impossible that he would ever be able to function normally again.

Upon reaching Gurion's hut he staggered to his room and sat on the proffered chair, swallowing the bile that rose in his throat when he saw the jagged trails of blood that now decorated the wood.

Lami took his leave and Gurion appeared. For a few seconds father and son locked eyes, but such was the vehemence of the unspoken words that passed between them, Gurion had to look away.

"Father!" accused Feda.

Gurion looked pained, but could not speak. He rallied, but again the words did not come. In the end, he nodded, eyes still downcast, and he left.

Feda gingerly transferred himself to his rattan bed, and then a moment later back to the chair, and then he stood and leaned his head against the wall, and then he crouched, and lay on the floor, and repeated the whole cycle again. Relief utterly eluded him. Each passing minute stretched for an hour, an hour felt like a week.

At some point Gurion brought him food, for which he had no appetite. Despite a scorching thirst he refused to drink any water. He must have slept for he woke startled by nightmares of peeing a painful spray of urine and blood.

Eventually – it might have been the next morning, although Feda had lost track of time – he was able to persuade himself that the pain was becoming a thing outside of him, a thing he could begin to put aside. He began to be able to think of other things. He toyed with the idea of leaving his room and getting something to eat.

But then he received a visitor.

mFana sashayed into his room while he was trying to dress. He put Lami's robe back on and turned to greet her. Her face was round and inviting, with a smile that could coax a blossom from a stone. Feda started saying something but his tongue became fat in his mouth.

"Feda, you're to be my husband," she said. He felt a childish love for the dimples in her cheeks. Her beaded hair and scent of shea nuts. Her body like a wood-carved sculpture. "If you're loyal, I'll repay you with a thousand kindnesses. I'll protect and defend you. I'll satisfy you and make you proud. Help me to make a home and it will be our spring of contentment."

Feda wanted to say a hundred things, but one rose above the others.

"I've been cut."

"Yes, I know. It'll take some time to heal. And then we can start our family." She rested a hand on her midriff. A flash of endearing mischief crossed her face, and she quietly closed the door to the room.

She gently pushed Feda down into his chair and stood above him. With one fluid movement she removed her camisole. Her skin was smooth as a wax leaf. Her breasts a perfect handful.

Her nipples like kola nuts.

But Feda's lustful trance was quickly overtaken by sudden alarm. He felt his penis becoming erect, and panicked, leaping to his feet. mFana laughed at him. He could feel the wound reopening and felt sick with the anticipated pain. With urgency she put her finger to her lips, dressed herself and left.

Again, the sensation of having wet himself. A crimson stain spread quickly across his robe. He whipped the robe off and stared at the blood pumping copiously out of the hole. He screamed. Loud enough to boil the river, he screamed.

He was only dimly aware of what happened next. His mind swam with disturbing visions; his body writhed constantly as if he were a snake shedding its skin. He allowed himself to be moved and manipulated without thinking to question why or who. Despite the oppressive heat, he shivered with cold. Trembled with thirst. Swam in sweat.

In brief moments of clarity he knew that he had succumbed to fever, brought on by an infection. The infection manifested in his mind as a parasitic scorpion in his lap. Several times he brushed the beast away, but the pain of its sting persisted.

At last, after some days, he woke feeling terrible, but once again present. A soothing compress rested against his forehead. Gurion sat by his bedside, holding his hand.

"Welcome back," whispered Gurion.

With his father's help, Feda was able to get out of bed to eat, wash and relieve himself. He could no longer pee standing up, he had to squat, and even then it was impossible not to get urine on his legs. He cleaned himself carefully, neglecting only the truncated stub of his penis which was still too tender to touch.

He found himself walking with shorter strides, even long after the pain had subsided. His whole stature had been somehow altered. He started helping his father with his woodworking again, lamely at first like a decrepit elder, but then increasingly with his former youthful vigour.

One day Mother mPene declared him fully recovered, and announced that he and mFana would be married that weekend.

mFana had not seen him much, having been busy harvesting coffee and qat, but with the wedding date set she became attentive, visiting him every evening and quietly watching him plane wood with Gurion. They were shy with each other.

On the morning of the wedding, there was electricity in the air. All the women of the village wore wraparound trousers of white linen, and ruched tops that accentuated the white teeth of their smiles. The men wore three-quarter shorts and diaphanous shirts in bold colours. Everyone had a dance in their step.

mFana held herself with grace and pride, frills at her sleeves and dyed feathers in her hair. Feda felt real awe at the sight of her; fear and wonder in equal measure. She was beautiful.

As was the tradition, the marital tent was designated. The people of the village stood by it in a circle, with Feda and mFana on opposite sides. Gurion and Mother mRoto led their respective offspring into the middle, nodded solemnly to each other, and entered the tent to negotiate the terms of the marriage.

The circle was quiet and still. In the centre, Feda and mFana locked eyes, but they were not permitted to touch. At first it felt uncomfortable to look so directly into a woman's eyes, but with infinitesimal gestures she coaxed him to relax.

mFana's eyes were deep and soft, full of intimacy, reassurance, perhaps even love. Feda asked those eyes a thousand questions, and the answer was singular: Trust, Feda. Trust.

Feda was stirred from his reverie by a sudden restlessness in the assembled crowd. mRoto and Gurion emerged from the tent, laughing gaily. Old Mother mRoto, her kindly face lined like windblown sand, raised a banana leaf above her head and muttered a prayer in the ancient tongue.

With the leaf she bound the couple's hands, and thus they were joined.

Immediately, the circle broke into cheers and dance. A fire was lit, food appeared, music played – djembe drums. The party would be wild and long. But Feda would not join in the revelry, for he had an important obligation to fulfil. A gentle pull on his arm from mFana told him that she was very keen to fulfil it.

She led him into the marital tent, which was empty save for a washbowl and a makeshift bed. Feda's stomach constricted. He only vaguely understood what was going to happen next, and the thought of it made him want to flee.

"Come," said mFana, sitting on the bed. "Kiss me, my husband."

Feda obliged. Their lips touched and opened. Her tongue flicked out like a snake's. Feda found himself distracted by the raucous sound of celebration just outside the tent. mFana laughed and the kiss was broken.

"Feda, husband, you are stiff as one of Gurion's planks. Come to me. Forget yourself." As she said this, she put her hand between Feda's legs. Feda knew he should submit, but he could not help squirming away.

"I don't want you to see," he said.

"Nonsense." She pulled his shorts down. She examined him, smiled tightly, and held his severed member tenderly. Feda stood stock still as if facing down a lioness. His throat was dry.

mFana removed her top and untied her wraparound trousers, letting them fall to the ground. She began touching herself, caressing her breasts. In her growing excitement she grabbed at Feda's penis.

"Ow!"

"Sorry. I'll be gentle." But she persisted, tugging at Feda until he became firm. Feda looked at his erect half-penis with bile in his throat. It was purple, lumpy-scarred and disgusting. But mFana didn't seem to notice as she guided Feda to lie on top of her and enter her.

Her eyes closed. She pressed his hips into her, and massaged her clitoris furiously. Feda's teeth gritted. He matched her rhythm, to help her reach satisfaction as quickly as possible. He tried closing his eyes, but saw a ghostly vision of his wound reopening and then had to check several times to convince himself that the moisture he felt was neither blood nor urine but mFana's natural lubrication.

She moaned; her face creased into something like an

expression of pain. Feda realised his face was similarly creased and he made a conscious effort to relax, without success. But there was something, despite the discomfort, something primal and attractive about this difficult, sweaty act. It reminded him of the one and only time he had tried smoking a cigarette – it had been revolting, yet as soon as he had finished he had been tempted to have another.

At last she climaxed and released him. He immediately sat up and inspected himself for damage. He turned away, ashamed to let mFana see his distress.

"You didn't finish," breathed mFana.

"Sorry. I'm a little sore."

"Ah, well, it's your first time." mFana sat up and hugged him. Her voice was affectionately mocking. "But you're going to have to do better next time, husband, if I'm to become pregnant."

Feda tried to take comfort in her embrace. He listened to the sounds of the party outside, and watched the flickering shadows cast against the sides of the tent by dancers in the firelight.

Married life started well. mFana was loving and considerate, and seemed pleased with Feda. He moved into her family residence, a large clay-brick house with individual bedrooms for Mother mRoto and three of her grandchildren: mFana and her younger sisters mGele and little Kampa. Feda was not used to the household's noise and bustle and welcomed the relative peace of his daily work with Gurion.

mFana became increasingly aggressive during their lovemaking until they found a reliable way of making Feda productive. When at last mFana fell pregnant, Feda wrestled with his conscience until he could no longer allow propriety to hold him back; while they rested in bed, he blurted out his ultimatum.

"If we have a son, we must not cut him."

Only after he had said it did he realise how heretical and dangerous the idea was, and yet how firmly he believed it. In the face of Mother mFana's silence he simultaneously wanted to defend his position, and undo it. The silence stretched for so long he wondered if she was pretending he had not spoken at all. But the mien of her body told otherwise.

Then she turned away from him. "I've decided," she said. "You will become a qat farmer."

"What? But I'm a woodworker and joiner like my father. That's my talent, that's what I love. I've started making my own chairs already, and Tromo says they're very fine. There's good money in that."

"You will become a qat farmer," she repeated, in a tone that invited no response.

Feda was baffled, until slowly he understood that he had been punished for rebelling against the ritual cut, even if only by thought. He was crestfallen. Sleep was elusive for him that night as his mind revisited the injustice endlessly in a self-amplifying spiral.

Thus Feda began learning a new trade. There was much to learn, and it so absorbed him at first that he was sometimes able to forget how much he missed working with wood. During this time, Feda grew closer to mFana's younger sisters, serving as a father figure although they were almost adults themselves. In the cool season little Kampa started menstruating and became Mother mKampa.

mKampa in particular seemed to admire Feda, and frequently flattered him with challenging questions about how the world worked, which he took great pride in answering in the most direct and practical way possible. She asked where the rain came from, and where it went. She asked why people valued money so much when it had no inherent usefulness. She asked what it was like to live in different parts of the world. Feda answered everything, glossing over details he wasn't sure of.

Once, when they had both wakened early and were sitting together on the terrace, she dropped her voice to ask him about the ritual cut.

"It's our way of balancing nature," he replied. "And tempering the male weakness for ego and violence."

"How can it do all that?" she said. "Anyway, you don't seem

convinced."

"It's been this way for generations."

"But what's actually cut? Ego and violence come from the heart, how can they be tempered by cutting a little finger – whether it's on your hand or between your legs?"

"A penis is more than a finger. It gathers . . ." Feda hesitated, trying to recall what Mother mPene had said about his foreskin. "Now, see. The evil thoughts of men physically gather as pus around the end of the penis. So the end of the penis is cut off."

He had tried to sound authoritative, but mKampa clearly saw through his act. "That's brutal!" she spat. "Didn't you think to protest?"

Feda blinked hard to suppress his emotion. "It's a high price to pay."

"To pay for what? My children will never suffer such degradation. I'll temper their violence and ego by teaching them, not maiming them."

Feda remained silent.

"I refuse to believe it," she said. "Show me."

Feda shook his head and stayed put, but did not dare to object. Even in her youth, this girl already had the practised and petulant authority of a Mother.

"Show me," she repeated.

"I must go now," said Feda.

He stood, but did not immediately leave. He desperately wanted to communicate how he felt: his gratitude that she too suspected the cut was an unconscionable hypocrisy; his fear that her innocent fervour would be tainted and forgotten as she grew. But how to put it into words? How to trust her?

mKampa's bright eyes shone up at him. She nodded, and Feda's heart bloomed with hope that she had understood. But in fact she had gravely misunderstood. Before Feda had a chance to react, she lifted her hands and pulled down his shorts.

"No!" he cried, but it was too late. She screwed up her face and grunted in disgust. Feda covered himself and sat, his cheeks flushing.

mKampa opened her mouth to speak, but at that moment Mother mRoto appeared on the terrace and shouted, "What are you doing?"

"Oma, he showed me his cut. I –"

"He showed you? He *showed* you?"

"She did it," Feda retorted, but this angered Mother mRoto even more. She roared, and slapped him.

"Get out of this house! Go!"

Feda ran. He beat his fist against his forehead as he headed into the jungle, squashing the dewy detritus underfoot. Reeling, he instinctively headed to Gurion's hut.

Gurion was there, as always, with his piles of wood ready to be cut and planed. He saw the tears on his son's face and instinctively knew that whatever trouble this was, it was deep. Wordlessly, he handed Feda an adze and gestured for him to sit and work the wood with him.

For the next hour, neither of them spoke as they worked side by side. Then the police came.

"Police?" said Gurion.

Feda shook his head. But they were police, two imposing women, stern and sweating in their uniform.

"Feda Agbola," said the broader of the two, "you're under arrest for adultery and fornication."

"I didn't commit adultery. I didn't even touch her."

"You must come with us."

"No. I refuse to accept the charge."

"Then get yourself a lawyer. We have a telephone at the station."

Feda looked pleadingly at his father. Gurion's mouth was slightly open, his busy hands still. When Feda's shoulders dropped, the police pulled him to his feet, and cuffed his wrists behind his back.

As they took Feda away, Gurion said only, "I love you."

For the next two days, Feda was kept in a solitary cell with almost no communication with the outside world. The cage served as an echo chamber for his shame and righteous rage.

By the time of his trial he brimmed with hatred, aimed both outwardly and in.

Thirsty and dirty, he railed at the police officer who escorted him to the court. There, he met his lawyer, a sharply dressed city Mother on a community-volunteering ticket. She asked for his story, which he told in detail although she looked summarily unconvinced. In the end, she advised him to say as little as possible.

The trial felt like a fantasy. Feda could not assimilate that the person being spoken of was himself. On one side of the courtroom sat most of the Mothers of the village, including mFana and mKampa; on the other side sat Gurion, Prior Lami and two strangers.

The prosecutor began by describing the events of the morning in question, concluding with: "Having seduced Mother mKampa, you prepared to copulate, with your wife's youngest sister no less. The act was interrupted by your wife's grandmother, but your intention was clear. You have viciously betrayed the trust placed in you by your devoted wife. What's more, you are cowardly enough to blame Mother mKampa. For such a flagrant breach of common morality you should suffer the most terminal penalty allowed by law."

The case for the defence rested on downgrading the charge from adultery and fornication to indecent exposure, which did not sit easily with Feda. Even the best possible outcome would be a gross injustice.

The cross-examination was particularly painful.

"Immediately prior to you exposing your genitals, were you having a heated debate about the legitimacy of the cut?" asked the prosecutor.

"She was –"

"Yes or no answers, please."

". . . Yes."

"Were you feeling angered and resentful about having undergone the cut?"

"No."

"So you approve of the cut?"

Feda did not answer.

"Is it true that you have in the past insisted to your wife that any sons of yours would not have the cut?"

Feda looked at the floor. "Yes."

"I put it to you that you were angry and resentful about the cut. You blamed your wife and wished to betray her out of vengeance and contempt."

"No!"

These manipulations continued, on and on, casting Feda as a lying, impulsive, conniving deviant. The spectating Mothers occasionally gasped and tutted, mFana loudest of all. Only mKampa was still, her expression inscrutable as she sat silently absorbing the proceedings. Whether she was protecting herself, or perhaps believed the prosecutor's argument that she had been exploited, Feda did not know.

The defence seemed weak in comparison, like trying to apply a sticking plaster to a shattered soul. But, after what seemed like hours, the judge accepted the defence. Feda was found innocent of adultery and fornication, but guilty of indecent exposure and breach of marital contract. The sentence was five years' imprisonment and mandated divorce. Feda would have plenty of time to reflect on his hollow victory.

The nearest prison was in the city, over a hundred miles away. His time there passed slowly. He resolved that as soon as he could think clearly he would reflect on how he had ended up here and what he could learn. But these revelations never came; each day was a paler imitation of the last, until his will atrophied. Five years seemed like a lifetime.

Worse than prison was returning home. He had changed. His small community seemed alien and hostile to him now. Even the things that used to comfort him felt empty. No one was uncivil to him, and he was allowed to work wood with Gurion again, yet he keenly felt his status as an outcast.

Not long after Feda's return, his son had his fifth birthday. Feda was not invited to see him. So when Tromo came to buy

Gurion and Feda's furniture, Feda asked for a ride to the city.

In the truck he asked Tromo if he had been cut.

"Of course," said Tromo. "Every man is cut."

Feda sighed disconsolately. "Then the city is not far enough for me. Take me to the port."

Eight years later, Prior Lami administered to Feda's son the ritual cut.

Mug

KEITH JARRETT

When the lady at the jobcentre – Janice her name is – when she asks you why you failed to turn up on the seventeenth day of your shiny new post in the daycentre, do not tell her – she won't believe you – do not tell her it was because you drank out of the wrong mug, which is the actual truth.

Say something non-committal or pithy. Either your friend died or another of your grandfathers – but remember to count them all first, all of your dead and dying grandparents, so she doesn't catch you out – or you overslept on the antidepressants. Practise in the mirror so your face gives away nothing. Janice will roll her eyes and say I don't know what to do with you, Mr Jarrett, this is the third placement I've found you.

This isn't the third "placement" she's found you, but that's of no consequence, so you won't split hairs over the particulars of the job you found yourself in, which lasted less than three weeks. And anyway, you like being called Mr Jarrett the way she says it, like you're a real man, not a boy waiting in the corridor outside the head teacher's office.

By way of bridging the gap between Janice scribbling notes into your file – and ain't her writing so full of loops and optimism? – and then typing things on the new computer that they've just had in – and there are some new machines for customers on the way, apparently, and you wonder when her job will be replaced by a machine and she'll be queuing up there with everyone else to punch in her jobseeker's too – you will tell her you want to be a writer or a musician. She'll say but there's nothing here for writing or musicking and there's no living off the dole for a bright young man like you. She's trying not to be patronising. Do not roll your eyes back at her, Mr Jarrett. Do not tut or kiss your teeth. Shrug and promise to continue searching. Show her the adverts you've circled. Flirt a little but don't be too bait, too blatant. ~~Say you like her new frilly blouse.~~ Ask her if she's done her hair. Say your hair looks kinda new, is it new? She'll purse her lips and put on her best teacher voice but she'll be pleased enough all right. Unbeweavable. That thing on her head will move when she scratches her scalp but you best transform your laugh into a compliant smile. Yes, your sister would be horrified – she's a hairdresser. She knows how to do weaves proper. Bonding. Extensions. Braids. Canerows. Relaxing. Your sister who you haven't seen for close to three years, just like your mother and father. It's funny how a city can do that – you've not so much as bumped into each other. You live less than five miles apart but sometimes it feels like time rather than distance that separates you.

As your mind wanders to your family – if you can call the disaster that raised you a family – and the carpet tiles begin to blur, you'll realise Janice has said something that requires an answer. She's looking expectantly at you. But all you can hear is your stomach growling a question that is more pressing, more real. You'll excuse yourself – you have bladder needs, hearing problems, a jumpy mind, dead grandparents haunting your thoughts, a pocket full of rye – I don't know how I'll excuse myself, but she'll ask you to take a minute. Perhaps you want to take some fresh air, and she'll let you sneak off for a ciggie. She's not going anywhere. She knows you're young and probably vulnerable – at least that's what her notes seem to say when you read them upside down. She writes a lot of notes but she doesn't treat you like you can't read, like they do at the Council. She's referred you to Connexions, to Open Centre and – very discreetly

– to God. She could lose her job for that and you have no more interest in God right now but it's nice she's not all shouty about it.

The jobcentre is just off Broadway – when you go for a snout, that's the direction you'll head in – which only sounds grand to those who don't know East London. Broadway. Maryland. There are so many places around there that seem to dream up America, small, dark places that want to be big. God Bless Hairdressers where your sister, in her pink synthetic wig, used to hire a chair, before she moved on. That's across the road, across all that traffic and horn-blaring, towards The Mall – even The Mall sounds American, isn't it? Your sister will be all finger waves now, like all the girls around these streets – hard, greasy strands of hair sticking to her forehead. She'll be finishing all her sentences with you get me? For all you know, she might have a kid by now. You better go back in though, before you get carried away. You'll get carried away walking and end up outside God Bless and it's been more than ten minutes. You best walk back quickly.

It's an ugly prefab building, the jobcentre is – temporary – but it's been there since the sixties, along with the strip lighting which flicks on and off once in a while, a nervous twitch as if to show even the electrics are on edge. You've seen fights there, plenty of fights. Someone loses it, goes all rago, maybe it's a mother with a kid in a pram – and another in her arms – shouting how you expect me to feed them? Or there'll be someone who doesn't speak English bursting into tears or falling on the floor. Without fail, every time you go, someone will knock over a bunch of forms. I'm not filling in another one of your fucking forms. I'm a fucking human. That's what they'll say. And of course, there's that tonk fella with the really high-pitch voice who keeps squealing I'm dying I'm dyiiiing. The older woman who starts speaking in tongues and walking around the place. She took out some olive oil and anointed your head once. I pray for you she said. I pray for you that the Lord release the demoned of darkness you have in you. Last week a kid came in and pulled out a knife and the police came, but it was business again within ten minutes flat. No one moved out of the queue. You miss your place in the queue, you might miss your money for the fortnight.

You're nearly back from your walk. Your eyes are wet. You're a day short of your nineteenth birthday and you're trying to rein in your hip sway, which always gets you in trouble somehow. Walk like a man. You bowl. You scowl. You arm yourself in maleness. Grr. Woof. That's it, dawg. You're ready. Now when she asks you about placement number three – Janice, that is, with her pager ready on the desk – and you feel the darkness come over you, and you want to bash someone's head in, just remember that charm is your weapon. It always has been, Keith. You have a face full of expression, you have wide eyes, you have a full-toothed grin. Use them well. If you're nice, it'll be over in a bit and you can use up the divers of weed you got, and swallow all the grey Stratford air again. Polluted, yes, but none of that lemon air freshener outside, designed to block out the damp and dead rats, the stink of desperate people being told they need to try harder.

Let's get you back outside as quick as we can. Outside is ~~fresh~~ air, is bus station, is In-Stores. A shopping centre within a shopping centre. Wheel within a wheel. Once you're out again, use your cheeky grin to steal a lemon at one stall, a tomato at another. Nothing blatant.

OK. Now you know the drill.

* * * * *

The daycentre was a short bus ride away, or a long walk.

On the first day, he took the short bus, so he would arrive on time. A dirty orange Skoda sped through a puddle and splashed him just after he got off, but he whistled 2Pac. *I Ain't Mad at Cha*. And then it morphed into the Blackstreet track, with the same melody. He'd worn the smartest clean things he could find: a pair of brown trousers, a little too tight maybe; a grey shirt with an ink stain on the cuff which he couldn't get rid of; a pair of shiny Clarks, polished with a smile.

The daycentre was an experimental project. They had a lot of funding and it was expanding. He didn't quite get everything they did at the centre but it sounded like a big deal, even though to him it looked like a holding space for homeless druggies. There was the woman who ran it and three other men who made up the permanent staff: the cook, the therapist, the something else he didn't catch. He was, well, he *was* gay, but the other men were *gay* gay. Properly gay. And old. At least forty.

On the second day, he walked there from his bedsit. The guy downstairs had been screaming all night. On the third day he walked and then ran through the sudden downpour. On the fourth day – after the weekend passed – it was Monday and he was late but he got the bus and wasn't as late as he could have been.

On the fifth day, he began to warm to the rhythm of his job: opening post, delivering letters, clearing his manager's desk, but leaving her mug alone, and obeying the various Post-its – put this in that file, put this in the other file. Once he'd washed up in the staff area, it was down to the food orders. The money was counted and receipts thoroughly inspected on his return. Any funny business would come off his wages at the end of the month. Then there were programmes to photocopy and staple. Then he could take his lunch, either outside, or in the staff area or in the common room with the "service users". On the tenth day, he tried the latter and found he couldn't meet eyes with the men whose table had a chair free. He heard them under their breath: not another pooftah. On the eleventh and twelfth days, he went outside and it didn't rain and it wasn't cold. On the thirteenth it was.

On the fourteenth, one of the old gays with more beard than face sat him down in the staff area, which was little more than a kitchen with a small wooden table. He didn't know half of what the old man was saying, he was busy looking at the man's beard and hoping he'd stop asking questions. Digging more and more about his family, his origins, his . . . On the fifteenth, he was more relaxed and that old man wasn't there but the other old man was, the therapist, and they ate sandwiches together in silence and smiles. The therapist excused himself after a while.

He was alone in the kitchen, windowless, the walls busy

with cupboards and posters. There was the tombstone poster. And there was a tin of coffee by the sink. And the mug his boss had said to leave alone. Have a Smiley Day it said. She'd hugged him the first day, said it was nice to meet him. Despite the sticky notes everywhere, she was hands-on. Those notes are more for me than anything else, she'd said. You got yourself a boyfriend yet, she'd asked him with a wink. Don't worry, she said, you're still young. But be careful. Be healthy. You don't want to get yourself . . . and she didn't say anything more because one of the other men came in.

WHO USED MY MUG? WHO USED MY FUCKING MUG?

The words bounced around in his head as he walked back home and the bus sped past. It was bloated with people and prams and shopping. The pavement was littered with chicken boxes and spat-out gum.

The therapist had looked him straight in the eyes before volunteering himself. I did it, the old man said. She'd slapped him in the face and he'd stood there and taken it, while the slap bounced between the walls then out the window onto the grass patch outside where kids were kicking a ball around. She'd apologised for slapping him but that was it. Nothing more said.

You have to understand, the therapist said, speaking into the silence of the room, after she left. Times are changing, but . . .

On the sixteenth day, he walked into the centre and straight into the office. There was a new mug on her desk. It had a Post-it note attached. Do not touch.

We're not lepers, he thought as he smashed the mug on the floor and flung a pile of her papers through the window. Next week he'd be back at the jobcentre, waiting for Janice's disappointed smile.

Take Me Out Tonight
GRACE JACOBSON

The Earth moves at a thousand and forty miles an hour. When things are in motion I feel OK – I don't have to think. Everything is still, this quiet suburban street does not murmur one bit, and I am willing the wind to disturb something, anything at all. On the scrap of paper in my hand, in my blue biro scrawl, are all the important details: 9th March, 9 a.m., 9 Verdant Lane. Seeing the number nine three times makes me smile, because I like odd numbers. I can't stop shaking, though: I don't want to be the one to tell Eve what's happening.

If my mother were here she'd say, "It's OK, Nell. I'll tell her for you." I always like to be the last to arrive and the first to leave, but this is no party. I turn and start walking with a purposeful stride. Halfway up the garden path, my body freezes. *Foot forward, other foot forward, that's right, there we go.* Eve's been living with Carol, the foster carer, for three weeks but this is my first visit to the house. Five more steps and my finger is on the doorbell.

After seven seconds Carol answers the door with rehearsed surprise, the "o" in her hello lingering as she beckons me into the hall. She is tall, black, younger than I had imagined, and reveals a wide gap between her two front teeth when she smiles. Her long pink nail extensions tap the door as she closes it behind me. The wall is lined with framed prints, all mantras: "Dance Like

Nobody's Watching"; "Be Happy, Be Bright, Be You"; "Believe you can and you're halfway there".

"Ooh, come round to see me, Mum? That's big of you." Eve, dark drawn-on eyebrows and bleached hair pinned like a pompom on top of her head, swings down the stairs, two at a time, one palm pressed flat against the wall and the other gripping the banister for support. She has the same nails as Carol and I wonder if they visited a salon together. I realise how I've missed Eve, the way she moves so skilfully everywhere, like a gymnast. "Actually, you can take me to Tesco. I've run out of fags and Tampax." She's wearing a crop-top and jeans, and her bones jut like ammunition over the top of her waistband; her pale midriff looks too taut, like there's no stretch, no space in there for a proper meal. *Skin and bone, skin and bone. You'll feel better if you eat something.*

I step further into the narrow hall and Eve jostles past me. She smells of Impulse and cigarettes. I want to wrap my arms around her but I know she will stiffen, go straight as a board in my embrace. Here in Carol's hall, with the paired shoes in size order, letters stacked neatly on the side table – everything with a slot, a place, a reason – there is no room for rejection. It's love, that's for sure, but holding her now seems as unnatural as violence. When she was little she'd rush to the front door to greet me; she'd plant snotty kisses all over my face, my hair. I would say, "Too much, too much, Eve, your kisses will kill me!" then fall to the floor, lie down like I'd fainted, smiling, and she'd continue pressing her lips on my cheeks, my forehead, my chin. Knowing how to be her mother then was as simple as making toast, but now all I dream about is keeping her safe.

"Tea?" Carol asks.

"Nah," says Eve.

"Yes please," I say.

Carol walks towards the kitchen at the far end of the house.

I follow Eve into the sitting room, look around and start counting the framed photos of children on the wall, stopping at twelve; they're posed school photographs mostly, many with fake blue-sky-and-cloud backgrounds. Some of the children sit next to their siblings, others sit on their own with gaps in their smiles. I picture the photographer asking them to recall a happy time. When I was young I thought about kissing boys.

"God, Mum, you're so nosy," says Eve, sitting down on the sofa. "Carol's been mum to loads of kids." I settle myself next to her and she shifts along, creating a large space between us before she looks at me, frowning. "You look old."

"I am old," I say.

"If you're here to ask about the Bermondsey thing last week it's all good. I'm good . . . I'm good." Eve elongates her words. "I'm staying indoors from now on. Ask Carol. It was just some bitch getting aggy and she thought it would be cool to try and knife me . . . No men involved this time so you can keep your hair on."

I have learned not to trust what Eve says any more: she lies to protect her abusers. Nobody really knows who gave her the impressive wound on her leg last week. She squirms on the sofa and looks first at the dead TV, then to the window. There's a people-carrier outside that I'm certain wasn't there before. I panic that Eve might see Joy, the social worker she despises. Glancing down at my phone, I see it's 9.25 a.m. Only five minutes to go until Joy knocks on the door.

I want to tell Eve that foster care was not what I wanted, but it was all that Social Services could offer. I want to tell her that before she moved to Carol's – when she'd escape from the house at night despite my attempts to stop her – I'd call the police to report her missing, then wait in the sitting room in darkness, listening out for the scratch of her key in the door. I want to say that I often drive late into the night looking for her, though I know that if she saw me she wouldn't come. Sometimes I just want to know that she's still alive. I want to tell her that I've spent days at Streatham police station begging for someone to make Social Services move her somewhere safe. Eve's pyjamas had been taken for forensic testing the night she returned home so drunk and drugged that I called for an ambulance. The semen of three men was discovered from that one night alone, and yet, according to her social worker, Eve "had to learn to keep herself safe".

Often, I wake at 3 a.m. and think of all the different ways I want to torture the men who'd raped Eve, who continue to abuse her. I think of how I'd tie them up (blue binder twine, so tight it cuts their wrists, their ankles), pour petrol on them, then strike a match until all that remains is the smell of burnt skin.

I check my watch and it's 9.27: only three minutes until Joy knocks on the door. My heart quickens.

"Eve, I need you to listen to me. I don't think you really understand how terrible everything is at the moment. I don't think you're allowing yourself to feel anything because you're scared that the men you keep going back to will hurt you if you don't do what they ask. It worries me sick, Eve. These . . . men and the things they do to you. You're a child. You have to believe that it's not your fault, my darling. Nothing that's happened is your fault."

Eve looks at me, mouth open, incredulous.

"What the fuck are you trying to say?"

I'm stalling. Eve is watching. *Spit it out, spit it out.*

"I've been trying to keep you safe. Desperately trying. So has everyone, but we can't, Eve. We can't. But Social Services have found . . . They managed to find a secure unit and these moves always happen straightaway. So Joy's going to come soon and take you –"

"You've got to be fucking joking." Eve lays the words out slowly, as if she's practising another language. She shakes her head from side to side, rises with arms uplifted, preacher-like. I hear the click of the kettle in the kitchen down the hall. The water has reached a rolling boil. Eve starts massaging the sides of her head frantically, then she takes her nails to the top of her cheekbones and pulls them down, and when she's finished she does it again like she's drawing chalk lines on a blackboard. Angry stripes appear on her skin. I stand and try to pull her hands away from her face, but she punches my arm.

"Stop, my love," I say.

"Nonononononono!" Eve's voice is deep, unfamiliar. "Carol!" The name echoes down the hall, and the distressed moan turns into a shrill cry, similar to the sound foxes make at night.

Carol enters the room, walking in the same measured way she always does, a cup in each hand. She places the tea on the coffee table and gently takes hold of Eve's wrists.

"No more scratching, baby girl," Carol says, shaking her head slowly. Her warm voice is so confident, unwavering. "Don't hurt yourself, baby girl . . . It's for the best. Your mum doesn't want this either. It's just what has to happen."

Eve wrestles free from Carol's grip, grabs a remote control from the table and hurls it against the wall; it hits a picture of two smiling schoolgirls and shatters the glass in the frame. She picks up a cup of tea and throws it out into the hallway.

Carol reaches out to stroke Eve's back, soothing her with, "It's OK, it's OK, baby girl." Eve turns around and buries her head in Carol's chest, kicking her flexed foot backwards into my shin. I cry out in pain and the warm tears that follow make my skin itch, but with the discomfort comes a welcome sense of relief as I dry my cheeks with the back of my hand. The steady flow of Carol's "baby girl"s brings down the fever in the room. She takes a hanky from her sleeve and wipes away Eve's tears before pointing to a tissue box on the coffee table. "Dry your eyes," she says to me. "Would you like some tea now, Eve?"

"Can I do anything to make this better?" I say, but Eve ignores me.

The doorbell rings and Carol goes to answer it, returning seconds later with Joy. She's short and wide, and stands awkwardly, hands by her side like a police sergeant. Everything about her irritates me, even though I rely on her to sign things off, move things along, make things official. She's dressed in her usual dark attire, her suit-jacket arms revealing only the tips of her fingers: she always looks as if she's borrowed her clothes from a much taller friend. Her eyes rarely look up when she speaks.

"Fuck it. I knew it. Did you get your little friend Joy in on this too?" Eve spits out her words, her eyes mocking me until I look away. Her body trembling, she moves into the hall and I follow, keeping my distance as I wait for another crescendo. But she stands still, looks at me through narrowed, kohl-smudged eyes.

"Shall we go and pack?" I ask.

"Burn everything," Eve says, sitting down at the bottom of the stairs.

Nobody told me to bring a suitcase. Upstairs I stuff clothes, a hairdryer, cosmetics and books into the bin liners that Joy pulls off a roll as we stand in Eve's bedroom. I feel like a trespasser. Pink carpet, pink walls, the smell of a hundred deodorants all sprayed at once. The pinboard is bare and Blu Tack marks remain from other people's photos; trainer boxes and box-fresh trainers litter the floor. *Where did you get the money?* Joy's sympathetic glances annoy me, her smile as limp as a blobfish. I hurry down the stairs carrying the bags, resisting her offers of help as she tries to keep up in boat-shaped shoes that slip off her heels. Outside, the bags look sinister lined up on the pavement. I've let Eve down again. She is better than this. I imagine cutting up the men who've hurt her, then shoving their bodies into the black bags and feeding them to the rubbish truck.

"Goodbye, baby girl. Be good," Carol says, hugging Eve, who is sitting upright on the back seat of the black people-carrier, eerily composed, her make-up fixed, her hair all neat.

I say thank you to Carol's back and count the sixteen seconds it takes for her to go inside her house and close the door.

Joy settles herself next to Eve. The driver, a fifty-something small man with white sideburns and a shaving rash, picks up the bin liners and puts them into the boot with such care that for a second I think that maybe, perhaps, I could run away with him. We'd take Eve, too. Just the three of us, up North. As he shuts the boot door I thank him three times.

"You move me around like furniture," Eve says, sticking her head out of the car window.

It stings. She's good with words, my girl. I put my hand through the window and press my palm against her forehead like I'm checking for a temperature. Her skin feels warm; I feel ridiculous. She brushes my hand away while looking straight ahead.

"Best speak to her when she arrives, Mum," Joy says as she puts lipstick on without a mirror. When she smiles at me, her front teeth are coral, and I'm glad. The way she calls me Mum makes my jaw tense, my fists clench.

I want to climb onto the back seat next to Eve, but I'm not allowed. "It'd be too distressing to come with us," Joy had said when we'd talked through the plans together.

Standing on the pavement I feel the tears coming, so I think about getting laid. I picture the men: tanned, taut, pale, bald, tall, shovel-handed, stocky. I've never had a type. Underneath, they pull me closer as they whisper things into my ear that make me cringe; behind me, loose flesh slaps my skin like a baker slaps dough. When I'm head down, bum up, my mouth is a lipsticked O that makes the pillow soggy and pink.

Then all the men float away like ghosts; the grunters, the shy ones, the men whose names I've forgotten. The pantomime is over, but strange thoughts have erased the lump in my throat.

The driver grinds a cigarette butt into the road with his shiny shoe. I feel a sudden desire to move closer, to see if he smells as strongly of aftershave as I imagine him to. If I met him on the street, alone, how would I convince him to come home with me? I don't find him attractive at all, but I've slept with loads of people I don't fancy. He smiles and performs an awkward salute before saying, "Roads look clear to me." Then he ducks out of view and into the driver's seat.

"Don't forget the shoes, Mum," Eve says, her eyes focused on the road ahead.

"I won't," I say, taking a biro from my bag and writing the word *SHOES* on the back of my hand. The letters hurt.

I show her my newly tattooed skin as the window slides up and I mouth the words, "I love you".

The shoes sit high on a shelf in Eve's bedroom in the house that we once shared. Stilettos: strappy, shiny with pin-thin heels and leather soles. They smell expensive. No doubt their sheen has been dulled by dust over the weeks. I once tried to squeeze my size-sevens into them but my feet looked like trussed-up meat.

"A tenner. British Heart Foundation," Eve said triumphantly when she first showed me the shoes. She slid her neat feet into them with impressive ease, like she'd buttered them up beforehand, and then she click-clacked up and down the hall. I knew Eve didn't buy anything second-hand.

"The next time the police get you there'll be no caution."

Eve gave me the middle finger.

"You should only wear heels if you can run in them," I said, pointing at the shoes as if to say "bad dog".

"You just don't get it, do you, Mum. I give zero fucks about what you think." Eve swooped down and pulled the shoe from her left foot, heel-spike out, saying: "Anyway . . . these could blind someone."

And now the shoes that have never been given a real outing are all that she is asking for. I look down at my feet, my once white plimsolls. My big toes strain against the canvas, almost poking through. I try to imagine plimsolls at the end of a strange man's bed. Would they, could they ever look sexy? I've not felt pretty for a while, but I am still better than plimsolls.

If the car has not moved in nine seconds, then I am going to die on my way back home. Odd numbers soothe me and the engine starts, a low grumble – I smile as I start to count. I'm behaving like the type of person who lights a cigarette at the bus stop because they want the bus to come. The car is still not moving by nine, even though I included halves, and near the end, quarters. So I return to one and start with something else: *If the car has not moved by ten then the man I have sex with tonight is going to kill me.* But the car does not budge so I change the criteria because maybe I'm not ready to die.

The car window whirrs down and Joy's head pops out.

"Sorry we're still here, Mum. Sat nav's playing up, so driver's just sorting it. Nearly there."

I turn my head to face Carol's door. Earlier, in my haste, I didn't notice the midnight-blue gloss, smart in comparison with all of its peeled-paint neighbours. Foster care failed, as I knew it would.

"She's a good, sweet girl at heart but the devil's found a gap in her soul," Carol had said when she too admitted that she couldn't keep Eve safe.

Joy wondered whether I'd have Eve home again. I asked her how many times she wanted Eve to fail. She didn't understand what the problem was, so I spelt it out, told her that Eve was being groomed, driven around in the back of cars by men who used her for sex.

"Can't you see, Joy? She thinks those men are her boyfriends. Not even the most brilliant therapist, or mother or foster carer, is going to be able to stop her from running back to them," I said, before putting down the phone.

And here we are, a week later. *Poor, poor Eve.* The car finally pulls away. When its number plate becomes impossible to read, I cry out into the marble sky. Next to my car, I pull down my jeans and squat over a drain, a steaming stream of pee splattering up and hitting the tips of my plimsolls.

When I'm done I shake my bum in the cool air, thrilled by this perfect feeling. I pull my knickers and trousers up at the same time, slip the plimsolls off my feet, open the nearest wheelie bin and throw them in.

Eve's small bedroom smells like the inside of my grandma's handbag: dust, perfume and dirty hair. It is the first time I've opened her door since she left to live at Carol's house. *Rooms need humans.* I grab the high heels from the shelf, and leave as quickly as I've come in; the cat, Fatso, leaps into the room and onto Eve's bed before I have a chance to shut the door again. *Dammit, dammit.* I don't want to look back but it's no use now he's in there. I lift Fatso to my chest and glance at the wall, checking to see if my memory is accurate and the photos are as I'd remembered. The magazine pages, the models' boobs cropped from bigger images so the focus is all on them, no face to distract from the tits – oh the tits and the arse and the teeth, all the things that can make someone wild. And next to the tits and the arse and the teeth are family snapshots of Eve riding her bike across the park, of Eve squeezed into a rubber ring on holiday in the swimming pool, of Eve nestled in the crook of her grandpa's arm, the man she called Oompa. The Eve who loved him and me and our trips to the park in summer for a swim in the Lido, followed by blue bubblegum ice cream.

When the shoes are wrapped up tight in a Jiffy bag I find Eve's new address in an email from Joy. How far away is the Lake District? Two hundred miles, perhaps? There is safety in that distance, but grief, too. My whole body aches as I write Eve's name and her new address on the parcel, then put it at the bottom of the stairs.

In the bath I rub soap in circular motions over my soft stomach, splash water over the gentle rise and fall, the place that had once been able to keep Eve safe. *Treasure the moments when she's a baby, Nell. They grow so fast.* I picture Eve's body, the body that was once straight and uncomplicated; within weeks, it seemed, she grew hips and breasts and men on the street turned to look at her. She noticed them watching, and soon, I was aware of a more exaggerated swing in her step, hips slinking silkily down the street. I didn't know what to say to her, what the *right* thing to say was. I wanted to cover her with a sheet like a museum piece. Too late now. No time to look back. *Stop looking at her like that. Do you know how old she is? She's only thirteen.*

Naked in front of my bedroom mirror, I contemplate the right kind of clothes for getting laid. The jeans I was wearing this morning are all wrong, a middle-aged blue that give me my aunt's bottom, which had also been my mum's bottom. "Flat bottoms run in the family," all the women in my family said to me at various times during my childhood, with no hint in their delivery as to whether this was a good or a bad thing. *Should I be proud?* Back then I thought flat sounded better than round.

I open up my wardrobe and scan the dry-clean-only clothes that hang like spectres in their plastic wrappers. They're made of silk and others' joy: weddings, fortieths, christenings. When I close the cupboard doors they fling open again almost immediately, protesting their unhappiness. *Take me out tonight. Go on, Nell. It's been a while.* My nicest bra, an expensive black lace push-up, sits in the top drawer away from tangled tights and grey knickers. When the light is right it makes my tits look kissable, full and young.

Dressed in tight black jeans, a T-shirt and high-heeled boots, I feel tall and powerful as I stand. I grab my handbag, walk carefully down the stairs, head-up-shoulders-back, check my reflection in the hall mirror, giving myself a score of six-and-a-half-verging-on-seven. *Fuckable, if the light is right.* Eve's parcel is on the stairs, and I scoop it up then take my coat down from the peg, before stepping outside.

In the car I decide on town, Soho, perhaps. The Congestion Charge and heavy parking fees don't bother me today. I want to spend money I don't have. According to my sat nav, I'll get to town by 13.03: the odd numbers and the vivid-green map lines that pierce the heart of the city give me butterflies in my stomach. They let me know that the traffic is flowing like water for once.

At the first set of red lights I fix my eyes on a man in the neighbouring lane for three seconds – it's harder than you'd think, longer than a furtive gaze. *I know you can do it, Eve, because I've seen you before and it's impressive.* When the three seconds are up I push my nose into my shoulder, inhaling the smell of toast and perfume. Sometimes driving is the closest thing to love.

The swelling of my heart stops as the sound of police sirens gets louder. I pull over, feeling the electric-blue lights, their screech and fury, pass me by. In my rear-view mirror I spot rooftops, church spires, trees; the safety of leisure centres, florists and train stations that are so much more familiar than the glittering view in front of me. In limbo is how I'd describe it, if somebody were to ask how I was feeling. Yes, in limbo. Those words make me think of not knowing how to be, or where to go or who to be with. My legs feel as if they're straddling a dangerous gap: I must not fall. If somebody could just come and lift me up, high up above the chasm, and carry me off somewhere for a while, that would be perfect, just perfect.

There's a space in the road, a chance for me to pull out, and my heart quickens as I work out what to do. The thought of heading into town now, to get laid in the afternoon, while people are eating sandwiches at their desks, or sorting laundry, or doing their shopping, seems ludicrous. *Make a U-turn, make a U-turn.* With my steering wheel on full lock and my foot on the accelerator, my car seems to decide for me as it takes its place on the road. Headed for home now, my body sighs as I take a deep breath in, then out, in then out, waiting for my heartbeat to slow.

On the South Circular, I spot schools I've visited, corner shops I've bought things from. Waiting at a red light at the bottom of the hill a woman sits high up in her 4x4, a half smile on her face. Two small children are strapped into seats behind her. I think of trips that Eve and I took when she was little; all the cafés, parks and museums; the satisfaction I felt then, when I could keep things moving till bedtime. Eve was safe and things were in motion.

Outside my house I see Rob from three doors down coming out of his front door. He chucks a black bag into his wheelie bin and I stay totally still, rigid in my seat, hoping he hasn't spotted me, or my car. He is tall, mid-forties and handsome, with a large lump and scar on his neck. I've never had the courage to ask him what happened. His shoelaces always bother me – he ties them too tight, like he's punishing his trainers. But he's the only person on the street who ever bothers to ask how Eve is. Everyone else pretends like she never existed. I wonder if this is what happens when people die.

Rob's dead-heading his daffodils now, and bending down to pick stubborn weeds out of the cracks in his garden path. Part of me wants to get out of the car and talk to him. Perhaps I could take him into my house, for lunch, then sex. But it would feel wrong, trying to seduce somebody I already know, on a street that is more familiar to me than any other place in the world.

I often imagine what Rob would be like in bed; scenes of

us fucking, slowly, come into my head. He is kind and careful and goes down on me again and again with surprising skill and patience. The thought of us is bearable, almost, until I imagine his strangled shoes by the side of my bed.

He retreats into his house and I open my car door, wondering how far along the M6, or the M4, or any one of the Ms, Eve is. I'm not sure where the North begins or where it ends.

The Ram

GILLI FRYZER

The ram staggered closer to the thicket, head lowered against sleet-spiked wind. Its breath pulsed in hard, dry gasps. Past dawn the Sussex sky lifted into the grey underbelly of a January morning, and under the thicket, the animal fell.

The padlocked gate bucked and rattled as Cath swung herself over its rails and into the field. Niall's spare binoculars had brought her running up the lane; showed her where the scarred fields ran into tangled copse and the grey shape lay. Beyond the gate, her trainers slipped and skidded on the dung-streaked grass.

The gorse thicket crested the field's long slope, snatched at Cath's ponytail as she ducked beneath its sharp sprays, one gloveless hand outstretched. The air beneath the thicket was rank with the gamey stench of untreated wool, the ram's half-closed eye a sliver of melting ice.

A quad bike skidded to a halt alongside, startling Cath as it spattered woman and animal with clotted arrowheads of orange clay.

"Leave it."

Cath rocked back on her heels. A brindle lurcher circled the edge of the gorse towards her, tail tucked like a comma, ears flat against its domed skull. The farmer choked the quad into silence, ignored the dog's low growl. Cath remained crouched.

"I came to see if I could help." It sounded ridiculous, now. Gorse was pricking into her back. Her thin tracksuit was useless here. She curled her fingers to stop the shaking.

"That's for me to do." The man filled the only gap in the thicket, swallowed the light from the field. The dog stood taut, hackles raised.

"I think it's dying."

The farmer's guffaw curled like steam into Cath's face as she rose.

"Beasted, more like." A muddied boot prodded the ram up.

"Beasted?" Cath looked up at the farmer, tucking her frozen hands into her armpits. This must be her neighbour. She tried a smile.

"Knackered." Narrowed eyes flicked over her bones. "So you'd be, girl, if you'd been hard at it."

He was already astride the ram, pulling a plastic tube from his pocket.

"I just saw . . . I live down –"

"I know where you live."

Blunt fingers dragged at the animal's jaw, forcing a drench between its yellowed teeth.

"I can't get over how rude he was, Lou."

Cath pushed their tennis racquets to one side and slid onto her kitchen stool.

Lou lifted her mug and glanced at her friend across the foam of coffee.

"Typical you, though. What were you going to do? Give it mouth-to-mouth?"

"No, of course not. I don't know. Call a vet? It was in trouble, I could see that."

"Bunny hugger." Lou grinned. "And of course Huggett knows where you live. So what?" She gestured at the great hammer beam that split the kitchen ceiling, the old forged hook above their heads. "He sees this place every day."

Cath knew Lou was right. The house barely tolerated their

presence. Grown from Wealden clay and oak to serve the farm, it had long ago been severed from its land; the old ways obliterated by the builders that demolished the pen where the house pig lived, paved over the gutter that carried away its blood, and polished up the hook on which its carcass swung when the time for sausage making came around.

"Don't we know it when he's muckspreading," she countered. "And no getting by his tractor, either."

A tennis court covered the ruins of the old kitchen garden; the farmhouse now as neat as a Sunday-dressed great-aunt amongst a confusion of roses. She and Niall had viewed its tile-hung walls in the flush of last June's honeymoon, when the nesting urge was high and the garden full of birdsong, its former farmland, sullen with summer thistles, lying quiet enough beyond the hedge. Niall, a wildlife cameraman, had promised to settle down; his house-warming present to Cath two docile feather bundles that had settled themselves, soft and warm, on her lap.

That first night, Cath and Niall had abandoned the packing cases and curled together in the centre of their new lawn, watching stars shoot across the late-summer sky, listening to the chirrup and rustle of the bantams as they settled into their coop. She recalled pressing her fingertips against still-warm soil, the sensation that she had tied herself to someone as brief and unpredictable as the meteors winking out above; remembered the urge to scrabble beneath the earth, as though she would otherwise fail to root, never breed. Cath swallowed her coffee. None of it had turned out as she had imagined. The bantams had scratched and squabbled until the night the fox decapitated each in turn, while the wild ducks spurned her newly painted duck house and continued to scatter eggs along the muddy farmland waterways.

Lou waved a manicured hand in front of Cath's face.

"Hey there, stop fretting. Doesn't sound like there was much you could do anyway."

"I know. Forget it. I'm just missing Niall, I guess."

"Where is he this time?"

Cath pictured her husband receiving yet another award.

"Conservation Black Rhino Month, so hanging upside down from a helicopter, probably."

* * * * *

The March wind blew onto Huggett's face as he braced himself behind the cab, rode the jolts as the pick-up bumped across rough ground, up towards the thicket where the ram had gone down that time. He rapped on the cab roof to signal the stop and held on as T-Bar killed the engine. Huggett powered up the Lazerlite as T-Bar opened the cab door, released the big lurcher. A tongue of light licked the wall of the distant farmhouse then travelled along the garden hedgerow, like a spotlight searching for its star. Below the beam the turf stretched away empty, the ripening ewes now safe in the lambing pens by Huggett's bungalow. Christ, that ram'd worked and then some, this winter. Huggett bared his teeth at the memory. The beast staggering with exhaustion, triumphant, that chilly young blonde quivering like a hare ready to run.

Now the ground lay clear between lambing pens and the woods, and the hunt was on. Huggett growled, soft and low.

"C'mon, Charlie."

Beside him the lurcher trembled, pale eyes fixed on the light. T-Bar cupped back of hand to mouth and made a tight sucking call, a cry of injury, distress, a noise that spoke of fear, and need. The sound whipped away on the breeze as he repeated it.

The light fingered the thin curtains of the bedroom, felt its way across the piles of discarded clothes, the half-empty suitcase, the pale walls of chalky paint, the open door. Cath could sense the warmth of Niall's skin, the sheet still cold between them. He'd driven back to her in the dusk, his cases full of camera equipment, his laptop full of images, his mind already on Alaska.

"The pregnant females lead the way. Spectacular sight from the air." His fork had waved over his cooling meal. "I need to get up there now, before full migration starts. I promise, we'll talk about it when I get back. I promise."

Cath caught the faint citrus of Niall's deodorant, the soft sigh of air through his slackened mouth. He'd fallen asleep before she'd climbed alongside.

The intruding beam swept the room, and moved on.

Huggett focused on the spotlight, tracked its path as T-Bar swung the lamp bit by bit along the boundary of the darkened garden and back across the field. The wind rose, sharp on the men's faces, spitting a little onto the windscreen. T-Bar started up again and slipped into gear; allowed the truck to roll almost silently down close under the treeline, spears of young bracken falling like ninepins under the tyres. From here the light arced across the field once more, T-Bar repeating his strange call from time to time, stiffened muscles twitching under the lurcher's brindled skin.

Time passed. A pinpoint light again, in the distance, caught by the beam. Huggett cradled the rifle, breathed out through his nose, gentle. Steady now, steady. Retinal red, thirty, maybe forty metres away, coming up from the lambing pens, heading back to the trees. Lamp off. Wait. T-Bar sucked on his hand once more, a fox's long-drawn-out wail of pain. Wait for the gap to close.

Lamp on.

The rifle cracked, once, and the red jerked, winked out.

Got it.

The lurcher was already streaking into the night, nose down.

The sound travelled like a nervous impulse and Cath's breath contracted in response. She lifted the curtain edge, watched the flashlight hunting along the dark line of trees on the other side of the slope. The precision of the moving beam unsettled her with its insistence, its unrelenting search for the unwary. From time to time it would vanish, and then as quickly reappear, the muffled crack that followed carrying above the wind.

Huggett tossed the final bloodied vixen onto the corpses already stretched across the tailgate, while T-Bar pulled out his phone, arranged the shot. The camera flash bounced off fixed pupils, the dark wetness staining the white and russet hair, the black pools congealing on cold metal.

Cath stared into the night, past the fields where the unseen predator hunted, beyond Huggett's bungalow and the ewes dozing close for comfort; seeing trails of caribou heading north to calving ground, each instinctive step slowed by the weight within, oblivious to the tracking helicopter, the snap of Niall's shutter. Her own belly lay concave beneath the thin silk of her nightshirt. The breeze pulled at the open window, and the curtain moved. She inhaled the odour of damp earth, mixed with the musk rising from her skin.

* * * * *

The bar was choked with waxed jackets and laughter, heavy with beer and Chanel. Huggett tossed a packet of crisps onto the table by the inglenook and passed Gordy his pint. He was glad to see Al had stacked the fire, April or no. Auctions always got him like that. All that piled-up machinery, the picking over another man's leavings like crows on roadkill, the hammer knocking the lid down on another farm, piece by rusting piece.

"I'm not stopping long." He jerked his head. "This lot can have it, Gordy."

The little jockey sucked at his beer, tongued the foam from his lip.

"Get that bit of tatty tinwork out the car park before Al sees it, you mean." Gordy's battered grin bared his broken teeth. "Bought a pup, you have."

"That harrow'll do a job as is, you watch." Huggett supped the froth off his ale. "Sound enough. He was a good bloke when all's said and done."

"Who, auctioneer?" Gordy lifted his beer, turned it this way and that.

"Old man Thomas. Sold me my first ram, way back. Got his

price for it an' all." Huggett still winced at the sting, the farmer stuffing notes into his tobacco pouch like an autumn squirrel.

"Didn't have nothing at the end though, did he?" Gordy squinted through the glass at the light. "This ale's not all it's cracked up to be, neither."

"Went downhill when his old woman legged it. Took what she wanted. She'd have took his kids'n all, only there weren't none left to take." Huggett kicked a smouldering log and the sparks rose around his boot. He'd not done more than poke his nose in the door of the place, that were enough. Full of cat piss and damp, that scrubbed table, sit ten easy, covered with china, lot numbers chalked on the plates. The smell of tobacco still there'n all, even though the farmer'd been stuck in that care home three month or more before he pegged.

"Pity young T-Bar missed it, him just setting up, like he is." Gordy drained his ale, looked to the other man for answer.

"What was that?" Huggett was staring at the blonde that had just come in, head up high, like a doe down a gunsight.

"T-Bar. Shame to miss a good auction, all said."

High-strung, that one, give some poor sod a real run for his money. Huggett's laugh was hard and short as he turned back.

"Ain't no scatter cushions at auctions. She's gone and dragged him up IKEA. Spending it good and proper – more fool him."

"Got him by the short'n curlies, then." Gordy nodded like that was the sum of it. He slid his empty glass towards Huggett. "I'll have the Spitfire, me."

"You're on your own, mate." Huggett banged his own glass down on the wood. "Gotta shift that harrow for a start."

Lou slipped from her bar stool and squeezed her way towards Cath.

"This place is heaving. Cheers."

The clink of glass on glass brought Cath back.

"Sorry, Lou, I wasn't listening. What was that?"

"I was saying that this place is packed, that's all. Bloody

beer festival. Someone's already knocked Spitfire all over my Converse. Oh and happy Easter. This one's for you." Lou bounced a chocolate rabbit up and down in front of Cath. "Eat me! Eat me!" She winked and nodded towards the bells and ribbons at the far end of the bar. "I'd neck it down if I were you. That lot are dancing again in a minute."

"Can't we get out of here?" Cath didn't wait for an answer, but started to push her way back towards the exit. "Too damn hot in here, for a start. Who needs a bloody fire?"

Lou tickled the back of Cath's neck with the golden rabbit.

"Maybe we should watch the dancers? Nothing like a fertility ritual to get everyone in the mood."

"Christ, Lou, everything's –" Cath stumbled as Huggett shouldered his way through the door and headed towards his pick-up. She inhaled the acrid odour of animals and sweat before cold air flooded backwards, like the draught at the mouth of an unstopped tunnel.

"Ooh, get you. What've you done to upset him now?"

"Nothing." Cath slammed the door on the noise from the bar. "And for God's sake stop waving that bloody rabbit about."

* * * * *

Huggett turned the new lambs out on the spring grass; began the long, slow job of checking the fencing for the places where the ground was flattened, the wire bent upwards by sly entry. As he worked his way around the lower meadow he could hear the smack of ball on racquet, and if he was lucky, catch a glimpse of tanned skin as one or other player stretched to serve.

Laughter drifted with the butterflies over the long grass. Huggett covered the boundary on all fours, pulling unnoticed at the stock fence, forcing hooks into the soil to pin the netting down; his face so close to the grass he could see the greasy sheen of fox smeared across the lower branches of the hedge, inhale the rank stench of its territorial marking. The women grunted with effort as racquet and ball collided, their white-clad bodies invulnerable as they leapt and turned behind the court's green wire.

* * * * *

The path across the field was hard underfoot, its clay shrinking in the May drought. Cath lengthened her stride up the hill, the beat in her earphones measuring out her flight. At the top of the rise she paused to suck in air, trying to shake the squeeze of anger in her chest. Across the field a tractor rolled its final arc of the day. The sun was still high, but the best of it had gone, waiting for Niall to call.

His face on the screen had been fractured, freezing and unfreezing like a poor recording.

"I'm heading over to the reserve at Katmai, going after the grizzlies." The image was blurred, but Cath could see his eyes shining, hear his tight-voiced excitement. "The absolute power of these animals, Cath – we tracked a female for a day, watched it take out the stragglers." Niall moved closer, his head filling the screen. He could be anywhere, right now, Cath thought, staring back. Anywhere. Just not here.

"Calves didn't stand a chance, that's for sure – got some fantastic kill shots. Flying back from Anchorage in a couple of weeks, honey, don't you worry."

Cath circuited the field and vaulted the wooden stile onto the lane. She pulled an earphone out and turned towards home, running more steadily now on the tarmac. The Wealden lane sank between steep banks, the leggy saplings twined like lovers' hands above her head. The shadows formed by their coupling were cooler, violet, filled with tiny insects indifferent to her path. Her pace eased as she reached the corner, heading downhill.

The tunnel of trees filled with noise as a tractor swung around the bend behind her, gaining fast. Cath ran on, breathing harder, legs stretching out as the tractor rolled along behind her, its harsh rattle and clang tight on her heels. As the lane opened out she sprinted onto the grass verge, saw the driver's expressionless face above the dust as the giant wheels swept by.

Huggett glanced at the wing mirror as he passed; saw those large eyes turned towards him, her slim body pressed against the hedge, at bay. She'd been running those footpaths since it turned dry, like she owned the earth of it. He'd seen her often enough these past weeks; from his bungalow, or up with the sheep, or that time when his dog had whined, wanting the chase – he'd cuffed it hard into silence and followed with his eyes instead. Same as ever, never paid him no mind, acknowledged him, even. Like he didn't count for nothing. Still, she'd know, next time.

On the road was better. Out here the ground was hard, the hill was steep, the weight of the tractor bearing down had pushed her along nicely. He'd tucked up good and close; seeing that scrap of a T-shirt sticking to her shoulder blades, tracking her ponytail, swinging like a lure in front of his cab.

Cath showered after her run, watched the water rinse away the dried salt rivulets, her belly tightening with the memory of the pursuit. Afterwards she pulled on one of Niall's old linen shirts and wandered into the garden in the dusk, as the pipistrelles dropped from behind the sun-warmed tiles to dance in crazy zigzags above the pond. She tugged the shirt across her body, remembering the basement club where she'd first seen Niall's flamboyant dancing, his darkened curls clinging wetly to his forehead. A stranger then, he'd wrapped his arms around her without words, as though her slight frame were weight enough to anchor his unquiet limbs to the dance floor's chequered tiles.

The breeze picked up a little, brushing the damp skin between her breasts.

Huggett sat long past supper, waiting for nightfall, feeling a need as bad as any lurcher. His chase down in the tractor had fuelled an uneasy appetite. A solitary steak had hissed and spat from the stove as he sliced bread in the cramped kitchen; he'd eaten both from the blackened pan, the bread turning pink as he rubbed its crust into the bloodied juice and lifted it, warm and pulpy, to his mouth. Now he pushed the remains to one side, lit a thin twist of tobacco, dragged hard and watched the smoke spread out and vanish like snow on water while the light faded and the fat congealed across the base of the pan.

His knuckles were still streaked with oil and the vivid smear of grass. Through the open door he could hear the distant bleat of a lamb, and closer to home, the shriek of the old tawny as she set out to hunt. There was a rustle in the tangle of weeds just outside; the lurcher raised its long muzzle and stared out into the twilight, nostrils flared. He picked up the remains of his steak, the thick yellow rind that dangled like a baby rabbit from his fingers, and tossed it to the dog. The owl's call pushed him to his feet; he thought of prey, of head shots that splintered bone, of unmarked pelts and warm bodies lying limp beneath his hands.

The sky was dark, moonless, cirrus-flecked. A warm wind blew from the woods as Huggett opened the field gate, shut it behind. Now the lurcher sensed work, slipping through the grass low-bellied and slow beside the farmer.

Huggett tucked his rifle crossways, and switched the scope on, then off again. No point in advertising. Man and dog pressed up the slope, nose to wind, heading for the warrens beneath the gorse where the ram had rested.

Heat pushed against the low ceilings. The bedroom windows were half open, and the first moths were drumming on the glass. Cath stretched out to pull a window shut, saw a lamp swing out along the field, picking out the tussocks in sharp relief. It vanished, and all was dark; and then the beam reappeared, and this time there was a muffled crack as the dark outline of a dog leapt forwards.

The light disappeared once more, and then returned, a few metres nearer to the lane, jumping slightly, echoing the gait of someone moving on foot across uneven turf. Cath bent over the warm wooden sill, watching for the hunter prowling below, seeing his familiar bulk silhouetted against the beam as he swung it across the grass. The light touched the house, and vanished. She jerked back behind the curtain, could hear the blood drumming in her ears. The light started moving again, steadily closer, pausing from time to time. Another shot.

Cath leaned her forehead against the cool glass of the window and tried to count the seconds of silence that followed the sound from the rifle. Under the thin linen shirt her limbs were shaking, as though the lamp would pull her body into the thickening dark.

The hunter was scanning the hedgerow now, its shadows twisting in etiolated shapes across the blue stretch of lawn. Cath knew herself to be part of a strange and elaborate dance, her heartbeat synchronising with the pulsing silences between shots. She felt blindly around in the bedside drawer for Niall's binoculars.

Huggett didn't need a sight; the dog's trembling flank told the farmer all he needed to know. The lamp was on quick as you like, flashed along the undergrowth and off. In those brief seconds Huggett had glimpsed another rabbit, its eye a ruby spark in the glow from the scope. He raised the rifle to his shoulder, hit the beam again and fired. The rabbit, illuminated for the briefest of moments, jerked and lay still. A milky doe, even better, thought Huggett, retrieving it, limp and leaking, from the lurcher's jaw. His penknife nicked the Achilles tendon; he slid the rabbit onto the game stick to dangle with the others, dripping, above the grass.

The tension had slipped from his shoulders, his breathing steady and quiet. The night was humming with life, he knew it; he could sense its force all around and feel himself part of that, the weight of the gun pulling him forward, king of his own fucking territory, life and death what it was all about.

Another rabbit checked, and turned to run.

The lawn was cool and damp underfoot, and the breeze twitched the hem of Niall's shirt, lifting it away from Cath's thigh. The light slid past again, raking along the garden's edge and back up the field's rise towards the gorse clumps at the top of the bank. Cath drifted with the moths towards the boundary. Something small darted across the grass, but otherwise the garden was empty, its clipped hedges stark against the ragged countryside beyond. Cath crouched at the base of a boundary oak and lifted her binoculars.

She breathed out. In the ruby-tinted lens his size was unmistakable.

The game stick was heavy across Huggett's back, its string of dangling pelts dripping slowly onto the ground. Huggett was beginning to sweat, the night breeze chilling the skin on forehead and chest. His muscles tensed as he stooped over a twitching rabbit. He'd winged this one, failed to get a clean kill, and now frustration returned as he gripped the animal's hind legs, pushed the ball of his thumb into the back of its neck. The rabbit pulsed in his grasp, its eyes bulging. He closed his fingers under its jaw and jerked, needing that crack of bone against thumb. The big buck swung from his fist as he released its head.

Huggett bent to retrieve his rifle from the grass. As he straightened, he wiped his forehead with his sleeve, sensing again the telltale twitch of the lurcher's skin against his leg. Steady, man, easy now. Huggett twisted his head in the direction the dog was staring, followed the long muzzle scenting the darkness, eyes fixed on the garden boundary.

"Hello, Charlie."

Flash of white, far end of the hedge. Huggett grinned at the unexpected gift, knew himself king again. Unmistakable, fox height. Slowly, carefully, breath held as he lifts the gun, scope focused along the sudden shaft of light; and now it rises, that gut-twisting thrill as he picks out the reddened glint of eyes, holding steady on him as the trigger shifts.

Choke

SOGOL SUR

I'm about to fall on the ground in Dean Street, but I hold on to a construction fence to steady myself. My scarf has turned into a snake again, choking me. I would love to collapse on the ground and fall into an everlasting coma, but people are already staring at me, some asking if I'm "all right" – to which I aggressively turn my head so they will leave me alone.

I know it must be around ten in the morning, the spring sun sprinkling on London, the day hideously stunning. Even though I am wearing my enormous sunglasses, I can still feel the glory of London and the decadence of Europe seducing me. The fast cars of Soho pass by me and I consider throwing myself under one of them – preferably a blood-red Lamborghini. But what if I survive the accident, stuck in a wheelchair, with my test results in my left hand? Like I was taught in my elementary school, that is the hand with which the sinners hold the result sheet of their deeds on the Judgement Day.

I am a sinner. I deserve to be judged and thrown into hell. Even though until two days ago I thought I was a liberated atheist. But who was I fooling?

I have slept with thirteen men since my arrival in England two years ago. Thirteen is an ominous number in our ancient culture. I used to think it was under ten men, but last night I stayed awake, not caring about getting my beauty sleep any more, counting, focusing, regretting. Not missing anyone: Steven, John, James, Liam, Stephen, Babatunde, Josh . . . and I do not remember all the names, but I recall their faces.

The only person I've confided in about my fear is my only Iranian friend in London. She was not surprised at my shameful secret because she had been suffering from the exact same fear until she entered a monogamous relationship with an old, dull man. She told me not to worry and added, "Your disease isn't AIDS. It's immigration."

I laughed insultingly at this accusation and attacked her by saying, "I'm not like you. I adore Europe. I've worked really hard to find this freedom. My mother is still angry that I've left Iran on my own – husbandless."

My mother. The God-lover. The history professor. At times, a bigger dictator than Iran's Supreme Leader, screaming at my dad for spoiling me and raising me as a non-religious human; at times praising us, even cooking for us the finest *zereshk polo* with saffroned chicken marinated in lemon juice overnight. My mother with her scary prophecies. The last one happened the night before I was leaving the country.

My father and I were in my orange-lit room, packing, me worrying about the lack of space and my father reassuring me that he could squeeze everything into my suitcase. Suddenly, I noticed how old his hands looked, and I couldn't take it any more. The tears I'd fought since that morning streamed down my face. "I don't want to leave without you," I confessed.

My father looked up from the suitcase; a pair of red sandals fell from his hands. "I'll come and visit you, I promise. And you'll come back in the holidays."

I managed a tearful smile and my father left my room. I knew my drama was too much for him but I couldn't help it. I knew he was going to the balcony to smoke and choke on his tears. Then my mother stepped into my room. I was still weeping into my overflowing suitcase, forcing a volume of Forough Farrokhzad's poetry amidst my shoes.

"You should be celebrating tonight!" my mother commanded. "You finally got what you wanted with the help of your beloved father."

For the first time in my life, I was completely honest with her. "I can't leave him."

Then my mother did something strange: she embraced me and caressed my head like when I was a child and we weren't shouting at each other about religion the whole time.

"Have the power to accept what you strived for. This is also what your father wants for you. Don't worry about him. I'll take care of him."

My tears finally stopped. I looked at her and said, "I'm glad you're finally supporting my decision."

"I still think you'll be disillusioned," she said, her dark eyes glued to mine. "Europe isn't as perfect as the utopia in your head."

"Nowhere is," I reasoned, "but it's definitely better than here."

"Your problem is you are more westernised than the West itself," she said. "You won't find peace there. Somebody with your attitudes should go live on Mars!"

How can I tell this lioness what I have done to her daughter's body?

I even know who gave it to me. It was James. A long-haired boy doing a PhD in war studies and video games, or something as absurd as that. James was living in Cockfosters with his parents – whom I never had the honour of meeting in person. He was so gorgeous that whenever we went out, men would look at him more. He was abnormally bony though, and he was into BDSM and sex parties – which at that time I considered to be the symbol of liberation and pleasure, but now I fear like death itself.

My vagina has started itching since he performed cunnilingus on me thirteen months ago. The worst part is that I didn't even come, because his teeth were too sharp, scrubbing my clitoris like a nail buffer. After our unsexy sex, James vanished. He didn't reply to my myriad text messages asking whether he had an STD and then closed down his online dating profile.

Once James left me with an itchy vagina, I became weaker by the day. Even now, today, as I am walking in my sacred Soho, I feel I need physical help. I can't even walk. I am also losing my looks; my once lively eyes look lifeless, encircled by brownish shadows. My strings of hair are falling as often as the London rain. My cheekbones are becoming hollower by the second. I look like a victim of AIDS, and get confused – and even upset – when people say I look "beautiful".

After mocking all my religious teachers for ten years and longing to escape to my fantastical Europe, now I am almost certain those backward *chadori* people were right: Europe is HIV positive.

I am now walking as slowly as I can, hoping I will not find the clinic. They will test you for free. These past few weeks I found myself crying under my red duvet, not leaving my room the whole day even though I was invited to a few parties. Yesterday, I almost missed a lecture. And when I finally made it, three of my classmates asked me worriedly, "Why do you look so tired?"

My gums have started bleeding whenever I brush my teeth. I Googled it and apparently it is one of the symptoms of either AIDS or diabetes. I have been tested for diabetes a hundred times. Unfortunately, I don't have it.

The tragi-comic part of my story is that after sleeping with numerous men, I've reached the conclusion that I'm not even into men – perhaps this explains why they're incapable of giving me orgasms and why I can't fall in love with them. I mostly fall in love with women, even though I haven't had the confidence to actually sleep with them. This is the ultimate tragedy: I am an AIDS-stricken lesbian. Good luck to me explaining that to my mother.

I should be in the library now, underlining *Orientalism*; instead I'm crawling to the sordid clinic taking deep breaths with a choking sound because I can't really breathe, because I don't know how to inform my parents of my disgraceful disease. They've sent me to England to prosper; instead I have destroyed myself with sex.

But I'll finally find the courage to tell them.

After all, my mother did tell me once that I look like "*viroos-e-AIDS*" after finding out I was not a virgin. But that was ages ago. I was eighteen. She's apologised a few times since. But it was a prophecy. I know my clever mother was right. I am human immunodeficiency virus.

Soho is crumbling before my eyes. I do not fancy Europe any more. Every English novel I read is filled with gay characters who end up being diagnosed with AIDS – my all-time favourite novel, Alan Hollinghurst's *The Line of Beauty*, is just one example. In London, on all the walls, there are hysterically happy advertisements of being tested for HIV "for free!" And I have avoided getting tested for more than a year. But I cannot take it any longer. I might need treatment. Perhaps, instead of paying my over-priced tuition fee, I need to spend this money to prolong the numbered days of my miserable life. But how can I tell my father what I am spending his hard-earned cash on?

I have finally arrived: 34 Dean Street. Unfortunately, I have found the clinic. A guillotine awaits me. This will not be a glorious death, but a disgraceful one. And I will bury the reason. I have already planned my suicide. It will happen this summer in Tehran, on the last day of being with my family. I will throw myself out of my bedroom window – we live on the eighteenth floor, so hopefully I shall be dead, not wheelchaired. I won't leave a suicide note.

The clinic is too bright, so I don't take off my H&M sunglasses; also, I don't want the tattooed receptionist to see the pathetic tears in my eyes.

Liam had extensive tattoos. I picked him up in Camden Town, blinded by his golden locks brightening up the Camden sky. We flirted under the guise of discussing the Arctic Monkeys' discography until the silver London rain started to fall. I offered him my black umbrella. He accepted and stood beside me. I touched his thin waist under my wet umbrella. We kissed near Camden Lock, his mouth small and minty; I invited him back to my place.

Tattooed people are more likely to be HIV positive. Where did I glean this helpful piece of information?

"Good morning!" the receptionist blurts out.

"He-llo!" I reply joyously – a sad imitation of the good old days when I was young and healthy and seductive. I force a smile which I know is dripping with sickness.

I fill out the form on the computer. It is asking whether I've fucked a bisexual man or not. I think hard. How the hell am I supposed to know the sexual orientation of people whose names I have difficulty recalling?

Yes, on a few occasions, the Boots condoms were torn . . . but that does not count as "unprotected sex" – or does it?

The happy receptionist asks me to go downstairs and wait for my name to be called.

I crawl down the serpentine staircase and find myself in a black and white room with three beautiful men. Their long legs fidgeting in sable and purple skinny jeans like the tantalising promise of hell. I ogle their sophisticated buns and anxious eyes. We give each other consoling smiles, regretting our self-sabotaging beauty.

In a few minutes, a tall woman saunters to the waiting room and calls my name.

I run after her like a shot puppy.

We enter a narrow corridor which I hope is an endless tunnel, but in a moment she opens a door and I find myself in a sunny office with a small white sink. I throw my body on the sink, my head hanging from my neck like the corpse of the puppy from a tree, and my mouth a deep well uttering whiny noises like "aaaaahhhhh" and then calling the god I was proud of not worshipping, "khodaaa". The woman stares at me, wildly mascaraed eyes wide with discomfort; her tone is cold and almost offended. "What's wrong?"

Realising she is extraordinarily gorgeous, I'm convinced she is the angel of death. I sit opposite her, feeling small – I am a sacrificed lamb at the altar of the goddess of death.

"Are you OK?"

"No," I bellow. "I think I might have AIDS."

"Why do you think that? Do you have any symptoms?"

"No." I find myself lying, not being able to tell her about my itchy vagina, bleeding gums and hair loss.

"Are you a sex worker?" she asks.

"No!" I reply, shaking. "I'm a student!" I think of my father, who claims to be proud of me. Should he be? I am shedding tears. I haven't seen him in a year, and now the child the old man is proud of has a self-inflicted disease. Instead of a successful doctor, I'll just be a dead student.

"Why are you so worried? Have you had unprotected sex with drug addicts?"

"No!"

"Then why are you so anxious? If you don't tell me, I can't help you."

"I have slept with thirteen men," I finally confess to the uninterested goddess.

"That doesn't mean you have AIDS." I am starting to feel a bit hopeful, but she adds, "Also, HIV isn't a death sentence. People live with it until they're eighty, ninety years old."

I have so much difficulty tolerating the mental image of my ninety-year-old HIV-positive self. "How long will it take?" I ask aggressively. "Sixty seconds?"

"I'm not going to do the sixty-second test with you. We'll text you the result in six hours. You're not high risk. Also, I won't be able to deal with you if it's a false positive."

"Six hours?" I scream. But she acts deaf.

My body trembles while she is taking my blood. But as soon as I see the red filling the plastic tube, I feel relieved. My blood looks so pure it shines.

"I'm sorry I behaved a bit dramatically earlier. I'm usually very well-mannered," I say to the woman, sounding even more insane as I am apologising to her while trying to convince her that I am "well-mannered".

"It's all right," she mutters.

I can feel she can't wait to get rid of me but I want to stick to her for the rest of my life. I'm considering ways of convincing her to become my carer if I happen to be HIV positive. But she is already kicking me out of her office. I crawl back to my room, not being able to eat lunch, awaiting the fateful text message.

When I reach my bed, I fall unconscious, having the same nightmare that I've had for the last eight months or so: I'm informed that I am HIV positive. I am in the same room with my mother, and when I finally manage to tell her, she just says, "I knew." And exits the claustrophobic room, leaving me behind with the result sheet in my left hand.

My phone vibrates and I wake up from this charming dream. *Your HIV test was negative (clear). Your syphilis test was negative (clear). You do not need any treatment.*

My heart pounds hard. I take a deep breath and feel like a newborn, until it occurs to me that the girl is too angelic to let me know the *real* result. She knows I can't handle the truth and would kill myself, hence she has sent me this life-giving lie.

I know I have it. I look in the mirror, and examine the pale face my numerous lovers have admired, and it looks like nothing but a true human immunodeficiency virus.

Kissing

ELINOR JOHNS

May grew up in the shadow of her older brothers, measuring her self-worth against the ebb and flow of her mother's attention. The urge to be noticed made her reckless. She would spit in the pudding bowl, or chalk words on the privy wall. Often, she spied on her brother Geraint, who was ten years older, following him into the long grass. She held her breath, unseen and quivering, while he smoked roll-ups and kissed first Eileen the Post and later, Rhian, the fishmonger's daughter. Spying was no good without telling: "Geraint's been kissing Rhian the Fish on the bench in the park."

Muma pulled in her lower lip when she heard such news. Then, she would get down on all fours with a brush and a wet rag, attacking the stone floor until she was puffed out and her knees were black and grimy with dirty water. Muma was all sharp angles on the outside, her cheekbones high, and her eyes hard as flint, but her heart was soft where her boys were concerned.

One time, May told on Geraint within earshot of her father. Their da could not bear the thought of his son sinning in the eyes of the Lord. When Geraint came home whistling Da whipped him with his belt before he had time to ask why. Muma grabbed May half by the pinafore dress and half by her plait and pushed her into the pantry. She hissed, "*Merch fach, twp!* Look what you've done with your tittle-tattle." May felt her mother's spittle on her cheek and an open hand cuffed her so that her temple caught against the pantry shelf. It did not sting as much as being told that she was a stupid little girl. She sat in the coal shed, in the dark, until the litter of kittens mewling in the corner got on her nerves. Muma served cawl for supper that was tepid and awash with leeks, guaranteed to give May heartburn. After just a few mouthfuls of the broth it sliced her in two, so that she doubled over and had to press her stomach across the wooden seat of her chair to find relief. Muma did not look at her once. Three weeks later, Geraint was sent to complete his carpentry apprenticeship in Pontyberem.

Muma would not allow her sons to be devoured by the pit-mouth, to be slaves to the machine. She would not see her lithe boys, with their peat-coloured hair and skin fresh as hen's eggs, dropped into the darkness and covered in coal dust. Their da could not walk up the hill to chapel without churning up sticky, black lumps in his spit and she would not have this happen to them. Nor would she let them spend hours in narrow tunnels that would cripple them. Her fears had tumbled through her dreams at night until Geraint became a carpenter and Dafydd went into the military, which in peacetime was far safer than the colliery.

May proved good at school. Muma was oblivious to the significance; it was May's teacher alone who had ambitions for her. Mrs Williams had been an ambulance driver, in Swansea, from 1942 until the end of the war. She had no time for girls who wanted only to get married, and pushed May to apply for teacher training at Trinity, Carmarthen. The day she applied, May's eyes glowed with amber flecks, and her heart swooped. Then in the summer of 1959, when the air was thick and stagnant, Da was caught in a crush between two coal trucks. His accident changed the natural order of things and she could not leave. Muma could not stand looking at her husband's mangled face nor his hands, the size of spades, lying idle in his lap. May was forced to take charge.

Every day for the best part of a year, May shaved her father, and once a week she washed him like a baby in the tin bath in front of the fire. May begrudged him nothing. She sought only to distract him while Muma reddened her lips with the damp edges of the New Testament and Dai the Fish dropped round with an extra piece of cod. Her da's defiant eyes were still watchful; it was just his jaw that was out of alignment and made him drool. His loss of purpose stifled him like a shroud, leaving him breathless, and it was his lungs that did for him in the end. Eleven months after the accident, he passed away from the miner's curse which the doctor called pneumoconiosis. Muma and May wordlessly struck a truce while they washed the body together, laying it out; his skin waxy in death, blurred to them both by tears. They agreed in the village that he'd timed his death very nicely. May could go to college now after all.

Her brothers and the men from the colliery paid their respects to Da. May would have attended the burial herself, but it was not the custom. Muma wept when the mourners returned to the house, and Dai the Fish stood next to her holding her hand in both his own, sighing in rhythm with her sobs. The old men shook Geraint by the hand and said it was an awful blow. May turned away, on pretence of helping in the kitchen. Once everyone was seated and supping in the front room, the mood changed; soon the miners told jokes and Muma sang *Count Your Blessings*, twice, on request. May's brothers got drunk on tales of their father down the pit, in ghoulish fascination with the hardship they themselves had escaped.

They listened to phlegmy old men tell how their da had been sent to work from childhood, tasked with opening and closing the doors for the coal trucks to pass; heard their talk of endless days with nothing but the scuttling in the darkness for company and how Da's own experience made him kind to the boys who were sent down in their turn. Of course these lads would fear the heavy closeting of the dark, their only company the nipping rats, sniffing around precious tuck. He knew they'd long for the rumble on the tracks, the whites of a man's eyes, and the gas lamps. At least then, they would be given fleeting knowledge of the tomb-like tunnel, as the older men crawled by, stinking of sweat. By all accounts Da was a sullen man but he would lighten up for the young lads who manned the doors.

"Transformed by their need, he was, mun," Alun Price told Geraint between fits of coughing that left him purple. He struggled to spit into a cotton hanky. "Your father would go for hours not saying a damn word, but as soon as he saw the lads he would start singing hymns in that big, gravelly voice of his and the rest of us would jump out of our bloody skins!" Alun rattled with laughter and May sat still on a hard-backed chair, listening in silence. She was sour with the sight of them eating bara brith and swilling beer when her father was freshly buried in the soil.

Eileen the Post had come back to Llefach at Geraint's request, and was pouring tea while the men reminisced. She looked up, teapot in one hand, pausing to catch May's eye. May reddened, aware of the scowl on her face, which contrasted so sharply with the warmth of Eileen's smile. Eileen passed her a teacup. Their heads were bowed close as she poured the tea and then Geraint called Eileen to him and any connection was lost. May couldn't take a sip. The overcrowded room was suffocating and she left the mourners to their revelry, taking refuge out the back, not expecting the other girl would follow her a minute later.

Outside, in the little yard, Eileen cupped a ready-rolled cigarette in her hand, shielding it from the wind to light it: an expert. She had spent the last five years in Llanelli, shunning a job at her parents' post office in Llefach. Two years ago, she'd gained a job in the new ball-bearings factory. The work had given her tall frame a slight stoop, but May had always found the older girl dashing and she seemed all the more impressive on her return to the village. The difference of five years away showed in the easy slur to her voice and the change in the clothes she wore. May envied her stylish slacks and was intrigued that instead of wrapping up in a shawl, as she used to, she now wore a woollen coat patterned with large black-and-white check. Eileen shunned both hats and headscarves and wore her thick, chestnut hair shorter than anyone else in Llefach, so that it emphasised the wide curve of her eyebrows and the slant of her cheeks. May thought it was the face of a goddess, but Muma's neighbours tutted and shook their heads when Eileen walked into the post office. "Pity for her," they said, spitting through their teeth.

The two young women leaned against the wall, holding themselves rigid in the chilly air. May could not look away when Eileen turned to her with eyes that glittered like cut coal.

"What are you doing out here in the cold, bach?"

"I've come to poody."

Eileen laughed. "Well, if you can't poody at a parent's funeral, when can you? Sulk away, little one."

May started to shiver so much that Eileen dropped the cigarette, grinding it under the heel of her penny loafer, and grasped May's hands between hers. "You're freezing, you poor dab," she said, chafing them into warmth and adding, "I'm sorry about your da." Her voice was low and she leaned in as she spoke, so that May felt Eileen's breath against her ear and her cheek. An unexpected quickening inside her urged Eileen's lips closer. Eileen paused only for a moment before kissing May full on the mouth, one hand pressing against the back of her head, the other still clasping May's fingers. May didn't pull away; no one had kissed her before. Eileen's lips were soft and bitter tasting and May felt little pulses like pins of fire darting deep inside her as the kiss took hold. The break in contact left them breathless. Then Eileen said, "You're a better kisser than your brother, you know. If you want a cwtch later, you know where I am."

May flushed at the glib tone in the face of such enormity. She felt guilty now Geraint had been mentioned, and flurried at the idea of a cuddle, what it might promise. She sank back against the wall, dropping Eileen's hand.

"Don't worry, no one saw," Eileen said with a short laugh, then more gently, "*Dewch mewn, cariad.* Come in, love." She pulled May by the sleeve, back through the kitchen door into the warm fug of smoke, a mix of fumes from the coal fire and pipe tobacco. There were still a dozen or so of their neighbours crowding around Muma and her sons. Someone had lit the candles in the long brass holders on the mantelpiece so that the front room glowed with heat and light and elongated shadows haunted the walls. Eileen perched on the arm of the big chair, next to Geraint, one foot against the floor, the other leg, bearing her weight, lifted and bent at the knee, so that her plaid slacks rode up and showed the milky whiteness of her calf. May felt heat prickle between her breasts as she watched from the doorway, and her fingers burned where Eileen had touched them. Geraint's voice trembled through the room as he led the singing of *Calon Lan* in a soft tenor, and the air vibrated with the pull of men's voices. The words of the hymn, *Pure Heart*, brought tears to their eyes at last.

When Eileen left with her parents, May was washing up in the kitchen. She hadn't said goodbye, perhaps still hoping May would come and find her, later. Mingled with May's grief was a longing that tilted her, like a boat unbalanced in the eye of a storm; but she did not go. Instead, she spent the night black-souled and fitful. In the morning, by the time May woke, Geraint was already waving Eileen off on the bus back to Llanelli. When Muma told her this, May clutched her side as though a rib had fractured. She would have wept had Muma not forbidden it. "Buck up, girl," Muma said, and made her clean the grate and fetch the coal, jobs she knew May hated.

It was a relief to leave for college a month later, but there was nothing of the thrill she had anticipated. Of necessity, she folded away all thoughts of Eileen. In her letters home she wrote only that the course was dull and the other girls unfriendly. She spent those first few months living in a tiny attic room that was musty and airless. Downstairs was dominated by ruddy-faced Betty Williams whose haunches, like her bosom, were mountainous, and who smelled like tinned soup. Her pale, wiry husband was a caretaker at the college and spent his wages supping ale at the Dog. Their twin babies screeched through the night, waking May with their cries, and in return May's footsteps on the floorboards were a source of waspish complaint.

May dreaded her daily walk to and from the college. The town dwarfed her, cars splashed her stockings, snaking past through oily puddles. Unfamiliar faces leered at her on the streets and old women, parsnip-skinned and foul-mouthed, elbowed her out of their way on market day. Carmarthen was all blackening brick and fetid air. On the horizon, she saw only the high curving wall in front of the municipal building that had once been the gaol. It mocked her longing for the hills of Llefach.

Her only refuge was the library, which smelled of wood and polish like a schoolroom. Here, she fooled others that she was content to cradle hefty textbooks on education theory, nursing them at the reading tables. Yet, she spent most of her time trailing her fingers along the shelves of fiction, thumbing through novels. Only Evan James, the librarian, noticed her restlessness. He was a small man, with a shock of black hair swept back off a high forehead. His eyes were deep-set behind gold-rimmed glasses. In his dark suit and tie he seemed much older than May. The first time he spoke to her properly she was reading *The Rainbow*. He tapped her shoulder and made her jump.

"Well, well, well," he said. "It is Mr D. H. Lawrence who has you hidden away behind the bookshelves, is it?"

She snapped the book shut. His tone made her flustered, and she touched her blotchy neck as though scalded. He licked the spittle from the corner of his lip, and asked her if she would like to join him on a drive out to the beach at the weekend. In her confusion she agreed. Later, she found that Betty Williams already knew she would be missing tea on Sunday. While washing out her smalls in the bathroom sink she mulled it over, regretful but duty-bound to let news of her courting chinwag its way to Llefach. It would, at least, please Muma.

They drove to Pendine in his Austin A35 which she duly admired for its comfy leather seats and the new-fangled indicator that lit up the dashboard when he turned the dial. She had been to the beach as a child, with Minister Bevan and the Sunday school, on the bus to Burry Port, but never before by car. Pendine was different because you could take the car onto the solid, flat sand and drive for miles along it. It was much too cold to enjoy the beach in December; it was windy and the tide far out. Evan wanted to walk to the shelter of the dunes, but the moment they left the car, it was as though they had been flung onto an arid planet. Sand whipped into May's eyes and they were forced back inside. Evan took charge then, holding her face in his moist hands, making her blink to rid herself of grit. While her eyes were streaming he pressed his lips against hers, his tongue greedy and slavering, pushing past her teeth, his right hand clawing at her clothing. He released her only when she struggled, protesting, "Evan! No! I can't!" In the years that followed, when May recalled the kissing she remembered only how her eyes stung.

"No, no, that's right," he said, when she resisted. Then he patted her on the arm before offering her half an egg sandwich. She sat there stunned while he told her facts he had gleaned from encyclopaedias in the library. May took in nothing of the conversation, transfixed only by the remains of the bread, pasted in the gaps between his teeth.

She turned away to watch through the window as the sea expanded from a belt at the horizon. The water made her think of the pages she had read at the library; of Ursula Brangwen and Miss Inger bathing naked and kissing in the moonlight. Slowly, the force of the insult she had suffered from this man beside her faded; Evan James was relevant only as her means of leaving the beach. All May could think of as he droned on was the intoxication of the other kiss. The memory of Eileen's lips on hers made her giddy so that she almost laughed out loud.

At the ramp, the sea came creeping forward, towards their wheels, grey and foaming with flotsam at the edges. Evan cursed under his breath until they were safely on the road. They drove back in silence and she hardly cared what he was thinking. He pulled the car up outside her digs and May reached for the door just as Evan stayed her hand, grazing her wrist with his thumbnail. Shrugging him off, May muttered goodbye and clambered out. She slammed the car door and the sound thudded in her chest.

She knew that Evan would see her turn away from the house, and that Betty Williams would be all judgement, bobbing wide-eyed at the window. She did not care that it was already getting dark and she was running in the street. The red telephone box was only yards ahead on the main road. May fumbled for thruppence in her purse. She had memorised the number. It was one of several she had found after the funeral, in Geraint's jacket pocket, scribbled in haste on scraps of paper, scrolled up and tied with an elastic band. She hauled open the telephone box, stepping over a bag of half-eaten chips squished in newspaper on the floor, vinegar masking the smell of something worse. Her fingers were deft as she dialled but the ringing went on and on and the thought that no one would answer constricted her chest. When someone picked up she felt dizzy with relief.

"Is Eileen there? Can I speak to Eileen Rees, please? It's May, tell her. May Jones."

The woman's voice on the other end was young, and brusque.

"Another call for Eileen! You'll have to wait while I see if she's in."

The thought of others ringing for Eileen jabbed at May, and she had to steady the heavy receiver against her ear with both hands. Then a startled voice said, "May? Is that you?" and the sense of Eileen being there at last, on the other end of the line, inflamed May so that she felt choked and incoherent. "Oh, Eileen – you're there! Really there! I was so . . . so worried you wouldn't be!"

"Calm down, *cariad fach*."

The familiar, sardonic edge to Eileen's voice, even as she called her "little love", made May bold.

"I need to see you," she said, and her voice was like quicksilver. "I don't care what Muma, or Geraint, or Minister Bevan, or anyone else thinks! *Iesu Grist*, Eileen, I think you are magnificent!" She waited for a second before rushing on, "Say something! Tell me what you're thinking! Quick, Eileen!"

"Well, I'm thinking this has been a long time coming," Eileen said, laughing in her throat. Then her tone changed to a new tenderness. "And I'm here," she said. "I am here, May, and I am waiting."

The money ran out then, just as May knew it would, and there was nothing for it but to make her way back to her digs. For once, May walked slowly. She let her raincoat flap open, and the wind loosen her curls. Then she paused and tipped her head back to feel the first drops of evening rain.

What to Do When You Can't Do Anything

STEPHANIE HUTTON

The consultant is still talking, fingertips poised on his desk as if he is about to play a concerto. Unsettling minor-key melodies fill the room, yet I feel nothing while I weep. Palliative is a pretty word. It masks a horror that should not wrap its spindly legs around my three-year-old. A greying moustache hangs over his top lip. I watch the curve of his tongue as he says that word again. His dishevelled hair flaps on his head as he nods along, looking down at his notes.

"Here are some leaflets on hospice care, support for you afterwards and so forth. The nurses will explain."

Then it comes. Fiery and raw, the strength blasts up from my stomach and down my arm. I grab the back of his head and slam his face into the desktop, crunching his glasses into podgy flesh. The force of my thrust pushes his head right through the oak. Cardboard files of nameless others fall through the gap and trap him under their weight.

I press Pause. A welcome silence holds me upright as the wall clock stops its countdown. Peering through the window I see a world that I can't allow to carry on, not yet. Traffic is frozen into patient queues; a bird dangles in the air mid-descent.

Hope pours down my veins and pools on the grey tiles underneath my feet like lost petrol on the driveway. I step out of the puddle and into the hospital corridor. The statues around me clutch clipboards, stare at phones, hold hands. My feet march to Ella's ward. I hate every pastel princess and tumbling clown painted on these walls, smiling down at our children's suffering.

In the first bay, a bony teenage boy is captured in the moment just before he unhooks himself from the tube going into his arm. The nurse caught striding across the shiny floor seems familiar. Her hair is scraped into a tight bun to help keep a smile on her face. My girl is curled up on a beanbag in the reading corner. She frowns in concentration. Wisps of new doll-like hair glow on her temples. In the stillness, I crouch down and try to find a smell that belongs to her. With my cheek against hers, I dream of a time before this. Of early Sunday mornings with her wriggling beside me, telling me jokes that make no sense. Both of us giggling without knowing why.

I place my hand over hers. I wish we could stay in this embrace for ever – but this is not a forever I wish for her. I kiss her head and whisper my love to her. The words turn to diamonds, glimmering at the corners of her eyes and cascading down her cheeks. Reaching into her, I steal a small ball of cells and place them in the locket around my neck.

Back in the car park, I remove the parking fine from the windscreen and throw it with the others on the seat behind me. In the next row, a woman in crumpled clothes holds her hand across her brow as if that will help her recall where she parked this morning, perhaps before she earned the title "widow". Mere moments have changed who we are. I unpause the scene. The woman turns her head from left to right, scanning each row helplessly.

My foot vibrates against the pedal as I race back to the village. At the health centre, I swing into a space marked "Doctors only". The receptionist shakes her head at me, her red talons tapping against the glass between us as I march past and throw open the door that leads to the doctor's office. Afternoon clinic does not start for another thirty minutes. I unfasten the locket and place the nest of cells in my left palm. He jumps as I burst into the room. His jaw tightens as he recognises me. This man who sent me and Ella away again and again. Who told me to stop worrying, to get some rest. Maybe have a spa day. He mumbles some formalities while looking at what must be an interesting spot on the wall. I fake a stumble and as he recoils from the discomfort of human contact, my left hand sneaks through his blue shirt and taut flesh. Tucked under his stomach, his pancreas squishes against my fingertips as I embed the cells into their new home. I pull back and apologise with a smile. He will feel unwell for a while. His wife will call it work stress. By the time he turns yellow, it will be too late to halt.

On my way out of the building, I smash my elbow against the fire alarm. As the bells scream at the staff to get out, I slam my hand onto the fire door and seal it shut with the heat of my rage. They will know the panic and confusion of realising there is no way out. For an hour or two, anyway.

Back at the house, I drop my bags in the hallway and check for lights. My husband is still in his bed after a night shift. I hadn't told him about today's appointment. Over the last eight months we have settled into a silence, swerving between stalagmites of unspoken words as we pass through the house doing those things that seem to need doing. Our shared bed broke in two from the weight of our pain. He moved to the spare room.

I stride the stairs and plan the words I must say. *They have done all they can do.* This man who can sleep as though there is no crying to be done. Who plays golf as I pull out clumps of my hair that are no use to anyone. He stirs as I enter. We look straight at each other. I curl up next to him on the bed. He cannot read my face and I cannot speak. His hand reaches up and touches my forehead, cups my chin. My face melts into his palm and he reads the Braille of my tears. He sobs from his stomach and holds me so tight I wonder what it would be like if I never inhaled again.

We Are Making You With Our Eyes

GEMMA WEEKES

We are making you with our eyes.

Don't forget this.

We've been hundreds of eyeballs.

We've been six hundred eyeballs trained on your YouTube channel.

A thousand eyeballs.

Three thousand eyeballs unblinking through your telly audition.

Ten thousand eyeballs watching you chuck your throat open and sing not-half-badly on *Saturday Night Sing-Off*. On that cookery reality show that got cancelled. That jungle reality show that got cancelled. Thirty thousand eyeballs watching you squabble with Whatshisface on that social-experiment reality show while we scooped garish food into our heads. Forty-two thousand eyeballs flooding their banks when you finally locked tongues. Ah. That kiss! (You-know-the-one.)

We've been fifty thousand eyeballs making a brand of your name. Scouring the internet for your latest faux pas and your newest fuck boy and eyebrow crayon tutorial and that time you twerked the alphabet in your Union Jack knickers. We liked that.

One hundred and twenty thousand eyeballs trolling your duck-faced Instagram selfies. Seven hundred thousand eyeballs peeled for bargains in your online sportswear shop, making of your pink hoodies something more than fabric and logos; making of them scenes from a life-worth-living; making you after our own image, but better: body ageless and smooth as a McDonald's burger bun. Nine hundred thousand. One-point-two million.

Lovingly, with our eyeballs, we have purged the grime of obscurity from your brow and burned away pimples and all superfluous pigment. In the fierce and benevolent light of our eyeballs, you have found yourself saved.

We have been three million eyeballs. Four million.

We have not looked away in boredom. We have not abandoned you. We've given you a new home and better clothes. Behold, we have made you blond not brunette. "Exotic" not coloured (sorry, a coloured person (sorry, a person of colour (sorry? Whatever.))). We've put you in high heels worth more than our organs on the black market. With our eyeballs we've tolerated that annoying way you catch your tongue between your teeth when you speak. We've tolerated the razor bumps in your armpits and that dress you wore to the British Film Awards that looked like a fucking lampshade.

You are nothing except what we've made of you.

You were not a you until we gave you to yourself.

Don't forget it.

Outside the sky is pissed off and about to bust open. You'll have to work hard to convince us you still belong up here, where the weather is always fair, temperature regulated, under the fat, meringue-coloured lights with Barbie and Ken, as bright and clean as the light from our own eyeballs. The floors shine. The couches are sweet shades of tangerine and custard.

The cameras will roll in five – four – three – two . . .

". . . And we have Galatéa in the studio! So nice to see you again!"

We are five million eyeballs aimed at your head: blinking, remoistening, looking right into the TV – not around the TV but right into the pupil of the eye of the TV – where you sit, on that famous couch, on that huge plastic ass, in that tight pink dress, under a veil of hair so thick it could never spring from one scalp unless that scalp was the size of Queen Elizabeth Olympic Stadium. Your race is "suntan". Hair the same colour as your skin; eyes the same colour as "your" hair; all of it a synthetic shade of caramel – not the type you make by burning sugar and adding cream, but the kind you'd get out of a tin, and you don't know what went into it, and it's gloopy and too sweet, and it smells rancid, and it tastes like metal.

You look like you would taste rancid and smell like metal.

One of your meaty legs is crossed over the other, in betrayal of your fitness video; and a platform heel dangles from your fat foot. It's gonna be a long fall back down into the gutter, girlfriend, in that pink dress and sandals.

Sandals! Aren't you cold?

Maybe you didn't know it's October.

Newsflash: it's October.

Do you think anyone wants to look at all that jelly while trying to keep down their cereal? This is not the time or the place. This is Breakfast Television.

Daytime.

Television.

You have four minutes.

"How are you feeling today, Galatéa? Lucky?"

You say nothing. Do something that might be a nod. You smile like a zombie at the Zombie Miss Universe Pageant. Your smile is a dogma. Your smile is novocaine. Your smile is titanium; like it would be impossible for you to stop smiling, even while taking a shit, or stabbing someone in the neck, or being run over by a coach, or hanging off a cliff by your gel-wrapped nails.

Your cheeks are oversmooth; all your contours painted in; your eyes two slits without context, without wrinkle. You might be about to break your face. Literally break your fucking face live on telly. Yeah, there was that one time we said you looked like Morgan Freeman's nutsack (in that magazine, after the break-up, you-know-the-one) but you've gone too far trying to look like a doll (and failing 'cause dolls look human but better. You don't look better. You look like a human that melted.). A million pounds couldn't fix how much of an eyesore you've become, even if you had that kind of cash. Which you don't.

The money's all spent, and so are you. Bet you wish you had your life to do over.

Say something.

We've seen the court papers online. All your coins have been drunk; trampled; totalled; repossessed; served up and eaten off posh plates; vomited on the side of the road and into reality-TV swimming pools. Seven million eyeballs watched you vomit into a swimming pool on that show (you-know-the-one). Ten million eyeballs gone wide at the sight of you falling drunk in the street two weeks later, twat on display for all to see. We had to watch it at least three times each and pass it on. Do you know how sickening that was?

Twelve million eyeballs forgotten what the fuck else you were famous for. Anything?

These days you probably can't even lip-sync in tune. It's eight a.m. but I bet you wish you had a drink right now, don't you? Drunken slag.

You have three minutes and thirty-three seconds.

Ken fiddles with his nice, light-blue shirt at the collar, then with the cuffs. Barbie does her concerned frown. They are our friends. With our eyeballs, we have made them more famous than ketchup, more loved than Christ. They are the neighbours everybody wants and nobody has, that would water our plants and feed our dogs and kindly maim anyone who tries to burgle our houses, if we could afford houses.

Behind them, huge windows look out over the muddy sky and the Thames. The studio is far above the Southbank: far above the laughs and shouts and sirens; beggars and street performers and bird-shat railings and carousel music.

"So there's been a lot of talk about your fashion choices lately . . ." says Barbie.

You manage, "Uh-huh." Still smiling.

Oh God, you've fucked your face up so bad it won't move. Is that it?

"What do you say to all your critics?"

Nothing.

"Some say you've wasted the opportunities we've given you," says Ken, pointedly. We love Ken.

"All the viewers at home have begun casting their votes, Galatéa . . ."

They're nudging you to make a case for yourself and eventually you're able to squeeze: "It's been really haaarrd . . ." out of those stiff, oversized lips in a mid-Atlantic accent, your native council-estate patois long gone. Are you British or American? Maybe you'd have more luck overseas with the Yanks.

But then, could you even afford to go? You should try swimming. Maybe you could use your fake tits as a flotation device. (A C cup would have sufficed. We told you so.)

". . . you know . . . just *haaard* . . ."

Barbie tilts her head sympathetically and when she does, her hair doesn't move.

This is how she sells hairspray – with an animated face and perfect hair. She is perfect in the gaze of our eyeballs; so fresh and perfectly made she might have no guts or sweat glands or pubic hair. Instead, she might have a hidden wire unfurling from a subtle hole in her back. It might be that when the cameras go off she is simply unplugged, her head sinking down gently onto her (34C) chest, into the folds of that pretty blouse, and she's wheeled into a storeroom until the next day while all the headlines of her life are made up in a special factory and printed in the magazines so we all know she's no different from us.

How amazing to be gently unplugged at the end of the day. Free and simple and empty of stench! Don't you wish your dramas were safety-tested in a factory?

You only have one hundred and forty seconds left to impress us. You've already spent one hundred seconds mostly just sitting there, with that grotesque smile on, like a mask, like this will be the mask you'll wear when you're dead, all the plastic parts of you unable to degrade, the white teeth and the hair and the ass and the tits lying around in a landfill until future civilisations dig you up and exhibit you as proof of our collective stupidity.

"One way or another, everything's going to change for you today . . . ! It's all going to be different for her, isn't it, Ken?"

"That's certainly true. Ha ha! So. Do you have anything to say to the viewers? What's your, you know, USP?"

Blank.

"The votes have already been flooding in and . . ." He grimaces. ". . . well it's not going well so far . . . !"

God, how we wish we could text in our own questions!

"Ken, shall we read out some tweets from the people at home?"

Oh, that's why we love Barbie!

What we want to know is: "Have you been forced to sell all your fancy furs on the internet, you mink-murdering, overspending . . . um, lady – overspending lady?"

We want to know: "How do you keep your face so plastic on a low income? Do you go down to your local cosmetic-surgery surgery and offer to clean their toilets and put their rubbish out?"

We want to know: "Do you rock up wearing a sign that says: 'Will Work For Botox'?"

What's it like?

Bad enough to be poor, but then having to live in the body of a caricature drawn by an adolescent boy who used, for inspiration, an overripe composite of all the bits of women he'd ever wanked to, but bigger, and without artistic skill. That's what you look like: a wank doodle.

We want to know: "What's it like to be a living wank doodle?"

And then the last of our comments is an actual slap, delivered by Barbie with vicious good humour. There has never been a more satisfying sound in all of creation.

By way of an answer, you start to leak yucky, masturbatory tears like the feral wailing of those crackheads who hang out around Tube stations trying to guilt us out of our loose change. You should have practised at home in the mirror.

You have ninety seconds and we are not voting for your redemption.

The gorgeous men are now at the ready. They're naked from the waist up, except for satin bow ties. The big window is open. Ready.

Go on.

Start blubbing to us about your wretched life. Your mum's life. Your mum's mum's life and so on. Your great-great-great maternal grandmother who was a slave. Your maternal great-grandmother who buried five of her sixteen children. Your grandmother who washed clothes in the river and shat in a hole. Your maternal great-great-grandfather who shot bows and arrows and whose people were almost entirely wiped out by the French and the English. Your maternal great-grandfather who was never commended for fighting in the First World War. Your mother who was born in a wooden house and raised in a flat the size of a rich man's toilet.

Blub to us about how you were abused by a family friend blah blah and went into care and about being poor and living in a high-rise flat with views over run-down car parks and shit-strewn patches of grass and about the struggles and the homelessness and the auditions and rejections and put-downs –

and being called monkey as a child and spat on in the street and are you from Jamaica but you weren't from Jamaica and blub to us about how you had the dream about the driveway and in that driveway a luxury car gleaming, colour of platinum, and up that driveway in the crotch of the driveway a front door of glossy red for good luck, and beyond that portal stretching out before one's eyes sparkle upon sparkle like the sun upon the seas –

gleaming wood and glass and chrome blinged out with sunshine. And how it felt to have the dream materialise, to be held in the gaze of all our eyeballs; how good it felt to have money and to be admired and to go waltzing through department stores buoyed by expensive clouds of perfume and classical music –

and to be free and buying whatever you wanted and being from an ethnic origin called "rich" and being a skin tone called "rich" and speaking a language called "rich". Going on posh sunny holidays and being loved by millions who didn't even know you and who just wanted to touch you while you passed them in the street with just a fingertip –

for a benediction –

and who wanted your photo, your signature, your news, your fake-eyelash line. Who wanted to know how it felt to almost be *there* . . .

at that place we all dream of . . . that any of us could reach if we were lucky . . .

if the light of five million eyeballs were turned upon us . . .

Tell us how you fought for everything you got.

Tell us how bad you want to live.

No don't tell us because we don't give a shit.

"We have some more tweets coming through, Galatéa . . . Apparently the crying thing isn't very popular. Everyone prefers your . . . what do you call it . . . twerking?"

"Oh yes, that was fantastic, wasn't it, Barbie?"

"Indeed it was, Ken! Can we have some music?"

The audience start clapping along with the *Wake Up Great Britain* theme tune.

You've leaned upon your own understanding before, and look where it's gotten you! Cleave to the moist wisdom of our eyeballs. The yang of our gaze. The yin of our blink. It's your own wilfulness blocking your throat, messing you up, kicking your voice down the back of your neck and down into the pit of your fat gut, where it crouches like a mangy rescue dog. You're trying to sit so you don't expose your cellulite but you're not doing it properly and we can all see it anyway! Do you really think you have anything else to lose?

"Twerk! Twerk! Twerk! Twerk!"

You still have sixty seconds. You still have fifty seconds.

You still have forty seconds.

Get up! That's right. Shake your ass!

Thirty.

Twenty.

Shake it!

Ten.

Shake your ass, go on. Shake your big lumpy ass in our faces, the ass that we made. Go on. Don't act like you're too good for it. Turn your face from the camera. We don't want to see your blubbing. Shut up.

We've got to be at work in thirty-five minutes staring into a screen not around the screen but right into the eye of the computer screen.

Shake it.

We're not blubbing about the no money and our self-harming kids and house prices rising faster than a dick on Viagra and the fumes and the radiated food and the cancer and the prime minister hunting rejected benefit claimants on the weekends and the everything and the everything else.

We made you up and we'll take you down. We'll chuck you out the studio window. We'll smash you into a thousand plastic bits and then we'll melt down those bits and reconfigure you into something actually useful like a suite of fucking furniture for the *Wake Up Great Britain* astroturfed garden.

You're not too good for it.

We're not too good for it.

Don't forget this.

We're all bad together, bitch.

"Looking great, Galatéa! The audience think you're pathetic but possibly in a funny way . . . Keep dancing. They definitely want some more time to laugh at you . . . You have another four minutes."

We are five million eyeballs aimed at your head: blinking, remoistening, looking right into the TV – not around the TV but right into the pupil of the eye of the TV.

You are nothing except what we've made of you.

Don't forget this.

We are making you with our eyes.

The Machine Gun Experiment
KEV PICK

"I'm not an artist," he said, apparently annoyed by the question. "Artists ask questions they don't need to answer. This is all about an answer."

"You're a philosopher?" Corey asked.

"Philosophers have never told you anything you couldn't tell yourself by looking out of a window to watch the rain." As if to demonstrate, he looked out of the window of the small café to the early-morning traffic beyond. He drained the last of his coffee. "Timewasters."

Corey nodded though he disagreed. "And you're not a scientist?"

"No –"

The waitress interrupted, asking if they'd like anything else after their breakfast. They declined. She took away their plates.

"– science has to be demonstrable. And repeatable. I don't think this can be repeated – at least, not by me. But I do need an observer."

Corey nodded again and turned a page in his notebook. He didn't write anything down. He hadn't written anything at all so far. "So, what do I call you?"

"Tom."

"No, I mean, how do I describe you? If not as a scientist, not as an artist, not –"

"I'm an explorer." Tom fished a pack of cigarettes from a coat slung across the back of his plastic chair. "I have a destination in mind and the view from the summit will be new to humanity."

"You're doing this for . . . humanity?" Corey found it difficult to disguise his incredulity.

Tom smiled. "Fair enough." He drew a cigarette into his fingers and turned it gently. "I just want to know." He stood up, took his raincoat and walked out into the street to smoke, the charming café bell tinkling as the door opened and closed.

Corey tried again to make some notes. Words fleeted across his mind, but none felt appropriate. Words like *depressed*, *egotistical* and *angry* swirled around with words like *determined*, *romantic* and *brave*. There was something here though, he thought. Something else. He suspected Tom was mentally ill. He thought about declining. He thought about calling his editor. He thought about calling the police. Was this illegal? It sounded illegal. It scared him.

He drew a smiley face.

The waitress returned with the bill. He gave her a generous note and went out into the rain.

Tom finished the last of his cigarette and dropped it to the wet pavement. "Well?" he said. "Are you in?"

Corey squinted and drew his collar up. He wished he was suave enough to carry an umbrella. "This might seem like an obvious question, but – are you suicidal?"

"No. Quite the opposite."

"Crawford Secondary," Tom told the taxi driver as they pulled away.

Corey screwed up his face. "Really? An abandoned school?"

"It isn't really abandoned. You can still rent the rooms. But yes – no – it isn't a school any more."

Corey composed a text to his editor, telling her where he would be. He still wasn't sure if he was going to take the story, but it was Wednesday, it was raining, and spending a morning with a mad scientist was better than sifting through piles of press releases. He corrected himself: an explorer, not a scientist.

"If you're not a scientist," Corey said, "why bother with us? We're a science platform."

"Your platform doesn't interest me," Tom said bluntly. "I've read some of your articles – the Schrödinger's Cat introduction, the stuff on tesseracts. You know the basics. Your older work, though – your Mexican diaries – the things you saw there. You can handle this."

Corey didn't say anything. He didn't want to think about that. It was already a miserable day. Instead, he looked at the rain beading on the taxi's window. He focused on an individual drop making its way down the glass, splitting and deforming, whipped about by the wind.

The car slowed as the school came into view, stopping by the gated entrance. As they got out of the taxi, Corey saw Tom pay the driver, alleviating some of his annoyance about being left to pay for breakfast. The school itself wasn't anything special, just a huddle of drab concrete buildings dumped by the side of an overgrown sports field. The old rugby posts were now a perch for sparrows. The old yard walls were a canvas for graffiti. The gates were chained and adorned with the appropriate public safety signs, one of them with the word *DERELICT* in large black letters.

Tom removed the padlock on the gates and let them both into the schoolyard, locking up behind them and then shoving his wet hands beneath his armpits. "The greenish building in the far corner," he said. "We're in there."

Corey followed along. He doubted that this place was available for rent, but was reassured by Tom having a key. His editor knew where he was, the taxi driver saw them. This would be OK.

Tom started jogging, keeping his head down against the rain. Corey made a half-hearted attempt at keeping pace, but he was already soaked and had stopped caring.

Inside the building, they shook off the weather and walked down a narrow corridor into a large classroom, poorly illuminated by the grey morning through the high windows. Some of the windows were covered by old sheets. The way their footsteps echoed made Corey feel nostalgic for his old schooldays. He remembered the clatter of assembly, the thunder of lunchtime, the hollow ring of detention. He remembered his last day and his old friends. He remembered the dismembered bodies that littered the scrub of Juarez Valley.

Tom switched on the lights. "This is it."

Three large metal screens were bolted together, almost cutting the room in two; the middle divider had a small window in it. On the side where they stood, all the furniture had been stacked up and pushed against the blackboard. Corey couldn't see what lay on the other side. "Come on," Tom chirped. He led Corey around the dividers, banging one of them as he passed. It boomed, bell-like. "Just in case it cooks and gets out of control. These will protect any observer." On the other side, their footsteps were deadened by sheets on the floor.

"Ta-dah!" Tom smiled proudly, pointing towards a machine gun attached to a low tripod that was screwed into the ground. It looked heavy and unforgiving. A few feet in front of the muzzle was a stool. The stool was watched by a video camera on another tripod in the corner of the room. More old sheets were hung around the walls.

Corey's hand went to his pocket. He gripped his phone.

"This," Tom said, "is a Browning M1919. Thirty calibre. Belt feed. About four hundred rounds per minute."

Corey looked at it, at the air-cooling holes along the cold black barrel jacket, at the golden rounds that slid from its side. He followed the ammunition belt with his eyes until it disappeared into a dull military-green box. The trigger mechanism seemed to have been removed and covered up with industrial tape. From beneath the tape, a long metal wire stretched down to the floor, curling and looping its way towards the stool. On the end of the wire was more tape and a mechanical button.

Tom caught him staring. "It's nice, isn't it?"

"Where did you get this?"

"Online. It cost me nearly six grand, all told – without ammunition."

Corey wanted to reach out and hold the grip, inhale the gunpowder and oil, but restrained himself. "Listen, if this is black market or some sort of –"

"I have a receipt," Tom said. "I have a permit. It's registered."

"It's a machine gun. You said you were using a quantum machine gun not . . . a . . . a machine gun. This is dangerous."

"It's extremely dangerous." Tom pointed towards the wall opposite where large chunks of plaster had fallen away, revealing a dented steel column.

Corey looked at the shattered stonework, noticing other holes and scratches near the ceiling. He turned to look at the metal room dividers, stood shoulder to shoulder. He saw scratches and dents, burn marks and discoloration. He felt his heart want to beat faster but ordered himself to calm down. He'd seen enough. He was a journalist now. "I don't see any melons," he said.

"What?"

"When we spoke this morning, you said you were experimenting with melons and complaining about the mess, but I don't see . . ."

Tom frowned. "Did I say that? I don't . . ."

"I don't see any books, either," Corey continued. "I don't see anything written on that blackboard. I don't see anything that suggests research."

Tom sighed and walked towards the video camera and turned it on. It beeped cheerfully. "All of my research is here. If you want equations, read quantum physics. If you want results, however . . . just watch."

"It's suicide," Corey said. He turned round and began to walk away.

"Quantum suicide," Tom called after him. "Not quite the same thing."

"I disagree." Corey walked around the metal dividers to the other side of the room but with every step towards the door, he felt his stomach pull towards the gun. It had been a long time since he'd done anything but write about dry experiments gleaned from universities in which he had little interest or involvement. It had been a long time since he'd stood in the blood-wet sands of Mexico, where he'd been so close to death he could do nothing but feel alive.

"Fine!" Tom shouted as Corey headed into the corridor. "Wait – you'll need the keys . . ."

Corey slowed his pace and stopped. He turned and waited for Tom to appear. He waited some more. It was suddenly quiet except for the gentle rain drumming on the flat roof. "Tom?"

Tom didn't answer.

Corey moved cautiously back through the door, his stomach doing a little flip of satisfaction as he stepped into the room and towards the dividers, towards the middle one, the one with the small window. He didn't say anything. A part of him knew he shouldn't look. He peered through.

Tom was sitting on the stool, facing the machine gun. The remote trigger was in his hand. In his other hand was a sheet of paper which he held up towards the video camera. He looked round at Corey and made eye contact through the glass.

"Just watch," Tom said. "I promise, we'll be OK." With that, he squeezed the trigger.

The Browning M1919 responded instantly, shattering the silence with a half-second of explosions. Three rounds ripped through the barrel as the ammo belt twitched and then fell still again.

Tom wasn't sitting on the stool any more. His body had fallen forward while bits of his head had flown behind him. The sheet beneath his body quickly bloomed with blood.

Corey had a ringing in his ears. The gunshots had died away, but he felt like the echoes would last for ever. He stared, taking in every detail he could tolerate. The open eyes. The shattered skull. The blood-slick hair. If this was to be a memory that would haunt him for ever, he wanted to know it well, to get comfortable with it, so when he inevitably recalled the scene, his mind would welcome him instead of turning him away.

He realised he'd been holding his breath. He exhaled and filled his lungs. Be professional, he thought. A flood of necessities came to him. Emergency. Authorities. Numbers. Forms. Who to call? What to say? Process.

He walked along the dividers and peered around to the other side. Tom had dropped the trigger. It lay on the floor near his hand. The gun was silent, as if it had never spoken. He moved closer to the body and looked at the sheet of paper Tom had been holding. It was face down. Gently, Corey knelt and turned it over, aware that the camera was still watching. All it had written on it was a large number four.

"Just watch," Tom said. "I promise, we'll be OK." With that, he squeezed the trigger.

The Browning M1919 responded instantly, but only with a dull click, and then immediately fell silent. Tom grinned and stood up. He raised his hands above his head and cheered towards the camera. "Four!" he shouted. He turned round and saw Corey still looking through the glass. "I told you. It works!"

Corey frowned. He wasn't sure what he'd just seen. Was the gun a fake? A copy? Was this a magic trick? A con? He walked around to the other side where Tom approached him and shook his hand for some reason. "Welcome to the fifth dimension," he said.

Corey scowled. "What?"

"It's a joke. Relax. But thank you for watching. It's important to be observed." He hurried towards the camera to check the footage.

"You knew it would jam," Corey said. It wasn't a question.

"Uh-huh."

"And the gun isn't rigged?"

"Uh, no," Tom said. "Sorry, I should have demonstrated that first, really. I'm not very organised. You can try it yourself."

Corey felt he should refuse, but walked towards the machine gun and picked up the remote trigger.

Tom gestured towards the gun's backplate. "You need to slide the –"

"I know." Corey bent down and drew back the bolt to re-arm the weapon.

"Take the trigger behind the screen," Tom insisted. "It might ricochet."

He did so, dragging the wire around to the other side to look through the window; followed by Tom. He thought about plugging his ears, but didn't really expect the gun to fire. He held down the trigger and jumped involuntarily as dozens of rounds blasted into the wall, barking and squealing until he let go of the button. His ears whined. A cloud of brick dust filled the room.

"Satisfied?" Tom said.

Corey looked at the button in his hand. "This thing could take down a plane."

"If you're going to do it again, use short bursts. That ammunition is expensive. Now, let's do five. Wait here."

"What?"

"Trial number five," Tom said. He took the trigger from Corey and disappeared round the divider to the other side. "We're going to do this ten times."

"Now?"

"Yes now." Tom reached into his pocket and pulled out a folded piece of paper. It had a large number five drawn on it. He showed it to the camera.

"Wait," Corey said. "I have some questions."

Tom ignored him. "Of course you do, but just watch. The chances of you observing me beating the gun twice in a row are . . . well, I don't know what they are. I'm not much of a mathematician, but the odds are huge, or small, or however it works."

"Wait," Corey said again. "I need to – Can we get some procedure here? What do you mean, 'trial number five'?"

Tom hesitated. "I've done some earlier work, that's all. I just . . . need you to not turn away."

Corey opened his mouth to speak but Tom was already settling himself on the stool and facing the muzzle of the gun. "It's going to work," he said. "In fact . . ." He stood up again. He held up his hand as if to stop any further questions then took a step to the side, away from the line of fire. "We'll be OK."

Some nobler part of Corey thought he should at least try to halt the experiment, but he didn't know how. "Stop it," he muttered, ineffectually. He watched Tom arm the weapon. The click of the latch prompted him to speak louder. "Tom! For God's sake!"

"For God's sake?" Tom snorted. Then shrugged. "If you like." He pressed the trigger. The machine gun roared into action, hammering the wall with a hail of bullets. The noise boomed and shook the walls and floor.

With barely a pause, Tom ducked his head low and walked directly into the gunfire. The bullets immediately ripped open his forehead and shattered the side of his skull, tearing away his features and sending his body into a spasm as he fell hard to the ground and twitched like a dying insect. His hand kept its grip on the trigger. The machine gun kept firing, the barrel growing hot and beginning to whine. It sucked in rounds at an incredible rate and spat them out for what felt like minutes, smashing into the ruptured wall, pounding the steel column until it glowed, until the last round from the ammo belt whipped into the loading chamber and the final shell was ejected. The bolt sprang forward and locked with a bright snap. It was quiet again. From behind the divide, Corey could see nothing but dust. When it had settled, Tom's body was still. The dust on his head was clumping and turning red.

With barely a pause, Tom ducked his head low and walked directly into the gunfire. The moment he did so was the moment the machine gun made another dull click and jammed. Tom stood upright, grinning and wide-eyed. He turned around and gave a nod to the camera. "Five."

"All right," Corey said, his heart thumping. "All right, I get it. This isn't . . . Let's take a break. Please. I don't want to watch you die."

"You've seen me die countless times, in countless realities,"

Tom said. He was fishing for his cigarettes again.

Corey didn't know what to do. He realised he hadn't been taking any notes. It didn't seem to matter. "Give me a cigarette."

"Let's open the doors." Tom coughed, waving his way through the dust. "Get some fresh air."

Out in the schoolyard, they sheltered from the rain under the porch of the main entrance. Tom was smoking aggressively, clearly excited. Corey, if he was honest with himself, felt alive. It was the kind of feeling that he'd learned to suppress, that he was well practised in burying. The nicotine helped, somehow.

Tom was rambling: "I used melons? Did I really tell you that? I can't believe I told you that. This is all about consciousness. The persistence of memory. I could have an infinite number of melons and I might see the gun jam once or twice, but what would be the point?"

"It was on the phone – the first time we spoke. You said they were preliminary tests."

"I told you, I'm not that organised," Tom said. "Listen, this isn't entirely unexpected. There could be some changes ahead. You might forget things, or remember things that I don't. It's nothing to worry about. It just means the experiment is working."

Corey didn't understand, so asked: "What exactly is your theory?"

"I'm testing a hypothesis: that I can only exist in the universe where my consciousness survives. There will be parallel universes where I am dead but, in a few of them, no matter how unlikely, the gun will fail. The only possible outcome for my consciousness is to experience survival. It's an old counter to the Copenhagen Interpretation."

"And you think you've proved it?"

Tom shook his head. "Look . . ." He held out his hand beyond the porch, into the cold light and the rain. "It's not much of a shadow, but there – see?"

Corey looked down and watched the shadow of Tom's hand blending with the reflections from the wet ground.

"My shadow is in the second dimension. I can move it side

to side and forward and back." He moved his hand around to demonstrate as the shadow danced across the raindrops. "But it can't go up and down because it's just a shadow of the third dimension. Us, and everything – we're in the third. But of course, there is a fourth and fifth dimension, and so on. Probably ten of them, according to string theory. We are nothing more than a shadow of the fourth dimension. That's all. We are merely the shapes that are cast from the dimension above us. The thing is, I can put my hand into darkness . . ." He did so, moving his hand out of the dim light and back under the porch. ". . . and the shadow simply doesn't exist any more. By affecting the dimension above, we can destroy the dimension below, and vice versa. That's all I'm doing here – removing the shadow of my consciousness from all parallel universes until I am the only version of me left, in any dimension. A kind of conscious singularity."

Corey thought for a moment, then asked: "Do you think you're immortal?"

Tom didn't say anything. He took a long drag of his cigarette and tried to explain. "Each time we do this, the probability of survival is tiny. So tiny that, while there are billions and billions of versions of me conducting this experiment right now, pretty much all of them will die every time a bullet is fired. Most of them are dead already. But with the intention of the gun and the gaze of an observer, this specific act, especially lethal, performed in unison, interdimensionally, will remove my consciousness from unimaginable numbers of realities. And then, standing as we are in this small pool of survivors, we simply repeat the experiment. If we do it ten times, then the odds of any version of me surviving are beyond zero. But it doesn't matter – my consciousness *must* survive. If we are one of the ways the universe knows itself, then the universe is obliged to remember us. For ever."

Corey nodded. "OK, but if there are infinite parallel worlds, won't this just go on infinitely?"

"The universe isn't infinite," Tom said. "That's a fairy tale which only describes the boundaries of our ignorance."

A lot of questions began to bother Corey. What about the

experiments that went wrong? What about the universes where injuries were endured? Realities where only the body survived? Paralysis? Comas? Where does consciousness lie then? He didn't know the first thing about string theory or if any of the numbers stacked up, but something about the idea appealed to him. The idea that consciousness had no choice but to survive, that everybody was alive, somewhere. "And in every world where the experiment fails, I get to clean up the mess?"

"I apologise to all of you," Tom said, grinning. "But you aren't afraid of a little mess. You're still here."

Corey wasn't sure if he was being flattered or pitied. He finished his cigarette. "How will you know if you're the last one? You might have already achieved it. You could be the only version of you left. Maybe this is it?" He waved his hand towards the empty schoolyard. "Just standing in the rain, about to kill yourself, kill the last you."

Tom shook his head. "If I was the last, I'd still survive all ten experiments. Success is inevitable."

"And after the tenth time? What happens then?"

Tom threw down his own cigarette and crushed it under his foot. "Let's find out."

Mercifully, there was a click. "Six!"

Tom got up from the stool, reset the bolt on the machine gun and checked the camera. He thought briefly about their conversation, about the versions of Corey that were about to watch a man commit suicide. He looked towards the glass window in the metal divider and smiled at Corey as he observed. He decided not to sympathise – the man could take it.

"Let me test the gun," he heard Corey shout from the other side. "To make sure it's working."

Tom picked up the trigger. "I'll do it." He moved to stand by the side of the gun.

"No – behind the screen," Corey said. "Ricochets."

Tom laughed. "I don't think that would matter, somehow." He pressed the button and fired seven or eight rounds. The machine gun barked happily, the muzzle flashing briefly. Satisfied, he positioned himself on the stool and looked down the barrel. He didn't feel any different, except his heart was pounding faster than usual and his muscles were tingling more than last time. To be expected, he told himself. He wondered about all the realities he'd affected. All those stories that would go on without him. All those funerals. But right now, here, he felt exactly the same. The pain in his shoulder he'd had for weeks was still there. The small cold sore on his bottom lip could still be felt with his tongue. One of his fingernails was still split. He was still the same person.

He showed another piece of paper to the camera.

Seven.

Click!

"Seven!" He stood up, careful not to let the sudden rush of euphoria overwhelm him. He breathed deeply to diffuse the buzzing feeling in his hands as he reset the bolt and checked the camera. He looked at the viewfinder to make sure that the battery was OK and he had plenty of time left, that the stool was still in frame and the observer's window was visible, with Corey watching carefully. Except, he couldn't see Corey through the glass.

He walked over to the middle divider and looked through. Corey wasn't there. He walked around to the other side. "Corey?"

Silence. He hurried to the back of the room and opened the door, looking out into the corridor beyond.

"Corey?"

There was a bang at the far end of the corridor. He breathed easy when he saw Corey come in from outside, slamming the door behind him. He heard the click of smart heels as he watched Corey approach, shaking off his umbrella.

Tom frowned. As Corey walked down the hallway, he noticed his hair and coat were reasonably dry.

"I promise, that's the last cigarette I steal from you," Corey said as he moved past Tom, back into the classroom.

Tom followed. "Where did you go?"

Corey looked at him quizzically, taking off his coat and withdrawing a notebook. "Outside."

"You were . . ." Tom stopped and looked at the umbrella again. ". . . wet."

Corey laughed. "Have you seen the weather? It's endless."

Tom shook his head and held up his hands. "Something's not right. Something's changed."

"More changes?" Corey asked, opening his notebook. Copious writing filled almost every page. He scanned to a blank area near the back. "Such as?"

"You. You were just here."

"I am here."

"No, you were here. You were here seconds ago. I didn't see you go outside."

"I've been outside for maybe ten minutes. Doesn't that sound right to you?"

"No it doesn't."

Corey nodded. "You said you expected this."

"Did I?"

"You said . . ." Corey skimmed through his notebook, through page after page of neatly written notes. "You called it 'conscious natural selection'."

"Those aren't my words!"

"This was . . ." Corey leafed back a few more pages. ". . . after trial three." He tapped his notebook with a pen. "You did say you expected this."

Tom felt uneasy. "Let's not panic," he said, more to himself than anyone else. "I'm just a little confused. I'll be OK. I just . . . I didn't know what the changes would feel like."

"It's probably best to continue," Corey said.

Tom tried to look Corey in the eye, but he was making more notes. He didn't seem troubled at all. Corey closed his notebook and walked around the dividers. "We're nearly at the end," he said. "I'll check the gun." Tom followed him, hesitantly, and sat on the stool. It crossed his mind that this could be it – that this was what it felt like to be in an unsuccessful universe. One where he didn't make it. He shook the thought away. This would have to work. He repeated his mantra inside his head: I can only survive.

"Number nine," Corey said.

"Eight. This is eight."

Corey frowned. "This is nine."

Tom felt in his pocket and pulled out two sheets of paper, unfolding them to confirm. One had a large number nine. One had a large number ten. He checked his pockets again. There was no eight. He stood up and walked to the camera. "I could have sworn this was . . . We've just done seven. We haven't done eight."

He rewound the video footage a little and watched the viewfinder. There was no audio, so he scrubbed back until he saw himself approach the stool and sit down. He watched himself hold up a sheet of paper. Drawn on it was a large number eight. He held it up clearly, though on its side. It looked like an infinity symbol. He watched himself drop the paper and push the button. He watched himself relax and smile and mouth the word "eight".

Tom shook his head. "Something has made me forget." He set the camera back to the end of the footage and resumed recording. He looked at Corey. "I just don't remember."

"Did you expect memory loss?" Corey asked. He narrowed his eyes. "Did we talk about that?"

"I thought about it. I thought that by the end some entangled memories may be lost. Or some new ones might be gained. I . . . It's just a little unsettling. I thought I would lose memories of childhood or holidays or something, not what happened five minutes ago."

"Do you want to take a break?"

"I can't." He left the camera and walked back to the stool and sat down. He tried to muster some pride, reminding himself that he was an explorer, climbing an unknown mountain, that he was near the summit, that the air was thin and it was playing tricks with his mind. That's all it was. All he had to do was keep moving. "I can't stay here."

Corey took the paper off him and held up the number nine to the camera. "We're almost there," he said reassuringly. He patted Tom on the shoulder then moved behind the divider and resumed his position at the observation window. "In your own time," he said.

Tom didn't like Corey's sudden calm, his sudden lack of excitement. He seemed too engaged. Too professional. Too intelligent. Together. Better. Perhaps it was . . . He shook his head – there were billions of variables. He reminded himself that they didn't matter. None of it mattered. All that mattered was one simple action. He looked down at his own hand. He held the trigger, though couldn't remember picking it up. He looked ahead, into the void of the machine gun's muzzle. Cold, quiet blackness. Is that what he had to look forward to? He imagined pressing the button. He imagined the storm of hot metal streaking towards his face. He shut his eyes and tried to block out the image. He thought about the stars as he repeated his mantra: I can only survive.

He kept his eyes closed and pressed the trigger.

He felt instant pain in his jaw and a wetness on the back of his head, moments after something thudded into his forehead. The shock of the noise barely registered. He felt himself fall and then the soft touch of a cotton sheet beneath his palms. He felt pressure on his chest as he breathed. His breath felt damp, like his throat was coated with honey. He smelled flowers.

He opened his eyes and through heavily blurred vision, he watched his blood seep into the cotton sheet. He felt no pain now. He felt himself being pulled upright. He felt arms around his chest. He smelled cigarette smoke as Corey held him and talked in his ear.

"You're fine," Corey said. "We're going to sit you down. You're doing fine."

Tom's dizziness faded as he was eased onto the stool. He raised his hands to touch his jaw, his fingers coming away bloody. He couldn't speak. He felt blood run down the back of his neck and down his spine. He looked up.

Corey was standing by the camera, resetting it. Next to the machine gun, holding the trigger, was himself.

Tom tried to speak, to shout his name, but he couldn't feel his own mouth any more. He tried to stand, but had no strength. He looked into the eyes of the man with the trigger. He was identical, almost. The same hair. The same face. But there was no sore on his lip. He looked at the finger on the trigger. It looked fine. Not bruised. Not split. Not like his own. The copy of Tom looked how Tom always hoped he'd look. Tall, healthy, in control. He didn't understand. *Who are you?* he thought.

Tom looked at Corey for help, but Corey was writing diligently in his notebook. He looked down at his body, to make sure he was still real. Blood was pouring down his legs and into the sheets on the floor. All over the floor were small splatters of blood and pink lumps of flesh, a few of them green and yellow. He realised it wasn't flesh. They were pieces of melon. His mind struggled to make any sense of what was happening. Most of all – why was he still alive?

"Let's do ten," the copy said, then looked at Tom. "Hello, Tom," it said with a small but sympathetic smile. "I'm sorry this didn't work out for you. I was right, conscious natural selection prevails and, well, I suppose not all consciousness is created equal. I win. I suppose I'm just a little more organised."

This made Corey laugh. Tom watched as Corey closed his notebook and walked around to the other side of the room. He looked back at the shadow of himself.

The copy of Tom held up the button as if it was a glass of champagne raised for a toast. "Anyway, as the last of us, all I want to say is thank you." He smiled and walked around to the other side of the divide.

Tom looked once more down the barrel of the machine gun. He would not close his eyes this time.

"Actually," he heard the copy say from the other side, "it doesn't really matter, but I thought you'd like to know – if only for a moment – that the universe is not infinite. Nor is it singular. It's binary." He saw his own face next to Corey's as they both stared through the observation window. "And we're about to break it in two."

The copy pressed the trigger.

The Wibbly Wobbly
MADELINE CROSS

We turn into Rainbow Dock and Toby starts swinging from my arm, whooping wildly. He lifts his feet off the ground, propelling his body forward. It is January and cold enough for snow. Chloe walks ahead, keeping enough distance between us that passers-by might believe we're not together. But when we turn out of the dock into the frozen shadows of the flats she looks back, just once, with a flick of her red plait and a blink, making it look like it is a physical reaction to something in the air rather than a need to check that we are still following.

I told Toby and Chloe once that there are rainbow fish living in Rainbow Dock. There is a view of the dock from my living-room window. I told them that the fish live at the very bottom where the water is as clear as glass. Each time he visits Toby climbs onto the window seat and scans the green water between the boat chains and floating rubbish, believing anything I tell him. There was a time when Chloe would look for them too.

We leave Rainbow Dock behind and turn into Greenland Dock where the Wibbly Wobbly is permanently anchored, its paint peeling back to reveal patches of metalwork like burnt bones. The floating pub's sign moves in the wind and a seagull bobs on the scummy water beneath the steps.

Joan rises stiffly as we enter, as if she has not needed to stand up in some time and slightly resents the effort of it. She is dressed in an oversized sweater, her grey-blue hair gathered and tied at the nape of her neck.

"It's cold out there," she says, watching us strip off our layers.

"Nice in here though," I reply.

"I've closed the deck – too icy. Hope the kids don't mind."

"I expected as much."

"Can I have some crisps, Daddy?" Toby asks, standing on tiptoes to try and see over the bar. Chloe strokes the black cat that is curled up between the Guinness and Foster's taps, loose black hairs escaping through her fingers onto the bar top. I remember someone once bravely embarking on a derogatory comment about cats and hygiene, but stopping short under Joan's hard stare.

"Usual drinks and a pack of cheese and onion please, Joan."

We sit beside the windows that look out across the deck and chained-up picnic tables to the ageing houseboats anchored in the dock. The jukebox is playing an old Bruce Springsteen track. A karaoke machine has been left set up from Friday night in front of the saloon doors that lead to the front of the boat, and there is still a dance mat on the floor which isn't hooked up to anything.

The only other person on the boat is Jack, sitting at a round table opposite us. He would have come straight from foraging on the banks of the Thames at low tide. He's yet to take off his wax coat and his crown of white hair has been swept back over his head by the wind. He fumbles through the pockets with mud-stained fingers, pulling out clay pipes and laying them in rows on the table in front of him. They are never whole pipes, just the stems, dozens of them, decades old and soft as young skin. I worked up the courage to ask him about the pipes once, which seemed to warm him to me. He told me in great detail about the art of "mudlarking" as he called it, and I did my best to seem intrigued so that I could have his company for longer.

"You eating?" Joan leans over us.

"Yes we are." I glance at Toby and Chloe who are distracted by beer mats. Chloe flicks them up into the air and Toby catches them with clumsy fists. "Three roasts."

Joan nods and writes down the order on a scrap of paper.

"Is Kian in the kitchen?" I ask, imagining her lanky son sweating over a chicken carcass.

"Yep – training him up, need him to earn his keep."

I imagine this means that she is not paying Kian a wage, which is not surprising considering the whisperings that the pub is not bringing in any money. Joan has never confirmed it, then again she doesn't strike me as the kind of person who would willingly share her troubles with punters.

A man and woman come through the door. Joan looks at them, seeming surprised. She doesn't move, scanning their faces as if she thinks they must be lost. New customers are not a common sight. The couple are smartly dressed in matching pea coats. Under their outer layers they are clearly young, though not so young for it to be illegal. The man's skin almost glows. They hover beside the bar until Joan finally shakes off her reservations and greets them. Still holding the woman's gloved hand, the man takes out his wallet and orders drinks. Chloe is watching them too.

"Fresh meat," I say to her. I heard the expression on TV.

She screws up her face. Toby is picking his nose. The woman takes off her hat and her chestnut hair falls down her back, catching the dusty light from the lamps and bouncing it around the room. I feel a painful tightening in my chest and I look up at the maps of south-east England and blurred images of the Thames estuary fading in blue and green hues on the wood.

The roast dinners arrive (hardly recognisable under smothering layers of brown gravy) at the same time as Mark and Chris. The midday football game must be over. They slide onto one of the red-cushioned benches, proudly displaying their Millwall shirts under their open jackets, scarves trailing over their shoulders, cheeks flushed. They are brothers, with equally stubbly and liver-spotted skin. Chris is slightly fleshier around the jaw and neck, and has a bent nose that I imagine was the result of a punch to the face from his brother. They never remember my name, but still nod politely in my direction. They don't come to the boat mid-week, so never have the opportunity to see me without the children, when I might have something to say to them, when I allow myself more than one beer and occasionally start to melt into the bar under the watchful eye of Joan, who is always ready to tell me when my tongue is getting too loose. It's unlikely the brothers recognise the pattern of my Sundays, but I recognise their patterns. I know the football fixtures because of their patterns.

I pull a piece of chicken gristle out of my teeth and put it on the side of my plate. Chloe frowns in disapproval and I wonder when it was that she started to judge me. I remember her sitting on my knees when she was small and me shouting "Hole in the boat!" while opening my legs so that she tumbled to the floor laughing. It was so much easier to make her laugh back then.

Toby is licking gravy off his sleeve.

"Stop that," I say.

"What's it matter?" Chloe asks.

"I don't think I was directing that at you."

She looks back at me stonily.

"Toby – eat properly."

He looks from me to Chloe. He is the spitting image of her as a younger child, dark-red hair, round cheeks, missing teeth. He shows them to me now as his face opens into a grin. He picks up a piece of chicken with his fingers and dangles it playfully in front of his mouth. It looks like a grey tongue. "You're too old for that," I try. He puts the grey tongue in his pink mouth.

Chloe is now watching the young couple studying a paper menu with their faces pressed close together.

"Why are they sharing a menu?" she asks, unable to disguise her disdain.

"I guess Joan only gave them one."

"Seems weird." She looks away. "There's plenty of menus. They don't need to share."

I go to the bar for more drinks.

"How did it go?" Jack asks cheerfully, reaching for the Guinness Joan has poured him.

"How did what go?"

"What do you think?"

Joan is listening too and I can't help being flattered at her interest in me. But there is nothing to tell.

I look over at the kids. Toby has managed to hurt his thumb somehow and Chloe is stroking it. "Not now, Jack," I say.

"They can't hear."

"Three lemonades please, Joan." I can still hear the sound of the scratching violin and the chewy scallops being churned up in our mouths. "It wasn't great."

Jack takes a slow sip of his pint and it leaves a white shimmer on his upper lip. "Ah well, a date's a date. It's a good sign. There's an app for it now too I heard."

"Yeah there is."

"Probably aren't many our age on it though."

Our age? I take in the wrinkles on his face – like contours on a map. "All right, Jack."

"Yeah, cheers."

We tap our glasses and I go back to the children.

The young couple are looking uneasily down at the food that Kian unceremoniously placed in front of them. Gravy has slopped onto the table top. The man takes a bite and smiles reassuringly at the woman as he swallows it down. I know for a fact that the food is not as good as his expression would have her believe. She leans against him and her hair brushes against his clean-shaven face. Instinctively my hand rises and feels my own chin, prickly and unsettling, with a dip in the middle, a dip a woman could press her nose into, a dip a woman once pressed her nose into. The man whispers something and they laugh. How happy can they actually be?

Jack stands up at his table. He looks like an old bird of prey that has just spotted a mouse, his shoulders back, his chin up. I am the only one watching him as he stands there, staring down at the carpet, his eyes moving back and forth. When he doesn't sit back down the others start to notice him. He raises his arm and his finger extends. At first I think he's pointing at Toby, but he's pointing at a pebble, a perfectly round white pebble that is now rolling along the carpet towards the saloon doors. I remember Toby picking up that pebble from the edge of the bath in the morning. He asked if he could keep it and of course I said yes and he slipped it into his pocket. Now it's rolling across the floor, and we're all watching it while our thoughts catch up with our eyes. It comes to a stop when it hits the frame of the doors. We all look back at Jack as if only he can offer any clarification. He lets us wait in an uncomfortable silence.

"I think we're sinking," he says.

Mark snorts into his beer.

"Don't be ridiculous." Joan comes out from behind the bar. "Why the hell would the boat be sinking?" She walks over to the pebble and picks it up off the floor, then she disappears through the swinging doors to the kitchen at the front of the boat.

Toby tugs my sleeve. "I can't swim well, Daddy. I haven't got my certificate yet."

"We're not swimming anywhere, Toby. We're in a dock."

He looks at me blankly.

Joan comes back into the room with her son Kian following behind her. Kian's hair is greasy and he smells like a roast dinner. He is only eighteen or so. He stands beside Joan, looking at each of our faces.

"The boat's sinking," Joan says, her face blank.

"You're taking the piss!" Chris bangs his glass down on the table and liquid splashes out onto Mark's arm.

"Watch it, Chris!" Mark barks. "You always overreact."

"What should we do?" The woman's voice is deeper than I'd expected, older.

"It's not exactly the Titanic," Joan replies.

"I suppose we better get off the boat then." Jack starts putting on his coat and filling his pockets with the clay pipes.

"That's probably a good idea." Joan walks back to the bar and stands behind it, facing us and the room which I can now see is quite clearly sloping slightly. I start to gather up the kids' things.

"What will happen to the boat, Dad?" Chloe asks. Her cheeks flush and for a fleeting moment she seems concerned and I lean forward to tell her the boat will be all right. But before I can she turns away and pulls her green bobble hat over her ears.

I scrabble around in my pockets and pull out some notes. I don't know how much I owe but can't bring myself to ask so overestimate. "I'm so sorry, Joan," I manage to say as I push them into her hand. She shrugs, and it occurs to me that she doesn't have a clue what to do. She just stands there, not looking directly at anything or anyone.

Jack appears beside me. "We should take stuff with us, Joan. You know – what's important. There'll be a lot of damage. What do you want saving?" His cheeks are red with beer and adrenalin.

Joan looks around her. "I don't know. Can't exactly save it all."

"There's enough of us," I say, surprised by her resignation. It's as if she's been waiting for something like this to happen, anticipating it. Maybe she didn't imagine this specific scenario. Maybe she imagined a sign going up outside, or a man with a clipboard leaning cockily on the bar as he told her she would have to leave.

Kian joins his mother. "We're all here, Mum. What should we do?" He is calm and suddenly capable. It seems to pull Joan back out of herself.

"Well then, I think the beer," she says.

"The beer?" I exchange an amused look with Jack.

"Yes, the beer bottles."

Jack turns to where Chris, Mark and the couple have all gathered by the door ready to escape. "Right, you all. There's no need to rush off. There's some empty crates there. Let's all grab one and take what we can off the boat. Wastage is a terrible thing and when it's alcohol its treacherous. Let's get to it – all the bottles we can carry."

"Leave the wine," Joan says. "It tastes like cat piss."

I grab one of the empty crates and go behind the bar. The kids follow me and kneel down on the floor to help.

When we've finished stacking I carry the full crate off the boat. Standing on the side of the dock we watch Jack carry out the last one with astonishing strength. There's a low-pitched gurgling sound and the boat tilts further. The afternoon light is already starting to fail and the water is marked by purplish ripples.

"What do we do now?" Chris asks.

"I don't know," Joan says. "Who do I call? The police?"

"The insurer might be a good shout," Mark says.

"What's the point?" Joan sits down on the bench. "Who's gonna stop it sinking?"

The front of the boat is considerably lower, the bow almost breaking the surface.

"What about the rainbow fish, Daddy?" Toby asks. "Will they be OK?"

"There are no rainbow fish in this dock, just green ones, and they're not very nice."

He looks perturbed by this, his bottom lip protruding. "Why aren't they nice?"

"They eat rainbow fish," I say. He stares thoughtfully at the water and I regret my bluntness.

"I don't feel we can just leave it to sink," Jack says, sitting beside Joan.

"No, I don't suppose we can. Would anyone like a drink?"

I do feel in need of a drink. It's the sight of Joan's body hunched over on the bench, and the boat looking old and crumpled but still not ready to be lost. I don't want to think ahead to another pub, another group of people, the awkward beginnings of conversations, those first few words dropping out of my mouth and sinking like stones. We open beers and huddle around with our breath rising in small clouds between us. The woman leaves her partner's side to dig around in the crates for bottles of juice which she offers to Toby and Chloe.

"What's that?" Mark points to the boat.

"The fucking cat!" Chris says.

"What?" Joan jumps up. The cat is looking at us through

the window. We see its mouth open but don't hear the noise it releases. There's another bubbling sound below us and the boat tips forward. The bow momentarily splits the blackening water and then rises again, only just visible now. The cat has managed to stay on the window ledge, but its eyes are wild and full of fear.

"Don't worry, Joan," Jack says. "I'll save her." He launches himself down the steps with long strides. He opens the door and disappears for a moment, before appearing through the windows in the slanted room beyond. He stands over the cat and hesitates, as if deciding whether he's actually willing to touch it, but then he looks out at us, scoops the cat up in his arms, and hurries off the sinking boat.

"That was your fault, Joan," he says, slightly out of breath as he passes her the cat. "You said save the beer – you didn't mention the cat."

The cat twists and turns in Joan's arms, and she puts it down on the ground. It walks off along the dock, stopping further on to sit and lick its paws. We go back to watching the boat, which hardly moves, but it is still tilting forward with the weight of the water that must be seeping through the front.

"Perhaps you should take the kids home now," Joan says to me. I am taken aback that in her own moment of need she remembers that I never normally keep the kids out this long.

Chloe looks over at us to see what I will say.

"Not just yet," I mumble.

Joan nods and I turn the other way, to where Chloe is now following Toby to the edge of the dock. They sit side by side with their legs dangling over the water and Toby describes to her the different ways he will catch the green fish and kill them.

The man with the clean chin and pea coat moves closer to me. "Great kids you got there," he says. I see the woman smile into her scarf and it occurs to me that maybe she's pregnant and then it occurs to me that's an odd thing for me to think, and I still haven't replied so I smile back at him. I'm waiting for him to ask me where their mother is when Jack comes up next to us.

"What brought you to the Wibbly Wobbly?" he asks the man.

"I read about it on the internet."

"The Wibbly Wobbly's on the internet?"

"Either of you a Millwall fan?" Chris interrupts.

"No, afraid not."

"Pity."

Joan opens another beer and stares down into it as if searching for something in the frothing liquid.

Chloe leaves Toby by the water and sits on the bench.

"Do you think you'll remember us coming here?" I ask, sitting down beside her and motioning towards the boat.

She shrugs, running her fingers over the buttons of her phone. She's too young for a phone. I said that. I'm almost certain I said that.

"Where's your mum taken you recently?"

She doesn't look at me. She knows I'm not supposed to ask these things.

"I'm interested," I say.

"We'll find somewhere else."

"Well yeah, of course! Plenty more boats in the sea and all that." I flash her what I think is a goofy grin. "Have you ever told her about it – the boat, I mean?"

"Yeah." She pauses. "It's come up."

"There won't be anywhere like this though, will there," I say, even though I know I shouldn't, even though I heard the pitch of my voice change and can now see her working out what to say to make me feel better.

"There'll be somewhere," is all she says.

"And Toby?"

"He'll remember it too."

"It's just an old boat."

"Exactly, Dad."

But I don't want her to agree with me. She pushes up her hat where it has started to fall down towards her eyes and turns her attention back to her phone.

I look over at Joan who is nursing a beer and staring intently at the boat. Her eyes seem to widen in recognition of something, and she drops her bottle, smashing it on the concrete. "I won't do this," she says, stepping over the broken glass. "I can't stop it sinking, but that doesn't mean I have to sit around watching it like this. I'm getting back on it!"

Kian has been standing apart from the group up until now, fading into the grey, but he comes to life and breaks through the group to his mother's side. He squeezes her hand. "Mum, don't be stupid. What's that going to do?"

"Bloody well nothing. I'm no idiot. But I want to be on that boat."

"What if you got hurt?" the woman says.

Joan shoots her a bitter look. "Hurt by what? I'm not too old to swim. We're not at sea."

"You're off your trolley," Mark contributes.

Toby joins us on the bench and pulls at my trouser pocket. "What's going on? I killed all the fish," he says. I lift him up onto my lap. I don't have anything to say to Joan to make her change her mind. I want her to do it, because this moment needs to be bigger and memorable. I don't want it to just disappear.

"Mum," Kian implores.

Joan shakes her head. "Just let me, Kian, there's no risk really. Just let me do it."

With Toby's head against my chest and Chloe's shoulder pressed against mine, unconsciously perhaps, but nonetheless there, we watch Joan walk onto the deck of the boat. She stands at the back facing forwards to where the bow is still only just visible above the water. The majority of the boat is free from harm, nodding delicately at an angle. The houseboats that line the other sides of the dock are lifeless in their scratchy greys and blues, which makes me wonder if anyone even lives on them and what they're doing there if that's the case. Who looks after them? Is everyone just waiting for them to sink too?

"Someone Google what to do when your boat sinks," Jack says.

"We could call the Thames river police," Kian replies. "Shit, Mum." He shakes his head with amazement.

Joan's expression is ferocious. Curls of hair skim her face and her cheeks are a cherry pink. She stands feet apart on the slippery wood, as if preparing to launch some kind of wrestling tackle on the boat. But before she can the bow is pulled down further as though someone or something has reached up out of the water and wrapped their arms around the metal. The front goes under like a seal slipping off a rock. Toby and Chloe rush forward and as Joan's position becomes more precarious she grips onto the railings that surround the deck. The boat tips and the angle widens. We all stand in a line, watching.

There is an unexpected thud as wood and metal meet algae-covered ground. Joan looks at us in shock, still clutching the railings.

Jack leans over the water. "I always wondered how deep it was," he says. "Isn't that something? Not deep at all!"

I feel my phone vibrate in my pocket. I try to ignore it but it won't stop and I realise it's getting late and through a gap in the thinning clouds I see a spoonful of moon above the roofs of the flats. Joan steps off the boat and walks over to Kian. "Think it's time we called someone," she says.

I take out my phone and look down at the screen and their mother's name blinking at me accusingly.

"Are you going to answer it?" Chloe asks.

I open my mouth but don't manage to say anything. The phone stops ringing.

"Fish!" Toby shouts.

Chloe takes his hand in hers and they bend over the water. I move forward to stand beside them. There is a fish below us, sent up startled by the sinking boat, rising to the surface. It is not a rainbow fish, if they even exist. It is grey and oily, with small swollen eyes, the kind of fish you would expect to see in the docks of south London. I can feel the warmth of the children's bodies as we lean in together. The fish seems to gasp at the air, its tail flapping, before it goes under again and glides out of sight.

Seasons
BRIDGET WESTAWAY

The sun drops like a blessing into my hands, uncurling the clawed fingers. I watch them open, as the warmth creeps up my arms. Georgie comes in, my smile mirroring hers – sudden, artless – as her small hand reaches out for mine. I lift her into my lap.

"Ba, bup, ba, bup," she half sings.

I rub her palm and say, "hand". I take her other one and repeat, "hand, hand".

"An, an, an," she says.

I lift her fingers and touch them to her face. "Ose, ose," she says.

Her nose is running and I wipe it with a tissue. "Nose," I say, tapping it gently, and again she says, "ose".

"Ickle," she says and I tickle her until she squeals and squirms herself onto the floor. She totters about the room for a bit, comes back to me, turns away and then back again, wiping her still dripping nose on the trouser of my unbroken leg before disappearing out of the door. I wait for a moment, half expecting her to reappear, and when she doesn't, I pick up my book.

The room is upstairs at the back, overlooking the garden. They call it my room, but it isn't. It's a room in their house – my son and daughter-in-law's, Laurence and Jessica. I have a room in my own house, more rooms, more house than I need, and now all empty. It bothered me sometimes when I was there, now it worries me more – this house of mine with no one in it. After the brief burst of spring when the sap stirred and blood ran more willingly in the veins, it's back to winter again. Bright today, but cold at night so in the morning the windows are coated in condensation. Will someone turn the heating on or will the walls become damp, the clothes moulder, corners of carpet rot? Did I hang up the washing?

The days pass quickly, hours I can fall into. Sometimes, when the pain in my leg stops me sleeping, I lie awake at night and then I doze through the morning. Time passes at different speeds. It takes me by surprise. Almost standing still in the floating hours before dawn and then flying in the afternoon as if it's rushing to catch a train. Sometimes it's sticky, itchy, difficult to get through. I want to be home and I wonder if I'll ever get back there. Occasionally, particularly when the air is buoyant with a hint of better days to come, time is a warm sea.

"Old bones take longer to heal," the doctor said.

I'm in bed, tired, but not asleep. My head is full of movement. From being lifted into the ambulance and out again. Wheeled around the hospital. Put onto a narrow trolley for the X-ray. The people. The noise. The traffic. Here it's quiet. Georgie whispers outside my room, in the way that children whisper – not in a muted voice, but as if they're telling you a secret that's busting to get out – all *fusch* and *whish* sounds. Jessica hurries her away, "Grandma is tired," she says.

Everything so bright and sharp. The fracture clinic. The children in the waiting area, playing, shouting, rushing, unwillingly contained as steam in a pressure cooker is held inside, and the ones with casts, the ones in wheelchairs looking longingly at the others. I felt so sorry for them and I wanted to tell them that – for most of them anyway – it'll only be a short time before they're free to run around again. But I didn't. Even if they paid heed to this old witch in a wheelchair (and I chuckle in amusement as I imagine them seeing me as this), even if they caught the words, they would have struggled to see beyond this moment, this hiatus in their lives.

I hear rustling outside the door. Heavy feet up the stairs – the new baby is almost due. I should be back home.

"What are you doing?" Jessica asks.

"Pic, pic, raw," Georgie answers. "Rama."

"Grandma," Jessica corrects her automatically. "You can draw in the kitchen." And I hear Georgie bumping down the stairs on her bottom.

I'm glad that she'll have a sibling. We married late, Tim and I. We were told we couldn't have children and then Laurence was born. He's an only and it must be hard. He worries about me I know – more so since his father died. Otherwise with the two of us we might have managed – people can often get along, help each other out, even if they are both ill or impaired. With one set of eyes and one set of legs two old souls can sometimes get by.

My leg isn't healing, they say. Why not? I ask, and they say it's because I'm old, it takes longer to knit together – as if it were a jumper. I feel some sympathy for this leg – my fingers won't knit any more either. It will mend, they say, it'll just take time. Well that is something I do have, I tell them – at least until Atropos, the oldest of the Ancient Greek Fates, finally clips my thread.

Are you moving your toes? they ask, and I nod. Better than a lie said out loud and Georgie sometimes pulls off the oversized sock that is pushed over the plaster and plays with my toes – does that count?

Georgie changes so quickly. I can almost see her growing, the increasing fluidity of her movements, of her language. She comes in with a book. "Mummy eeping," she says.

She scrambles onto my lap and we snuggle down together. She points at the pictures, pressing the page with a sticky finger. I think of telling her to go and wash her hands but Jessica is probably asleep on the sofa – she needs the break. The story progresses in fits and starts as Georgie turns the pages in both directions – forwards and backwards, sometimes several at a time – but eventually all the animals are safely home, the doors and windows are shut, the fire lit and supper cooked for everyone. Georgie slams it shut and rushes through the door calling out, "nuther one".

But she doesn't come back.

I wait, listening for her step on the landing. There is something going on downstairs. The front door opens and shuts, phones are ringing, I hear voices – then it goes quiet. Sometime later Laurence comes into the room. "Are you all right?" he asks and I nod.

"It's Jessica, I'm taking her to hospital," he says and quickly continues, "Everything's fine. We had the midwife round and it's all good but they want her in hospital just in case."

I nod again. What can I say? I wish I wasn't here or as I am here I wish I could be of help.

"Georgie's gone to Dinah's." I've met Dinah. She's a sweet child, beautiful, unable to keep still. "Will you be all right?" he asks.

"Of course."

"I'll bring some sandwiches up and some fruit. And Dinah's mother brought a cake. You sure you'll be OK? I don't know when I'll be back."

I can get to the bathroom but not downstairs. I have my phone. I assure him I'll be fine.

The house breathes in and stops. Without people to animate it the air is still. I imagine Jessica and Laurence at the hospital – the rush to get there, the confusion of their arrival and then the long wait behind thin curtains, in anxious rooms. I pick up my book and put it down again. All this activity makes me restless and yet I'm tired – a disconcerting mix. I shut my eyes, opening them as I hear a sound. A scraping. Or maybe a rustle of voices. I glance towards the door, looking for Georgie. Is the noise close at hand or out in the street? It stops. I think of Georgie. What will she make of her new brother or sister?

Laurence comes back late the next morning. After calling in to tell me I have a small but healthy grandson, he sleeps. It looks like he's slept in his clothes when he comes into my room a few hours later. He brings me more provisions, before returning to the hospital.

They all come home together, Jessica, the baby, Laurence and Georgie. The baby and the parents sleep. Georgie comes up to see me. Instead of running straight in, she peers round the door, checking, it seems, to see if everything is as before. Then she rushes into my arms, burying her face as I embrace her. I can feel her chest, her stomach, the whole of her body as it rises and falls with her breathing. It is surprisingly strong. Two quick breaths come swiftly together and she twists her head up to look at me.

"Rama," she says.

"Yes?" I wait for her to continue.

"Rama." She looks puzzled, jumps down and runs away.

Soon she's back, with a toy rabbit this time. She gives the rabbit to me and dashes out. I hear her going down the stairs, into the sitting room and up again. "He's cold," she says, handing me a small jumper. This continues for a while. The house is quiet apart from Georgie going up and down the stairs and thrusting things at me. By the time Laurence stands yawning in the doorway I have quite a collection.

Georgie tells me the rabbit wants "a nack".

"No Rama," she laughs in derision as I pick up a small brick. "Not a kit, apes."

Apparently he is to have grapes for his snack, not biscuits.

"Don't be so bossy," Laurence says to Georgie. He offers to make coffee. "I need something to keep myself awake."

Georgie follows her father downstairs and then back up as he brings the coffee. He sits to drink it with me and Georgie builds rabbit a house in the corner.

"Grandma doesn't want all this stuff in here," Jessica says as she passes the room.

"I don't mind," I say, and, over the next few days, all round the edge of the room and under the bed, Rabbit's house and garden spread out.

Georgie talks to herself as she makes and unmakes Rabbit's world.

Her words lack beginnings – 'abbit acquires an 'arden outside his 'ouse. It is a non-stop scramble of consonants and loose vowels. The few dozen words she's used for the last month or two are joined by others I can't make out. But there's no doubt they have meaning. She's starting to talk in whole sentences – seeming to relish the syllables she shapes so seriously – with appropriate intonation and large gestures. But there's one word I haven't heard her say since her brother's birth: 'aby. She never mentions him.

"I'm big," she says, standing on tiptoe and lifting her arms above her head, but something in her eyes doesn't ring true and I don't think she believes what she says.

She looks more carefully at me now when I speak to her. And I take more care of what I say – having her solemn eyes, so full of curiosity, fixed on my face seems to lend every word I utter a meaning greater than it can bear.

Rabbit's house and garden are replaced first by a hospital (one where legs are mended but no babies born), then a school and more recently by a town which, in need of extra space, keeps extending onto the landing. Even though this corridor outpost lacks planning consent and is demolished each evening, every morning, full of optimism, Georgie builds it again. One night she has a victory of sorts because the bricks and assorted toys that make it up aren't put back inside my room, but just pushed out of the way against the wall – with, I'd guess, a weary foot acting as a bulldozer.

"Rama," she says, and I look up. Outside it's windy. I can see the treetops staggering as they're blown under a preternaturally blue sky. "You know I'm big?"

I nod. "Yes, I know."

"Max spits." She screws up her nose as she thinks of her brother.

"Yes," I say. He's a greedy baby, seeming to want to grow faster than time will allow.

"Rama, will you have a baby?" Her expression switches from disgust as she considers the regurgitated milk, to concern as she forms the question.

"Of course not." I laugh. "I'm much too old."

She smiles and throws her arms around me.

My leg is getting better. The plaster is removed and I start to walk with two sticks. It's slow and cumbersome, more so when Georgie tries to help, but it is an enormous relief to be vertical again. Soon I should be able to go home. It's really spring now and I can't wait to be back in the garden there. I don't think of it as my garden because I can't imagine it without Tim bent over a flower bed, picking at weeds, so I call it the garden.

I go downstairs, for the first time in weeks, and out into my son's garden. I've looked down at it from the window for such a long time it seems strange to be standing on the lawn and looking up at the window. Like being transported to the moon and able to look up at the world from there. It's such a good feeling, to walk in the land of the living. The air feels clean and new, everything is fresher, more clearly defined and, as the sun warms me deep inside, my spirits start to brighten.

I spend days following Georgie as she plays in the garden. We sit in hidden corners on layers of leaf mould and just as we get comfortable with Rabbit and Teddy, with snacks for them and snacks for us, the signal is given – by Georgie – to decamp and set up somewhere else. We circle the garden. It's our land. She talks, all the time, to herself, to her toys, to me.

"Whassat?" she asks a hundred times a day and I answer her – a blackbird singing, a helicopter, a broken plant pot, a beetle. She particularly likes the 'eetle and I try to get her to give it its "b".

"Ub, ub, ub, bub, bub," she says. We get as far as "ub eetle", which sounds just like "a beetle", which I choose to count as an achievement and give her fifty pence.

I'm not quite sure why I do this. I know it will come in its time, this fluency with language, and that someone to answer her questions is all she needs to help it along. Maybe it's vanity – perhaps I like to think I've played more of a part than just being a soundboard. Perhaps I want part of her triumph to be my own.

I'm looking up at the trees when I feel it, something split inside my head. The leaves are freewheeling, falling, rising, tumbling through the air. Then they stop, they become fixed, all the colour is drained away and the black shapes in front of the white sky look like metal fretwork covering a vacant space. The pain is sharp and spreading, until it's the only thing there is and I can't tell what I remember, where I am, what's true.

I'm in hospital again and I want desperately to be out. Nothing is quite right. I lift my arm to reach the drink which stands on the table beside the bed. I manage to touch the plastic beaker which has a lid on top of it with a straw poking through – a bit like one of Georgie's cups, I think, and smile – but my fingers go right past it and knock over a bottle of squash which crashes to the floor and breaks. A nurse comes over to see what's happened and they section off the area as if it's roadworks or I'm a murder victim – I laugh to myself as the thoughts float like cartoons above the bed. A cleaner looks at me. Did I laugh out loud? How can I tell? I shut my eyes and try not to hear the commotion that's going on in the ward.

Laurence comes, sits on the bed, talks to me. He listens but seems to take no notice of what I say. Can you bring me some oranges? I ask, but they never arrive. I see him speaking to a doctor. They seem to be agreeing with each other, they nod and look over at my bed.

I feel like I'm inside a drum – every noise, even the rustle of papers from the next bed, hurts my head. I say this to a doctor and he writes something down. I try to answer his questions but it's difficult. I think he keeps asking the same things but I can't be sure, there's too much noise. I don't know if I've seen this doctor before. He doesn't look familiar but, before I've had time to take a proper look at him, he's gone.

They come and go like sparrows – indistinguishable from

each other on the lawn – these doctors or nurses or whatever they are. It's like being at a theatrical performance. One of those plays where the actors mingle with the audience. Where nothing is fixed and it's hard to tell reality from make-believe. Everything is random, muddled up, it all collides, seeps into itself and then breaks away. Sometimes, it seems, breakfast appears just after I've gone to sleep.

The next day I'm got up, wheeled over into a small side section and a young woman comes to talk to me. She's nice but a bit dim. She doesn't seem to listen to what I say. She starts to make strange noises, indicating her mouth and her tongue, and then she wants me to point at pictures. I do this to humour her. Water, a banana, a newspaper – she seems pleased – then she says, "Orange." I find the picture among the others on the card and say, "Yes please, can I have an orange?" She smiles as she gets up, saying, "I'll be back tomorrow." The next day she comes with more cards but no orange.

I'm back in my room – no, their room – my room, if it's still there, is not here – I look at my leg – it's thinner than the other – a nasty whitish yellow colour – with red blotches – but the plaster is gone – when did that happen? – I sleep – I wake – I eat – with difficulty I load it on the spoon – the distance to my mouth seems like a chasm – it's porridge – is it morning? – Jessica looks at the bowl, helps me with a few spoonfuls and then dashes out – the sky is dark – is it getting darker or will it lighten into morning? – how can I tell? – I'm tired – I shut my eyes – the sun is shining – there's a mug on the table next to me – it wasn't there before – I'm thirsty – I look at it – I lift my arm – it waves in the air – a thing with its own volition – I move it towards the table – I'm lying down – I sit up – three, four times I try – I manage it – breathe out – rest my head back against the pillows – I see the mug – I think about moving my arm – raising it to my lips – I try – I try again – some spills on the sheets – it's warm – not cold or hot – brown – tea or coffee? – I sip – the edge of the mug is thick between my teeth – coffee – I smile.

Night and day displace each other as if the sun and the

moon are competitors and neither will allow the other its proper time. Laurence brings me food, drink. Jessica opens or closes the curtains, asks me how I am. I hear Georgie rustle outside on the landing, a mouse along the wainscot. I wish she'd come in. Her head appears round the door. "Rama," she whispers. I smile.

Another day – days are beginning to regain their pattern – Georgie creeps in. I say something to her and she laughs. We laugh together. Now I know the problem I have with words is not with the hearing of them or with the understanding – I can order the ideas in my mind – but with giving voice to them. I practise some of the exercises the nice but dim woman in hospital taught me. Georgie hears and she laughs again, helping me with my vowel sounds – "Ee, ee, ee, easy," she says, as if it's a game. A secret game we play together.

Georgie sits on the bottom of the bed and bounces up and down. Again she's spending large parts of the day in my room.

"Can't we go in the garden?" she asks.

I shake my head and try to say, "Soon" – I point to the word on one of the cards Laurence has made for me, but of course she can't read it. Although she is learning. I help her, picking out the word "apple" on the card in my hand and passing her one from the fruit bowl next to my bed. She's learning fast, faster than I am, I think, as I struggle to turn the syllables around my tongue into meaningful sounds.

Inside Georgie two things are happening at once. With me she's become a mini adult – as she is occasionally with one or other of her parents. I hear them downstairs. But when they're all together she's a baby again. I can hear Max crying – urgently, as if his life depends on it, which, in a way, I suppose it might. Georgie is shouting insistently, objects are being thrown or dropped, either Jessica or Laurence is getting cross as the other tries to bring peace to this cacophony.

One day Jessica dumps Max in my lap. "Do you mind?" she asks.

I shake my head. I've got better at making gestures now and at looking at people in such a way as to get their attention so they can see every inflection of my hands, every raised eyebrow or movement of my head.

Last time I held him he was stiff as iron, full of fight, but now his muscles are soft, floppy, milk runs from the corners of his mouth as his eyelids drop. It's Sunday, Laurence has taken Georgie out, Jessica is downstairs, Max sleeps, the house is quiet.

I think. My words, I know, are like my leg was – they no longer knit together. I feel this as a loss. Almost as if they're misplaced inside my mind and I try to scan my brain to find them. As if it's the words that are lost and not the saying of them. Sometimes when I speak it seems all right but I know this isn't really true because when I asked for juice yesterday Laurence handed me a newspaper. I took it without complaint. I don't want him to think that I've become an imbecile, that he'll be saddled with me for ever.

I listen as they return, father and daughter. They come in lightly, with laughter. It's good to hear. Georgie comes up to my room, sees Max, turns to go, before spinning round and squeezing him. He looks alarmed – as much as a small baby can.

Jessica comes in and quickly Georgie says, "I uddled him."

It's autumn, nearly winter again – I don't know what happened to the summer – the leaves pile up on the balcony. Carefully, holding on with both hands, I step over the sill and through the long windows. It's not quite a balcony – these aren't doors – it's only a small space on top of the bay window below. But it is outside and I feel a transgressive elation as a cold east wind whips my face. I've felt so little for so long – sensations limited to the crisp texture of clean sheets, the touch of Georgie's skin, hot liquid in my throat – that even this icy blast is welcome. Am I really so circumscribed, so hemmed in? How did this happen? But of course I know – how piece by unsuspecting piece a world is lost. The rail is a bit rickety and quite low – too low for a proper balcony. I watch the leaves being lifted, played with, until slowly, randomly, inexorably, they end up on the ground. And me, I think, would it blow me like that? It's just a thought, a whimsy. I like the idea of floating above the treetops.

I've tried to write, but my hand won't form the letters. I'm so fed up of using the cards Laurence made me – often I can't find the one I want and I can't make my own. I haven't looked at a paper for weeks, since the time he brought me one and I got nowhere with it. This morning – for a moment I feel hopeful – I ask for another. He brings me an apple and although I feel like throwing it into the wind with the leaves, I eat it.

Jessica puts a bird table outside the window. I see a robin fly past with nesting material – it must be nearly spring again. I've been here for a year. The seasons are like my words, indecipherable – this can't go on. I'm no better and feel myself becoming cantankerous – that's a good word, I think, one I'll never be able to say aloud again, I'm like an old tree with canker. I hardly know myself, or maybe, I wonder, am I getting to know myself too well, was I always like this? I still play the word game with Georgie but her language is so good now it's mostly her helping me which doesn't bring the same joy. I'm getting no better and she comes in less. Just now I hear Jessica tell her to go and see Grandma and she answers in a new whine she's developed, "Do I have to?"

I think more and more of those falling leaves.

Sometimes a nurse comes or the physiotherapist. I don't know what's happening – they keep me in the dark, telling me a few inconsequentialities like a soldier on manoeuvres. "One step at a time," they say, smiling, and I think, yes, I know all about this precarious motion. I miss Tim. It was after he died that time started to speed up, and everything – good or bad – passes so quickly things hardly seem to matter because, whatever they are, they'll soon be gone. But when I look at Georgie I know that she exists in a different rhythm – I can sense the importance, the imperative, of every moment. She misses nothing.

I watch the robin and two blue tits. They're a bit like Georgie, so busy, so alert. A commotion in a sycamore some distance away sends them flying. It seems silly, but I feel as if I need to know how they do it, as if at some time my body might forget its connection to the ground and take to the air. Nothing is solid – everything is fluid, mutable, shifting. My mind ricochets, without pause, from one place to another.

I'm not getting any better, I know that. I think I had another stroke yesterday – only a small one, but I believe it's cumulative, the toll they take. I've only ever been in hospital once before, when Laurence was born – now I've been from there to Laurence and Jessica's, and again, and I still haven't been back to my empty house. This can't go on. I mustn't become incapacitated. I watch these thoughts form and disappear like a shoal of fish swimming through a child's fingers. What was I thinking of before?

I remember Georgie sitting on my lap and reading a book together – she'll be here soon, we can look at a book. Here she is. No, it's not her. Georgie runs. Who's this? She's frowning. Georgie smiles. "Go away," I try to say to this strange girl, and she does – immediately.

Laurence comes and sits next to me. "Mum," he says, and I look at him. He's so large now, he's grown into his name. I remember us choosing it – it always seemed like a mouthful. We thought it would become Laurie – I like Laurie. I think if we'd had another we would have chosen a shorter name – Dan maybe. Laurie and Dan. But by itself Laurence remained unshortened until it was too late.

"Georgie's upset," he says. "She told me you shouted at her." Did I? I can hardly talk, how would I shout?

"Don't worry," Laurence says, "you'll be better soon." He touches my arm, my hand. I point at the curtain. He starts to draw it. I nod. He closes it. I sleep.

When I wake up I can remember Georgie creeping into the room and telling her to go away. I can't bear it. It's wrong. I'm wrong. But I can't tell her that. I can't tell her anything.

When I was young I was frightened of an old man in our street. His face, the whole of his head, was like a skeleton, you could see the bones through his skin. Whenever I saw him I crossed the road, keeping as far away as I could, and held my breath until I reckoned he'd be out of sight. And every time I passed his house I fixed my eyes on the ground and tried not to imagine what was inside.

I think of that old man now and feel shame, but also something else – I can't, I mustn't let myself become my own version of him in Georgie's head. Laurence and Jessica are both kind, busy and optimistic. But I'm not getting better as I should be – things go up and down, round and round, but there is no general direction, no real progress. Was there ever? I wonder as my mind finds this track. Is there ever?

I feel sad, lost, angry, bewildered. What happens to all these emotions? These odd, troublesome fragments that snag the surface of my mind. They can't be squashed or harried or hurried away. All I can do is to recognise them, give them the air they crave, bear witness, until hopefully, satisfied, replete, they leave of their own accord.

I go out onto the balcony. It's raining but I don't care. I try to pull the tall window behind me so it's not quite shut. My bare feet pad about in a cold puddle as my head seems to float. My body between is stretched, insubstantial. What to do? I hold Georgie in my mind, so bright, so vital. And if not now, will I still be capable later?

I see her in the garden with a friend, both wrapped up in gloves and hats – winter is hanging on. They're throwing things, balls, sticks, old conkers, up as high as they can. Their red and blue wellies, tight jeans and waterproof jackets with pictures of starfish and butterflies make them a riot of energy and colour. They don't glance up at my window and I don't want them to.

It's just before dawn, that time when each day has to choose whether it's winter or spring. There are snowdrops under the apple tree and a few stray crocuses on the lawn. Although the room is only one storey up, the house is on a hill and the ground drops away at the back so it's nearly two storeys down to the ground. Enough? I think so. The rail is quite low. Although in my mind I can imagine this final act – over and over again I've run through the sequence – I can't name it. And however hard I try to extinguish the delusion, I can't help but see myself rising into the sky instead of hitting the concrete below. I watch the sun slip behind a cluster of fir trees at the bottom of next door's garden and, realising how cold it is, glance back inside.

I can hear a blackbird singing. It must look like an accident. Well that should be easy, I think, and smile. I don't think I've ever smiled as much as I do now. Is it something to do with being unable to speak? Did I catch it from Georgie? Or is it something else, something I don't understand?

Outside everything is different. The trees are leaning towards each other, whispering. The sky is clean, each blade of grass on the lawn sharper, greener than it was before. The sun touches an old leaf, left over from autumn, and it curls in on itself. It's beautiful. I shut my eyes and smile as I step nearer the edge. What will happen to Georgie? How will Laurence and Jessica cope? These are harsh questions and my mind, struggling to escape, turns back to the leaf. A light gust lifts it up and my eyes follow. I raise a foot and pause.

The Flower
LEILA SEGAL

1.

A flock of blue, brown and white doves on a wall.

A large cockroach with wings flew in through the window. It looked like a cockroach but flew like a moth, batting frantically against the sides of the room. Yamil came in and caught it by the antlers, took it out hanging from his hand, then killed it with one sharp thwack of a shoe.

It's funny how you don't see things unless they look as you expect them to. It took me two weeks to see a supermarket's shiny blue sign near my new flat in Havana, simply because the front of the building was a dull colour and the windows empty, not like the ones at home, which blare themselves out to the world.

2.

I was dancing in the kitchen with Yamil, for it was the morning

. . . a place where I can lock eyes with them . . . lock eyes with the key . . .
I looked up, and where a dead fly would usually suck out its life
in my hand – steel.

And in this way, I held my arms up to him, still sweating
from my sleep. A dance of the morning – the radio sang and the
beat swayed – out of a pink silk slip barely reaching the thigh. He
was cooking half-way into the kitchen and a fly trailed ants up
the side of a greasy pane of glass open to vermilion baking blue.

Over the water a tiny man could sit all day, his chest slumping,
belly big – he always leaned towards quiet, all day; the building
was broken but its sun blazed and he waited. He was tiny but he
sat with me, often, eating. We two faced one another.

And Yamil sweated before bathing, from sleep on the black
vinyl, cooking up the pineapple rinds into a morning brew – a
baby-blue enamel pan and sweet-smelling gas.

Two cockroaches. They were dying. Helmets and armour,
belly-up; legs struggled slowly, waving in the sweet air. They
died for a day till I had to end it, sweeping them into the pink
plastic pan with rinds, decaying mango juice and ash.

So we danced in the morning and he cooked tea with a pan
over my shoulder, and I ran to the window to watch the day till
ants bit my arms, streaming up the side of the house.

And Yamil knew how it was to dance in the morning with
sweat on him from the night before.

3.
Night lightning flashes flashes. I thought it was a lighthouse or
an aeroplane but when I opened my eyes, the sky was dip dip

dipping a Morse code of palest grey on black.

Surrounded, in the beating kettledrum.

The door slammed. I went to close the bathroom window, still in the silence of my sleep. A fuzz of rain blurred the street below; a square of light held two women in white, shelling peas.

4.

26 July – Revolution Day. I awoke that morning with square eyes; bits of dirt were stuck to them. Yamil was in the kitchen making juice out of all the leftover fruit in the fridge – mangoes with bruises, yellow and brown guavas. I was curled up in a ball on the bed; my eyes flickered open and shut. There was a fresh-fruit smell. He was padding around the apartment like a leopard.

I felt a sprinkling of water on my eyelids. I had been struggling to stay asleep because I so loved the world I found there; he pulled me gently back.

"It's eleven o'clock, Maya."

I sat up, pleased. Sleep was always so difficult to find. For days I had been waking at five, the cock crow dragging me from my dreams. Pleased. But it was only nine. Still, it had been a good night.

Yamil was working on the computer. He liked it. I had taught him how to use it and now he took it up alone, working consummate, professional, in one corner. He didn't need to ask me what to do. Sometimes I had the impression of living with a man and his work, not knowing exactly what was going on.

I could hear strains of music coming from outside. I went into the bathroom and peered out of the window into early-morning sun. People were walking slowly up Calle 23 in their best clothes, holding Cuban flags and wearing T-shirts with the faces of the five men imprisoned for spying in Florida bearing the slogan

Inocientes! The music was coming from speakers placed all the way along the road. They were marching towards La Tribuna Abierta; it was a moving sight – calm, peaceful, united. I felt a sense of pride and wanted to join them.

Adelante Cubanos!

Liberen a los heroes que defienden su pueblo de muerte.

We were right in the middle of everything there on 23. On TV millions of people were marching to the US Interests Section along the Malecón, and through the open windows I could hear rousing trumpets, marching music booming out, a baking salsa beat. The people were carrying red Che Guevara flags.

Big trucks of people were collecting; trucks and buses were moving past our windows packed with Cubans sitting and standing, most wearing the T-shirts bearing five faces – los heroes que defienden su pueblo.

Sometimes I think Yamil just doesn't understand the tone in his voice when he speaks. I have told him but he doesn't hear me.

5.

The garden. I opened the flower before it was born, peeled back the bud for a peep of vermilion hunched up inside and lovely red-lined green. Its petals were new, crushed like fingers in the bath or a baby's new-born scalp. The stamens were perfect tough rods and a single petal was speckled with white.

6.

Writing is not an empty experience.

It is a whole round thing.

Writing is not just the words – first it is the knowledge; the words translate the knowledge into common property.

7.

Thunder in Havana. Rain strings across the city, globules of yellow-white rain, ripping through the sky till a brighter white splits open pearly grey. Rushing from the gutter of the neighbours' roof. Two people running under the forked lightning in shorts, a man and a woman in cold suddenly come.

You see that giant electric energy spark rip open the sky and the sun is still shining. Gnats cross-fly with the rain and the light is a neon flickering on on on. Patting tin roof. Where is the cockerel? Dog trotting, hurries away as someone cracks sticks in the fire. I can see white rain in balls falling on the sky; streamers curtain the space between me and them, not far, huge blocks and hotels. The people are running on the roof, splashing water over themselves from the tank with a big tin jug. Clouds from Botticelli or older, from a painting of doom at sea, and each one has been lit by lightning and the sun. I am ripping open, firing a gun, artillery drum; a tearing giant is splitting open our world. I have never seen it before, in the midst of a war, afraid – but the music hasn't stopped and soon the heat will come.

I heard the cock crow; he's all right somewhere. Where are the chicks? I saw them on the dirt path, before, at the back of the house. I still see the sun. Lemons, limes sublime eat rain for the green we have. It's all dirty yellow and crunching underfoot, rain on tin. A bomb. I dive for cover. The man is still singing, quietly, next door.

8.

And what is it? What is it that we find here? A brutal part of us that resonates with the symphony of Cuban life. You could call it a cacophony for there is always noise here, noise that assaults me, unruly, offends my tranquil ear – but it is the white noise of home I cannot stand: when noise sears and cuts, it can kill because it is ugly. Harmony, integrity, I have learned from this cacophony, can present themselves in various guises we have yet to understand. I never shout, unlike my neighbours on the stairs; for me, tension collects as rancid poison in my bones.

We live here in a drum. The lightning flashes constant, noiseless, over the sea.

I love this place where a sincere smile will always meet you without a price. I love this place where I can lock eyes with them and my moves are understood.

All I want is to develop my writing. I have seen my ambition – it has flown from under my wings into this sacred tropical place. I know what I am, see myself from the inside. To devote the rest of my life to my writing, because I live like this, like this I understand. Like this, the world holds me as its partner and my spirit finds its heart. Like this I speak, I am at last known . . . in words, the words my lips cannot form.

The neighbours on the third floor had the TV on very loud with the door open; music burst forth at the same time. She shouted at her husband over the noise of both – pause – he shouted back. There seemed to be no thought of reducing background noise for effective communication. All conversation was conducted this way regardless, and their door was mostly kept open.

9.
I don't think writing should ever require effort. My writing should come easily, slip off the edge of my thoughts like cream

melting down the side of pavlova from the oven. A pavlova from the rain.

Yes, slipping off the side of my thoughts, skimming froth off the water as it boils.

You think and think and think and feel and live, and from that should exit your work – a by-product of your life, of the way you have chosen to live – el sale de tu vida . . . el sale.

In a way there is no point in *trying* to write at all. Because you can't *try* – it should be obvious; it should be a complete bloom that issues from the plant of your living, the pinnacle of everything you are and do.

Your talent, such as it is, is that you know how to find the words.

Your talent, such as it is, is to live your own life, because often that seems almost impossible, as it is stolen from your infancy – me lo has robado desde que era niña – or to exit from your own grave, which was one you came to after much suffering.

10.

I know how you can love another, no matter that you're separate as night and day.

And all the while I was conscious of this, hope tumbling, another shoot broke through – of truth, crystal hard the truth we had.

I was crying in the garden and he asked me whether I'd like a flower and I said yes.

Which one? he asked. That one over there or this one here?

I chose a strawberry-red bloom like a long foxglove on a dark-green bush. The red broke through a sea of foliage crouching under the night.

But when he brought it to me, the red was not a flower –

it was leaves opening from the stem like a pineapple, blushing pubescent as they sank themselves into darker shades of maturity.

He reached up to pluck the other flower as it hung like a red star over us.

I held it in my hand. It was like crêpe paper wound on a stiff wire stem. The flower shone out between us as we both looked down at it. It seemed to calm us, to soak up the sad or to change it with its lack of understanding. Unknowing bloom.

11.
And then I began to wake up and see the pink things, the sparkly nail varnish and the flowers on the side and Yamil's eyes move in his dream.

12.
We didn't argue; it just all went wrong, and I am not sure I understand why. There we were walking down the street, and one minute we were talking, then the next he had left me. I couldn't understand. And then I walked home, where he was waiting on the step; as I tried to unlock the door I dropped the water, but he didn't pick it up.

Now he is sorry. He left me alone and he didn't care. Now he is sorry. But he doesn't know what he should do; I shall not tell him.

We went for a walk along the Malecón and he wouldn't speak to me all the way because he said his head hurt, and every time I tried to talk to him he got angry with me and said I didn't respect him and I cried and he tutted and walked at a distance from me and ignored me, and then we came home and I couldn't stop crying and he ignored me and he sat on the sofa and watched TV and tutted and ignored me even though I was lying on the bed in tears. Then he went to bed and wouldn't speak to me. And I said I couldn't be with someone who didn't speak to me and he told me to find someone else who spoke to me a lot.

inside   every drop of breath I draw is a silent shock
outside   the breath is of death, of silent dying

I liked Yamil at first because we had no words, so all seemed pure and true. I couldn't use my tortured untrue words to get in between us. I was prevented from being the me I didn't like.

He was with me always, all the time, there was no distance between us; I never had to feel alone, to find a time and place where that could be. There were no words that needed to be said that might not be said, no painful silences, even though we spoke hardly the same language.

Soon, soon this time will be over – these inhabited words of mine will be gone. Soon, soon, this all too painful time will reach out over the billions of particles in the universe and be another dust.

There is a time, and it is only moments, a time of light. When the waves close over you, and the night, there is nothing left but the ripple of your imagination on this sea of living.

And this place we call memory – where does it live? I saw the light shining on us in the café talking, but all too soon it was gone and the shades of peace were replaced by winds of desire and ugly yellow sands of change.

13.
A new day. A cave in my belly, hollow and sickening, as if all the bad from yesterday had collected there as bile during the night.

Yamil knows how to make tea out of pineapple skins. He boiled them up in the blue enamel pan and made a plastic bottle of yellow tea to put in the fridge.

My mind is like crushed petals or knives, layers impenetrable bruising. Fug of the morning heat, blue haze that swept in through the window I went to open in the bathroom. The other shutters were closed for the cockerel who sang all night and day.

Inside me is a big hollow eating up. This is a difficult time.

Leaving soon – leaving Yamil and the time of here. Only three weeks: this time is gold, keep it here. This is my time. I can't remember life at home – don't know it now. I know here and heat and light and beat, here and faces hard or alive that meet me with their looks.

Time is like sand that runs through your fingers on the beach when you hold them up with it. There is no way to live time. Only to face it now, and look at time as if it will never leave.

Yamil's eyes say so much, then the shutters close him off. I am not helping him. He is struggling, but he must come to me. He went away from me. He has to learn and if he doesn't know . . . But I think he understands.

14.
The words have stopped now. Murmuring of music almost continuous . . .

15.

I can see a leaf, crimson scarlet; it is a foot from my big toe, crimson scarlet also.

So tall, where did it grow to? Up above everything. That one has spurted out all alone, for its own, unknown reasons. Other trees, true, may know – even I may be allowed to know, if I can sit here long enough and listen, gain their trust.

I have done many calculations in this garden; an age has passed as I try to get still.

What is the feeling of rain? Chill, skin shivers, prickle – we know.

Darkens. You see how . . . one of us is marvel – oh how can we know? And the other – well – it does, automatic . . . senses . . . the obvious things. The strangeness is only in the delight I have of my knowing how soon the rain will come.

Wind, shivers over me.

Here, the smells are exclusive; they exclude sweet faint smells of home – except now one flew . . . or was it memory? Where did it fly in to – from where?

I like sheltering under the dark trees and I like to disappear into them. They hover in layers over the red brick path, calling me in. Further . . . deeper birdsong, more real, mixed in with the soothing Caribe music, and drops of moisture that are home.

Green is . . . it is darker than you remembered, darker than it should be in such a sun-bleached place.

Under the arch, over the red brick – dark red or green, can't see for lack of light – it calls you into its silence. If you squat still, so you feel damp rising from the earth, *smell* it, they start to speak. And a colder wind blows the crimson scarlet leaves along the terracotta path, so chill against damp; warmth freezes. The Madonna bends her head, folds her hands in some unknown, unsung humility.

16.

I've learned here how everything is about currents of air. It's all about moving the air. I hated coming back into the stairwell of the flat. I would open the front door of the building and come into a filthy humid stairwell of trapped air – still air that had sat there rotting all afternoon. It was so hot that air – hot because it did not move, did not have anywhere to go. I realised, then, how it was all about moving air. Move the air, live. Fans that move the air. Air moving through a car. That was life, and still air was not.

17.

Leaving begins today. I felt it come inside, small in the pit of my stomach. Leaving, when each time gets shorter shorter, slipping out of your careful hands, and a slight sickness as time begins again.

Wanting to hold the gold dust between your fingers, and knowing how soon it will be only the dust of memory. Making pictures, inscribing words, calling ghosts – how time deceives us. How she tricks us into imagining we live here for ever, when all there is, is the endlessly shifting kaleidoscope of bright plastic jewels to tempt our beginning.

All of our words are an attempt to hold on to time, all of our images an attempt to hold off our fear of the void left after the candle dies. A picture holds what we want to believe about what happened. I defy them.

Fault Lines

ELLEN HARDY

The bus is hissy and gassy, a spiteful old goose. It's pissing rain, and the driver's got the heating on full so the inside is claggy with wet and stink – sweat and chewing gum and last night's chicken nuggets. The Year Nines make smudgy circles in the misted-up windows with their sleeves: a row of portholes along the length of the X90, everywhere but the front seats by the driver.

Jonah Hardcastle sits near the front, but he doesn't wipe himself a view. The movement might be something they could remark on, so he sits quietly, concentrating as hard as he can on making the back of his head disappear. It doesn't seem to be working. The first missile hit the window a minute ago; a fat gobbet of masticated bus ticket. It missed him, but slid slowly down the pane an inch from his cheek – lumpy, like a premonition. The next one catches him in the crease of his ear, next to the hairline. He feels it slobber slowly down between his shirt collar and his skin, and it's cold. A direct hit, and there's an answering flutter of excitement from the back rows of the bus. Now they have something to do.

Flump. Spat. The nape of his neck, the crown of his head. *Pah.* Another one hits his shoulder, as if the bus were hosting a seagull with the shits. The volley continues until they reach the centre of town, where most of the kids get off. Now spattered with gummy paper mash, Jonah grips the fuzzy bus seat, wondering whether they'll make him go with them. But it's Friday; they've got other plans. So he submits only to an almost celebratory succession of cuffs to his right ear as they troop past him towards the exit. The last one to leave is Alex Hall, who Jonah thinks of only as Hell. He looms over Jonah, at fourteen already massive, already beery.

"Fuck, Hardcastle. Look at you." His thick thumb probes Jonah's jawline, rubbing wet paper and acne together. "You should stop squeezing that shit in public."

"Alex, hurry up!" call the girls from outside, already rolling their skirts over at the waist. Hell lets fly with a final, hefty cuff that bounces Jonah's head off the saliva-smeared window, and the swipe of his hair finally clears the mist enough to let in the outside world. Through streaming eyes, Jonah looks over the leering faces of his classmates into the grimy display window of the hardware shop next to the bus stop. Above the plastic trays of spring bulbs and rat poison, there's a rack of autumn fireworks. It's illustrated with green cartoon rockets, red-and-yellow explosions and silhouettes of sexy girls. He reads the rockets' names to himself slowly, like a charm. They are strong, brave names, names that have adventures: *Sky Salute*, *Star Chaser*, *Zulu*. *Stealth Rising*, *Hurricane Blitz*, *Mini Gods*.

Jonah is the last one off the bus, where it wheezes to a stop at the end of the valley beyond the town. The driver doesn't glance down from behind his Perspex shield, and as soon as Jonah's feet hit the ground the vehicle is off, with a spritely efficiency it never demonstrates when in service. Jonah takes galoshes out of his backpack and puts them on over his school shoes, then heads down the unpaved track towards the farm. His hair is still daubed with bus-ticket spit, so when he arrives he skirts the courtyard and goes to use the sink in the farm shed, scrubbing himself with Swarfega and freezing water. He checks himself for debris in the rusted mirror fragment on the shelf above the sink. Dark eyes, dark curls. Spots. A scar below his eyebrow where Pa hit him once, by accident, with the butt end of a mattock.

He finds Pa inside, as usual, in the chair by the kitchen window. There's a farm-supplies catalogue folded open on the arm of the chair, but his reading glasses are still hanging on the hook by the stove. Books and papers cluster around him under a light blanket of dust and dirt, and onions spill from a canvas bag in the corner of the kitchen. The whole room smells faintly of soggy, rotting onion flesh; they have long gone sour inside the bag, beaded with black, but will not be moved. Jonah could do it, but he no longer knows what will incur his father's wrath. Pa turns towards him and his skin is the skin of curdled milk, his hair the wispy grey of dandelion clocks.

"Did you get caught in the storm?" Pa sneers. There's a weak sunshine leaking through the window now, but Jonah is still dripping wet from the farm tap, his hair plastered to his scalp.

"No, Pa."

"What, then?"

"I got dirty, Pa."

"Of course you did. You're worse than Bessie, and she's got old age as an excuse."

Jonah notices that the dog has pissed on the floor under the kitchen table. Bessie raises her head in his direction, gazing uncertainly through cataract-clouded eyes, and thumps her tail. She's huddled by the door to the yard, a sure sign she needs to go again. Jonah lets her out, then fetches J-cloths and a plastic bowl from under the sink, starts to run water. The activity stirs Pa from his chair. Jonah still has his back to him, finger under the tap waiting for the stream to turn hot, but he can feel the resentment shivering through his father's awkward frame, the unhappy skin stretched too tight across his bones. All *right* then, say Pa's half-mast shoulders, his stiffened knees. If you *must* crash about like that, I'll *go*. As if Jonah's action of releasing the dog had intruded rudely on some private, intensely important project. It probably has. Except Jonah knows from the pattern of the toast crumbs on the table, from the stale air and the untouched coffee cup, that his father has barely moved from his chair since Jonah left that morning for school.

167

He hears Pa cough and swing his dirty waxed jacket up from the back of the chair and over his shoulders. It catches the empty bottles ranked on the windowsill and a line of them fall, the glass shattering and skittering into inconvenient corners of the room. Pa seems barely to notice but staggers past Jonah in pursuit of his dog, close enough that Jonah catches a whiff of stale wine and vomit. He turns from the sink to look at his father, who has paused briefly in front of the open door onto the yard. He notes collarbones like coat hooks, the stained edge of his shirt, eyes cast deeper into milky shadows by the light from outside. Pa's gaze scans back into the room, catches Jonah watching. "Christ," he says. "Can't you leave me alone?"

It's not his fault. Mama died, so it's not his fault. It's Jonah's. Jonah who should have been there. Jonah who should have come home from school quicker, instead of being made to chew on his own underwear behind the Co-op recycling bins. Jonah, who should have found her before it was too late, not opened the door to the sheep pen and found her hanging, already cold, the rope around the beam too far for him to reach. Jonah who ran to her but couldn't touch, frightened of the rigid flesh beneath her woollen tights. He screamed then, but there were only sheep to hear. They regarded him steadily, their ears flickering.

Jonah finishes cleaning glass and piss from the floor, then sits at the kitchen table to attempt his homework. The letters swim strangely in front of his eyes, and he has trouble concentrating on the geographical significance of attrition in river basins – rock and water pounded ceaselessly together, so that rock becomes grain and the riverbed itself mutates, over time, creating something entirely new. Not entirely, though, he thinks. For rock and grain and riverbed are all one – the same streams that snake their way from side to side across the map over millennia, nibbling delicately at the rim of their shores – here, there, a little further, back again – cleaving the land into its constituent parts with the patience of rain. Jonah's head is full of splintered stone and foaming estuaries, his pen lying forgotten by his exercise book, when the chainsaw grind of a vehicle in the yard brings him back to the kitchen table. Half relieved, half fearful, Jonah moves to the door to see what's happening.

Pa and Bessie are standing by a mud-streaked Land Rover, their hackles up. Inside the vehicle, a red-faced figure rests an over-familiar elbow on the rolled-down window, and is talking to Pa in cheerful tones. The man speaks with the local Hereford accent, the one Jonah can't perfect in school. Despite his best efforts, Jonah still speaks like Pa – clear and aloof, like the radio.

"Be doing me a proper favour, Mick. Can't keep this stuff at home, the missus won't have it."

"So because there's no 'missus' here, I should feel some obligation?"

"Now, Mick, you know I don't mean anything by it. But you've space, no small kids running around, quiet time of year. You'd not notice them."

"No."

"It's only until Sunday. The school can't keep them, but it's a proper lovely evening they've got planned. Hot dogs, toffee apples, Guy Fawkes got up to look like the man from Defra."

"Why the fuck should I do a favour for that bunch of clowns?"

Land Rover man's self-possession falters slightly in the face of Pa's fury. His red face flushes a slightly deeper shade of puce.

"Two grand's worth we've got here. Sure I could find somewhere else to stash it, but given what you've not put into the community lately, I reckon gunning for Arsehole of the Year isn't your smartest move."

Jonah has been so absorbed in the exchange that he has forgotten to stay inconspicuous. Land Rover man turns suddenly, looking straight at him.

"Hiya, mate. Sure you'd appreciate your pa putting up these here firecrackers for a night or two, eh?"

Jonah stares at him, levelly. Picks his words as if they were shot.

"Do you have . . . Star Chasers?"

"Probably, mate. Got all the good stuff in here. No expense spared. You'll be down for the show, won't you? Won't want to miss it."

"Fuck, then," Pa spits, intervening. "Put them over there." He gestures towards a small lean-to shed with a metal latch.

"That's it, Mick. Knew you'd come through." Land Rover man leaps down from his cab and starts lifting boxes out of the back. For all he pretends not to be afraid of Pa, he doesn't want to waste time. On one of his trips from the boot to the shed he nods towards Jonah and mutters to Pa in a stage whisper. "Funny one, that one. Did you ever think of getting him looked at?"

"Get out before I put the dog on you."

Say what you like about Pa, he doesn't take any crap. And Land Rover man didn't look at Bessie properly before she ambled off back to the kitchen, so takes the threat as meaningful. He finishes unloading the long boxes of fireworks, ten or fifteen in all, then clambers genially back into the Land Rover cab and sets off. "See you Sunday!" he shouts as the engine starts to roar, raising a jovial hand in salute. Jonah reads the number plate as the vehicle churns out of the yard: *H8LL W1N5*. Forgetting everything he turns to his father, eyes wide.

"Don't look at me like that. You're not fucking going."

Jonah fucking knows, but is not about to say so.

That night Jonah lies half awake, half sleeping. The air captured between his skin and the sheets is hot, almost feverish, but he can't quite break the surface into consciousness and lift his arm to peel them back. Fireworks sputter and fizz past his closed eyes, burning hot bright trails across the inside of the lids. They whine their names to him as they go by, the same names printed on the long boxes in the locked shed. *Cyclone Wheels. Star Busters. Sizzling Sentinels. Gunsmoke.* He lingers over their bold stars and comet tails, their backdrop of deep night; his lashes flicker in time to their whistles and screams, the crackling spray of their tacky cloudbursts. Vaguely, he wonders if it's not just in his head – perhaps the explosions have begun already, in back gardens and fenced-off parks further down the valley. Maybe it's real, what he hears, the booms and pops releasing whooshes of light that illuminate the houses clustering along the old road, tumbling their spent cartridges from the sky over the town. They're comforting, these noises outside in the dark; they keep away the lurking claws and bat-things. They suggest that somewhere out there, someone is having a good time. Now their deeper notes begin to sound: heavy drum beats that obliterate the dark, entwine lovers' arms and draw children into safe embraces. Finally, Jonah sleeps.

It's Saturday afternoon, and Jonah is scrambling up the hillside beyond the farm. There's a loose sheep somewhere, a sturdy matron who managed to heave away as he checked her for fly strike and was off across the fields as if he had snapped her from a rubber band. Pa: "That sheep's maggoty arse is more use to me than you are. Go!" He should have a dog, but Bessie is too old and no one has mentioned getting a replacement so he's equipped to catch a Shetland pony, with a bucket of feed and a small halter. It's the first properly chill day of autumn, cold streams of air burning at the skin through his jeans. The mist thickens as he climbs higher towards the beginning of the woods, halfway up the steep slope that bleeds, eventually, into the Brecons.

When he reaches the woods he pauses and turns to look back the way he came, across hummocked fields and wool-snagged wire to the farm buildings. He's seen them from here before. But it was different then: a sunny day in another lifetime, spreadeagled at the edge of a tartan blanket while Mama read aloud from *The Wind in the Willows*. Bees hummed in the flower heads and there were sandwiches and glass jars of lemonade – impractical, but Mama wanted everything to be perfect. Pa lay a little further off, snoozing under a hat tipped forward over his eyes. They were new to the farm then, but full of hope. Not for them the grey emptiness of the city: they had come to be part of the land. They would brew their own cordials and make preserves, store food for winter, grow vegetables and care for animals. They were pioneers, forging a new life in their country's own Eden.

That was before the farm became a lonely place, which Mama both hated and was frightened to leave. Before the front gate became the furthest limit of her world. Later she wasn't allowed to go out, for fear she'd turn up dead or disgraced in another part of the country, wherever she'd been seeking her next escape. She began to run her head along the walls of the kitchen like a zoo animal, and to look through Jonah at something beyond, or inside, his living flesh.

Jonah blinks the sour mist out of his eyes and imagines the farm at the bottom of a river. Loosened from its foundations, a broken flagstone topped with tiny buildings making its stop-start journey between the clatter of weedy rocks. Air bubbles escape from its empty windows and trout flick by, their rainbow scales gleaming next to corrugated-iron roofs that are already coming away from the walls. It's the very first stages of attrition: there are miles and years to go before the farm is ground down into fine particles, welcomed into the shifting mud of old stone and pulverised invertebrates. Now Jonah sees the farm caught in a crevasse, a fast current beating at its fragile walls. The outbuildings go first, snapping off along the fault lines of their gateways and windows, fragments of their structure careening away with the swift water. Then the farmhouse itself: roof tiles, chimney stacks, floorboards, doors and lintels, all stripped from their framework and tumbled off out of sight. At last the farm splits and shatters away cleanly, leaving nothing behind but people's useless memories of it.

Suddenly the sheep is there next to him, hurrying along the path back down towards the farm. Jonah starts and moves towards her unthinking, too quickly, catches his toe on a tussock of grass and pitches forward onto his knees. He's winded, his jeans are soaked, and the startled sheep gives an insulted bleat and swerves back the way she came. He fumbles for the spilled bucket, attempts a soothing noise from his tightened throat, but she's already far out of reach and gathering speed.

"Fuck off then!" he shouts after her, as she ricochets gracelessly away through the trees. The mist slaps his words back at him wetly, bitter on his tongue. He hurls a final cry against the silent woodland: "*Mama!*"

Jonah stands motionless, disbelieving, feeling the pointless echoes of his voice disappear into freezing leaf mulch and moisture-spangled spider webs.

He returns to the farm as darkness falls. His father will be in bed already, two bottles in, the escaped sheep forgotten until it feeds his rage the next morning. Jonah's legs ache as he trudges across the yard and pauses in front of the locked door of the lean-to shed. The metal catch is a joke, and the whole fixture comes away easily with a few twists of a screwdriver. The fireworks are dry and safe inside, the boxes stacked carefully in the middle of the space, sharp and clean against the shed's habitual accumulations of old paint tins and broken tools. Jonah approaches them carefully. He runs his fingers along the edges of the boxes, lifts the lids and reads their names aloud to himself, quietly: *Treasure Chest. Carpet Bomber. Angel Dust. Vengeance.* Each smooth explosive has a printed slip of paper taped to its neon plastic shell, with a tantalising legend. *Fires red stars with silver and blue tails, then gold brocades, before a final volley of crackling mines. A pretty little firework, ninety-six shots of coloured pearls and pops. A single hit of scarlet streaks to four bursts of silver glitter.*

Jonah is a hunched figure, scurrying back and forth across the yard from the shed to the sheep pen. When all the fireworks are stacked inside the barn door, he draws it to and looks the sheep full in their petri-dish eyes. They rustle quietly in the dim yellow light cast by the single wall lamp, their waxy fleeces and carelessly hewn heads subdued by the autumn dark. He considers the pen; its flat concrete floor, bales of straw, metal fencing. High wooden beams. The sheep watch him blankly.

"Did you get caught in the pen?" he asks them, sing-song,

mocking, and goes to work. It's tricky at first, the heavy ewes rushing stupidly about, but he fetches a bucket of pellets and then it's just a matter of choosing where to begin. Before too long the sheep are hobbled with firecrackers, crowned with comets strapped to their woolly skulls. *Phantom*, he whispers to himself as he moves among them, binder twine in hand. *Blast Off*. *Screaming Eagles*. Catherine wheels are slung from their necks like herder's bells, Roman candles tethered to their jiggling tails. *Red, purple and green rosettes with a crackling pistil make this totally unique.* He takes the rockets last – a clutch of them, six War Hawks with slender stems and pointed red caps. *Each one produces a different effect, but all on a gold willow theme.* Stands them firmly in a bucket of loose hay in the centre of the pen. *Fires nineteen shots of thick titanium crackling comet tails.* He takes matches from a high alcove in the wall, and turns towards the pen one final time. He breathes deeply but the scene swims slightly, sheep and straw blurring together, and he shakes his head as he holds the matchbox against the heel of his hand, ready to strike.

Perhaps he shouldn't be surprised when the door behind him slams back and he feels Pa's hand close around his. The inevitability of it makes him gasp, and they stand there unmoving for long moments, their breath blooming white in the freezing air. Jonah waits – he can't raise his eyes from the matchbox, where Pa's large coarse hand frames his smaller one. Then Pa's hand moves to his elbow, turning him around. He still doesn't raise his eyes as Pa holds out his hand for the matches, and Jonah passes them over.

Pa opens the box, picks out a match, and lights it millimetres from Jonah's face. Jonah feels the brightness of its flame sear the back of his eye socket and inhales its puff of sulphur. Then Pa starts to feed the flame back into the box, so all two hundred matches start to pop and flare. He slides the lid back and lifts the box high, making Jonah flinch away. But Pa's arm completes a longer arc, and he lobs the matches towards the bucket of War Hawks.

Jonah turns in amazement. Together he and Pa watch the

hay catch, and the sheep start to circle nervously around the fire.

"Fucking things," says Pa.

He doesn't look at Jonah, but stares at the sheep as if they held the answers to questions he hadn't known to ask.

"Come on," he says. "It's show time."

Together they back steadily away. At the last moment before they reach the door the War Hawks explode, setting the mass of ewes screaming and alight. Jonah darts back and unhooks the gate of the pen, and the animals stream past him in a staccato rush of sharp shitsmell and singed wool. Outside in the yard, panic and pain. The crowns and hobbles fizz to life, sending up scorching flares between the farm buildings.

It's extraordinary, like a funeral pyre. Jonah and Pa stand together in the doorway of the shed, looking out onto the yard over a sea of misting gunpowder and blistering flesh. They raise their eyes to the sky above the turmoil, awestruck by the entirely new beauty they have created. Hung flauntingly in the air above the farm is a whole new landscape: crackling peonies, coloured pearls, spinning turrets. Golden willows, dazzling fountains, white brocade.

Fish Fingers

AMY J. KIRKWOOD

Ellie's grandmother came back from the dead on a Tuesday just before tea.

There were no fireworks. The lights did not flicker or dim. It's just that one moment she wasn't there, and the next she was perched on the landing, her large boat-like feet resting on the edge of the top stair.

Ellie didn't know that Granny Moo was dead, so it didn't occur to her to be afraid as she continued down towards the kitchen, thinking mainly of crisps. Her grandmother looked a little bit misty around the edges, a smudgy charcoal sketch. But, Ellie decided, that probably happened when you were old. Lots of sad things happened when you were old, like not wanting to dress up as frogs any more and having to go to church in a smart outfit every Sunday to pay your bus fare to Heaven. Smudgy edges were a logical next step.

"We'll need to set another place for tea. Granny Moo's here," Ellie announced solemnly as she took two crisps from the snack bowl next to her father and made them fight each other to the death before eating the loser as punishment and then the winner too because she was nothing if not fair.

Ellie's parents gave each other the kind of look that normally accompanies a "Yes, but . . ."

"Granny Moo's not coming today." Mum threaded her

fingers through Ellie's hair. "I know this is her day to come for fish fingers, but she can't make it. Can you go and see if Andrew'll come down for tea?"

For a moment, Ellie's eyebrows criss-crossed together as she tried to work out why Mum and Dad were trying to keep Granny Moo's arrival a secret. Was she getting a present? It wasn't her birthday. Confused, she returned to the question in hand. "Andrew shouldn't have tea. He's too fat. The doctor said so. And he won't come anyway. He only ever eats in his room."

Every day Ellie would call her brother for tea, and every day he would tell her to go away, so she did. But sometimes late at night when she couldn't sleep she heard the familiar crackle of packets and fluh-flump of footsteps. By morning, all the good biscuits would be gone. Mum and Dad sighed and frowned but Andrew never got told off.

"Dad just doesn't get it." Her brother had told her that three summers ago as they sat waiting for the cows to pass at a spot near Granny Moo's cottage. Andrew used to call it the Top of the World because when you drove up the winding track to the top of the hill it looked like you were going to plunge over the edge into nothingness. But after her first few scares, Ellie had learned that there was always road the other side, that even nothingness ends. She'd tried to tell Andrew that everything would get better, but he'd just laughed – the sad kind of laugh, not the funny kind.

That was when Andrew had been a bit younger, and still spoke to her sometimes. But the older he got, the sadder he got. Now, the only things bigger than the fat rolls that choked his stomach were his eyes, which were wide and wet and starey and twitching.

"Just go and at least call him. Please," Mum repeated, in the tone of voice that meant there would be no chocolate pudding if she didn't get a move on.

Ellie trudged upstairs, but not before she heard Dad's low, cross whisper, "You're going to have to tell her."

She heard Mum breathe in sharply, almost gurgling, and then there was the thuh-thunk of Dad's leather boots as he moved across the room. Not guarding the crisp bowl any more, Ellie thought wistfully, but she carried on climbing upstairs all the same.

Granny Moo was sat waiting for her in the same place, greyish hair curling in bottle-cap ringlets around her head, dressed in her smartest bus-fare-to-Heaven outfit, her eyes piercing.

"Hullo," Ellie said. Granny Moo's edges were a little more smudged now. "Mum said you can't come for tea. Don't you want fish fingers? Andrew'll only eat them later if you don't."

"I can't eat fish fingers. I'm dead." Ellie's grandmother spoke just like the Queen.

"Oh." Ellie bit her lip. She reached out a hand for the banister, her legs suddenly wobbly. "Is it . . . ? Does it . . . ?"

"Come and sit next to me." Granny Moo moved over to make room, smiling kindly. "Honestly, I've always hated your mum's fish fingers."

"I know." Ellie nodded as she sat down, uneasiness forgotten. "They're horrid. I keep telling her she should just go and buy them from Sainsbury's, but she always wants to make them herself. They're so much . . . *healthier.*" Ellie paused to chew the nail on her little finger. "It's probably because of Andrew," she added thoughtfully.

"Andrew's what I wanted to talk to you about." Granny Moo's voice sounded a bit like Mum's at bedtime, so Ellie stopped chewing her nail and met her grandmother's gaze. "Andrew's very sad."

"But he doesn't cry," Ellie reasoned. "I cry when I'm sad."

Granny Moo's owl-like eyes softened. She tried to rest her hand on Ellie's as they sat side by side, but her fuzzy edges kept slipping through Ellie's arm, so she gave up, just letting her hand hover slightly awkwardly. "I know," she persisted, "but Andrew is a different type of sad. He talked to me about it sometimes. Can you imagine being in a bubble? A bit like a hamster in one of those plastic balls they use for exercise?"

"Yes," said Ellie, because she was excellent at imagining

things. That wasn't boasting. Her Year 3 teacher, Mrs Foster, had written it on her most recent report.

"Now," Granny Moo continued, "imagine that all your feelings, like your happy and your sad and your angry and your scared, and other people's feelings too, are outside that ball. You're inside it – and you can sort of see where they are but you can't get to them, and they can't get to you."

Ellie chewed on her nail once more. "So . . . not a crying sad, but sort of a . . . an empty sad?"

"Exactly." Granny Moo's eyes crinkled up at the corners like the curled sides of a dried leaf.

"Can I – I mean, can Andrew . . . can he get out of the hamster ball?" Ellie asked, knees knocking together as she shifted her weight from left to right. She wondered how polite it would be to try to reach all the way through Granny Moo's stomach where it was smudgier at the edges.

"Yes. I think so. He wants to."

"Why can't you tell Mum?" Ellie asked, as she threw manners out of the window and pushed one forefinger through Granny Moo and out the other side. It felt a bit like wrapping a wet flannel around her hand. She tried again.

Granny Moo raised an eyebrow. "I did before I died, but I couldn't make her understand, not fully. Andrew's not like you or Mum or Dad – he's more like me. Your dad thinks he should just cheer up by himself, but he can't. He needs someone to help him, because he won't ask – a bit like those proud ninjas you like to read about so much. I kept telling Mum that, when I was alive. But now she thinks I'm dead, she won't listen."

"But you *are* dead," Ellie insisted, logically.

"Yes, I know," replied Granny Moo, and again, without noise or colour or – disappointingly – fireworks, one moment she was there and the next she wasn't.

Ellie felt sad that she hadn't had a chance to ask whether being dead hurt very much, because after watching a nature programme about how polar bears sometimes ate their own young, she had been wondering about that quite a bit. Then, remembering her original mission, she rolled herself sideways up the next flight of stairs like a hamster in a plastic ball.

She knocked on Andrew's door.

"Go away," he said.

For once, she ignored him and went in.

Andrew was lying on top of his bed, still in yesterday's pyjamas, staring at the ceiling.

"It's teatime. There're fish fingers," Ellie informed him, poking his flabby shoulder.

"I don't feel like tea," he replied in a flat voice.

"I know. Granny Moo says you don't feel anything much." Ellie squirmed up onto his double bed and sat cross-legged.

"When did she say that?" Andrew sat up slowly.

"Just now."

"But Ellie . . ." Andrew's froggy eyes flickered, opening and closing rapidly. "She's dead."

"I know." Ellie sighed, irritated.

"Oh. Who told you she was dead? Mum wanted to wait for the right moment."

"Granny Moo did. Just now."

"Oh."

There was a long pause. Andrew's mouth stretched sideways and up like he might say something, but he didn't.

"So, are you coming down for tea?" Ellie asked impatiently, jumping off the bed, an astronaut taking one giant leap for mankind. By the time she was in a standing position though, she was a masked ninja – one of the proud ones from her books. Combat-rolling towards the door, she hid behind it, crouched, waiting.

Andrew heaved himself up to a standing position and shuffled across the room, a brown bear trying to blend into a crowd of racoons. She wished he would stand up a bit taller.

"Do you think," Ellie asked, still crouched in her ninja pose, "that if we got you a hamster and put it in a ball, that you wouldn't feel like it's just you all alone by yourself?"

"Maybe. A bit." Andrew looked at her like he was trying

very hard to remember something.

Ellie was reminded of how her brother's face had looked after a jellyfish stung him in Egypt. His eyes had been all wet and glistening but he hadn't cried because Dad had told him to smile and the tingling would go away. Ellie remembered the red blotchy sting spreading over Andrew's leg like a birthmark – her brother had grinned in a stretched, scary way all day, but when the lights were out in their shared room she had heard him sobbing from the pain.

Andrew reached out for her hand and Ellie stood up and took it. It was clammy and sweaty and not very nice. What *was* nice, though, was that they'd probably get a hamster now that she'd got Andrew to come out of his room.

She made her way downstairs slowly, ahead of Andrew, leading him.

When they got to the kitchen, Mum and Dad's mouths were big round Cheerios of surprise.

"Hullo," Andrew said, looking at the floor.

"Son." Dad crossed the room and gripped Andrew's shoulder like he was trying to stop it from falling off.

"I'll set a place at the table for you, sweetheart." Mum started to busy herself in the cutlery drawer. She seemed to need to crouch right down and cover her face to look at it more closely, even though Ellie was sure she knew it off by heart.

Seeing that the three of them were occupied, Ellie took full advantage of the now unguarded snack bowl. She was a lion, the crisps were antelopes and she hunted them one by one.

And then she remembered. "Mum, Dad, I saw Granny Moo. She said we need to get a hamster." That's what she thought Granny Moo had said anyway. Hamsters had definitely been mentioned.

Mum and Dad looked at Andrew and at each other. Dad nodded and Mum took a deep breath. "Ellie, Granny Moo died last week. I'm sorry you didn't get to say goodbye. It was very sudden. Do you understand what I mean when I say she died?"

Ellie rolled her eyes and licked her fingertips so that they stuck to the crumbs in the bowl. She sucked the crisp dust off her fingers one at a time. "I *know* she's dead. She told me. Is tea ready yet?"

Mum nodded without speaking, eyes wide.

Ellie sat down at the table, and then she remembered one more thing Granny Moo had told her. "Oh, Mum. Granny Moo said she hates your fish fingers. She thinks you should get them from Sainsbury's, like me."

Important information shared, she waited as Mum and Dad stared at each other. Were hamster shops open this late? They were probably trying to decide which breed would be best. While they thought about it, Ellie absorbed herself in trying to make her knife and fork move into battle using only her eyes. And maybe it was just her imagination but she thought – just a little bit – that she might be managing it.

Talking Loud and Saying Nothing

SARAH EVANS

He is asked to crouch froglike on the table. Knees out wide, feet apart. Head resting on his intertwined fingers. Bare arse stuck up high. The world's most undignified posture.

The air is crisp and clinical. A hushed male voice talks him through what is happening. A routine procedure. Ten to fifteen minutes max.

Gut-screw fear subsides, giving way to the freeze of submission: the only way out is forward. He feels the warm, slippery wetness as he is washed, the softly dabbing towel, the slight sting as antiseptic is liberally applied. He tries to distance his mind from the present, as firm, latex-covered hands grab and manipulate his genitals. A clamp is positioned: uncomfortable, but no worse.

"Just a small prick," the snooker-commentator voice says as a needle pierces scrotal skin, shooting a sliver of white-hot pain up to fill his balls. His body jerks in reflex, teeth biting down on knuckles, toes curling within the socks he is still wearing. "There we are," the voice says, its gentleness not delivering reassurance.

He thinks how this is all Eileen's fault.

Three weeks ago last Friday and the prospect of dinner with old friends brought an undertow of pure dread.

"Should be fun tonight," he said to Eileen, and thought how

fun had always seemed an alien, somewhat threatening, concept.

"Yeah." But in the wardrobe mirror, her eyebrows drew together, sparking off anxiety: had he let something slip? "Bit of a headache," she added. "But I'll be fine."

Patrick exhaled the air he hadn't known he was retaining. He came close behind, index fingers and thumbs spanning her waist, burying his face in her cropped hair and ocean-fresh scent. "We can call off if you want."

"Oh no. No," she said. "They're expecting us. And you're looking forward to it."

Disappointment stabbed, irrationally acute. "Sure." He wondered what it would be like, just for once, to be completely honest. *I don't want to go; I've had a lousy day.* It's one of the first things he learnt, back in schooldays, that lying is a far more natural reflex than telling the truth.

They discarded their office grooming, exposing pallid, goosebump flesh. Over the years, his muscle tone has softened and spread, while her angles have sharpened. His hair is beginning to thin and both of them are slowly turning grey. He doesn't mind himself. Life is passing and he is muddling through and that seems enough. Whilst Eileen . . . But he didn't want to dwell on that.

He pulled on sharp-crease chinos and a linen shirt. Eileen's geometric-print shift dress was rather classier. "You look nice," he said.

She grimaced at the mirror, then smiled and said, "Thanks. So do you." Both of them were handling each other carefully, still a little bruised, neither of them wanting to reignite the recent disagreements which had started so slowly he barely noticed – some seemingly offhand remark – but which have become more heated with every round, each attempt at explanation pushing them more rigidly into opposing views.

"Guess it's my turn to do the driving," he said.

"If that's OK."

"Sure." Saying it, he realised how badly he needed some proper alcohol. Always, he seems to be a step behind himself, mind catching up only after he's spoken or acted. It feels a very singular failing, the way he is always wishing he had said or done things differently.

The town-centre snarl-up was quickly left behind, leaving them winding through hedgerow-tunnelled, narrow lanes, darkness pushing against the pooled light of headlamps. The routine of driving; Eileen chatting through the minutiae of her day: these externalities occupied surface layers, not impinging on his stream of consciousness, a vague fantasy regarding an actress in a period drama they saw recently. *What are you thinking?* Eileen asks him from time to time. *Nothing*, is his stock response. Constantly, he invents a version of himself that bears little relation to the inner narrative.

The road running round the village green was parked up. Eileen distracted him mid tricky manoeuvre and the car was left skew-whiff, rear end sticking out.

He bit down on irritation.

Stars glittered in the void; a thump of music spilled out from the pub; jaundiced light puddled beneath street lamps. He set his expression, smoothing away the strain, and placed his hand in the small of his wife's back as they walked up the driveway to where the door opened spontaneously. He felt exhaustion pressing down as his face distorted into an effusive grin, echoing the delight of their hostess, Katie.

Their pricey bottle of Châteauneuf was handed over. "Ooh wonderful." They entered the overheated hall, the air dense with kitchen smells along with Katie's over-intense perfume. Greetings were exchanged, first there in the slate-flagged hallway and then with the group of people already gathered in the Charentais-tinted living room. Seven of them in all. Two old college friends of Eileen's plus one add-on. Another couple appended somewhere along the way. All of them knowing each other so long that the history of who originally befriended who no longer mattered. Not really.

He forced an ease with all the touchy-feely stuff, hugs and

air-kisses with the women, handshakes with the men, along with shoulder squeezes. Drinks were offered. Alcohol is removed from the bloodstream at a rate of one unit an hour, thereabouts, so drinking early increases the total allowance. "Just a small one," he said. Eileen frowned at him. Pete never ever pours anything small.

Those all-occasion reflexes flicked into action and he was easing into the flow of trivial conversation, latching onto the discussion about football, all of them talking loud and saying nothing. He's never given a shit about the game (hated, hated mud-bath playing fields at school and the stinging punch of leather against grasshopper-thin legs) but sport is an essential social lubricant and the guy he shares a lift to work with plays nonstop Radio 5 Live. He has learned to offer strident opinions he doesn't hold, whilst never affirming tribal loyalty. Pete was dismayed at the abrupt dismissal of a manager after some scandal involving a teenage girl. "Like she didn't know what she was doing," Pete said. "Poor guy."

He took the counter view. "But I expect he'll find a lawyer guaranteed to win his case. His type can pay their way out of anything." He enjoyed his coolness set against Pete's red-faced exasperation and wondered what it would be like to care quite so much.

Half of one ear homed in on the female chit-chat. Katie detailing the kitchen renovation. Sian's latest far-flung travels, hiking the Inca Trail. Eileen's job. Nina hijacking the conversation to monologue about the travails of motherhood – the terrible twos – but with an indulgence in her voice, implying that all the difficulties were eminently worth it. "I've got some photos on my phone."

"*Awww*," the women said.

He could picture, without actually looking, the melting-down of Eileen's face.

Four months ago, Eileen had started off apologetic. "I know it's perverse . . . I know I said . . . I just didn't realise . . ." The note of contrition has since morphed into one of accusation. Somehow, *he* is the one being unreasonable. He sipped more whisky, trying to tame the resentment bubbling beneath his skin, his arguments resurfacing in a handy one to three.

1. We agreed that neither of us wanted kids right from the beginning. 2. You even made it a condition of dating. 3. I'm not the one to have changed.

The groupings shifted. Further drinks were offered. Katie disappeared into her kitchen with its oak wood cabinets and Yorkstone floor, while Nina needed to check in on her babysitter.

Sian and Eileen nudged their way into the all-male group. "You can't talk football all evening," Sian said and rolled her eyes before smiling in unmeant apology.

Patrick sipped his single malt, swallowing his annoyance.

"What do people think about . . ." the two of them said in unison.

". . . the Oscars?" Sian said, her words overlapping with his: ". . . the referendum?"

His hands tightened in dread, and then in triumph as his question prevailed.

Immigrants. Trade deals. Payments in and out. Britain's standing in the world. Everyone offered loud opinions, as if individual views make any difference.

Food was ready and they began the shoulder-bumping foray into the dining room. He put his glass down: empty, when he'd intended to leave half.

"Go easy, Patrick," Eileen said in sotto voce caution, her disapproval spurring him towards the opposite.

People shuffled round the table. Instructions were issued. They should mix themselves up and not sit with the person they came with. He smiled what he hoped was a good-natured smile. *For Christ's sake.*

At least sitting at the far end from Eileen meant she couldn't kick him under the table when he accepted Pete's offer of wine. "Just a small one."

They started with lobster tails in garlic butter. Discount supermarkets sell frozen packs of this stuff these days, so he didn't need to ponder the living creature, pacified by refrigeration before being placed in a pot of cold water, the temperature rising, degree by slow degree, and the poor sod not realising he's being boiled alive until it's too frigging late. It might well have happened, only not in Katie's newly Aga-ed kitchen. The meat wasn't tasty and the texture was terrible, like chewing on skipping rope. "Delicious," he said.

Exchanges about jobs and holidays sprang up. Plates were cleared away. They moved on to the next course. *Meat on Friday.* The lamb was pink when he prefers it thoroughly done. The roast potatoes were soggy and the vegetables virtually raw. No salt on the table. He thought of being at home, eating high-sodium, microwave meals on the sofa, removed from the necessity of talk by the white noise of the TV and able to drink unmonitored.

Consciously, he unclamped his jaw, seeking signs that the alcohol was beginning to unwind him, trying to view the candlelit evening in a softer light. He'd had a lousy day, that was all. Just give things a chance and he'd be fine. He turned to Nina.

"How's your job?" she asked, smile bright.

Insurance broking hardly constituted the ideal starter topic. "Oh, you know. Fine. Busy." What else was there – really – to say? Politeness demanded he now ask about her sproggling. "How's Emma?" Surely she would get that his enquiry was as casual as hers.

But, as usual, Nina seemed unable to comprehend that others might not be as obsessed with her baby as she is. He's seen it before, the transition from intelligent adult with a range of interests into a person he no longer recognises, someone fixated by a single thing, who appears to derive no pleasure, none whatsoever, from parenthood – depicting it as a non-ending litany of sleepless nights, of crying and tantrums and mess, of all-encompassing exhaustion, anxiety and guilt – and yet claims it's the best thing they've ever done.

"I seem to be going on and on," she said. Eventually.

He ought to have provided reassurance, but she *had* been going on and on. He smiled noncommittally and his eyes strayed over to her partner, Chris, who has aged a decade in the time their offspring has aged two years.

"All worth it of course," she asserted and then added, "You and Eileen have never thought about it?" *Because she had of course just provided the perfect advert.* Her question sounded a little too offhand and he wondered what exactly Eileen had told her.

"Well we've thought about it," he said. "Obviously." Not true; his views on the subject require no reflection at all. He can remember the presumptions he grew up with, that having kids was simply something everyone did, the natural consequence of within-marriage, contraceptive-free sex. One generation ago and people ploughed into parenthood without stopping to consider and debate. He has always been deeply grateful that that is no longer the case. "Never get beyond the thinking." He couldn't be as dismissive as he'd have liked, because Eileen *has* started thinking. Rethinking. When until recently she agreed with him. All that time ago, their second date for God's sake, she brought it up.

"Might as well tell you upfront," she'd said. "I don't date guys who want children." She paused and pulled a face. "I know that sounds weird. And I'm not getting all heavy or anything. It's just it's such a fundamental thing."

"Fine," he said.

She stared back at him. "I'm serious."

"I'm serious too. I don't want kids. Never have. Never will."

She continued probing, as if fearing *he* might be the one to change his mind. "It's just it's so easy for guys," she said and talked about how important her career was – brimming with enthusiasm: *biomedical research could make such a difference* – how there were far more interesting things to do in life. "And it's always women who end up giving stuff up."

He has never thought it sounded remotely easy. But it wasn't worth setting out his case when they agreed on the basic point, albeit for different reasons. Likewise they shared a secular outlook, liberal politics and a taste for art-house films:

they had such a lot in common.

Still have.

"Well anyway," Nina continued. "You'd have to get a move on."
Parroting Eileen. Late thirties and it's pretty much now or never,
she says.

His thighs tightened reflexively as he remembered his idle
Googling at work. He was not going to pursue either his passing
thought – the plan that was not yet a plan – or this conversation
line. He applied himself to sawing through flaccid meat. Slugged
back wine. Their own lull coincided with a general one.

"What about films?" someone said, the question spreading
across the table on which every square inch of polished fruitwood
was covered with handcrafted serving dishes, plates and glasses,
bottles, candlesticks and condiments. "Anything good on?"

His lungs constricted. What would normally be a bog-
standard opener felt venomous tonight, only a few days after the
Oscars. Around the table, faces were alive with alcohol cheer and
he wondered, the way he often does, what it is like to experience
existence so smoothly. Or do others fake it too? He pushed himself
to start talking about the latest must-see Icelandic film. His real
opinion – tedious and pretentious – was spun into something
more nuanced. But he and Eileen were the only ones to have seen
it and she contributed little – "interesting, perhaps a little long"
– and he was nowhere near inebriated enough to hold forth for
more than a couple of minutes.

"What about . . . ?" Katie said and, there it lay, the name
of the thing he'd been hoping against hope to avoid. "The one
about child-abuse cover-ups," she clarified.

The vipers in his stomach stirred. "Great cast," he said. "Not
sure I'd have given it best film though." Best to get in early with
some sort of opinion. He couldn't deny having been with Eileen
sitting there. He'd desperately wanted to avoid it, had failed to
find a sufficiently convincing reason to say no. Afterwards, his
lack of opinion had disappointed her.

He sipped from his glass and tackled more chewy lamb,

hoping the conversation would dwindle and move on. He had at the ready the name of the costume-drama thing Eileen dragged him to last month, the one with that actress, and tried to formulate a way of making his dismissal of it humorous.

But isn't it just the way things go, the one topic he was frantic to dodge was the one whose initial spark took hold and started building. There was so much to discuss. The film, its script and the acting, sure. But this was *based on a true story*. He makes a point of disliking films that claim that, most of them bearing no closer relation to reality than those that are thoroughly made up. *What's wrong with imagination?* After all, it's where he spends ninety percent plus of his own time.

"It's just so shocking," Katie said, her face a parody of shockedness, heaped fork hovering mid-air. "Not just the extent of abuse by priests. But the way the Catholic hierarchy covered it up."

Everyone was appalled, scandalised, found it unbelievable. All of them talking loud. "It's just so awful," the women agreed, drawing out the *awww*, like when they were looking at baby pictures on Nina's phone.

Ever since the Savile scandal broke, everyone wants to talk about the one thing that previously no one spoke about at all.

He thought of the message left on his answer machine at work that morning, the way it had pitched him from office tedium into a state of panic, innards melting down, bringing back with sickening precision that other call, the one he had badly wanted to ignore, then, on reflection, hadn't.

1. Refusing the request to meet might've suggested he had something to hide. 2. He needed to make his position plain in the hope he would not be hounded again. 3. If revelations were afoot he wanted to have advance warning, rather than be hit with them out of the blue.

"Patrick wasn't keen on the film," Eileen said and her eyes were glinting spotlights of disapproval.

He shrugged. "I didn't think it was bad." Everyone waited for him to say more. But what could he possibly want to say on this subject?

"Not like you to be so quiet," Nina said. And he smiled what he hoped was an inscrutable smile.

"Well everyone else is so noisy." He aimed to interject the correct degree of levity and certainly people laughed, while his mind remained blank of anything he could plausibly say. He reached for the bottle of Sémillon and avoided Eileen's eye. Condensation trickled down the outside of the bottle and his blood was running cold.

In the cinema, he had closed his eyes and wished he could close his ears. Why hadn't evolution allowed his species to do that? He fisted his hands and concentrated very hard on a problem from work and on not letting the build-up of lava explode. He couldn't identify who he was most furious at. Eileen for insisting they go. The filmmakers who consider this entertainment. The events portrayed: the perpetrators and those who allowed it to happen. His fellow cinema-goers, who would emerge, somehow imagining they now understood everything so much better.

Dishes were cleared. New ones appeared, the centrepiece an enormous chocolate tart with gooey centre. Plates were passed. Forks dug in. Appreciation was expressed. And yet still, the topic was not done.

"At least it's good that people are talking about these things," Nina opined. "Everything's so much more open these days."

He heard the smug assumptions: 1. that talking is an all-purpose cure; 2. that these things no longer happen; and 3. her own offspring are immune. As if words automatically help and the human race has been genetically reprogrammed. And the stupid cow not realising how completely powerless parents are.

"But Patrick," Pete said, "weren't you at . . ." And he provided the name of the well-renowned Catholic boarding school with its Gothic buildings set amidst bleak moors. Patrick was such a lucky boy to win a scholarship there, so everyone had said.

The sugar-scented air felt thick and unbreathable.

"He was." Eileen answered for him.

The eyes around the table felt invasive, prurient. His skin

itched. He longed for a long, hot shower, scrubbing every inch of himself with tea-tree shower gel and loofah.

He sipped his wine, unpleasantly dry against the cloying gunge that clogged his throat. Very carefully he put his glass down, the clink on polished wood resonating unnaturally loud.

"Weren't they in the news?" Pete persisted.

"Hasn't everywhere been?" he said.

"Patrick says he wasn't aware of anything at the time." Eileen had picked up on the story when it broke; she sounded a little apologetic now for his lack of observational skills.

"No," he'd kept saying to that detective several years ago, the two of them meeting at a carefully anonymous location. "No, I don't know anything about that. Sorry that I can't help." He had focused intently on maintaining control of voice, hands, face, gut, on refusing to allow the shaking and squirming and throwing up. The past could not be changed and the best he could do was shore up defences against it piercing through into his present.

Eileen proceeded to reel off facts and figures. She seems to have made it a personal project, rummaging around in all the sordid details.

Thirty to forty victims identified by the police, but the true number thought to be many times that. Boys as young as eight told to strip from the waist down then caned to provide sexual kicks. Night-time checks on sleeping boys and the cover of dormitory darkness covering up so much more. Shoulder massages during piano lessons, with hands working their way lower, slipping inside elasticated waistbands, then slipping lower still.

And worse, much worse.

Three decades of it.

"Just as well you were never musical," Pete said.

No one laughed and Katie's eyes widened in mock admonishment. "Pete!"

"I was only . . ." Pete added more cream to his plate.

Patrick could feel the weight of ghost hands on his shoulders, the cool of glossy wood beneath his seized-up fingers. "Yes. Just as well." His voice sounded deep and strange.

"So how does it feel?" Nina asked. "I mean now? Knowing all *that* was going on? Was it a terrible place to be? Did you know any of the victims? Have you kept in touch with people?"

He pulled a face; she seemed to have fired off a dozen questions without allowing him time to reply to even one. "I don't feel anything really." What might he be supposed to feel? "I didn't like school much." Understatement of the century. "Wasn't keen on some of the teachers." Ditto. "But it was all pretty routine stuff that got to me. The usual petty bullying." *Petty* not being quite the right word. "Missing home and being bored in lessons. I lost touch with people once I'd left." Very deliberately so. Childhood is pure endurance, but at least eventually you grow up; you move on.

He thought of Neville's voice message, recalling a skinny boy with a stammer whose freckles and bony knees formed a mirror of his own. He tried to imagine the man he might have become, to picture sitting across from him in a bar, pint in hand. And what? *Discussing certain things from the past.* That was the phrase Neville used. Perhaps it wasn't what he thought. Yet, what else could it be, in the current climate, when there seems to be only one thing everyone in the whole wide frigging world wants to talk about?

Around the table, people seemed let down; he was failing to be sufficiently entertaining. They carried on scooping up chocolate pudding. Seconds were offered.

He emptied his wine glass, acid pooling in his stomach alongside sickly goo, and wondered just how long this evening, this scrutiny, would continue.

Outside, the cold doused him like an ice-water bucket. The air smelled of burning wood and damp green. Alongside the car, Eileen insisted, "You should let me drive."

"I'm fine." She'd been drinking too and was less alcohol tolerant.

She conceded the steering wheel – freezing to the touch – but continued to harangue him. His manner was boorish. He'd offended Nina by being so curt. And then later he drifted into sullen muteness.

While she was obsessed with monitoring his every move.

They bickered back and forth, then lapsed into petulant silence, the two of them locked within their bubble of metal. Driving – ultra-cautious – the lanes seemed ever darker, winding tighter; he felt the control between his hands. It would be so easy. Misjudging a corner. A swift, sharp swerve. Veering abruptly left into the dark solidity of a tree. His blood-alcohol would provide sufficient excuse in the autopsy.

He remembered his teenage road-to-Damascus moment, the instant when, sitting in the ancient chapel with its acrid scent of incense, the bluebottle buzz of the priest, it came to him like a divine revelation: *I don't believe this.* He did not believe in a heavenly being, benign or otherwise, and with his unconversion came the comfort of insignificance, the pure relief of knowing that no matter how bad things get, there is always an end. Definitive. Absolute.

Arriving – safely – home, he parked the car conspicuously well. They ought just to have headed for bed, but somehow didn't. "You should've seen Nina's photos," Eileen said, so seemingly innocent. "So sweet."

He was standing by the kitchen sink, gulping water to rehydrate, his thoughts fuggy, disconnected threads twisting round one another, aware of needing an excuse in order for his vague musings to crystallise into an actual happening. A simple medical procedure would put an end to all this.

"Talking of Nina. What the fuck have you been telling her?" he asked, opening the evening up to full-blown row.

Eileen paused, her eyes glinting obsidian black, sucking in all warmth. He had a terrifying sense of staring into loneliness, a life empty of the day-to-day rhythms of companionship and love. "This isn't about Nina, is it?" Her tone was artificially measured. "Explain it to me again. What exactly you're against?"

"One," he started. It isn't just that he doesn't want the complete upheaval to their comfortable lives that a baby would bring (though he doesn't, he really doesn't). His objection is existential and he knows exactly how pretentious that sounds.

"Oh no you don't! Not another of your *one to* fucking *three*s."

They glared at one another. He wanted to punch through the veneer of civility, unleashing his greater strength. His hands had clenched to iron. Though he would never. Of course not. He wouldn't. He breathed in deeply. "We're middle-aged for Christ's sake. Aren't we past all that?"

"You're forty-one, not geriatric. You've become so stuck. Wanting to carry on same old, same old until we're dead and buried."

"I hadn't realised that completely reversing opinion was mandatory."

"It's our last chance. If we don't at least try, we'll end up regretting it for the rest of our lives."

"You might regret it, you mean."

"You might too."

"I won't."

"You can't know that."

"I can."

"No one ever regrets having kids."

"You don't know that."

"Tell me someone who does."

"People aren't always honest."

"Tell me about it!"

They paused. She seemed totally unknown, this lean, tight woman he regularly professes love for. *What about the kids themselves?* Except he couldn't ask that without giving too much away.

"I want this," she said, eyes dipping and voice turning quiet. "I was too young to know what I wanted before. But isn't it the whole point of life? Giving life."

He thought of her slow disillusionment with work, the

corrosive drip of realism: corporate profit margins matter more than human suffering. He felt his anger hissing out of him, like air from a punctured beach ball. His counter arguments felt so annihilating, his solid belief that life has no point and perpetuating pointlessness is . . . well, pointless. That consciousness is simply a quirk of evolution, because developing a theory of mind led to competitive advantage. Like a peacock's feathers, or outlandishly large antlers on a buck: survival of the fittest delivers absurd outcomes. He was too deeply tired, inadequately drunk, to even attempt to explain.

In bed they turned definitively away from one another, none of the usual exchange of *goodnight*s and kisses.

He was knackered. Wasn't going to sleep, could already tell how the night would pass, minute by agitated minute, and the need to not disturb Eileen would ensure the frustration would grow. She lay unnaturally still.

He coughed away an irritation in his throat, feeling the dark urge that sometimes lurked there, like his vipered anxiety, never fully swallowed down, as if being honest about one thing might serve to absolve him from other failings. Confessing was supposed to leave you feeling light and clean.

He remembered the dim-lit claustrophobia, the smell of mint-breath and coal-tar soap, the sound of nasal breathing from behind the grill. *Bless me Father because I have sinned.* He felt again the writhing up of wordless panic in which he knew that naming things would only grant them greater power. He heard his voice – high and childish – gabbling idiotically, a whole list of made-up misdemeanours, at the end of which he would always add, "and I've told fibs." And as he listened to his absolution, he felt the diarrhoeal flood of shame and loathing. It was all his fault. *He* was the one who should have found a way to make those things that happened stop.

* * * * *

The pain ebbs from his bollocks, remaining etched onto his mind.

He tries to block the murmurs of the medical staff as

instruments and swabs are passed back and forth. Inner tubing tugs; clamps pinch. He inhales the metallic air and tries not to think about snips, cauterising, stitches.

They must be at least halfway through. Seven minutes max to go.

He thinks of a drawn-curtained room, his own bed, the pack of paracetamol on the bedside table, of sleeping through the afternoon, perhaps a warm bath, more sleep. And then a further day, time to rest and recover before Eileen returns from visiting her mother.

Earlier, the mandatory counselling, he told the woman that his wife was in full agreement, his manner outwardly composed, alarm knifing through. He'd meant to tell Eileen. Still will. Only it is desperately hard to find the right moment. The right words. He pictures her eyes turning ice-hole cold.

"We're nearly through. Just some tidying up," that soft voice says.

And inside his head he is talking loud, explaining how his reasons for this are existential. He refuses to inflict the ordeal of existence on another being. It is that simple. On yet another goofball of vulnerability who will be too stupidly naive to spot the ways you are lulled into defencelessness and lies, heat rising so slowly you hardly notice, until it is just too fucking late.

Mrs Mackie Waits

JENN ASHWORTH

Mrs Mackie waits in her car. She unfastens the top button of her good jacket, then she fastens it again. Just a couple of minutes to the hour, according to the dashboard clock. Two pigeons peck at the dirty grass on the verge between the road and the pavement, are scattered by passing traffic, then drift back downwards. She's parked in front of a newsagent's, on a side street slightly away from but in view of the main gate. This is so she can see him as soon as he comes out, before he can spot her. She wants the advantage and she doesn't think he'll look in this direction – why should he? – and see her first.

She fiddles with the button again. The coat is too tight across her chest and under her armpits; it's her good wool one and has been in the back of the wardrobe inside a plastic sleeve from the dry cleaner's for a long time. She's left the engine ticking over. This is so she can run the heater and the radio without making the battery go flat. It is so she can drive off quickly if the man behind the counter in the newsagent's comes out and tells her to get away from the front of his shop. It's so she can change her mind if she wants to, without fuss. Her foot rests on the clutch. She doesn't know how punctual these things tend to be, but she's here, at least, and in good time. The pigeons nod and stoop their grey-and-pink heads to the grass.

Mrs Mackie finally leaves her jacket alone and pulls an

envelope out of her pocket. She doesn't open it because she knows the letter inside off by heart now. She has never been written to by a vicar before. She corrects herself: precision is important and there's no way to tell for certain the man who wrote the letter actually is a vicar. It says "HMP Chaplain" at the bottom, under his signature. Chaplains can be anything and she doesn't even want to think about how he got her address. She is in the phone book, she supposes, and there's always the internet. But still. The letter-writer's name is Peter. *Forgive me for the intrusion,* he wrote – this vicar or priest or whatever he is – *but I am writing about Danny, who you taught some time ago and probably won't remember. He remembers you.* She holds the envelope lightly between her hands.

Danny. She'd had to rack her brains. She doesn't remember all of them; sometimes they come up to her in the supermarket with their children (it is strange, that – she's more likely to recognise them by some familiar arrangement of features in their children's upturned faces than their own, these days), and once in the park, with a dog that jumped up on her leg and left mud on her cotton-blend skirt. When that happens – especially in recent years – she has been forced to let them lead the conversation and, without actually lying, pretend she knows them and recalls more clearly than she does the days they were awkward teenagers in her classroom.

It is to be expected: that the slow hours they spent during the tumult of their adolescences sitting in what she'd always hoped was the relative calm of her upper-set history class would leave a greater impression on them than they did on her. They shared the hours, but they went more quickly for her. She sometimes felt the best years of her life were sifting through the hourglass faster than she could stand. These days as she waits with her trolley in front of the chiller cabinet, her progress through her list interrupted, embarrassed by her ready meals, the intrusion is starting to irritate her. This belief they have, that she holds each of them in mind and that their names and faces – every single one – a hundred or more a year, for forty years, for God's sake – her entire working life – have impressed themselves indelibly upon her, is unfair. It is a burden she didn't ask for. That even in retirement her job is only to hold them in mind and remember them. She nods and asks after children and houses and jobs, shares a vague, all-purpose memory about a school trip, clicks her tongue in fake surprise at her watch and looks for the moment she can push her trolley away. Mrs Mackie, they always call her, or just Miss, as if she was still their teacher, and that's how she can tell where they know her from.

But yes, she does remember Danny.

The man from the newsagent's is standing in the doorway of his shop. It's a dull day, not the kind of weather you'd expect anyone to come outside to enjoy, though she supposes that watching the cars throb by and the council-planted daffodils sway in their beds is bound to be more interesting than an afternoon spent rearranging packets of crisps and counting newspapers. She hopes he isn't going to light a cigarette, and winds up her window as gently as she can, so as not to draw attention to herself.

It seems strange to have a prison so near to the town centre. It's very old: the front of it looks like a castle, though there are modern additions, and wire fence panels boosting the height of the old brick walls. Right in the middle there is a great wooden gate they must be able to open in its entirety when a van goes through, but which has a smaller door cut into it, which is where, the website has told her, they'll come out. Right onto the street. She's expecting a little group of them to come out together. Then they'll have a choice. They can take a right turn past the daffodils and into the town centre, or a left, towards the bus station. Maybe they'll linger there at the opening, on the threshold. *Class of March 2017, graduated with honours.*

She shouldn't let herself get silly. She is waiting here for Danny because he remembers her, perhaps with kindness, and because she is surprised to find that she remembers him. There's no reason for him to remember her with anything other than kindness. She was – she's confident in this – a skilled and experienced teacher. She taught him origins of the Second World War in his fifth year, it would be. Some thirty years ago now. She'd have to check her records to know if he passed his exams, or not. But she supposes he did. He never had the right uniform. She had to stop letting him take his textbook home and instead just kept it for him in her desk, because every time he took it home, it went missing. Vanished. God knows what he was doing with them. She thinks he had his dad at home, but she couldn't say for sure. She never met his parents.

Danny was not special. Not especially good-looking but not ugly either. He wasn't a smoker, as far as Mrs Mackie could recall, having taken her fair share of the behind-the-bike-sheds patrolling duties over the years. She tries to conjure up his face and only just manages it. He didn't wear glasses. He was nondescript. If the police ever asked her to make a statement that involved giving a description of him that's what she would say.

Was it strange that she never met his mother or father? That nobody ever bothered to turn up to a parents' evening? Mrs Mackie decides no, it was not. There are hundreds of bright boys (and he was bright, she remembers that; she remembers the neatness of his handwriting, the flourish with which he looped the tails of his gs and his ys) with parents who are too depressed or exhausted or drunk or just too uninterested to come to parents' evening. They aren't compulsory, after all. Perhaps it was their version of trusting him. Leaving him to it. Letting him have his independence. A fifteen-year-old is a man, in some cultures. The head of his own family. Well, Mrs Mackie thinks. Look how that turned out for him. No. She should be kinder. Apparently his mother was ill, though she never knew with what. That would have been the Head's role. She never tried to get involved in the pastoral side of things. She played to her strengths, let others play to theirs. It was called being part of a team.

Chaplain Peter – she can only imagine him as a vicar, someone round and rosy, with a dog collar and a cardigan – did not enclose a photograph. Just a note that said Danny would be let out of the gate at 3 p.m. sharp and wouldn't it be nice if she was there waiting for him. *You probably won't remember. He remembers you.*

She avoids the temptation of pulling the letter out of the envelope to reread it: the man from the newsagent's is still standing there, staring into space, and she doesn't want to open the envelope while under observation. Doesn't want to get absorbed and have Danny come out of the gate and spot her without her being ready for him. But she knows what it says. And it does not say what he did. Only that his sentence was a long one, and *he's got good reason to think there'll be nobody there to greet him at the gate when he comes out.* He says that's important to Danny. That someone be there. A friendly face to welcome him from his old life into his new one. That's how he put it. *His new life.*

A religious person would put it like that, but Mrs Mackie imagines that's how it was: for years, until his youth was all gone, Danny has been behind those brick walls listening to the traffic go by on the road outside, just waiting. And the only people he's known in this time have been fellow prisoners or those in charge of the daily details of his life. Without equality, there can be no intimacy. She does believe that. So he must have been lonely. Very, very lonely.

She is letting her thoughts run away with her again. She has had colleagues who have taught inside prisons. They have libraries and whole FE colleges in there now. Courses for the vocationally minded, and A levels and Open University for the rest. There's no reason he won't have had a full life in there. If he's decided not to make something of his time, well, that would have been his choice, and him free, despite everything, to make it. You can lead a horse to water, etc. Hadn't she learned that in all her years as a teacher?

She looks at the walls; the red bricks. At the top, just under the join where the metal fence panels have been joined on to the top of the wall, a stray elderflower plant has taken root, and its cat's-eye leaves and grey, springy stems lean out and bounce in the wind. Elsewhere, there's a streak of moss marking the route water tracks down the brickwork from a leak in the cast-iron gutter. He'll be forty-six now.

You're under no obligation at all. I haven't told him I am writing to you, so you mustn't feel that you'd be disappointing him if you find that you are simply too busy. I know it's a weekday.

The vicar's meaning comes across loud and clear. She didn't have to go. Didn't have to be here now, at all. She should have written back. Should have asked if it was drugs, or pimping, or if he'd killed or raped somebody. You don't get a long sentence – Peter didn't say how long, but long – without doing something serious. Without hurting someone. He could be dangerous. She hopes they don't let them out if they're still dangerous, and comforts herself with the thought of checks. Interviews. Assessments and the like. All his housing and his benefits are sorted; there are people to take care of that. He's got somewhere to go, and money to get there. But nobody to meet him at the gate. That's all he wants. All Peter the Chaplain, unconfirmed vicar, wants her to do for him. A friendly face. *Perhaps a lift into town, or a coffee in a public place, if that makes you feel more comfortable.* Her hand twitches towards her keys, still dangling in the ignition. The comforting rattle of the engine, quietly ticking over. She could slip the car into gear right now. The digital display on the clock flickers; it's 3 p.m. now. She glances at the gate. No sign.

She was cruel to him once, when he turned up to her classroom late. Not very late: the others were still unpacking their books and getting settled. But late enough. She opens the glove compartment. Inside, beside the folder with her documents and the travel first-aid kit, there is a small red-and-white tin of mints. She thumbs it open, takes one, puts the tin back and carefully shuts the compartment. Glances over her shoulder: the newsagent has gone back inside the shop. She can see him standing behind the counter, through a window covered in stickers advertising ice lollies and soft drinks. She wonders if that's what Danny remembers. Her minor act of cruelty. It is the correct word for it. She won't sit here and exculpate herself. The mint dissolves on her tongue and she feels its cooling effect on the tender skin on the inside of her cheeks. She wonders if that is why, when he thinks about his school days, it's her face that comes to mind and nobody else's. Her throat is dry.

She could have ignored him or made him wait behind and given him a dressing-down after class. She could have given him a lunchtime litter pick. She could have done any number of things. What she did do, she was not ashamed of at the time and she will not, if that is Danny's plan, allow herself to be shamed for it now. She made him stand at the front of the class for the entire lesson. That's all. Just stand there. He kept dropping his pen because it was so awkward to hold his exercise book in one hand and write in it with the other. The other pupils laughed. He asked if he could sit at his desk and she shook her head. The other pupils laughed again and she did not intervene.

It is not a punishment – they don't even use that word any more – that would find itself in favour in the modern classroom. And Mrs Mackie does remember that Danny was not one of the clownish types who would have enjoyed that kind of attention. That is of course why she gave it. He blushed. She remembers his neck: red and mottled. The way his embarrassment seemed to provoke more laughter. The way the pen kept sliding from between his fingers. She did not ask him why he had been late. His blazer was dirty. It comes to her very quickly, that detail. Yes. Not the mud and dust of a football game played at lunchtime sort of dirty. But a not been washed this term dirty. She'd not looked at him carefully before. But then – standing at the front of the class – he'd been one on his own. The other children – young people, they'd be called now – saw it too. A sort of unkemptness – a lack of washing – what you'd think of as parental neglect in a younger child, and perhaps a symptom of unhappiness in an older one. It was noted. Loudly, that day, by the other children. And quietly, in sniggers and whispers in the corridors and changing rooms in the following days – all his remaining days at school. His shabbiness. Perhaps there was a smell, too. And he'd passed under the radar successfully up until that point. Not her fault. Things were different then. Teaching has changed but she knows she did the best she could, given the climate of the times and the training given to her by those responsible for her work.

Mrs Mackie has been – in spite of everything – avoiding looking at the gate. She glances at it now but nothing is happening. The letter is still inside its envelope on her lap, the torn edge soft with handling. She folds it in half and jams it into the little space between the handbrake and the passenger seat. Her hands are clammy. How ridiculous. She will admit to herself – because what will become of her if she isn't able to look herself in the eye with dignity in the privacy of her own car, valeted and paid for?– that it has crossed her mind more than once that when the two of them get face to face with each other – if they come face to face with each other, because she is still not decided, she is going to leave the decision until the last minute – he will come close to her and laugh in her face. He will spit at her. Perhaps even strike her. She has worried – in the small hours – that perhaps his years in that cell have encouraged him to look backwards for causes, to trace the origins of his own behaviour, the bad seed of his poor choices. And perhaps his looking led him to her. To that moment when he sauntered into her classroom a full five minutes late and was not given the chance to explain. Was set up before the others as an example. Of what? She forgets now, exactly what her intention was.

Mrs Mackie stifles a yawn because at first light this morning she was up, padding around the sunroom in her bare feet, watering her succulents and wondering about this. About causes. About being somebody else's cause. She'd chided herself for her arrogance – and that is what it was, this daydreaming about being so important to another person's life. Just arrogance. It was a watery dawn; the chill from the sunroom floor tiles sank into the soles of her feet. She was convinced then, and had managed another hour in bed. Less so now.

She doesn't know what she's going to say to him. That's the real matter in hand. Today. Not some half-remembered moment from the ancient past. She and Danny will have nothing in common. No easy point of reference to get the conversation going. If it were her in there she'd have imagined this moment the whole time: the day when she got to wear her own clothes again and come out of the gates and do exactly what she pleased, when it pleased her, without having to answer to anybody. It might be, she allows herself to wonder, a little like her own retirement: long awaited and anticlimactic.

The gate opens. She hears it rattle before she sees it. It's like a little mouth and it slides open and there's only one man coming out and so it must be him. No *must be* about it. That's Danny. Her hands flutter to the steering wheel. He's a bit grey and fat and his face is pale and he looks – what does he look like? He looks scared, hunched and he nearly flinches at the sky. He looks clean, by which she means, washed, and groomed. Neat. He says a few words to the officer in the black-and-white uniform who is behind him, and smiles, and they shake hands. That surprises her. The friendliness. The familiarity of people who have known each other a long time. Did she sign Danny's shirt on his last day of school? Write a little note – something to the effect of his old school always being there for him? Wanting to hear how his life turned out? Was that what he remembers? Did she write that? If she did, she truthfully cannot recall it. The gate closes behind him and he's looking left and right, up and down, and Chaplain Peter hasn't told him that Mrs Mackie, his old history teacher, will be out there waiting for him. But he has seen her. He crosses the road and approaches her car. Her hand gropes around for the handbrake as if it is a weapon.

"You're here," he says, mouthing the words in an exaggerated way, speaking loudly, so she can hear him through the window, which is open just a crack. "I asked Peter to write. I didn't . . . I hope you don't . . ."

His voice is deep and gruff. He looks at her without looking at her. Without making eye contact. As if he is seeing only his own reflection in the window between them, rather than her.

She should get out of the car. She should stand and shake his hand. She should do something. She looks away from him, at the vicar's letter, folded up and shoved into the little gap next to the handbrake. She recalls his handwriting, neat like Danny's. He might not be a vicar. He could be a priest or an imam or a bloody Druid for all she knows – they have all sorts. Even the humanist types, who don't believe in anything at all, so far as she can see, other than turning up. She rolls the window down.

"Daniel Wilkinson, I was told 3 p.m. Sharp. You're" – she glances at the dashboard – "four minutes late." She doesn't know why she says it. If she'd planned what to say, this would not have been it. It's her teacher voice. The one she finds herself using in shops, at slow waitresses, sometimes at the receptionist in her GP's surgery. She can't help it – that tone of impatience and authority. That tone that claims rights to things. The right not to be kept waiting. The right to point out deficiencies and areas for improvement. She hears it as if for the first time and she wants to tell Danny that. She can't help it. It's her training. She doesn't know how else to be.

This man who used to be Danny meets her eye. Sees something in there, perhaps, that he recognises.

"I am, Miss," he says, still smiling. "I'm late again."

He has a rucksack over his shoulder. He straightens up and adjusts its straps. Puts his hands into his pockets. Takes them out again.

"It's all right. I waited for you," Mrs Mackie says. She gestures towards the passenger seat of her car, recently valeted. "Don't call me Miss. Charlotte will do. Not Charlie. Shall we go and find a café?"

The Lodger
RESHMA RUIA

Old age. It still catches them by surprise.

"Not that we are terribly old," Mandy tells the bathroom mirror as she brushes her teeth. She stares at her face as though it were a map that needed a compass.

"How did this happen?" asks Bill, her husband, a protective hand on his heart. He scowls at the pills that crowd his plate, a rainbow of marbles.

"It's high time you guys moved into a care home. This house is too big and you're too old," their daughter Abigail observes, lying on the couch. Her left leg is raised as she paints her toenails crimson.

Abigail lives in Nevada on a cactus plantation with a woman who is her girlfriend. They run an aloe vera business. The juice is extracted and shipped in neat little silver cartons with the tag line, *Juice up your insides*. The Grahams only know this from the company website.

"You sure messed up. Look at the both of you. Not even eighty yet but hobbling around like a pair of whackos. I mean, deal with it," Abigail says. She uncurls herself and sits up straight, her legs extended, blowing on her newly painted toes one by one. Her quick, healthy puffs of breath dazzle her parents.

"I'm not moving out, if that's what you mean. I'm staying right here," Mandy says, trying to keep the quiver out of her voice. "You could visit more often."

"We could get a lodger," Bill suggests. His voice dips, low and uncertain. "He can keep an eye on us and we'd get some income too. It'll be a win win."

Now that Bill has retired from his job as the maintenance man at Delaunay High School in Chantilly, and Mandy's left knee flares with arthritis every winter, they find their pension isn't enough to cover the expenses of old age.

Bill darts an anxious glance at his daughter. The plan would need her blessing.

Abigail approves. "Yeah . . . I like that. A lodger. Some nice guy who keeps an eye on you like you say. He could even help Mom clean up this shit." Her eyes sweep over the room.

It is late afternoon. The smells of the previous night linger stale in the living room, like a set of unwashed teeth in the morning. Mugs of coffee and Pyrex bowls of microwave-fresh popcorn and cheesy nachos balance on old copies of *Sports Illustrated* and crochet magazines. Mandy sucks Sprite through a straw while listening to her daughter. Her husband dunks his hand in and out of the bowl. From time to time he sniffs his fingers, inhaling the popcorn's greasy salty smell.

Abigail raises her voice. "Just look at this mess, Mom."

Mandy gets up to shut her bedroom door. She doesn't want Abigail to see her unmade bed or the dropped towels that carry red and brown streaks of her make-up like battle wounds.

"Dad's right, Abigail. We'll get someone. The money wouldn't hurt, especially now that Dad's got his angina to deal with." Mandy pauses, and examines her hands sitting like a pair of discarded gloves in her lap.

A lodger will perk them up; give them an excuse to get out of bed, plump up the cushions, buy the lettuce, change into jeans rather than stay Velcro-strapped inside their elasticated sweatpants.

She continues, "Did you know that in England you can get your medicines free? That's what the radio said."

"That's bullshit. Nothing's ever free." Abigail gives a snort.

"I'll put an ad on Craigslist for the lodger. Dad, get me my iPad will you?"

Bill shuffles out of the room and hands it to her like a trophy. "There you go, honey."

Abigail runs her tongue over her bottom lip and pulls at a strand of her dark-brown hair as she hunches over her iPad. Bill eats the popcorn quietly while Mandy trains her eyes on the patched spot on the blue Navajo rug. They had a pet once, a German shepherd who'd chewed his way through the house and had to be put down.

Abigail writes, *Elderly retired couple living in a quiet neighbourhood would welcome a lodger. Low rent in exchange for light household help. A well-furnished basement bedroom. Wi-Fi and utilities and use of kitchen included in the deal. No probing into the past or future. Just be present . . .*

She grins as she reads this out to her parents.

Mandy objects to the ending.

"But, you don't mention the rental amount and what if he is a rapist or a child-molester. Of course we'll probe. We're Americans not Buddhists."

Abigail rolls her eyes.

She won't say it, but Mandy is glad about the advert. A lodger means company. As much as the radio babbles, the TV gurgles, the husband snores, she can't deny she is lonely. Not lonely in a vein-cutting, circus-clown way, but alone in a silent, window-watching way. She spends hours sitting on her plastic chair on the back step looking at her yard, making a mental inventory of things each season left behind. In the summer there was the barbecue set, burger fat congealed on its insides, and the paddling pool where tadpoles breaststroked in rain water. Fall came with its shower of fallen leaves shored up at the borders and the empty hammock swinging under the bald-headed tree that could be elm or chestnut, she's never quite sure.

"It'll be good to have company," she tells her husband after Abigail has left.

"He can clear the crap in the yard." Bill grunts. He is fixing himself a sandwich.

The Grahams eat sandwiches most days. The only exception is the last Sunday of the month, when Mandy defrosts a chicken. Bill zips up his anorak, crams his feet into a pair of Crocs and drives to the Chicken Out at the end of the road where he picks up some mash, peas and cornbread. They eat the meal in silence, the TV tuned to a John Wayne film.

A week passes. And then one day Mandy hears the doorbell ring.

"I'll get it," she shouts to Bill, who has his headphones on. He is watching the baseball, eyes deep inside the television screen.

A young man stands on the front step. He is chubby, with rounded shoulders and a head of tight brown curls. A questioning tilt on the sides of his dark eyes gives him a foreign look. Mandy looks at his hands, checking for any leaflets, but he is only holding a cell phone and a map.

"We're not Jehovahs," Mandy says, her fingers firm around the door knob.

The man shakes his head.

"I rang last week. I think I spoke to your husband. You advertised a room for rent and I would like to see it," he says, his foot already inside the door.

She can't place the accent and then she spots his shoes. He's wearing red Nike trainers. They look brand new. She narrows her eyes; she's seen a similar pair on QVC, top of the range, at least ninety bucks.

"Oh, the room! Yes, we got a room all right." Mandy moves forward, her girth blocking the front door while she tries to remember the last time she hoovered the room in the basement.

He stands close and she can smell the aftershave steaming off his neck.

"You just wait here. I'll call my husband."

"Bill," she hollers. "We got a lodger."

The young man smiles and extends his hand.

"Hi, my name is Yousef. Yousef Kemal."

She's not heard such a name before, but confused by his

outstretched hand and aware that she's still in her pyjama bottoms and Bill's old, washing-machine-shrunk fleece, she nods and says, "Mildred Graham. But call me Mandy."

"Mandy," he repeats. "My favourite singer, Barry Manilow, wrote a song about you." He grins.

Mandy's unsure whether to return the compliment, but she doesn't know any songs with Yousef in them. *Yousef*. She can't pin the geography or the flag behind the name.

"We'll call you Youz, if that's OK. Sits more comfortably on the tongue," Bill says, slapping Yousef on the back.

"So, what do you think? He's foreign," Mandy whispers to Bill, while the young man is checking out the room.

"Seems a good enough chap. He works down at Georgetown, doing research of some sort. Student visa, so he's kosher," Bill says, pocketing the first month's deposit in crisp hundred-dollar bills.

Yousef reappears.

"May I see the kitchen please?" He stands aside respectfully, as Mandy leads the way to the sunroom that doubles as a kitchen.

Years ago, when Bill was still agile around the house, he'd cleared one wall, fixed the shelves and installed the plumbing for the fridge, the dishwasher and the hob.

"This way you look out and see the kid playing in the yard," he told Mandy.

"This cupboard can be yours," Mandy says to Yousef, pointing vaguely in the direction of the cupboard nearest to the door. She is making up the rules as she goes along. "And I'll clear the bottom shelf of the freezer and the fridge. And yes, don't use the dishwasher after seven p.m. It makes a hell of a noise."

Yousef shakes his head. "No freezer for me, Mrs Mandy. I only cook fresh."

"Suit yourself." Mandy shrugs. "We only cook on Sundays."

It takes him three days to transfer his belongings from the motel to his new accommodation.

"Looks like he's setting up home," Bill says.

Mandy notes down each item as it enters her house.

"Shouldn't it be in reverse?" Bill asks. "Shouldn't you be making an inventory of what we've got, so when he leaves, we got an idea that he's not made off with our stuff?"

"We got nothing worth taking," Mandy replies.

She drags the beanbag to the front door and carefully writes down each item on a notepad, watching as Yousef unloads his luggage from the hired minivan. She mentions the following:

1. A blue checked comforter
2. Velvet slippers
3. 2 Samsonite suitcases
4. A black lacquer tray inlaid with a mother-of-pearl stork design
5. Herb pots in a wooden crate and two bags of tomatoes and red onions

"What's that?" She points to a brown ceramic pot with a cone-shaped lid that Yousef is cradling in his arms like a baby.

"This is a tagine." He spells out the word slowly. T-A-G-I-N-E.

"It is Moroccan. I use it to cook lamb with chickpeas and apricots. Do you like chickpeas, Mandy?"

"Not really," Mandy says. "Chickpeas give me gas."

On Sunday Mandy remembers they have a lodger in the house, and she forces herself out of bed. The clock by her bedside says eleven and there is noise in the kitchen. She reaches for her sweatpants and then, changing her mind, pulls on her JCPenney jeans. The waistband cuts into her stomach, but at least she looks decent. Crayoning some lipstick onto her mouth and dabbing powder on her chin she enters the kitchen.

And there he stands, an apron tied around his rotund belly, busy cracking eggs into a bowl, stirring it with a spatula.

Hey, this is my space, Mandy almost shouts out. Instead she opens a cupboard and reaches for her stash of Mrs Fields soft-baked cookies. She likes dunking them in her morning coffee.

"Try my pancakes," Yousef says.

"What's that brown thing?" She points to the brown twig in his hand.

"It's a vanilla pod." He waves it under her nose. She steps back. The smell reminds Mandy of the perfume counter at Macy's.

Whistling under his breath, Yousef snaps open an aluminium box and pours two drops of rose-coloured liquid from a glass vial into the mixture.

Mandy edges closer to get a better look. Rows of glass bottles stand tightly wedged together. Each bottle filled to the brim with different-coloured powders, nuts, and liquid.

A spice rack . . . She used to have one of those, hanging just above the hob . . . Paprika and rock salt and Cajun spice mix, rosemary, thyme. Even goddamn verbena.

How she'd loved cooking the drumsticks, coating them with honey and cornflour, then leaning out the window, yelling at the kid to come in and eat.

She rings her daughter. "Hey, Abigail, guess what your dad and I had for brunch?"

"Let me see . . . Pork scratchings and an Oreo milkshake?" Abigail's voice is impatient.

"No sir. We had pancakes. Proper fresh ones with fresh-squeezed vanilla and roses. The whole thing was like a garden growing inside my mouth. That Youz sure got magic in his fingers."

They begin to look forward to Yousef's return from work each evening. He comes home, his arms loaded with groceries. He's been to the Korean store.

"So much cheaper than Safeway," he tells them. "And you get fresh parsley, apricots and even Medjool dates." He is smiling as he goes down to his room to change.

When he comes back up he is wearing a loose blue-silk tunic that reaches his ankles and carrying his tagine.

"Tonight I make you some lamb tagine. The lamb so tender it will melt in your mouth."

He kisses his fingertips, making loud smacking noises that

frighten the Grahams.

They push their couch nearer to the kitchen door so they can catch the aromas that drift in.

Mandy wanders into the kitchen, watching his hands as they chop and slice and purée.

"You use a lot of garlic," she observes. "And way too many tomatoes."

Yousef's hands are busy stirring a pot in which the tomatoes and the meat dance around in a thick broth.

Her mouth waters.

He scoops the food into small orange terracotta bowls and carries it to them on his lacquer tray with its mother-of-pearl storks.

Bill points to his ham sandwich and Mandy slaps her stomach to show how full she is. But they give in. "I quite like his foreign food," Bill confides to Mandy at night. "It tastes kind of homey."

Sometimes, Yousef comes home early and sits with them, sharing their couch.

"You guys watch a lot of TV," he says, and looks away when news comes on of soldiers marching through towns. The houses blow up on the screen like a Fourth of July firework display.

"Are you from those parts?" Bill asks.

"Yes . . ." He hesitates before continuing. "But one day my wife and child will be here and we will all be full-time Americans like you." He bows his head and shuts his eyes. "Inshallah," he whispers.

"Interstellar," Mandy repeats after him, making the sign of a cross.

He grins and Mandy notices his teeth are Hollywood white and perfect, or maybe it is the contrast with his skin, which, in the lamplight with the curtains drawn, looks coffee brown.

While Yousef's at the university, Mandy likes prowling around among his things.

"Just going down to check on the boiler," she says to Bill.

Bill grunts and reaches for his pills. His back is giving him trouble and he spends much of the day stretched out on the sofa, a hot-water bottle cushioning his lower spine, his face turned to the television screen, like a child gazing at the moon.

It is an effort for Mandy to climb down the stairs. She grips the banister and pauses at the bottom tread to catch her breath.

She knocks on the door, just to make sure, and enters. The room smells different. A lit incense stick presses its orange nub against the window pane. She holds the incense stick under her nose and sneezes. It smells of jasmine. Could be a fire hazard, she thinks, and snuffs it out.

Velvet slippers wait quietly at the foot of the bed and the comforter is folded in two. She lifts the pillow, plumps it and then presses it against her cheek.

A flash of colour under the bed catches her eye. She bends down and pulls out a small orange rug, rolled up tight. It reminds her of Abigail's yoga mat. She unrolls it. Nestling inside is a small book. She flicks through the pages with their swirly and curly alphabet.

Just as she's about to put it away, a photo of a young woman slips out of the book. A green scarf covers the woman's head. The small child she's holding in her arms gazes unsmiling at the camera.

Mandy walks to the window and holds the photo up to the light. She sees Yousef in the defiant thrust of the little girl's chin and the brown curls that cover her head like a crown.

That night, with Bill snore-deep in sleep beside her, Mandy gets up and opens her underwear drawer, lifts the purple Leonidas box, prises open the lid and takes out a photo. She takes it with her to the bathroom, locks the door, flicks down the toilet seat, sits on it and stares at the picture.

Seasons turn. The trees in the backyard slowly strip off their leaves. Mandy hauls the electric blanket from the garage and tucks it around Bill's lap as he sits watching the commercials on TV.

She offers to buy Yousef a coat.

"That jacket of yours." She shakes her head. "No good for our American winter."

He tells her he's from the mountains; he's used to the cold.

"It will be Christmas soon," Mandy says. She can't make up her mind whether she likes or dislikes this fact. "I suppose you'll be staying, so I'll get a Christmas tree from Home Depot."

"No going home this year," Yousef says. "But I can't wait to show my daughter the Christmas lights. You Americans know how to put on a good show." His face beams.

Mandy squeezes his hand.

"We will make sure you're not homesick."

There is talk of turkey, of stuffing it with dates. "It will be a good change," Yousef assures Mandy. "Your daughter Abigail, she will love it."

"She is vegetarian and she may not be coming home," Mandy says.

He raises his eyebrows. "Not coming home for Christmas? She doesn't want to drive around and see the lights with you?"

"She's a businesswoman, very busy," Mandy says and changes the subject. "Now tell me, are you sure you'll be able to cook the turkey?"

That evening Yousef asks for Mandy's help in peeling some potatoes. He wants to make a Spanish frittata.

"My little girl, her name is Miriam. It's her favourite."

There is something shy and proud in his confession. Mandy is curious. She leans forward.

"Where exactly are your folks, Youz?"

He shrugs and says it is a little place on a big map. The name won't mean anything to her.

"Is it where the fighting is?" Mandy says, showing off her radio-heard knowledge.

Yousef's lips shrink into a thin line.

"The fighting is everywhere, Mrs Mandy. We just choose not to see it."

There is a hissing sound as the oil burns in the frying pan

and sets off the smoke alarm. The frittata is burnt but Yousef doesn't seem to notice.

"The world is cruel, Mrs Mandy."

"Life is cruel," she agrees and starts buttering the bread.

And then a week before Christmas, Mandy sees Yousef in the backyard, the phone pressed to his ear while his free hand dives inside his trouser pocket to pull out a packet of Marlboros.

"I didn't know Youz smoked," she says to her husband as she stands at the window watching her lodger pace up and down the hard grey patch of bare lawn.

Bill leans towards her and whispers, "We mustn't forget he's foreign. That type always got a lot of light and shade in them."

The change is immediate. Yousef rushes down to his room when he comes home from work. The cheerful waving stops. The "How is your back today, Bill?" conversations halt. The kitchen no longer hums to the sound of his cooking.

One day Mandy finds him microwaving a packet of macaroni cheese.

"Hey, no bad news from home, I hope?" Mandy keeps her voice cheerful.

Yousef frowns at her and she's not sure if it's a film of water clouding his eyes or just her cataract playing up.

"You won't understand." His voice is flat, without emotion.

He goes down to his room and stays there.

Two days pass and he's still in his room. At night voices float up through the floorboards to reach Mandy's anxious ear.

"That boy is in trouble," she tells her husband.

"Shall we call a doctor?" Bill's eyes are frightened. "Does he even have health insurance? Is he a terrorist?"

They are old. They have worries of their own.

The next day Mandy drags herself down the front step, gets into the car and drives off to the shops.

When Mandy enters Yousef's room she finds him slumped against the pillows. Dark shadows smudge his eyes and a book lies face down on his chest.

"What's wrong, Youz?" she asks. She's holding a bowl in her hands.

He tells her his daughter is in hospital with an infection in her lungs.

"She will get better," Mandy says, placing the bowl on the bedside table. She pats his cheek.

"I feel helpless, so far from her. My only child . . . It's not good." Yousef's words fade. His accent thickens. "She is in a refugee camp in Lebanon. No good doctors there."

"Lebanon?" Mandy looks puzzled. "Is that near Europe?"

"Oh my God . . ." Yousef turns his head to the wall and there is a catch in his voice. "There is a big world outside this house, Mrs Mandy. Please pay attention to it."

"I will. I will," she promises, sitting on the side of his bed. She lifts the bowl and wedges it firmly between her thighs. Her right hand fishes out the spoon from her T-shirt pocket.

She clears her throat. "Yousef Kemal" – she calls him by his full name – "Yousef Kemal, you must not give up. You must eat this so you get strong. Strong enough to bring your family home. To America." She tilts his face towards her and scoops a spoon up to his mouth, not stopping until the bowl is glistening white and empty.

Yousef's face softens. He smiles.

"Very tasty. Did you make this? I thought you Americans don't know how to cook."

"This chicken soup was the kid's favourite," Mandy says. She is blinking hard and the words rush out.

"Abigail likes this? You told me she's vegetarian." He knows all about Abigail.

Mandy shakes her head. "No, no, not her. It was my son's favourite. I fed him a bowl every day to strengthen his bones."

"I didn't know you had a son. Is he married? Does he live far away?"

The questions come thick and fast. Yousef sits up, his back pressed against the blue gingham headboard, his eyes alert.

Mandy lowers her head and carefully places the empty bowl on the table.

"Jamie died young. Only six. An accident in the swimming pool at school. He was on life support at Chantilly Medical for four months." Her lips curl into a snarl. "The lifeguard was sick that day, but still they went ahead with the swimming. The assholes." She spits out the last word and turns to Yousef, tears like uneven footsteps running down her cheeks. "We adopted Abigail after he died. She never met her brother."

She pauses and looks at Yousef to check if he's understood her words. He nods and she continues.

"I hated cooking after he died."

Her hand lies on the comforter. Yousef entwines his fingers through hers.

"Please don't cry, Mrs Mandy. There is a God somewhere beyond the edge of night watching over our children."

A Thousand Grains of Sand

SARAH HEGARTY

The winter moon is high. The poplars cast their barred shadows on the empty road. Beyond the crossroads, just outside the arc of lamplight, a bicycle silently circles.

The rider is Liu Qiang. Despite his woollen gloves, his fingers, gripping the handlebars, are cold. The Beijing air seeps through his padded jacket, chilling his bones.

From nowhere comes the thought: Is this how death would feel? Last week he went with his work-unit comrades to pay his respects at the Great Leader's mausoleum in Tiananmen. Three years after his death, the Great Leader's embalmed body was swollen and yellow, his skin waxy. But it was definitely him. The old man has really gone.

And now, a new year – with the luckiest of numbers – has begun. In 1980, everything will be different.

Liu pats his breast pocket, feeling the outline of his papers. If any Public Security Bureau comrades appear, he has his story ready: he had to get out of the house – away from his wife and son. You know how it is, comrade – a man needs a little peace. A former Red Guard will be believed. His heart beats, hard, through the layers of his clothes.

Hallo. I am very pleased to make your acquaintance. The sentence circles his head; the language as slippery, and full of hisses, as a bucket of snakes; that he longs for, as a starving man dreams of rice. The universities have only recently reopened, and he has not been chosen to study English. But in the spirit of the new Paramount Leader Deng Xiaoping, Liu is making changes.

He watches the road. The two English girls are late. When he invited them, he spoke slowly, in his simplest Mandarin. He thought they might laugh; confusingly, they often do. But clever Ka Lin understood straightaway, pushing her glasses up her pointed nose in excitement. She explained to Zhu Li. Then Ka Lin got out her big dictionary and found the word: adventure. They practised saying it in Mandarin: "*m-a-o–x-i-a-n*". They didn't notice that one of the meanings is "risk". As if Liu was the one who needed to understand, Zhu Li wrote the characters out, over and over again, in a lumpy line.

Liu thinks of his father's writing, the strokes and dashes as beautiful as music, that in the *luan* – chaos – of recent years he had to forget he knew. The curves and sweeps became black squares – Big Character slogans, daubed on posters and walls: "Rebellion is just!" Liu remembers with unease the crunch of spectacles under his shoe.

The girls' writing is poor. He wonders about their education at the Foreign Languages Institute. When he heard that English students had arrived there, he knew he had to meet them, but he couldn't work out how. In the end, he plucked up his courage, and it was easy: to cycle past the guardhouse, after dark, in a crowd of students, and whisper, "Hallo," to a tall, light-haired girl standing there. Luckily for him, it was the soft-hearted Ka Lin. She introduced him to Zhu Li, who looked at him suspiciously.

The girls are nineteen: ten years younger than Liu. At their age, he was working in the countryside, digging the frozen earth to plant cabbages with an old peasant couple, whose one-room home he shared. In the evenings, he read to them from the Great Leader's thoughts, ignoring his cut hands, and their mocking laughter.

When he returned to the city he met Han Mei at a rally. And then, two years ago, Han Mei produced Pangpang. Now, under the new policy, there can be no more children. It is hope for his son's future, too, that is tangled up in Liu Qiang's plan.

He finds it hard to concentrate on his work at the East Wind bicycle factory, but none of his comrades has accused him of having a Bad Attitude. Nor has he been summoned to a Self-Criticism Meeting, where he would have to explain his lack of enthusiasm for fitting spokes into iron rims. On the production line, he smiles when he imagines living in the West: in a big house, with three cars, like all Westerners.

The shadows ripple, becoming two bulky outlines. Could they be PSB? Liu's feet are poised, ready to push. Now the lamplight shows the gleam of new bicycles, and the dark fur collars of expensive coats. Liu releases his breath. The girls have understood his instruction to push their hats down, and their collars up. But in between, their faces are pale.

He whistles, and sets off along the street. If the girls are stopped, he will go on ahead. They would be escorted to the main road, and warned not to be out after dark again.

Liu turns left, then right, then doubles back into the *hutongs*. The single-storey buildings are dark; here and there, a light shows behind a blind. Liu cycles past his courtyard and turns back. A little way from his house he stops, and signals to the girls to walk.

In the small room lit by a fluorescent strip, Han Mei sets the special chopsticks on the table, and tastes the seasoning in the pork-offal soup. Her hand wobbles, and a scalding drip lands on her chin. She rearranges the plate of fried tofu, and the mutton, and takes a spoon to push the boiled peanuts into a bigger heap. She tries not to think of the ration coupons she has used up. In the queue this afternoon old Mrs Zhang said, loudly, "So much food for one family, comrade?" Quick as a whip, Han Mei replied, "I suppose you've forgotten how much a hungry husband and a growing son can eat?" That shut the old witch up. Her husband, Teacher Zhang, hasn't been seen since he was arrested, four years ago, for being a counter-revolutionary.

On the bench seat against the wall, Pangpang is quiet, his

head drooping on his chest. Han Mei nudges him awake. She knows that these Foreign Friends, as they must now be called, will be impressed with her son. She tries to picture the students, who, her husband said, want to see how worker-comrades live. "Let them find out from someone else," said Han Mei. Her friend, who works near the Languages Institute, has stood next to foreign students on the bus. They smell of milk, like babies.

The sound of the latch, lifting; a rush of cold air. Han Mei feels her chest tighten.

Her husband is first through the door. He nods at her, full of self-importance. Now, two dark figures. Han Mei can't help staring. Foreign Devils, right here in her house! She straightens her jacket, glad she has mended the rip in the padding.

Like visiting Party comrades the girls look around, as if they are checking up on her. They have big noses, just as her friend said, and round eyes, although the taller girl's are hidden by glasses. They are wearing expensive cotton shoes, and it's true: their feet are as big as men's.

They introduce themselves, and Han Mei wants to laugh. "What kind of family names are those?" she says to Liu, behind her hand.

"Don't be stupid." He fusses with a chair. "Their teachers made them up."

Han Mei waits for the girls to praise her cooking, but Liu gets in the way, waving his arms about like an actor in the Beijing Opera. Squashed at the small table, on the bench along the wall, she thinks of a work-unit meeting, or a Self-Denunciation Session. She puts her arm round her son.

"*Chi ba, chi ba.* Eat!" Liu spoons rice into the students' bowls.

Han Mei studies the visitors. Even with her glasses, the light-haired girl, Ka Lin, is better-looking than the dark-haired one, but they are both so white they could be actors in face paint. Their hair is curly: does it grow like that? Now that permed hair is allowed, she has hers done regularly at the hairdresser's on the corner. When Liu said he didn't like it, she pretended not to care – why should a revolutionary woman worry what her husband thinks?

Until he started going out on a Tuesday evening, and coming back late.

When at last she confronted him, his story was so strange it had to be true. She could hardly speak. "Meeting Foreign Devils? You'll lose your job!"

But Liu just smiled. "I'm getting a better job." He spoke slowly, as if she wouldn't understand. "Interpreter with a Trade Delegation."

"Those jobs are only for high-ups."

"My work-unit comrades will put my name forward," he said. "The students say my English is very good." Before she could ask anything else he added, "Think of the presents I'll bring back from England."

Since then, whenever she is bored working the sewing machine at the Number Five underwear factory, Han Mei imagines her husband, smart in his Party uniform, returning from a foreign trip with a new plastic suitcase. Inside are toys for Pangpang, and shoes with a heel for her. Perhaps even a radio. Of course, there are obstacles to overcome – one of them, these Foreign Devils coming here tonight. But as Liu always says, *A thousand grains of sand build a tower.*

"Do they speak Mandarin?" Han Mei asks.

"I speak English to them, they speak Mandarin to me." Liu leans over the table and makes strange hissing noises. The girls smile, and say something about the weather. Their pronunciation is terrible.

Han Mei pictures an official car, waiting at the end of the alleyway, its blue paint and chrome trim gleaming, and Liu climbing into it, waving to her, before pulling the curtains closed and setting off.

The girls open their backpacks, and Han Mei sits forward to see what they have brought for Pangpang from the foreigners' Friendship Store. Like all her friends, she's wheeled her bicycle slowly past the windows, studying the displays of silk scarves and jade ornaments, but there must be toys in there too. Pangpang would be happy with a bat and ball, although that might be hard to explain to the neighbours. Perhaps a picture book, or some pencils, would be better. He can hold a pencil now.

Smiling, the girls take out their own chopsticks.

Han Mei pulls Pangpang onto her lap, where he squirms and cries until she puts her little finger in his mouth. At last, he settles in her arms and falls asleep.

The dark-haired girl tries to pick up some tofu. When it falls to the oilcloth, she grabs it with her fingers.

"They have no manners," says Han Mei.

When Liu doesn't reply, she leans back against the seat, and shuts out the girls' ugly talk. She sees the food in the congealing sauces, and remembers queueing for the meat in the cold afternoon. The clock on the shelf says eight thirty; she is on an early shift tomorrow. Weariness pulls at her like the waves on the lake at Beihai, where they once hired a boat, before they were married. It was Liu's idea, but he couldn't row. After going in circles, Han Mei took the oars, and rowed them back to the bank.

Her head is as heavy as an iron bell. She lays Pangpang down on the bench next to her, covering him with her jacket. She folds her arms on the table and puts her head down, as she was taught to do at school.

She is aware of a commotion, but she is far away: on the lake at Beihai, the oars firm beneath her hands.

She bumps the bank.

A prod on her arm wakes her. Liu's face is in hers. "What do you think you're doing?"

The two girls jump up, as if they've been burned. The dark-haired one says something that makes no sense.

Han Mei sits up. "Are they going?"

"Of course not!"

Liu feels Han Mei watching him. The questions he wants to ask Ka Lin – *How near to the airport is your house? Which bus should I catch?* – will have to wait for a Tuesday evening. He is keeping the conversation general. But the girls are so slow to understand. Of course, when he gets to England, and Ka Lin introduces him to her high-up *guanxi* – contacts – they will all speak the same language.

A headache is beginning at his temples. He looks around the room for inspiration, and spots the studio photo of Pangpang taken at New Year. The little boy, in his new padded jacket, stares seriously into the camera.

Zhu Li has noticed too. "Son good picture," she says.

"Lucky no daughter!" Liu smiles. "Please to tell me, how are you spent Chinese New Year?"

She looks confused.

"New Year," he repeats, his neck growing hot.

"Ah! New Year," says Ka Lin, across the table. "Xian," she says. "We go to Xian." She looks at him and his heart stutters. If only he could talk to her alone.

"Xian very . . . beautiful," he says, carefully. "From Beijing long way."

"Did she say Xian?" His wife looks up. She's always wanted to see the old city in the west.

"We no allow travel in countryside," Liu says. He wonders how to explain "restrictions on internal movements", but the girls are nodding, as if they understand.

"Sorry," says Ka Lin.

"Xian very old city," he says. "You like, yes?"

The girls whisper together.

"You see Drum Tower? Wild Goose Pagoda?" He is surprised at the longing he feels for the ancient names; places he has seen only in photographs. He waits for Ka Lin to translate.

But Zhu Li speaks. "We see very bad thing."

Ka Lin touches her friend's arm. "We see much old things." She smiles at Liu; as if trying to tell him something more.

Zhu Li mutters under her breath. She takes a cloth from her pocket, and empties her nose into it.

"Ugh," says Han Mei.

"Something at Xian, we no like," Zhu Li persists.

"No good to Foreign Friends?"

The girl shakes her head.

Han Mei nudges him. "What's wrong with that one?"

"Stop interrupting."

"Prisoners," says Zhu Li, as if she has just remembered the word.

"What?" says Liu.

"We see, at Xian."

Liu racks his brains. Foreigners wouldn't be allowed anywhere near prisoners. The girls often use the wrong word – or the wrong tone, which completely changes the meaning. He remembers news stories about the Xian excavations. "Soldiers!" He laughs with relief. "You see Terracotta Army!"

"No army," says Zhu Li. She reminds him of a dog he saw once in the alley: it had a rat by the tail but wouldn't let go, and the rat was leading it in circles. In fact, her long nose and small eyes make her look more like the rat. "Prisoners, in lorry."

"No, not possible." Liu smiles.

"They no have hair."

Liu pictures shaved heads. "No, no," he says, laughing. "You make mistake." He leans over the table, finds the tastiest pieces of liver in the soup and drops them onto Ka Lin's rice. "This food better than Institute, yes?"

"Why do you keep talking to her?" says Han Mei.

Liu feels heat rise to his face. His wife holds their son close. The child's eyelids flicker, but he is lost in sleep.

"Much people watch prisoners," says Zhu Li.

"Did she say prisoners?" Han Mei reaches to pull the blind down, but it can go no further.

"Shut up. She's not talking to you." Liu catches Ka Lin's eye and raises his eyebrows, willing her to stop this nonsense.

"Prisoners have signs," she says.

He imagines the placards swinging at the men's necks, as the lorry carried them towards a crowded stadium. His pulse is beating loudly in his ears. He casts around for something to say. "But you no good read Mandarin!"

The girls laugh, and Liu dares to hope the subject is closed. He smiles at Zhu Li, but she doesn't notice. With a mixture of miming, and odd words, the girls explain: the signs at the prisoners' necks described their crimes.

"So small things." Ka Lin puts her finger and thumb close together.

"Thief only," says Zhu Li, frowning.

He hopes she lives far away from Ka Lin in England; when he gets there, he does not want to meet her.

"But they go be kill." Ka Lin mimes a gun, aimed at her head.

Han Mei nudges him. "What the hell is she doing?"

Liu cannot look at his wife. The conversation is sliding away from him like water out of a bowl.

Zhu Li peers at him. "You think kill is right?"

"What does she want?" says Han Mei.

Liu's head is a muddle of half-remembered English phrases. He knows the students hear the news on the loudspeaker at the Institute every morning: they complain that it wakes them up. He has a vision of Ka Lin, waking up, her pale skin next to his. He is sure Han Mei knows what he's thinking. He feels sweat under his arms.

"At Xian you see – Bad Elements." He drops his voice, but the words explode in his mouth.

Han Mei stares. "What on earth are you saying?"

Ka Lin mutters to her friend.

"Why do they keep whispering?" asks Han Mei.

"Stop asking stupid questions!"

Zhu Li pulls a face that makes her look even more like a rat. "Bad Elements?" Her voice is loud in the small room.

Liu glances at the door.

"Bad Elements," the girl repeats, laughing. She looks at him as if he is stupid. As if he has spent all his life believing the wrong things. Liu is transported back to the peasants' hut; explaining to the old couple the Great Leader's thoughts.

Ka Lin whispers something, but that makes Zhu Li laugh even more.

Han Mei prods him. "What's so funny?"

"I don't know."

"So much for you speaking English." She sounds like his work-unit comrades.

Liu wishes his wife had stayed asleep. He would like to put his head down on his arms himself. He stares at the oilcloth, where Han Mei's special chopsticks lie, unused; at the trail of dropped food in front of the girls; and their soft, pale hands. He looks up to see them watching him: amused, curious – as if he should be in a cage at Beijing Zoo.

"England, China, not same," he says at last.

"No," Ka Lin says. "No right, kill thief."

Liu feels his face burn. What kind of country would this be, if people who broke the law were not punished for it? "You know," he says slowly, *"Zhong-guo ren tai duo-le."*

The students repeat: *There are too many Chinese people.*

He smiles. "So, no matter if some die."

Behind her glasses, Ka Lin's eyes are cold.

Zhu Li looks at him. "State kill prisoners, State is Bad Element."

Han Mei straightens. "What did she say?"

"Nothing," says Liu.

"You must think I'm stupid." She leans across the table at the students. "That's enough from you," she says, wagging her finger in their faces.

The girls sit back, startled.

Liu elbows her. "Shut up, you ignorant woman."

"Interpreter! The only plan you have is to bring shame on us."

Liu glances at Ka Lin, but she is on her feet. "Now look what you've done." He grabs the back of her chair. "Sit, please. Stay! Please, Ka Lin."

The girl smiles, in a vague, irritated way.

"Get them out of here," says Han Mei. "Ignorant Foreign Devils."

"They don't understand."

"But I do." Han Mei reaches for Ka Lin's coat and shoves it at the girl. "Goodbye, goodbye, stupid students!"

Zhu Li is smiling like a dazed goat. Ka Lin says something that could be "Sorry, sorry."

Pangpang wakes up and wails, and Han Mei pulls him to her. She says, slowly and clearly, "You're a useless liar. I wish I'd never married you."

Liu stares at the shabby room, in the yellowy light; at his wife's lumpy body in her faded jacket. The students stand next to her, their hair and clothes gleaming.

"And I the same."

He opens the outside door.

"Goodbye! Goodbye! *Zaijian, zaijian,*" the students call, their words barely understandable.

"Tell the silly bitches to be quiet."

The air is icy. Liu pulls his jacket collar up, and his cap down. The girls follow him across the courtyard. Silently they wheel their bicycles into the lane.

He cycles in front. When the main road and its lamp posts are in sight, he turns back. Perhaps they say goodbye; he doesn't hear. Their bulky silhouettes are soon swallowed by the night.

In his head their laughter is shrill; his wife's angry face clear.

He remembers the sharp edge of frozen earth in the cabbage fields at dawn, and how his torn fingertips refused to bleed.

"*Hallo. I am very pleased to make your acquaintance,*" he whispers.

The moon is high. The poplars cast their barred shadows on the empty road.

Beyond the crossroads, just outside the arc of lamplight, a bicycle silently circles.

The Katie Merrick Case

JO HOLLOWAY

The Jury Act (2030)

An Act to make provision for a fairer and more transparent trial by jury.

[16th March 2030]

BE IT ENACTED by the King's most Excellent Majesty, by and with the advice and consent of the Lords Spiritual and Temporal, and Commons, in this present Parliament assembled, and by the authority of the same, as follows:–

1. The Secretary of State for Justice has a duty to provide a fully representative jury for criminal trials. All British citizens will be able to vote "guilty" or "not guilty" via the GovVote website. This will constitute one seat on a jury of twelve.

2. "British citizen" refers to anyone living in England, Scotland, Wales and Northern Ireland with full citizenship status.

3. "GovVote website" is the government-run and -monitored website used for referendums, general elections . . .

* * * * *

My professional career, and to some extent my life, can be split into two distinct sections: before the Katie Merrick case, and after. Before it, success, a job, a strong Twitter following. Now I'm driving as fast as I can away from all that. I look in the rearview mirror. Max is still asleep, still holding one of his comics. He has no idea where he's going. I have no idea what to tell him.

The day it started, I'd gone upstairs to find my son and his friend furtively watching a video on his phone.

"What's going on?" I asked, suspiciously.

"Nothing," Max said, far too quickly.

Looking back, I wish I'd insisted on seeing what he was watching then. I didn't, though. I thought teenage boys should have some level of privacy. Laughable really, given that my son's generation is the one without any privacy at all, apart from what's inside their heads. And I'm not even sure there's much inside there, given the amount of time they spend looking at a screen.

"It's dinner time in five minutes. Come and have some food," I said.

They talked a million miles an hour at the dinner table, as I served up the meal.

"Did you hear what she did?"

"Yeah, everyone did. It was some boys in Year Ten apparently!"

My phone buzzed in my pocket. I have a no-phones rule at the dinner table, so I ignored it.

"Yeah, those boys who are always smoking and stuff."

It buzzed again. I was itching to have a look.

"She went ballistic at them! Mad Merrick!" Dylan exclaimed.

It buzzed a third time. And a fourth. Then a fifth.

"Yeah!" Max exclaimed in response. "That's so Miss Merrick!" They fell about laughing.

"What's this about Miss Merrick?" I asked. I felt my phone buzzing repeatedly now. It was a call. I let it go to voicemail.

"Nothing, Mum, she's just crazy," Max responded, like it was no big deal.

"Max, that's not a nice thing to say. She's a really nice –"

"No, Mum, really, she went crazy today."

I frowned. I looked at my phone. Five Twitter notifications, a text message from the school, and a missed call from my boss. Oh God, I'd clearly missed something.

"Mum! You always tell me no phones at the table! That's really unfair!"

"Max, give me your phone. Show me that video you were looking at earlier."

He didn't move, probably thought I was playing some strange trick. "Now, Max!"

He pulled the phone from his pocket and found the video. He handed it over. I noticed it had already received over ten thousand views. There were over four hundred comments. I watched it, mouth open in horror.

I scrolled down the comments:

> Bitch!
> What a sycho
> No way, she should b put in prison
> Lock away the key
> Haha kid deserved it!
> No kid deserves that, don't say that
> I can say what the fuck I like
> Fuck you
> She's mental AF. Fucking crazy bitch
> Women r all mental
> STFU. Not all women r crazy
> Bitches b craaaazzyy lol
> I still would
> Bitch should be raped. Teach her a lesson
> Lmfao
> LOL :p

I remember that my first reaction was not shock at the rape threats or the blatant sexism, but was simply frustration at the inarticulacy of Generation Z.

My second reaction to the video was full-on work mode.

"Max, when was this posted?"

"Today, after school."

"Three hours ago?" This was bad – ten thousand views in three hours was really bad. My phone rang again. I answered it this time.

"Liz, it's Jack." My boss. "Have you seen?" He sounded stressed.

"Yes. Just seen. Sorry. Can't believe it's taken me this long. Sorry."

He ignored my apology. "I want you on the case."

"Jack, I don't know. She's a teacher at my son's school."

"I don't care, this will be a big case, and you're the best. Call her, get her signed up. We can't let one of the other firms get her. She's probably had a ton of offers already, and judging from the video, it will almost definitely go to court. Anyway, get her. Play on the woman thing," he said.

"The woman thing? Really?"

"Liz, you know what I mean. Don't get all feminist on me now. She's much more likely to accept help from another woman than from a man. And let's be honest, most social media lawyers are men. Chances are she might not have been approached by a woman yet."

I hated it when he was right. "Fine," I said. "But still, the woman thing. You're a lawyer, Jack."

"Just call her, Liz." He hung up.

At this point, maybe I should explain what I do. Remember years ago, if you had an accident, you'd have someone call up and ask if you wanted to sue? Sometimes you'd even get a call if you hadn't been in an accident, but they'd try to convince you that you had been? Well, I guess I do that. Except instead of having an accident in your car you've had a social media blunder that's about to ruin your life, and if it's illegal, maybe help send you to prison. You see, nowadays it's more important that you have representation in public as well as in court. It might only be one vote on the jury, but now that everyone's business is on the internet, it's impossible for the rest of the jurors not to be influenced, despite the oath they take to remain impartial. Firms like mine have sprung up ever since the Jury Act.

I tried to call her that evening, but there was no answer. No doubt she was trying to ignore everyone. In the end I went round, dropping the boys off to Dylan's mum on the way. This was going to be an all-nighter. I drove to Stoke Newington where she lived in a small one-bedroom flat, one of those nice Victorian conversions. I parked down the road slightly, but I could see a small crowd already outside her door. Thankfully, there were only about twenty people, mainly lawyers like me, and journalists, but there were a few youths there too. Everyone had their smartphones and smartwatches at the ready, just in case she made an appearance. One of the youths pulled out a can of spray paint. The crowd stood by while a spotty teenager spray-painted *cunt* on her front door. This was my chance. I found my baseball cap in my glove compartment and my parka on the back seat. I pulled the cap low over my head, zipped the coat all the way up and I ran forward.

"What are you doing?" I shouted. "That's my front door, you little sod!"

"Wait, you live here? With Katie Merrick?" a journalist asked. I was thankful for the short winter days and the dull street lights of Hackney. This guy definitely knew who I was. In fact, he'd done me a few favours in the past. I turned my face away, pretending to find my keys in my bag.

"She lives downstairs. I don't know what you're doing here though. I've just seen her climb over that fence and leg it down Church Street." A wave of excitement and adrenalin spread through the crowd. A few of the lawyers had already sprinted off.

"What? Where? Church Street?"

They scurried off, and once several had gone, the others simply followed.

"Hey! What about my bloody door?" I yelled, for dramatic effect.

The road went quiet. Now for the hard bit. I crouched down and opened the letter box.

"Katie?" I said, in a loud whisper. "It's Liz. We met at a parents' evening? My son, Max, is in your Year Seven class. I just want to talk. I might be able to help."

There was nothing.

"Katie?"

Nothing. I stood up, my hand sticky with yellow paint. Perfect. I was thinking about what to do next, when I saw the hall light go on through the mottled glass panels in the door.

The door opened as far as the chain would allow. One puffy red eye looked at me warily. "Is there anyone else there?"

I shook my head. "They've all gone. It's just me."

The door closed again and I heard the rattle of the chain being taken off.

She stood, looking tiny and tired. She held a thick grey cardigan tightly around her, and wore black sweatpants and Ugg boots. Her long black hair was tied into a messy ponytail. She closed the door quickly after me.

I followed her into her living room, where she sat down on the edge of the sofa and began to bite her nails, staring at the floor. I sat down next to her and put my hand gently on her shoulder. Her eyes welled up then, and she swallowed hard. Finally, she looked at me, her lip quivering ever so slightly.

"What should I do? I'm going to lose everything. Everyone hates me, and it was just so awful. I shouldn't have done it. I wish –" She stopped abruptly, pulled her sleeves down over her hands and looked away again.

I tried to instil some confidence in her. "We need a strategy and we need your story. But it will get better. The first twenty-four hours are always the worst."

"I've had death threats. And worse. Somebody put a note through my door threatening to rape me in my sleep." She paused. "What if they do?" Her voice cracked as she said it.

"They won't, they never do. They say those things, but it doesn't happen, I promise." I wasn't lying either. I'd never heard of these threats becoming reality before. People write a lot of things they would never speak aloud, let alone actually follow through.

Katie was silent. She tucked some stray hair behind her ear. Her hand was shaking. I felt my phone vibrate in my pocket. By this point I had set up alerts that told me anything that contained her name or the school. I checked. Two hundred and fifteen notifications. Shit. And a hashtag had been started on Twitter – #crazykatiemerrick. There was a text from Jack: *Hurry*. Helpful.

"Come on, you need to pack a bag. We can't stay here. You can stay at mine. We'll get the contract drawn up and then we can start on the case."

"I'm not sure I can afford –"

"Katie, we will figure that out. We have finance plans. And if we – *when* we win, we can claim damages." I'd obviously take a cut, not that I'd tell her yet.

She leaned her elbows on her knees then and pressed the heels of her hands to her forehead. When she looked up, her eyes were red and she suddenly looked a lot older than her twenty-eight years.

"Katie," I said, gently. "They will come back when they realise I was lying. We need to go."

She nodded. She got up slowly and went into her bedroom, where I heard her finally let out a sob.

I studied some of the notifications.

The video had now been viewed more than forty thousand times and reposted on Facebook, Twitter, Snapchat, Tumblr and YouTube. Someone had screen-grabbed a shot of Katie's angry, twisted face from the video and turned it into a meme with captions like *I don't have PMS!* and *Telling a woman to calm down*. The internet had a vast collection of apparently hilarious quotes from which to make these memes. And through it all, the rape threats continued.

I took this opportunity to call a few of my contacts.

"Hi, it's Liz . . . Yes, good thanks, I'm representing Katie

Merrick now . . . Yep, the teacher who . . . Yes, that one . . . Listen, I need a favour. Post an article about teacher stress and workload. Get a quote from those lefties at the National Union of Teachers." I heard Katie go to the bathroom and close the door. I slipped into her bedroom and snooped around. There they were on her bedside table. Yes! Antidepressants! "She's been suffering from depression . . . Yes, going through a really tough time, not sure about the details yet." I heard the toilet flush and went back to the living room. "I'll call you later. Start the article."

Katie reappeared in the doorway with a half-packed bag.

"OK?" I asked. She nodded.

We were walking out of the living room, when a brick came flying through the window, sending small daggers of glass towards us. They fell short, but the brick flew directly into a photo frame on top of her mantelpiece. That too shattered.

Katie screamed, and I grabbed her and ducked down, and we were still in that position, thankfully, when I heard the fake shutter sound from an iPhone camera. Katie made to look but I pulled her head back round. Instead I held her hand and, still crouched, led her through to the hallway, reached up to kill the light. I can't remember if I was scared at that point. I don't think so, I think I was just concentrating on getting Katie out. But now, looking back, that should have been a sign that something had changed. I'd never had a brick thrown through a window before.

"I think it was just kids, but to be safe, here." I put my baseball cap on her and pulled the peak down low. "Ready?"

She nodded. All the colour had drained from her face and she swallowed hard.

I opened the door, but I had gambled correctly. The kids who had thrown the brick had already run away and the mob hadn't quite worked out that I'd lied about Church Street. We ran silently across the road to my car. I heard a familiar yell. The pack was definitely on its way back.

I looked in my rear-view mirror; I half expected to see pitchforks and torches, but instead I saw the press guy running full pelt.

"Liz! Is that you? Are you representing her? Liz!"

I started the car as the mob returned. I ignored them and tried to get Katie to do the same, but her eyes were fixed on the mirror. I sped away as the press guy banged a fist on my car. Katie jumped.

We drove, mostly in silence at first, to my house. The only noise was my phone bleeping and buzzing.

"Liz?" Katie said in a small voice. "What happens when they find me? When they get me?"

"Don't think about that, it won't happen. I need to call the police, tell them you're staying with me. We don't want them to think you've done a runner. That wouldn't do our case any good."

I remember her face so clearly in the car that night; her big brown eyes pleading for a miracle, and she'd started to chew on her bottom lip. She looked really vulnerable then. Whenever I'd seen her before she'd been smiley and confident. She'd seemed so together. It was hard to believe this was the same face that the internet had turned into an angry meme.

"Katie, you have to tell me what happened. From beginning to end."

"You've not seen the video?" she asked, hopefully.

"Oh no, I've seen it, but I need to know everything. What's work been like? Why are you taking antidepressants? Weren't you off for a while near Christmas?"

"Wait, how do you know about the antidepressants?"

Some people don't get urgency. They see these trials by Twitter all the time: the dentist who killed that lion, the man who refused to move his BMW out of the way of an ambulance, the countless idiots who pushed cyclists off their bikes – but they don't get how important it is to have their stories, their sob stories, out there quickly. The people who comment on social media are more than just the jury now, they are the trial. Everything they say affects how people vote. If someone Googles her name and a fake story comes up, or a meme, then they start to think she's guilty. People don't really care about truth any more, just entertainment.

"Katie, I need to know everything. Preferably by the time we get to my flat."

She did tell me everything. We arrived back to my house, and she collapsed onto the sofa. By the time I'd made her a cup of tea, she'd fallen into a deep sleep. While she slept, I made progress on the case. I drew up the contract, and rang my contact back at *HuffPost* and another woman at *BuzzFeed* and gave them the exclusive. Katie's dirty laundry would be aired first thing tomorrow. I yawned, and looked at the clock. It was already past midnight.

The next morning Katie was formally arrested and charged. A colleague of mine went to the station with her, so that I could stay home and concentrate on the more important task of changing the public's opinion. I wrote an article about the prevalence of sexism online and my friend at the *Guardian* posted it on her blog. In another article, I explained that the student who had been filming Katie secretly had provoked her. In fact, she'd put up with a lot before she'd finally cracked.

It was this article where Katie first got some online support:

> What a nasty kid.
> I'd have done the same
> Little twat deserved it
> Not so crazy after all, it seems.
> I think anyone would have done what she did if
> someone spoke to them like that.
> See, this is why I hate kids.

I sat at my computer all day, trying to ensure that everybody with an online presence had seen the article. My diet consisted of three bags of Hula Hoops and a Coke, which I sipped between vaping and typing. I showed her when she got home from the police station. She read the comments, and with each positive statement she seemed to feel just a little bit more vindicated. Eventually, she smiled.

"Liz, I can't thank you enough for what you've done." She ran her fingers through her thick black hair, which was unbelievably shiny since she'd washed it that morning. She looked at me and the shadow of a smile appeared.

"It'll be fine, Katie. People will see it from your point of view. How did it go at the station?"

"OK, I guess." She looked down. She had the perfect face for court. Very pretty, humble, slightly self-conscious. And best of all, she had an air of childish innocence. "It was pretty intense. They questioned me for hours. They watched the video again, and we saw others from the kid's phone. That was hard – I had no idea she had been filming me. I've got to stay with you until the bail hearing."

"That's good, Katie. That's a really good sign. There will be another scandal on the front page tomorrow, so we won't have to worry as much about the internet and what the trolls think. We can focus on preparing for the hearing."

That night I convinced her to have a celebratory glass of white wine. I called Max and told him he could probably come home tomorrow, although he was having a lot of fun at Dylan's and didn't sound too bothered, putting my guilt at ease.

The next morning, I finally persuaded Katie it was OK to go out in public. Her brother had invited her to Cambridge for the day. At first she was adamant that she couldn't go, that someone would recognise her, but I typed her name into Google and she changed her mind. The top results were my article and a blog by the NUT about stress in teaching. So eventually she went. I was sure we'd beaten the internet, and usually by this point it was pretty much plain sailing. As I'd said to Katie, the first twenty-four hours are the worst.

My phone buzzed. The first Katie Merrick-related notification that day.

Bikini Babe! Crazy Katie Merrick shows off a hot bod in pink bikini in Thailand!

The *Daily Mail*. I felt the optimism drain from my body, the disappointment washing over me, causing me to sink into the nearest chair. I had to steel myself before I read the article.

They'd found some pictures from ten years ago of Katie on her gap year, dancing in next to nothing on stage at a full-moon party in Thailand. She must've been about eighteen.

The article was mostly pictures – first the original, then zoomed on her breasts, then her bum, then her pouty lips and drunken eyes. They kindly recapped Katie's rise to notoriety in between. And so, a fresh round of abusive comments began. *Not what I needed.*

My phone rang. I rolled my head, clicking my neck, took a deep breath.

"Liz." It was Jack. "Have you seen? The fucking *Mail*."

"Yep, I've seen." I stood up, making my way to my study. "I'll keep pushing the other articles, see if we can stop it from too many searches." I slumped at my computer.

"Where is she?"

"She's out for the day at her brother's. She probably won't have seen it yet."

"Don't leave it too long to tell her. Liz, fix it." He hung up.

I got to work, re-posting the more sympathetic articles, trying to keep them at the top of the Google search. I sat at my computer for most of the day, struggling to stop the flow of aggression and hatred. I wrote yet another article, letting my anger out onto the page. I criticised the *Daily Mail* for invading Katie's privacy and implied that her photos had been hacked. It was a risky strategy, potentially libellous, but I had to make out that they were the bad guys, not Katie.

I had decided to tell her when she got home. Hopefully by then I could say "The *Daily Mail* almost ruined it all, but I saved it, don't worry," instead of "The *Daily Mail* have screwed us all over. Especially you."

That's the bit I really regret. If I'd called her, maybe it would have been different.

She never came home. I called the police at eleven p.m. and by that point I was really worried. I couldn't get hold of her and her brother said she'd left hours before. Of course, I found out what had happened by social media. A notification on my phone:

#crazykatiemerrick bitch got owned, with the photo that has burned itself for ever in my mind.

Her body was naked and her arms positioned above her head, her legs tucked up to one side. She was lying on concrete, covered in blood and scratches. I threw my phone across the room and dropped to my knees, struggling to catch my breath.

I don't know how long I stayed on my bedroom floor. Eventually, I pulled myself up and got a drink of water to steady myself. Then went to my computer.

Twitter tried to remove it, but every time they took it down, it was posted from a new account. The police found it impossible to discover who was posting the pictures, and it was retweeted hundreds of times in the first couple of hours. I joined the effort to remove the picture from the internet. I sat in my study for hours, the screen the only light on in my house. I angrily reported the photo, every time I received a notification of the hashtag. There was widespread condemnation of the attack, but through it all support continued:

> Teacher got taught a lesson LOL
> Justice been done
> Deserved what she got

I think I knew then what would happen next. I sat at my computer, hearing the clock in the kitchen, the small, night-time noises. At some point, I got up and drew the curtains.

In the early hours of the morning, one of the trolls, this horrible mob, mentioned me.

At first it wasn't really anything to worry about. Just a reference to "her lawyer trying to save her". But still, I grew uneasy. Then the questions started.

> Who was her lawyer again?
> She wrote loads of shit articles about Katie, all lies apparently.

It felt like they were literally closing in on me. I tried telling myself that I was being paranoid, that this was silly and stupid. I looked over at the screen and could see the tweets piling up. I went back to my desk and sat down but I stopped trying to report the photo and watched my Twitter feed as the trolls came for me.

Hey, wasn't it Liz something?

My stomach seemed to shrink and my heart began to hammer in my chest. I stared at my laptop, my eyes dry from the tiredness. I reread it, in the hope that maybe I'd somehow misunderstood.

Then one Twitter notification. They'd found my Twitter handle.

@lizziemay how do you feel huh? Little Merrick is dead. You lost, we won.

It wouldn't normally have scared me. But now, I froze.
Two notifications.
Three.
Five.
Eight.
I stood up and turned my back to the screen. I rubbed my eyes, and told myself to think straight.
Max.
I called Max's mobile, despite it being 5.30 a.m.
It rang and rang. "Come on, Max, pick up, pick up."
"Hello?" he said groggily.
"Max!" I said. "Are you all right?"
"Mum?"
He was half asleep.
"Max, I'm coming to get you. Get dressed for me, OK?"
"Mum, what's going on?"
"Max, just do it. Please. I need to come and get you."

"OK, OK," he said. He hung up and I turned around. My laptop was still on, the white blinding in the dark room. I walked over to close it, but then my photo appeared. It was one of the pap shots from three nights ago outside Katie's house.

Within minutes my face was plastered all over Twitter, I was condemned for supporting her, and it wasn't long before the death threats started.

I didn't wait for the police or sympathetic members of the public to support me, and I didn't try to stop it myself. I didn't even bother putting the laptop away. I grabbed a few belongings for Max, some clothes and two comic books to keep him entertained, and shoved a few clothes of my own into a carrier bag. I called the police and reported the threats, and then I left my house. I picked up Max and drove.

Max's dad owns a little B&B in the Cotswolds. He's proud that it has no Wi-Fi and no signal. He says it's the only holiday home in Britain where you can truly get away from it all. It's why we separated – he had said that I'm too obsessed with the virtual world. I'd said it is my job to be obsessed with the virtual world. As I drive further into the countryside, the 4G on my phone gets weaker and weaker, each bar dropping one by one. Eventually it disappears altogether. I wonder how long I will need to lie low before somebody else becomes the target and I'm forgotten. I hope it will be Katie's killer, but in a way, I know it won't be. He was too obviously guilty. No. Somewhere, another Katie is making a mistake that will go viral.

Act IV
KATIE WINFIELD

Out of spite, you go alone to the theatre.

"What will we say to the LeSauters?" you had asked, and he looked at you as though the script you were reading was tiresome.

You fantasise that you are leaving for more than just the evening. Prise your rings off your puffy fingers and slip them into your purse.

This is your rebellion: sitting in the Upper Circle, seat F32 empty beside you, your hand, audacious, conducting.

At the interval, you stand at the bar, attempting nonchalance. Have to ask the barmaid to repeat herself – "Card machine's broke." Watch her pass your glass to another customer and the approach of the LeSauters.

"Brave of you –" Stuart begins, but Patricia bends to thank you for the Dartington vase and though he isn't the type to be silenced, he doesn't try again.

The pair of them are unusually attentive, her manicured hand on your sleeve. You feel a flush prickling at the hollow of your neck. That his absence should be so predictable. That you, his dumpy wife, should be left alone to face his competent friends and their complacent unity.

"He's just popped to the men's room," you say, inexplicably.

As the tannoy requests that you return to your seats, Stuart reappears, balancing on a tray four Pinot Grigios. You take two and see them exchange a glance as they float towards Door E.

The wine swills in your stomach. You hear the faint music of the Act III prelude and imagine them straining to see you. Confirming the emptiness of F32.

Outside, you hail a taxi. The wine has diluted your resentment towards William and it strikes you that he might find it amusing. The joke will be on the LeSauters. The two of you will pretend he'd come along after all. And they will feel chastised. You fish your rings out of your purse and stack them onto your finger.

But, when the taxi pulls up, the house is dark.

The Last Empress of Calcutta

DANE BUCKLEY

We must go home, even if we've never been. That was Daddy's mantra. I've no idea what will be waiting for us, but it has to be better than this blessed jungle. Blighty is doing a runner, tiptoeing back, leaving our kind behind. Calcutta won't be safe for Anglo-Indians any more: the Raj might have forgotten about our mixed blood but an independent India will not.

I walked across Daddy's lawn, away from the hullabaloo and noise of the servants packing up everything, anything that could fetch a price. I'd taken another cigarette from Cook's stash, knew his hiding place – full of pinched things it was. Things that left the pantry, but never reached our supper table. So we are even.

I lit it, stopping where Daddy's lawn ended and the long grass began; the borders of our land. I lifted my dress a little to let my leg-backs air. The grass was as high as my navel and full of cobras now, probably. Jagat has grown very lazy. Servants aren't so willing to work now, near the end, but willing to take Daddy's – my – money. I blew smoke out over the long grass.

In the shade of Daddy's Java-plum trees, away from the white-hot sky, I watched something slither across the lower branches, a victim of my own prophecy. I listened for the hiss. Pea-green skin slipped over the fruits. It turned its prying eyes towards me – not a tree viper, thank God! But a vine snake. The bird-like face confirmed it.

I flicked the cigarette out as far as it would spin. If Daddy was still alive, he would have something to say about my smoking. *Lilly, it is not fitting.* But cigarettes dull the throbbing in my head, always keeping time with the cicadas and their racket. In England, all must be calm. Servants work with you, not against you, and a garden is a place of rest and birdsong. I left the sticky heat and returned inside. I was sure God had chosen today, of all days, to test me. He would have to be patient. We both would.

I found Mother's silverware still in the dresser and the dresser still in the bloody dining room. These items should have left for the auction house already. Must I do everything? Daddy's old maps were stacked on the mora where he used to sit, like catch-paper for the fire. Maxwell and Glen's old baby-clothes were folded up on the piano. In England, we will need money – my boys can't eat a piano. I put the clothes on the growing pile to be donated to one of the Christian orphanages and took out the silverware from the dresser, laying it on the floor. Were it not for me, my family's belongings would become the property of the schoolmaster. I sold him the house, not our possessions. Better we make some small profit. I walked into the hallway and quickly felt the shadow of Ranjini scuttling alongside me.

"Can't find Cook," she said.

"Don't know where he's gone," I answered. "Look in the outhouse or fields."

"Yes Mistress, but who will –"

"If Cook can't be found, has done a runner, then yourl have to do the cooking, isn't it? Don't bother me with this. Make do." I sounded like Mother, or how Mother used to sound in the stories told by the elderly servants.

She went to say something else, but I walked to the end of the hall and opened the coatroom. "I need you to make some alterations for the boys, okay?" I chose two handsome blazers for Maxwell and Glen and held them out to her.

"I will come and show how I want them. Let's eat in the kitchen tonight." I left her standing there and went into Daddy's room.

My case was full of clothes and the fine cloth that Uncle Larry and Aunty Violet had sent. I tried to close it, pushing with my hands, leaning all my weight, and I am no weakling – during my nurse's training they called upon me to hold down the difficult patients – but I couldn't force it shut. I sat on the bed, and you know what I saw out of Daddy's window? My boys, by the outhouse, half naked and rubbing themselves down with a bottle of something or other. Bloody buggers!

I jumped off the bed and tried to open the window. It wouldn't budge. "Ranjini," I called, "come help with this blessed thing!" I rapped at it like some ting-tong wallah selling at the door, and caught their eyes, holding them to the spot with my finger. I ran to the hallway, taking my slippers off as I got outside. I would give them such a hiding!

"What yourl doing?" I said, grabbing the bottle from Maxwell. They stood to attention, angel-faced, reeking of mustard oil. "We leave for England in two days and yourl are doing this?"

"But you told us to," Maxwell, image-of-his-father, said.

"Not any more. I told you stop. We are going to England, isn't it? No need to lighten your skin . . ."

Glen started crying before I had barely said a word. What a soft child. Maxwell stepped forward. "You told us to rub it on before going out to play, because of what happened to Marcus Creed." He pointed his finger up at me.

"Don't cheek me up, or I will slipper your tonsils," I said. "You want that?" Poor Marcus Creed. He'd been too dark, and beaten because the Muslims thought he was Hindu, only letting him be when they ripped the clothes from him and saw his crucifix pendant.

I picked Glen up and held him, bobbing him gently on my hip the way the nanny used to. "Look at this fellow now, huh? He looks like a chokra-boy." I smiled at the glistening, confused look on his face. "Yourl know I stopped Ranjini putting the oil on when we found a way for England. Where did you get it from? Glen?"

"Maxwell took it because of Cook."

"No I didn't – be quiet," Maxwell said, jumping forward.

"Mamma, he called us *kutcha-butcha*," Glen said, struggling to say the words.

Half-baked. "Cook called you this?" I bent down, letting Glen stand on his own, trying to control my temper. I could throttle that man!

"Listen to me . . ." I was so tired of having to be peacemaker, protector and bloody inquisitor. I was never meant to be doing this on my own. "Do you know who yourls father is?"

"The East India Company," Maxwell said, proudly.

"No, not like that," I said. "I mean, who is your daddy?"

"Corporal Gordon C. Mockey."

"Yes, Maxwell, very good. And he was what?"

"Missing in action –"

"No! You've got it arse-about-face. He was white. 'Member? A white man from England." They both nodded. "Means you are even one up from me." Glen smiled. "And if anyone calls you *kutcha-butcha* again, you remind them that you are proud to be Anglo – Maxwell!" I snapped my fingers to get his attention back. "Yourl understand? You are nearly seven years old and the big brother, yourl must listen."

"Yes, Mamma," he said, taking his hands out of his pockets.

"Now go, *jaldi*. Tell Ranjini to give yourl a bath. Scrub! And no more oil. Come Thursday we go to Blighty, isn't it?" The little gundas ran back towards the house, holding each other's hand. *Missing in action*. Gordon better stay missing in action! In England, a war-widow's pension would help a lot more than that boozard could have.

I lifted my hair to let the nape of my neck breathe. A house lizard ran across my foot, towards the big tree. The vine snake I'd spied earlier lay curled around the lower branches, resting its head on a Java-plum. It snapped the lizard up in one. I knew exactly what to do. I sought its tail, unknotting it from the tree. It hissed as I cupped its head in my hand and cooed back to it, gently. The elderly servants taught me palm and leaf reading but I cut my teeth on snakes long before arithmetic and calligraphy were important.

I wrapped its small body around my arm and held its head out in front of me, like a torchlight. I knew where to find Cook and Jagat – all the pariahs. I walked around to the side of the house, along the little stream. The snake tested the air, flicking its tongue to and fro. By Daddy's vegetable patch I found Cook and Atul, smoking and talking, all in their language. They laughed as they saw me come, I know. But they weren't so cocksure as I got closer. It was as if the snake was in my employment – it hissed at Atul and lifted its head up out of my grip.

"Cook, look what I found," I said. "Very dangerous." He flinched. I knew he feared them above all else, even hard work. Atul mumbled something and ran back towards his field hut, arse-over-kettle.

"Has the kitchen been moved? Didn't know. Don't remember telling it so," I said.

"Yes Mistress, so sorry Mistress," he said. But I didn't hear any sorrow in his voice.

"You were busy today, no? Talking with my boys earlier, isn't it?" He eyed me as if I was about to curse him with a manja-ball and hurried towards the house. Daddy would not have put up with this. I dropped the snake onto the vegetable patch.

"What is this?" Jagat said, coming out from his hiding place with his clean shovel propped over his shoulder.

"Oh," I said, straightening myself up, "might have known you'd be around." He watched the snake uncoil and slither away. I knew he didn't fear it; this one was too proud for that.

"Why do this? It's dangerous," he said.

"What danger? Just teaching Cook a lesson. It was only a vine snake, Jagat."

His handsome face looked angry with me, knotted. But why? All knew I didn't suffer fools – and Cook had overstepped the mark. "Why are you sulking? Because I'm going to England?" I stepped closer to him, but he moved back in protest.

"Fine," I said, "if you want to be like that." He wasn't even listening, transfixed on something other than me. I looked over my shoulder, half expecting Ranjini to have found us out, but saw our neighbour, Joseph, waving his arms and half jogging down the hill towards us. And he was no young man – Daddy's friend from the railway.

"Uncle," I said, "why yourl running? What's the matter?"

"They've gone crazy," he said, stopping to catch his breath. "Hindus and Muslims killing each other."

"What?" I said.

"Calcutta is being razed to the ground!"

"They're rioting in the streets . . . So many dead," I said, sat at the kitchen table.

"Mistress, what about Jagat?"

"Jagat? Your precious Jagat? The world has gone topsy-turvy and that's all you worry about? What about England? If there aren't any ships departing, we'll have to stay in this bloody place."

"So sorry Mistress."

"You should be. What is the matter with yourl? Why are you people doing this?" I asked.

"Because of Pakistan," she answered, throwing another chapatti onto the pan.

"What? Have yourl not got what you want? Hindus will have India and Muslims will have a country of their own."

"It will break India, Mistress –"

"Then we should have left it under British rule, isn't it?"

She eyed me as she flipped the chapatti in the pan. "Mistress, what about Jag–"

"For God's sake! I sent him to the schoolmaster, okay? We won't be able to leave on Thursday now, and he's gone to ask for more time," I said. "And Atul I've sent to check on Uncle Larry. Let us see if he even comes back. I never should've listened to you – to pay yourls' last wage early. I've nothing to hold anyone to their work now."

I stood up from the table, the better to see. "You're burning it, Ranjini."

She flipped the chapatti and, turning around, let it slide onto the plate.

"Not burnt," she said, but I didn't like the smirk on her face; my Ranjini was getting very *kunny*.

"Boys – come get!" I called, putting a dollop of blackcurrant jam into the middle of a second chapatti and rolling them up into cigars. "One each only, there's no more jam," I said, as they came running and sat up at the table.

"Mamma, do they eat jampatti in England?" Glen said, in between blowing and biting.

"Of course, my son. They eat the same – meats and the like and cutlets and gram dahl, even Grumpy's favourite," I said, nodding at Maxwell, "country captain chicken."

"And jampatti," Glen said again.

"Yes jampatti. Yourl jampatti-mad. When yourl finish, go and brush your teeth and I'll come up for Hail Marys."

When the boys left the table, I got the bottle of ginger wine from the pantry and poured a glass. "You want?" I asked Ranjini, but she shook her head and sat to eat her own jampatti.

I picked up the blazers we'd been working on, reinspecting her work.

"Good?" she said, tilting her head down at the hidden pockets along the inner seam.

"Yes, nice – don't gloat. We can put extra in these pockets, they won't check children."

"Three pounds," she said.

"What?"

"Three pounds for you and two pounds for children. That's what you're allowed."

"So you're an expert now? Three pounds won't get us far in England. Why should I leave my money here? For who? *India* is to tell me how much I can take? You wouldn't want that for the boys, would you, Ranjini, that they go hungry?"

She shook her head furiously.

"I'll wear my money." I stood up and went to Daddy's old safe, built into the kitchen wall. I pointed for Ranjini to face the opposite corner, then turned the dial and opened it, taking out bangles, rings and necklaces, all made from Indian gold. And a fine jewelled brooch and my mother's pearl-and-shell tiara, with empty holes where the pearls had once been.

There were brand-new bangles for the boys. The Sen Brothers Jewellers had made them specially. I put the hoard on the table.

"If you go through the authorities' limits with a fine comb, there is nothing that bans jewellery from leaving the country." I put on some of the rings, testing the fit. "Do it up," I said, beckoning her over to help fasten a necklace.

She fetched Mother's hand mirror. I laughed when I saw myself.

"Mistress, you look like an empress."

"Ranjini, you have me looking like some trollop," I joked, "a chutney Mary, all marinated up."

On the ship I would have to wear my jewellery under my clothes. The gold was too pure, too shiny and would draw attention. In England, I might start a new trend, but more importantly, I might buy a house with what I was wearing.

Later, when I'd tucked the boys in with another telling of our ancestor, a Goan princess burnt alive in her palace for being too mean in a time of famine, Ranjini took a glass of ginger wine. She wanted me to sing my best song, Daddy's favourite: the Andrews Sisters' take on *Sonny Boy*. Ranjini had no skill for harmony so I had to carry it. She applauded afterwards and I stood up and bowed. I placed Mother's empty tiara on her head and told her she could keep it on condition that she promised to stay away from Jagat.

I told her I'd read his leaves, that he was a charlatan. She wouldn't hear of it and offered to make me jalebis. I let her change the subject, but told her that he couldn't be trusted. She got up, and started heating oil in a pan.

I wanted to learn how to make them myself. Daddy said the English sweetshops probably sold them, but homemade was best. Ranjini, the silly cow, near cried when I told her I would have to cook for my boys in England, that not everyone had servants. "Yourl have to give up your recipes, Ranjini." She'd taught me a few basic dishes and everyone had commented on my dhal being tempered just so.

I watched her making a saffron sugar syrup, slowly, quietly, with the empty tiara half sitting on her head, like some hill-folk princess. While the syrup was boiling, she made a batter and said she wasn't sure who she'd miss more, Maxwell or Glen.

"Oh, the ginger wine is talking now!" I said. "What about me?" Ranjini smiled. She will miss me too; it's not everyone that will eat with their servants.

I don't know how I thought jalebis were prepared, but I was not expecting such chemistry. She made it look simple: filling her piping set, squeezing and spinning a web of batter into the hot oil. I told her it looked like a Catherine wheel sputtering in the pan.

"You don't know that?" I said, explaining what it was.

She took the jalebis out of the oil and submerged them in the carrot-coloured syrup, before putting them on Daddy's dinner plate.

This was the last of Ranjini's sweets I would eat. It sat there like a sticky amber trinket. I bit into it. I wasn't sure if I'd know this taste again. Unplanned and unlooked for, a tear rolled down my cheek. I cracked through the sugary glaze to the chewy centre. I could taste the syrup bleeding out.

"Too hot – you've made them too hot," I said, embarrassed. She knew I could take hot things; didn't I drink down tea the quickest, eager to read the findings?

She took my plate and put two more on there. Turning back to me, she dropped it in her rush. It smashed all over Daddy's tiles, and we both jumped. I watched the floor and then heard the fizz of another jalebi being made. In England, some things would be so different, but I didn't know what. I told Ranjini to give me a hug.

"Tea?" I asked, trying my best to steer the conversation away from the blasted troubles in Calcutta.

Mrs Lindsey nodded. "Please."

I handed her the cup and saucer. I still felt nauseous, like some monsoon had passed through my stomach. On waking,

I'd messed myself all down my front. I suspected my body was in mourning; the dock had been closed due to the riots and passenger ships were no longer departing.

The auctioneers had closed too and I'd no choice other than to sell our possessions to the schoolmaster who was buying Daddy's house. He wanted them for next to nothing on account of letting us stay on, walking from room to room completing an inventory. I'd intervened over the boys' carom board, explaining it was a family heirloom and not for taking.

He brought with him his fat wife dressed in a sari, and Mrs Lindsey, an English woman with an unrecognisable accent, who'd donated money to their school. With Cook and Atul having scarpered, Ranjini and I had rushed the kitchen table out into the garden to accommodate our guests.

"Where are your family from?" the schoolmaster's wife said, turning to me and taking a fistful of hot-gram from the bowl.

"British India," I said. I wasn't going to get into the nitty-gritty and what have you.

"But where are you coming from?" She grinned and I could see the hardened peas swirling around her mouth.

"Why are you asking?"

"Conversation, isn't it?" she said.

Mrs Lindsey looked at me, and I knew she thought I was the one being rude.

"Kharagpur."

"Such a small village," the schoolmaster's wife said, smiling.

"Big enough for a school," I reminded her. "I trained in Calcutta as a nurse," I added, to shut her up.

"Very nice," she said, sitting back and fanning herself with her hand.

"In England, there'll be plenty of work for nurses with my training." I spoke to Mrs Lindsey now; I didn't want her thinking I was the same as the schoolmaster's wife. "We'll take lodgings in London," I continued, clearer. "I'm a widow so I'll only work part time, while I raise my boys." Daddy always said the English favoured good hard work above all else and, failing that, tragedy. And who could do the job better than a hard-working war-widow? Even if the paperwork had not yet come.

"Lovely, Mrs Mockey," Mrs Lindsey said. "It sounds like you've got it all planned out."

"He passed in the war?" the schoolmaster's wife asked. I was surprised she'd followed the conversation. I knew what she was. *Charlie Billy PoPo.* Not like me – who can trace the white relative back. She was desperate to be so very English, sipping tea and talking about the war. I nodded, more in agreement to what I suspected, than to my husband's possible fate.

"It will be hard for you, no?" she asked, but I didn't want her pity.

"Not at all," I said.

"Mrs Mockey, you have a beautiful garden. Are they mango trees?" Mrs Lindsey asked, looking over to the far side of the lawn. I was glad for her polite curiosity.

"Call me Lilly, please. Yes, thank you. Daddy loved his garden and we have many fruits. Mangoes were his favourite. Mine also," I said, looking over my shoulder to the trees. "I wonder how English mangoes will compare."

"What?" the schoolmaster's wife said, looking pleased. "There aren't mangoes in England, even I know that."

"You don't know all," I said, leaning forward. I wanted the ground to swallow me whole.

She laughed at me and started to choke on her hot-gram. I watched her, letting it play out, forgetting my vow as a nurse, while Mrs Lindsey fussed and passed her a hanky. Daddy never said . . .

"I know," I said, tapping my chest, "about England."

"Child – come," the schoolmaster's wife said. "Anglos are just playing dress-up, everybody says."

"Rubbish." I flicked her comment away with a turn of my hand. I wanted to jhap her gluttonous face. She had no manners, the woman. I stopped myself from saying any more. We needed somewhere to stay and I didn't want to give this junglee the satisfaction.

When Ranjini brought the boys out to join us, the schoolmaster's wife spoke to her in their language and left us sitting there not knowing what was being said. I told the boys to say hello to Mrs Lindsey, but it was the schoolmaster's wife who was taken with them, pinching Maxwell's face and commenting on how well turned out they were.

When the schoolmaster followed, he told us that Jagat had been most helpful with his inventory and that he wanted him and Ranjini to stay on. That they would be needed. Ranjini didn't look too shocked to hear the news, or else didn't fully understand, and I wondered if she'd already known. I was beginning to feel like a guest in my own home.

I stood up to return to the kitchen and supervise lunch. As I excused myself the schoolmaster's wife caught my arm.

"Lilly," she said, looking up, "I wish you all the best and good health for England." I hadn't seen that coming – oh, this one was very *kunny*.

A few days later, on the Saturday afternoon, Uncle Larry visited with some of the cousins and Merrill, his neighbour. We played cards and he prepared my favourite: kofta ball curry.

After dinner, I asked if it was true that many were fleeing Calcutta. He said evacuees were all making their way along the Hooghly River, heading for Howrah station. I told him what I'd heard on the wireless about an Anglo being made to prove that he wasn't a Muslim – forced to show his nakedness.

"Christians are safe," he said. "They're not touching us, too busy fighting over the partition. And somebody's got to man the trains."

I didn't have his confidence. We were too far out to be in any real danger, but Fr Varghese was still advising all Anglos to carry their prayer books and recite the Lord's Prayer if they were stopped.

After several glasses of scotch, Uncle Larry petitioned me to think about staying and marrying a nice Anglo boy – said I'd been too isolated from the community.

"And what?" I said. "Go to Anglo dances with some cotton Johnny?"

"Anglos are the most thoroughbred half-castes," he said, grinning. "Can't get better." I had to admire his pride.

"Uncle," I said, "I married Gordon for opportunities. And Daddy liked –"

"Let me tell you one thing only," he said, cupping my hand between his own. "Your father married Anglo. And he thought your mother was the prettiest girl . . . until you came along."

He was trying to get one up on me. This didn't change anything. From what I could remember, Mother was always jealous of Daddy and me; it felt bittersweet now, to hear there'd been a time that she was his number one.

"Lilly . . ." Uncle said. "Stay."

On my last night in India, I lay in Daddy's bed thinking about how nice it would be to have a house full of furniture that was nobody else's but my own. The dock had reopened and passenger ships were departing once again. Come the morning we'd travel to Calcutta to meet Uncle Larry and then in the afternoon we'd sail for England, finally.

I was just drifting off, thinking about red buses on well-built roads and how, in England, yourl can have a day trip any day of the week for no reason other than, when I heard somebody outside the bedroom door. The handle turned and a shadow stepped inside.

"Mistress," Jagat said.

"Mistress?" I answered. "Oh, you're giving me proper titles now."

"Lilly," he whispered, like a password, closing the door behind and approaching my bedside.

"What yourl want?" I said. "Don't think you can charm your way –"

"One more time, please." He leaned forward and kissed me.

I could smell the drink on him and I would not have a drunk in my bed. But I let him be. No doubt he was still upset; they'd found Atul cut down on the road towards Calcutta, the carrion picking at the body.

He took his clothes off, watching me. He looked so handsome, so simple. His skin was too dark, but everything else was perfectly balanced: his nose, his eyes, lips – all working together. I sat up, pulled the covers off and let him lift my nightdress up, over my head. It was tight, most likely too much of Ranjini's cooking. He got into the bed and began kissing my neck, just the way I liked.

"Yourl can't stay the night," I said. If Glen had another nightmare about a Bengal tiger gobbling him up, I didn't want him running in to find this man in my bed.

"We'll see," he said, kissing my breasts.

I tutted, pushing him back. "Gently," I warned.

He whispered to himself as he kissed along my breastbone and then down towards my navel.

"You have ideas above your station," I said, chuckling, as his lips tickled my skin. I'd promised myself that I wouldn't do this again, but I was glad of his company.

Afterwards, I let him sleep a short while. Turning from me, he kicked the blankets off in the heat. His legs and buttocks were no darker than mine; like tea made from milk. I stroked the muscles on his back and wondered if Ranjini suspected us. Stupid girl. But there was a part of me that wanted her to find someone better; Jagat was not a man to have long term.

I woke before anyone else, even Ranjini. Jagat had given me such a look when I'd told him to return to his own bed. Sat on the back doorstep, I calmly watched the dawn, perhaps my last Indian sunrise. *England will be like stepping out into the light, after skulking in the shade.* Everything I knew about England had come from Daddy's fables. Yet, I couldn't think of him without thinking too of a mango tree, or bandicoots, or mulligatawny.

I stood and went inside to wake the boys. Ushering them towards the kitchen, I told them to sit up at the table. I was about to go and find out what was keeping Ranjini when Maxwell asked, "Will we see Daddy in England?"

"No, my son, we've been through all this." I sat down next to him; Glen slid in between us, not wanting to miss out. "Daddy loves you – both. Like my daddy loves me. But he's not coming back, because of the war." I didn't know what else to say.

"But he might be in England," Maxwell added, "like when we lost Solomon and he found a way back to his kennel."

"Maybe. How about we get another doggy, would yourl like that?" They cheered and I got up and put some eggs on to boil.

By the servants' quarters at the back of the house, I heard Ranjini and Jagat speaking in their language. I don't know why I didn't make myself known. I stayed put, spying from the edge of the doorway. Ranjini was sat in the chair and Jagat stood next to her, rabbiting on. This was what they'd be, without me.

Then he spoke in English in a false high voice, ordering Ranjini to get this and do that, with his back straight and his arms folded. I realised he was mocking me. It was a cruel impression. Ranjini laughed and clapped her hands and then Jagat pulled her up out of the chair, into his arms. How talented he was. When he touched me, it felt like it was just for me, but look at him now. Pariah. I headed back to the kitchen.

After breakfast, I styled my hair into victory rolls, just like Vivien Leigh. All agreed it suited. Jagat carried our cases the short distance to the train station, employing a coolie for porterage. Ranjini prepared some food for the journey to Calcutta, then set about helping with my jewellery. She coaxed the bangles over my wrists and fastened the necklaces, making sure they were concealed underneath the collar and sleeves of my blouse.

"Lilly," Ranjini said, testing my name with tear-filled eyes and throwing her arms around me. I breathed in the scent of Daddy's room and told her it would soon be time.

When Jagat returned, I felt him trying to catch my eye, but I ignored him. By the front door, the boys were looking very pleased with themselves, all togged up – suit-boot-and-gramophone, as

Daddy used to say. I told them to keep their blazers on despite the heat; money was sown into the hidden pockets.

Once outside, the boys raced one another to the gate and back like rascal mutts kicking up the dust, and I called out to them not to get their clothes dirty. Joseph, our neighbour, and a handful of others, had come to see us off. Ranjini had insisted on accompanying us to the station but I told her no, and let her fuss over the boys one last time.

I held their hands as we walked away from Daddy's house. I'd planned on not looking back, but I couldn't help myself; they were waving us off our own land. Oh Daddy, we've lived our whole lives getting ready for England, let's hope England will be ready for us.

We walked out of the gate and turned towards the station. Then it hit me, like a shot to the back of the head. I let go of the boys' hands and stopped in my tracks. I felt the blood drain from my face. I was late. Weeks late. Please no! I, a nurse, and I'd not seen the signs: sickness, weight – my breasts. It was true. I felt it in my gut like some eel lurking in the shallows.

"Come on, Mamma," Maxwell said.

But how? When I lost my daughter – I knew it was a girl – they said I'd never bear a child again. Gordon's temper had seen to that. My head was reeling. It wouldn't take much to bring me to the ground now. I tried to think of a little garden with calm and birdsong.

And Jagat is so dark, people will see. England suddenly scared me. Don't know where I found my strength. I looked down at my boys, their faces searching mine. Everything had led to this.

"Come," I say, taking their hands. "Let's go home."

White-Bread Sandwiches
TOM HEATON

When the doors slid open, the four boys entered and processed smallest to tallest down the aisle with bags held aloft. They all had the same broad brow and the sharp Decan nose, like a lump of pinched putty. They wore camo print and T-shirts with slogans, shorts with deliberate rips and superfluous pockets, clean trainers with no socks – summer clothes bought in a spree the week after the cremation. They spaced themselves across the facing seats of the carriage, dropped their bags and slouched in the nook between seat and window or splayed against the upholstery, long legs angled sharply, arms dangling over seat edges.

They didn't talk much. Michael Decan scrutinised his comic and snickered at it and looked up at the others, hoping they'd ask him why, which they never did. Johan Decan watched the rush of pine trunks through the window, some cut clean with chainsaws and bleeding a garish orange sap. Occasionally he pointed out objects of interest to Edwin Decan. "Look, a red tractor, Edwin. It's pulling a rack thing. What do you think that is?" Edwin's pale watery eyes gazed earnestly at what he was shown. He was the youngest, only six. His blotched cheeks puffed with air. Johan continued his questions. "It's for making rows for seeds. When do you put the seed in? What time of year?"

"We'll eat nearer London," said Anthony Decan. He expected

no argument. He was almost a man: soft patchy stubble graced his chin, creeping in ragged lines along his jaw, and he was in his last year of school. "Remember what Mum said."

"What did she say?" Michael asked.

"If you eat sooner, you'll be hungry later," Anthony said.

"Doesn't make any sense," Michael said.

"Sure it does," Johan said. "You'll be hungry later. It's obvious."

At Woking the train started to fill. Some girls sat near them with canvas bags on their knees; they wore bright cherry lipstick and talked in urgent whispers. This was where he planned to eat, but the girls made Anthony self-conscious and even ashamed, and it wasn't until the others nagged him that he produced the cheese sandwiches made with soft white thick-cut bread. They were large and square and hadn't been halved, so required the use of both hands. They smelled sterile and steamy with a tang of yeast like fresh paint. The boys ate in silence, with an intensity to the way they bit and chewed the dough, like novices at a rite that hadn't yet lost its charm. None of them looked out of the window now, just at their own sandwich: their pristine square of white.

That morning little Edwin had been sent to the shop at the corner to buy the bread on his own for the first time, his fist buried in his pocket, where a ten-pound note was scrunched around a shopping list in his own clumsy handwriting: bread, cheese, margarine, pickle. He walked back along the shady side of the street with its privet hedges and low brick walls – roses about to hit the first bloom, buddleia already in flower – swinging the loaf high and singing a song from a TV show he used to watch, the tune carrying on the crisp air, until Anthony, waiting on the wall of their front garden, called him to hurry back.

Johan made the sandwiches the same way he'd seen his mother make them, scraping the margarine as thinly as he could over the bread and recycling the leftover globs for the next slice. He cut thin rectangles of the Cheddar and arranged them on the bread so there were no gaps. Then he handed the slices to

Michael, who dolloped on some pickle and spread it evenly, laying another slice of bread on top.

It was only the previous evening that they'd decided to go. Anthony had tapped on the door under the stairs and leaned into the long room behind it, the one their father used as a study, and which these days he left only to eat or sleep and sometimes not even then.

"We're going to see it tomorrow," he said.

"Come on in," his father said.

Anthony had to cross the threshold into that dark space; his father kept the curtains closed and never used the main light. The tip of his cigarette glowed amber. A layer of smoke hung from the ceiling and formed an inverted landscape of smooth hills and soft curling valleys. His father made a noise in his throat – a sort of grunt. "See what?" he said.

"The painting." Anthony didn't need to say any more than that.

His father was tall and top heavy, but as he turned his chair a quarter circle to face Anthony, he looked almost delicate. He dusted something off the knee of his corduroys and nodded, with half an eye on the pair of glowing monitors on his desk. Anthony braced himself to offer an invitation, for form's sake, but his father spoke first. "Do you like art, then?"

"Some art," Anthony said.

"I don't," his father said. "I can't be bothered with it." Something came alive on one of the monitors, and he jabbed at his keyboard in response. "I liked it when I was younger. I tolerated it. It was good for talking to girls." He blew smoke in the air. "Art or money?" he said as a challenge.

"What do you mean?"

"Which would you prefer, if you had to devote your life to one or the other?"

"Do I have to choose?" Anthony said.

"It's not a difficult question."

"I only said I liked art."

"Money, then, that's good. And you can go to a gallery on a Sunday, or to a theatre, pay your respects."

"Yes." But Anthony was not sure if he understood. "We were wondering if you wanted to come with us."

"No, you lot go," his father said. "I'm busy at the moment, can't really take a day out, and it's better that way, hmm?" His large thumb straightened a ridge of corduroy. "That's how it always was with those trips, wasn't it? Not really my thing."

Anthony waited.

"Oh, you need money," his father said. "I should have thought. Art needs money, same as always. How much?"

"Thirty for the train, another ten for food. There'll be some change."

"You should have said. Just say what you want, that's how business works. Business is better than art. Things mean what they mean. That's best in the end."

From his backpack, Michael Decan took a long, fine headscarf – dyed a vivid, almost violent, green – and held it against the train window so that sunlight filtered through it.

"Why've you got that?" asked Anthony, but Michael didn't answer. Instead he crushed it against his nose and mouth and breathed in through it.

Johan took the scarf and wound it round his head as tight as it would go and tucked it in like a turban. Anthony grinned, and Michael laughed out loud, but Edwin started to cry. Anthony crooked him in his arm and told the middle boys to put the scarf away. Edwin's glasses were steamed up and dirty, so Johan polished them, but Edwin shook his head and wouldn't take them back and sniffed against his eldest brother all the way into Waterloo, and Anthony breathed the musky, gummy-sweet scent of Edwin's scalp.

They were carried along in the flow through the Underground, Anthony holding Edwin's hand, the other two close enough behind to reach out and touch. They all knew the way. The dense air swaddled them and smelled of ground metal, cooking oil, baked mud. Trains screamed through hidden tunnels, rushing suddenly close to them and driving a sultry wind down the ancient corridors. Michael sang, "You put your left leg in, you put your left leg out," along the platform and kicked his leg over the drop to the tracks, and no one told him not to.

Outside they found themselves in London's blazing summer embrace of exhaust fumes and hot engine oil and the sweet stickiness of softened tarmac. Cars queued behind buses with heat shimmering from their bonnets. Bikes cut through the gaps. Tieless men in tailored suits swerved briskly around each other. Women with bare arms and soft golden hair and plain office skirts talked into mobile phones about what they were going to do that evening and who would be there. Everything was swirling and alive, bright and primary-coloured in the heat. There was a soundless pulse like a heartbeat; it pulsed in the bright things, in the fast-food cartons and the flashes of Lycra and the adverts for vitamin supplements on the sides of the buses.

The boys lingered at the fountains. Johan ran his hands through the water, Edwin and Michael climbed the base of a lion, Anthony let the sun rest on his face until he felt it burn.

Even Edwin knew the steps up to the gallery were serious. The boys looked straight ahead and not at one another, as solemn and silent as a funeral cortège, but where the coffin should have been, there was an absence that moved among them, that touched one boy and the next, until Johan skipped ahead and gestured them through the entrance with a low bow like a doorman.

When Anthony asked for Dr John Wilson FSA, the man at the information desk raised an eyebrow and consulted a laminated sheet of yellow paper and ran his finger down it, looking for the number. The Decan boys studied the rack of guidebooks while they waited.

Dr Wilson was tall and balding, wearing a banana-yellow shirt open at the neck. He had a stoop and bent forward nervously as if hinged at the hip, smiling and shaking his head at the same time. Anthony gave him the bag of books he'd taken from his mother's office that morning. "She asked us to return these." Among the books were loose-leaf papers, which Dr Wilson examined quickly. He read the first page and then flicked through to read later pages. The early pages were typed, but the later pages were written in their mother's tiny looping script in lines that slanted across the page.

Then Dr Wilson FSA made bashful conversation with them. He asked how everyone was, how their father was getting along. He seemed about to ask something else but decided against it. He crouched down to hear Edwin recount how he went to the shop by himself and clapped him firmly on the shoulder. "Splendid," he said. "Good man!" As if Edwin had scaled a mountain. "Have you come all this way just to return these old books?" he asked.

"We have to find one of the pictures," Anthony said. "She told us to."

The old man scratched at a point above his eyebrows. "Which picture?"

"*The Doge*, by Bellini."

Dr Wilson led them through the Renaissance halls, through rooms filled with vibrant reds and greens, rooms that smelled of ripeness: the sweet fruitiness of wood polish. People spoke in whispers and trod lightly, reverentially, but the floorboards groaned and creaked beneath their feet without restraint.

He hung back at the edge of the room so they'd find it themselves. Other gallery visitors shuffled from painting to painting, their heads bowed over audio guides that they fingered like prayer books, but the four boys stood still in hushed communion before the portrait. The Doge sat against a brilliant blue background. Soft, loose skin sagged under his neck. A string of heavy beads like chestnuts or ancient brown knucklebones hung below his collar. They studied the solemn expression, the curious hat which gripped his forehead and made him strangely hairless, the sunken cheeks and sad eyes which creased around the edges. The fine noble nose.

"The weight loss has actually fixed my nose," Anthony remembered his mother saying to friends gathered around the kitchen table, before taking a sip of whichever blended-up bunch of nutrients she was then on. "Saved on the price of a plastic surgeon, look." And she'd held her face to the side for them to admire the new sleekness of her profile.

The Doge's thin sallow lips were drawn into a grim smile.

"Is it a man?" Edwin asked.

"Yes," Michael said.

"It looks like her," Johan whispered.

Anthony nodded. "She said it would."

At home, Anthony picked the crusts of white bread out of the plastic bag. He thought about the picture of the Doge. It didn't look like his mother really. There was some likeness in the bloodless lips. Some ghost of her, too, in that strong but hairless brow. But his mother's skin was silky, not leathery like the Doge's, and hadn't aged into such serious lines.

His father emerged from the office under the stairs and squinted into the brightness of the kitchen. "How was it?"

"It was all right," Anthony said. He swept the crumbs from the counter surface into his open palm. He couldn't quite piece together his mother's face in his mind. He rolled the crumbs between his fingers; they'd become dry and hard.

"Did you find it?"

Anthony nodded.

"I suppose it wasn't easy," his father said.

"Dr Wilson showed us," Anthony said, though he knew that wasn't what his father meant. He held the crumbs over the gaping mouth of the bin, but his hand clutched around them. He had to rehearse the gesture mentally before he could open his fingers. He would teach his fingers to unclasp from things that were no longer needed. That was how a man must behave. He would relearn the old gestures. He had time. There was no hurry any longer. It was only a matter of waiting. He would wait, and the movement would come naturally, without thought, like remembering how to swing a loaf of bread high in the air on a crisp summer morning, like starting to sing again.

Bavaria

RUTH IVO

I started bleeding the moment lightning struck Berghain on the hottest night of the Berlin summer. I was standing in the middle of the dance floor, eyes closed, palms open to the sky, feeling the edges of myself dissolve into the pounding bass, when I sensed rather than saw the blinding flash that illuminated the cavernous turbine hall of the old power station. At the same time, I was dragged back into my body by an unmistakable twist somewhere low in my belly and the sensation of something hot trickling down my legs. The white safety lights flickered on overhead, flooding the darkness and killing the lasers' sweeping green searchlights, starkly revealing the faces of the bug-eyed ravers, who blinked about them in the unfamiliar glare, while the music thundered on.

I reached down and drew a finger up the inside of my thigh and looked at the glistening, ruby tip. *Fuck.*

Around me the dance floor accepted the night's new, bright order and continued its twitching, tribal stomp towards oblivion.

I wove through the sea of thrashing limbs to the unisex toilets, where I put out an SOS along the underground railroad of the few women scattered amongst the testosterone throng. Five minutes later a handful of supplies of various sizes were delivered to me by two helpful German girls and I shut myself inside one of the cubicles where I attempted to deal with my too-real body, punch-drunk as I was after ten hours under the club's sonic-anaesthetic.

The air con was down and soon the vast Temple of Techno was swampy with the steam of a thousand bodies. Skin became slick with sweat as clothes were soaked through and removed. I bought an icy bottle of Berliner at the bar and went to the balcony overlooking the main dance floor to watch the sea of naked flesh – a Hieronymus Bosch nightmare – in which I could almost see the currents of impulse and instinct ebb and flow.

I pushed my forefinger into the glass neck of the bottle and feeling it grip, let it hang suspended above the swarm below. I watched as it slid slowly down my finger, catching it at the last second as it fell.

Draining the dregs, I turned and headed upstairs to the Panorama Bar.

I was drifting through the crowd, dreamy with heat – here the music was less fierce, the bass more sensual – when a prickling awareness of a presence at my back made me turn around.

Behind me a beautiful boy with golden skin and hair stood swaying out of rhythm to the beat.

He smiled at me, revealing a row of perfect white teeth, and held out his hands. I tilted my head to one side and smiled back. Our hot fingers closed around one another's.

"The way you smile, I think you look like such a sweetheart," he said, his accent blurring the Ws into Vs.

His eyes danced and fluttered in the way of the Very High. He looked like a Hitler Youth poster boy.

"And you look like an angel," I said in the moments before we kissed.

I had an impression of hunger and salt.

"Come with me," he said. "I know a place we can go."

He led me downstairs and along a corridor towards The Darkroom, usually a pitch-black space where a distant stutter of strobe revealed in flashes the tangled bodies pumping in the dark, and your hand might touch bare flesh as you reached out to steady yourself. But now the room was deserted, transformed by the safety lights into a small, sparse cell strung with chains. Broken glass littered the floor. I looked at the boy and shook my head.

"You are right," he said. "I think you are too special to fuck with you like this, in this nightclub."

"Thank you," I replied. "Also I'm bleeding."

His eyes grew round, his mouth forming an O of comprehension.

We spent the rest of the night entwined in one of the secret booths on the side of the dance floor, battered by the bass as it shuddered through the walls, making out like teenagers in the pure white noise.

In the pauses in between, he attempted to tell me, over the ear-splitting music, of his life as a trainee at a *Waldkindergarten* in rural Bavaria.

"What's a *Waldkindergarten*?" I shouted.

"I am teaching kids in nature!" he shouted back.

"Seriously?" I laughed.

His face fell, suddenly grave. "I know something bad, but I don't know if to tell you."

"Tell me."

"Someone dies at this nightclub, one month ago. Here" – he gestured at the padded seat – "in this place where we sit. All night people think he is only sleeping. They carry him out in secret the next day."

I pictured the bouncers attempting to wake the curled body.

"Does it make you feel strange, or . . . ?" he asked.

"Well I'm sure he's not the first person to die here," I said. "At least he died having a good time."

"I think the same."

Eventually we fell asleep, wrapped around each other in a hot womb of sound, until he woke me at 9 a.m. to tell me he had to catch his bus back to Munich.

We parted company on the kerb outside the club, steam rising from our wet clothes like vampires vanishing in the new morning light.

I drove past him in the taxi on the way back to the apartment in Neukölln and turned to watch as he receded into the distance, a slender, tow-headed figure wandering alone into the city's concrete wasteland.

In the apartment I dropped a watermelon on the floor and lay down next to its shattered pink flesh on the cool kitchen tiles, pushing chunks of it into my mouth and staring at the ceiling as I waited for the humming in my bones and ears to dissipate.

My phone buzzed with a text: *The first message of the day is: I miss you.*

I squinted at it and laughed and sent back a parade of Xs in return.

And then I finished the watermelon, crawled to my bed, slept.

* * * * *

I flew back to London on the last day of August, packing up my memories of the long, strange summer. Every night in the weeks that followed, a painstakingly constructed message from the boy would appear on my phone, accompanied by pictures and videos of his home, his work, his little dog. Once there was a video of him smiling in a forest surrounded by a gaggle of blond tots all peering into the camera and greeting me by name. And always the words: *I miss you. I want to see you again.*

To my surprise, I enjoyed talking back. He was by now a disembodied presence, my fragmented memories of him reduced to a lingering impression – of his hand in my hair, pulling it until my back arched – that I kept returning to like a stuck record. The distance made the conversation intimate and unreal. I sent him a video of me drowning in the bath, my hair making black water snakes as the last bubbles rose, eyes open under the water. *You're beautiful*, he wrote in reply.

October brought with it slate skies and shorter days as the

chill autumn nights crept in and the last traces of sun faded from my skin. One day I looked in the mirror at my own pale face, trying to see beneath my skin to what he saw, and decided.

My thoughts kept me awake the night before I flew and I arrived early to the airport, blinking and shaky under the harsh neon lights of the departures hall. I used the extra time to visit Duty Free, where I stole a cashmere scarf from Burberry. More awake, I headed towards my gate.

I moved like a sleepwalker through the silent corridors of Munich airport, until finally I emerged into cool, grey daylight.

I looked around, searching for his face.

A boy in a hoodie, barely out of his teens, walked towards me eating a pretzel.

He smiled and while I was still registering my confusion, took my face in his hands and covered my mouth with salty pretzel kisses.

"My girl."

I searched for him inside the kiss, but it was over too quickly.

On the walk to the car park, my eyes slid sideways to study the boy beside me, scanning the contours of his features for clues. Reality bent and stretched, trying to accommodate the new version.

At his car I was greeted by the high-pitched barking of a malevolent-looking chihuahua that I recognised from the videos. It growled up at me from the passenger seat. It had odd, misted eyes like blind marbles.

"Shhh Lulu, shhh boy." He picked it up and planted a kiss on the creature's tawny fur, setting it on a sheepskin blanket in the back of the car.

"Why does he have a girl's name?"

"He has this name when I rescue him."

Inside the car Lulu scrabbled his way into my lap and attempted to mount my arm. The boy shook his head and muttered something in German, depositing him once more on the back seat. The little dog immediately crawled back and continued his assault, punctuating his thrusts with strangled, yapping yowls, his penis protruding like an angry red lipstick.

"He likes you," the boy said, laughing.

The boy lived in a gingerbread house that was one of a cluster of gingerbread houses in the middle of the Bavarian countryside. All around were fields just teetering on the edge of autumn, and in the distance, the darker green of pine forest. He told me that his parents had built the house themselves.

"And where are they now?"

"They are here," he said.

His father was a thin, stooped man of around sixty, his shoulders and neck following one another in the shape of an S. His mother had the same face as her son and the same slanted dark eyes, her silver hair hanging loose down her back. They both wore felt slippers with curling toes.

They looked at me as if an exotic animal had wandered into their hallway. His mother said: "*Spricht sie nicht Deutsch?*" And something else that I did not understand. The boy rattled off several brisk phrases to her and ushered me up a flight of stairs that were strewn, curiously, with red apples.

"What did you say to them?"

"I say that you are a very nice girl from a very good family," he said. "My mother is a lovely woman but she can also be evil."

He lived in a separate apartment on the second floor. The walls were painted a warm yellow and there were plants and books and artwork all around. He presented me with my own pair of curly-toed house shoes. I put them on and sat down on the sofa, contemplating my new elf-feet.

Around the apartment were little towers of concrete bricks that held candles of various shapes and sizes and I watched as he padded around lighting them, noting that his shoulders curved slightly forward. One day he too would become an S like his father.

When he had lit all the candles he came over and lay down with his head on my chest, his eyes closed.

"You are here," he said. "It feels like a dream."

I rested my hand on his hair and looked at his lovely profile. He had changed into a dark cashmere sweater and felt soft and warm. His mouth tasted clean and sweet.

After a while he said: "Come with me," and we slipped across the floor to his bedroom and the low wooden bed.

Not long after, recognising the feel of his golden skin, the air in the room expanded with desire and I caught it like a sail.

I woke the next day with Lulu's foul breath in my face as he snuffled pawing at my chest with his tiny claws. I pushed him away and sat up in bed trying to orientate myself. I remembered being kissed awake in total darkness, a voice telling me that it was morning and later, as I'd drifted back to sleep, hearing over and over: "My girl, oh my girl, my girl."

Bright sun shone through an open door leading to a balcony and I could hear the boy somewhere in the apartment. He came in holding a saucepan.

"I made chocolate tea. Please tell me if it's too hot for you, or too sweet."

I went out to the balcony in my felt slippers and one of his jumpers. He had arranged an elaborate breakfast of pastries, fruit and yoghurt on a wooden bench next to two cushions. I bit into a doughnut, sugar falling like snow onto his jumper, and leaned my head against the wooden wall, watching him as he poured the tea.

"I have something for you."

He held out a package wrapped in coloured paper and tied with twine. Inside was a leather-bound notebook.

"Maybe one day you will write our story inside," he said.

I opened the notebook and looked at blank pages.

"I have a present for you too," I said.

I gave him the Burberry scarf.

He looked at it gravely. "If it was very expensive then I

cannot accept it."

"Don't worry," I told him, "I stole it for you."

"Really?" He laughed and wound the scarf around his neck. "Then it is even more precious for me."

That afternoon we went for a drive. He called to the little dog as we got ready to leave.

"Is Lulu coming?" I asked.

"Do you like Lulu?"

"Of course," I said, arranging my mouth into something like a smile.

We drove to a tower like a pale cylinder, that was perched on a hill overlooking a river valley. Inside, the stone walls were lined with statues of great, blank-eyed angels, who stared down at us, their faces stern.

"It is the Tower of Liberation," the boy said, his voice echoing around the chamber.

"Liberation from what?"

"I don't know," he said, laughing. "I wanted to show you where I climbed."

I followed his gaze towards the glass ceiling two hundred feet above us.

"Up there?"

He nodded, grinning. "I stay here the night in my car and when it is near morning I climb up the outside to the top."

I imagined his distant silhouette pinned against the dawn sky.

"What did you do when you got there?"

"I lie down and I watch the sun rise."

My eyes came to rest on Lulu, who was pissing on the foot of one of the angels.

"And if you fell?"

"Then I fall."

We visited a sauna in a neighbouring small town, where he surprised me, steering me into one of the changing rooms, whispering filth and locking the door behind us. We had sex against the wall, while on the other side families chattered as they stashed their belongings inside the lockers.

Afterwards we sat in the silent steam room, observed through the veils of mist by the locals, who listened benignly as we giggled softly to one another in English.

We arrived back at his apartment as the sun was setting across the fields. I stood on the balcony and watched a wheeling flock of black birds flickering against the soft apricot sky. All was quiet but for their evening song.

I went back inside and joined the boy on the sofa. Lulu was asleep and we curled up together in uninterrupted silence as night crept into the room.

"I want to take a picture of us together," I told him.

I went to find my phone, then came back and lay down with him, flipping the viewfinder around and holding it up so we were looking at ourselves from above. The screen showed an image of two lovers, one dark and one fair, their faces open and peaceful. I took a picture and laughed at our innocent expressions.

"We don't look like ourselves."

"I don't know what to do with myself," he said.

And then he said: "I know."

The gun was in a special case. I'd never seen one before. I'd never realised what sensual objects they could be. Sleek and powerful, its surface had a deep granite sheen.

"It is a Luger," he said, "a very nice gun."

He started to tell me where it had come from but I did not hear the words. The gun had an aura of its own that demanded your complete attention.

I leaned back on him and we gazed up at the screen as he held the gun to my head, his arm wrapped around my neck. We mugged for the camera, his face twisted into a deranged grin, mine distorted in mock fear. I pressed the button and I examined the picture.

"It's perfect," I said.

I reached for the gun and felt my fingers close over the cool silky metal, but the boy pulled it away out of my reach.

"Careful," he said, "it might be loaded."

He opened the chamber. Inside, two golden bullets nestled like jewels.

He shook them into his palm and laid them carefully on the table, handing me back the gun, somehow drained of all its power. I looked down at the toothless weapon in my hand and searched for the appropriate response.

"You pointed a loaded gun at my head?"

He looked at me with a confused smile.

"Yes . . . but there's no danger? Because I love you."

The next day brought with it a perfect autumn sun that saturated the colours of the surrounding countryside until the trees and fields took on a hyper-real glow. I stood on the balcony looking out and drinking in the sensation of the warm light on my skin.

"The weather today is a gift," he said over breakfast, "and later I would like to fuck with you in nature."

We drove to an outdoor antiques market. Leaving Lulu in the car, we spent the morning strolling hand in hand as we walked amongst tables presided over by good-natured stallholders on which curios and treasures were laid out. An enormous man with calluses on his hands the size and texture of walnuts said something to the boy as I investigated an unfamiliar object on his stall.

"He says you are a sweet little mouse," the boy translated.

He insisted on buying me everything I liked the look of and I came away carrying a tiny articulated sewing machine made from tin, a carved wooden owl and a beautiful jewellery box covered in embroidered silk.

We bought bratwursts and beer from a small café and got gently drunk sitting in the shade amongst the roots of a broad-branched chestnut tree.

"Today is our last day together and tomorrow I will be

crying," he said.

I leaned my head on his shoulder and touched the soft place on his hand where his forefinger met his thumb.

We got back in the car and drove through the glowing countryside to the outskirts of a small lake that was bordered by flaming-yellow trees. Its surface showed a perfect mirror of the surrounding woods and the mountains behind and the burning blue sky above.

I stopped motionless next to the car and stared. I put my hand on his arm.

"Wait. I just want to look for a minute."

My head felt swollen with bright air and light. Untranslatable thoughts seemed to sing somewhere above me. I closed my eyes. Far away from myself, the word *high* rose like a balloon.

Lulu started to yap.

"We will take Lulu to walk around the lake," said the boy.

I felt the feeling start to slip. I grasped for it but it had already gone.

Something like grief welled in my chest and I fell into sullen silence as we followed the little dog which waddled along the grassy bank next to the water.

"Are you OK?" the boy asked. "Your face is sad-looking."

I nodded in reply, lost in loss.

He stopped suddenly, his eyes wide with alarm.

"What is it?" I asked.

"The car keys. I think I leave them inside?"

I looked at him, uncaring.

"I will check. Lulu stay."

He bounded away, back towards the trees where we had parked.

Left alone, the little dog and I regarded one another. Lulu's mossy eyes stared through me and he started to pant.

"Fuck off," I said as he came snuffling over to me. "Don't even think about it."

Straddling my foot, he started to hump my ankle. I shook

him off and the force of it sent him skittering backwards.

"I will kick you into the fucking lake," I told him.

The little dog started to bark.

I looked at Lulu and I looked at the icy water. I took a step towards him and he backed towards the verge, his high-pitched yaps echoing across the lake's pristine hush.

"Shhh," I said and took another step.

Lulu's stumpy legs scrabbled for purchase where the grass dropped off to a steep slope leading down to the water. Murky reeds tangled underneath and I wondered if chihuahuas could swim like other dogs, or if their barrel-shaped bodies would overwhelm their stunted limbs and drag them under.

Lulu was going crazy now, baring his tiny teeth and snarling.

"You're a monster," I told him, and kicked him into the lake.

He hit the water with a dull splash. Ripples rolled out, distorting the lake's green glass surface. The sky's reflection folded and disappeared.

I watched the little dog for a while, his ineffectual paws paddling frantically as he struggled to stay afloat, his pink-ridged mouth spasming, his barks muted now as if someone had turned the volume down.

A deep quiet settled inside of me. The only sound was a delicate splashing and the strangled gasps of lungs the size of a thumb. I looked across the lake to the still grey mountains beyond.

"Lulu!"

The boy sprinted across the grass.

I stepped quickly away from the edge and turned towards him, pointing dumbly at the little dog in the lake.

The boy splashed down the bank and reached Lulu in two strides, scooping him from the water.

Deposited back on the grass, the bedraggled creature sprang towards me barking hysterically, his eyes bulging white in their sockets. The boy hauled himself out, holding onto his hand, which bore the bloody pinpricks of Lulu's teeth.

"What happened?"

"I can't swim," I told him.

Lulu was gurgling and frothing. I looked at him with distaste.

The boy looked at the little dog and then at me.

"Are you angry, or . . . ?" he asked. He was looking at me strangely.

I exhaled. "I'm not angry," I said, laying my words out like cards, "I'm impatient. And right now I'm wondering if you're going to take me into the trees and fuck me while the sun is still shining or if we're going to keep walking the fucking dog for the rest of the day."

The boy burst out laughing. "You are amazing right now," he said. "Before you were amazing yes, but now even more so."

And he went to lock Lulu in the car.

The next morning I packed my bag in the cool dawn light as he watched me from the bed, before carefully wrapping the silk-covered jewellery box, which held the rest of my treasures, in the brown paper the boy had provided. I sealed the box and wrote my name and address on it.

"You'll post this to me?"

"On my way back from the airport," he said smiling. "You won't have to wait."

I said goodbye to his parents in the downstairs hallway. His mother had appeared with her head wrapped in a towel, and gave me a bag of red apples to take for the journey. His father put both his hands on my shoulders and said something to me in German.

"He is telling you to be happy and to be healthy," the boy translated.

In the car on the way to the airport I told him: "You've made me happy."

The boy kissed his hand three times and pressed it over my mouth.

He waited at the top of the escalator while I stood in the queue for airport security. I looked back at him and he traced the path of a tear down his cheek.

I folded my fingers into a silent gun, pointed it at him and fired, before blowing him a kiss over the smoking barrel, making him laugh.

I smiled at him and thought of the other gun with its two golden bullets, tucked away safely inside the jewellery box and wrapped in brown paper, and wondered how long it would take to arrive.

And then I turned and walked away, holding out my open passport to the waiting security officer.

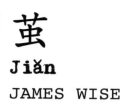

Jiǎn

JAMES WISE

Sun Phase One

Jiànyǔ inched his way along the main branch towards the Silk
Pavilion. He was used to being summoned by the Magistrate,
but not this early. His skinny green-and-yellow body humped
and arched and his stumpy legs scrabbled, pushing him forward.

On a broad leaf outside the Pavilion, a group of young pre-
shedders were sat round in a circle listening to Yè. Jiànyǔ stopped
for a moment and leaned against the stem of an overhanging
frond. Like Jiànyǔ, Yè had broad dabs of dark red on the sides
of her head, framing her green face and ending in points on her
chin. These false-eyes were sharper on Yè, though, more angular,
and striking, giving her a severe expression.

An iridescent Silk Weaver was sat up on his hind legs,
waving a shiny black foreleg in the air. "But Miss, *why* do we
shed our skins four times?"

"Well, what do *you* think?" asked Yè.

"I dunno, Miss." The little caterpillar, suddenly finding
himself on the spot, looked around at the others.

"Could it be because we find the number four all around us?"

"Like the seasons?"

"Yes, very good. And all the caterpillars we share the Tree
with – the Weavers and the Stingers, the Metalmarks and the
Dew Mouths."

Jiànyǔ saw Yè look from caste to caste, sitting in their groups, as she listed them. He caught her eye and winked. The raised spots running down her smooth green body grew a little pinker.

"So," Yè said, returning her attention to the class, "that's why we must treasure the time we have between each shedding and, no matter how hungry we might be, eat as little as we can. That way we live much longer, giving ourselves more time to –" Yè paused for a moment. Jiànyǔ noticed she'd been secretly spooling a silk ball with her spinnerets. She flicked it over her head and into the group. "– play!"

The class cheered and butted the soft milky ball to each other with their heads.

Jiànyǔ smiled and moved on. He went past the Pavilion's silk spans, stretched between the branches, and up to the flat fan of leaves where the Magistrate would be waiting for him.

Jiànyǔ found the Magistrate on the easternmost leaf of the Gathering Place.

"We've got another one," the Magistrate said through his pale-yellow maw, "and already infected too." He was standing by a swollen mass lying on its side. The pupa, bloated and shot through with white streaks, was quite old, maybe as many as three or four sun phases.

"Plenty of time for a Reaper to have injected its eggs," Jiànyǔ said. He moved closer and inspected the body. It still bore strips of dried silk but where it'd flaked off, eroded by wind and rain, pallid segments showed through. Jiànyǔ traced a pattern of faded pink spots with a tentative foreleg. He looked at the Magistrate.

"Yes," the Magistrate said. "We're certain it's her."

Jiànyǔ looked back down across the leaves to the Pavilion. Yè and her class were still playing with the ball.

"Where did you find her?" Jiànyǔ asked.

"A Weaver found her two branches down. It took a long time to spin enough silk to haul her back up."

Jiànyǔ looked up into the criss-crossed canopy.

"Yè's sister's been missing for some time, hasn't she?" the

Magistrate asked.

Jiànyǔ gritted his mandibles. "Not missing, exactly. Yè said she'd gone to join the Myriad."

The Magistrate shook his head, making the short spines running down his back quiver. "They've got something to do with this, I'm sure of it," he said. "They're forcing these poor twice-shed and even once-shedders to their deaths."

"But how? What for?" Jiànyǔ asked.

The Magistrate just shrugged a few of his foremost shoulders.

Jiànyǔ tentatively peeled the flaking pupa with his jaws.

"What's that?" the Magistrate asked.

"It's like a cocoon, only it isn't her silk. This was spun by a Metalmark, you can tell by the texture and, here, the spinneret markings."

"That was on the others. We thought it was just weathering."

Before Jiànyǔ could reply, they were interrupted by the Undertaker inching his way towards them, with a brush in his mouth and two assistants trailing behind with pots of ochre. The Magistrate greeted the Undertaker and Jiànyǔ nodded to him.

"Magistrate Héng. If you're done here, we need to attend to the poor girl before the ceremony," he said through thick black bristles that covered his face and most of his body.

"We're not quite finished –"

"Of course," the Magistrate said. "Undertaker, we want to give her the most reverent ceremony we can. And quick too – before the damn thing hatches and infects anyone else."

The Undertaker nodded and issued instructions to his assistants, who put down their pots and set about preparing the body.

Sun Phase Two

Yè lived out on a limb, a branch above the Gathering Place. Jiànyǔ found her sitting on the tip of her leaf looking out through the trees and sat down next to her, slightly back from the edge. Steam rose from the forest floor, damp from recent rains, as the morning sun broke through the dense canopy. Jiànyǔ absorbed the scent of dank soil and drying vegetation drifting up to him.

"The monsoon is ending," Yè remarked.

"Yes."

"They'll be gathering the raindrops." Yè looked down, her pale eyes surveying the ferns far below.

"Yes."

"And preparing for the festival."

"Yes," Jiànyǔ said.

Yè looked at him, her green face flushed with yellow. "She didn't kill herself," she said quietly.

"I know. It was like the others."

"Héng is claiming they're all suicides, or the Myriad is force-feeding them, or . . ."

Jiànyǔ put a foreleg around Yè's middle segment and said, "The community will believe whatever Magistrate Héng tells them. Look at this." Jiànyǔ regurgitated the silk strip he had managed to secrete earlier and smoothed it out on the leaf.

Yè stared at it. "Was this found on the others too?"

Jiànyǔ nodded. "And I noticed something else," he said, pointing to some faint black markings just visible on the material.

"Are those . . . *characters*?"

"Some kind of inscription, yes, but not in any language I can read."

Yè peered at the writing. "Me neither," she said. "Old Téngfēi might know. We should try to find him."

"If Téngfēi's the leader of the Myriad like Héng claims, he might know what happened to Qiū too."

"Or had something to do with it," Yè said, clicking her mandibles.

"One thing at a time, Yè." Jiànyǔ patted her middle segment. "The ceremony's this afternoon."

"Will you take me?"

"I came to get you."

Yè hooked a silk thread to the leaf and made to start weaving herself down.

"Mind if we go down the trunk?" Jiànyǔ asked.

"Of course, Jiànyǔ. Sorry, I was forgetting."

Rain began to fall as Jiànyǔ and Yè approached the Gathering Place. The leaves above offered some shelter, but the fat drops bounced and splashed, showering the crowd. Yè stopped.

"The whole community's here," she said.

"You'll be all right, Yè." Jiànyǔ looked at her, widening his false-eyes sympathetically.

Together they made their way through the rows of caterpillars; past a red mass of Stingers, their spines collapsed, smoothed and turned down in respect. Past the Tent Weavers, whose iridescent bodies were dulled by the grey cloud. At a normal service they'd stop now and join the Moon Weavers, their own kind, sitting still in bright-green rows, but today they would be with the Dew Mouths at the front. Magistrate Héng, sat with his Administrators, had kept two places free.

"Looks like the monsoon's not quite done with us yet," the Magistrate said.

Yè smiled weakly at him.

The congregation faced the northernmost leaf of the Gathering Place. The Cenotaph, a slender structure of twigs bound together with spirals of silk, stood there tall and straight in the rain. Jiànyǔ wondered how many times the frame and silk windings had been replaced over the seasons. It had been cleared of moss and was decorated with purple seeds and dusted with pollen. At its base was a woven platform of green strips, surrounded by dark-red berries, where Qiū's body would be lain.

Jiànyǔ took one of Yè's forelegs in his and patted it gently. The murmur of the crowd quietened and then ceased as the Priest took up his place in front of the Cenotaph. His long, wild white hair stuck out in all directions despite the damp. The hair hid the Metalmark's entire body but his brown face and little black eyes stuck out clearly and surveyed the ranks of caterpillars.

"We are gathered here today to pay our respects to one of our fallen sisters." The Priest paused to look at Yè.

Jiànyǔ felt her shrink back under the scrutiny.

"I would like to recite, now, a passage from the *Jueju of Life*. A fitting passage, I think, and one to remind us all of our time and place here."

The leaf swayed slightly as the caterpillars bowed their heads as one and the Priest began his recital.

> *"Silk threads strum in the soft breeze.*
> *Seven sisters, spinning yarns*
> *Strung from the very first stars,*
> *Hear our tale, as the Year turns.*
>
> *Angels of Life scatter eggs*
> *As jade orbs on emerald leaves;*
> *We caterpillars emerge*
> *To live out bright but brief lives.*
>
> *Though pupation is the end,*
> *We can stave the Reaper Moth –*
> *Eat less! Pray more! – 'fore our time*
> *Comes to spin the cerecloth.*
>
> *Overconsumption is death;*
> *We chew our way to green ends.*
> *Abstinence is key to life,*
> *For all we leave are legends."*

The Priest then nodded to the Undertakers, who were huddled in a circle on the far side of the eastern leaf. They reached down and lifted Qiū onto their shoulders. Yè couldn't look, but Jiànyǔ turned to follow them as they passed around the congregation, to the south, the west and the north. They laid Qiū's body on the platform at the foot of the Cenotaph and ushered themselves back to their place. Qiū had been painted perfectly, her body the same deep shade of red as the berries around her.

"The departed has been adorned according to the rites of sky-burial," the Priest announced. "We deny the Reaper the chance to claim her and call on the Sunbird to take her from us and on to the next life." He beckoned to Yè.

As she made her way to say her final goodbyes to Qiū, the Priest turned back to the crowd. "I ask you to think of your loved ones, to give thanks for this life and remember, no matter how hungry you may be, we owe it to each other to live a life of abstinence and serve long, productive lives."

Magistrate Héng and a few of the Administrators nodded emphatically. The rain eased and a little sun shone through the clouds and leaves. Despite the silence, nature played its own indifferent song; mosquitoes buzzed, a breeze swayed the branches sending down more raindrops, and cicadas started up their thrumming. Jiànyǔ heard the shrill call of the Sunbird.

The Priest escorted an ashen Yè back to her place and joined the Dew Mouths on the other side of the aisle. The Sunbird called again, louder this time, and a murmuring grew amongst the crowd, silenced only by a glare from the Priest. Then, in a whirl of dark feathers and a flash of turquoise the giant bird was upon them and, in a moment, Qiū's body was gone.

Sun Phase Three

"You didn't have to come, you know," Jiànyǔ said to Yè as they crawled up the rough bark of the trunk. "You've been through so much, you should be resting."

"Qiū was my sister. I have to find out what happened."

"It could be dangerous, Yè."

"What, you mean like sheer drops and dizzying heights?" Yè chided.

Jiànyǔ stared at her, open-jawed.

"Two spinnerets are better than one," Yè said, a gleam in her eye. She spun another thread, tied it around Jiànyǔ's middle and inched ahead.

Jiànyǔ resisted the urge to look down and crept after Yè. Even at this height mists hung in the air, scattering shafts of golden sunlight. Ahead were circles of vines, where an orchid had wound its stem around the trunk. They clambered over the smooth, green fibres, as white-and-purple angular flowers towered above them. A sweet, wispy fragrance enveloped Jiànyǔ.

"They're beautiful," breathed Yè.

Out of the corner of his eye, Jiànyǔ saw one of the flowers move the opposite way from the others in the breeze.

"Yè, I think . . . Get out of the way!" Jiànyǔ pushed Yè aside just as what looked at first like the edge of a petal stabbed down into the vine where Yè had been. Jiànyǔ rolled out of the way as another pink leg jabbed at him. A flower seemed to detach itself from the orchids and stalked towards them. The creature swivelled its triangular head, purple dots for eyes fixed on the caterpillars.

Jiànyǔ felt toxins coursing through his skin, pulsing into the tufts of black hair that protruded from red bumps running down his body. If only I were a Stinger, he thought, then I could fight back and not just taste vile.

The mantis made up its mind and turned towards Yè.

"Jiànyǔ," she yelled, "what do I do?"

Jiànyǔ saw vicious barbs running down the backs of the creature's legs and along the flanks of its upturned purple abdomen.

"Over here," Jiànyǔ shouted. "Hey you, not her, me. I'm much tastier."

The mantis turned, fixed both dots on Jiànyǔ.

"Run, Yè," Jiànyǔ called.

The mantis raised one of its thorn-sharp front legs.

"I'm not leaving you."

"Get out of here –"

In a blur of pink and white, the mantis stabbed its leg down into Jiànyǔ with lightning speed, piercing his hind segment and pinning him to the trunk.

It raised its other leg.

Jiànyǔ peered up at the merciless face staring down at him. Something moved behind the creature's head. Something green. Yè had climbed up over the mantis and was aiming her spinnerets downwards. She fired. A stream of silk splattered its head and covered its eyes. It gnashed its mandibles and writhed and raised its front legs defensively. The barbs tore Jiànyǔ's flesh as the leg pinning him down was withdrawn. Jiànyǔ cried out as green hemolin splashed from the wound and pooled around him.

Yè fell from the swaying mantis' head and rolled towards Jiànyǔ. They watched as it pitched and staggered and stabbed its forelegs blindly.

They lay very still until it was gone.

Jiànyǔ clenched his jaw as Yè wrapped thick silk bandages around his hind segments.

"That should stop the bleeding for now," Yè said. She tied more silk threads to Jiànyǔ's midsection and bound him tightly behind her. She started inching down the trunk, away from the orchids.

"What are you doing?" Jiànyǔ asked.

"Getting you home. To a healer."

"But what about finding Téngfēi?"

"I'm not losing you as well," Yè said.

"Téngfēi's a healer as well as a scribe. Maybe he can help?"

"We don't even know if he's still up there. No one's seen him in many moon phases. It's too risky with your injury." She humped her way down the trunk. "Stupid thing you did." Her midsection arched and lowered, arched and lowered. "But thank you."

Jiànyǔ gazed back up through the canopy as he was dragged and bumped back down the trunk.

"Qiū must have fallen from up there," he said.

"Why do you say that?"

"She'd been cocooned and exposed to the elements for at least a few sun phases. If she'd been in the village, someone would have seen her."

"But she was found *below* us."

"Yes, but not hanging there. Fallen."

"And someone else must have spun the silk around her with

the writing on it, I suppose," Yè said.

"Which doesn't make any sense. I can't help thinking . . ."

"What?"

"That it might have been a message. A message meant for –"
Jiànyǔ heard a shrill call in the distance.

Yè froze. "Is that . . . ?"

"Don't move," Jiànyǔ breathed.

The call came again, louder this time. A shadow fell across
them.

"Jiànyǔ, it's the –" but before Yè could finish there was a
whirl of dark feathers and a flash of turquoise. The Sunbird
snatched Yè in its long, curved beak and flew upwards, with
Jiànyǔ swinging by silk threads below. He could see down. All
the way to the forest floor. The world spun and went black.

Sun Phase Four

Jiànyǔ was sure he'd opened his eyes, but whether he opened or
closed them he saw nothing but darkness.

"So, this must be pupation," he said out loud, "entombed in
dark silk for ever." He shivered.

"I prefer to think of it as just a phase," a voice said.

"Who . . . who's that?" Jiànyǔ asked.

"A friend," the voice said.

"Where's Yè? Is she OK? Is she . . . ?"

"Easy now, you've had quite a shock. Light, please."

A blue glow appeared above Jiànyǔ. Then another and
another. He was in a small, gloomy space. Dried, brown leaves
formed a pointed roof above him, supported with twigs and
dried silk. Glow-worms clung to the ceiling, their abdomens
emitting the soft blue light. He turned to where the voice had
been coming from and let out a cry.

Crouching next to him was a giant caterpillar, but one that
looked like it was made from black bone. Two knobbled, curving
black antennae as long as its body protruded from its forehead.
Two more rose from the back of its head, rising almost to the
ceiling and ending in tight curls. Smaller spines ran down its

back. Its body was flanked by peach-coloured blotches that met huge, pale false-eye patterns on the sides of its head. It was using its two front forelegs to stir something in a seed husk.

"Don't worry, I'm used to it. Téngfēi. And you must be Jiànyŭ." Clasping a brush made from dried leaf fibres, Téngfēi dipped it in the husk and applied the substance to Jiànyŭ's hind segment. Jiànyŭ felt a burning sensation and winced.

"Téngfēi? But you're a Metalmark."

"Is that what the Priest told you? Let me guess. He said I'm just a crazy old hermit with wild white hair, eking out a solitary existence in the high branches?"

"Pretty much."

"Magistrate Héng and that Priest sure know how to keep things just the way they like them."

"How do you know my name?" Jiànyŭ asked.

"Your friend, Yè. That's her name, isn't it? Means *leaf*. Not very imaginative parents, but poetic, I'll grant, if you put her and her sister's names together."

"Autumn Leaf," Jiànyŭ sighed.

"She's fine," Téngfēi said. "She's outside. You can see her when we're done here."

"But how –?"

"All in good time, Jiànyŭ, all in good time."

Téngfēi helped Jiànyŭ up and led him outside. They emerged from a pagoda made of dried leaves and silk that stood in the centre of a large hollow in the Tree. More glow-worms lit the space from above. Around them were caterpillars of all shapes, sizes and colours; most were feasting and gorging themselves on piles of green leaves.

A red-and-green Puss Mouth with a square face was dipping a brush in pots of ochre with its mouth and painting spirals, dots and patterns on one wall.

A Metalmark, long hairs blackened and grubby, stood in front of a canvas of silk, stretched between two twigs, writing characters in black ink.

By the entrance, a Bagworm sat strumming an instrument made from half a cicada shell strung with strands of silk.

Téngfēi led Jiànyǔ through the entrance into the daylight and onto the branch in front of the hollow. In the centre lay Qiū's cocoon, Yè hunched next to it.

Seeing Jiànyǔ, she rushed over and embraced him with every single one of her forelegs. "You're OK," she cried.

"You're alive," he replied. "I don't know how, but you're alive."

Yè turned and looked up. Jiànyǔ followed her gaze. On a branch above was a round nest of twigs and bits of bark. The Sunbird sat in the centre, gulping down red berries.

Jiànyǔ, open-jawed, turned to Téngfēi.

"He was quite easy to tame, given a steady supply of berries."

Jiànyǔ edged back from Qiū's cocoon. "But when that thing hatches . . . aren't you worried it'll infect you?"

Téngfēi laughed. "Jiànyǔ, that 'thing' is no monster."

Yè took one of Jiànyǔ's forelegs in hers. "It's Qiū, Jiànyǔ. It's Qiū in there."

"I don't understand."

Téngfēi and Yè looked at each other. "The Puss Mouth" – Yè gestured to the hollow – "he paints the patterns of every caterpillar here. Once they hatch and fly away, he records the patterns on their wings. He's found a way to identify every one after they . . . change."

"It's not Puss *Mouth*," said Téngfēi, "it's Puss *Moth*. Not Dew Mouth, as Héng would have you believe, it's Dew Moth. You and Yè and the rest of the Moon Weavers, you are Luna Moths, perhaps the most spectacular in all the forest."

"But . . . but that means . . . we've been . . ."

"Yes," Téngfēi said. "That's why we tamed the Sunbird. It was too late for some of your kin, but we've saved hundreds now. We bring them up here, allow them to hatch and fly away."

"And the others?" Jiànyǔ asked. "The young who've joined you here, gorging themselves and growing fat, hastening their –"

"Deaths? Is that what you were going to say? We spread messages, so once they learn the truth they can decide for themselves. Brave souls like Qiū agree to be lowered down so that others may hear the good news, knowing that another bird may take them or Héng might even have them killed."

Jiànyǔ produced the fragment of silk he'd found on Qiū.

"Ah yes," Téngfēi said. "Let's see.

Crawl, our cruel rulers.
I fly to a better place.
You will listen now.

Hear trees in the wind,
Feel soft light inside your heart;
You are the angel.

Shed your skin four times,
Travel to the Cenotaph;
I will not be there.

From where does life stem?
Who can explain its branches
Once upon a time?"

"I don't understand," said Jiànyǔ. "Why all this cryptic stuff? Why not just come down and tell us?"

"I tried that, many moon phases ago," said Téngfēi. "Héng and that Priest of his had me banished, claimed I was crazy. I lived up here on my own for a long time, but eventually was joined by more and more misfits, all the Myriad brethren who wouldn't fit neatly into Héng's castes."

"But that's no reason to hasten your deaths or 'change' or whatever."

"Don't you see, Jiànyǔ?" Yè pleaded. "It's beautiful. We don't die, we change and we fly away."

Qiū's cocoon sat immobile on the branch, a droplet-shaped husk swaddled in silk. Veins and the suggestion of a wing curling towards the tip. A berry to the Sunbird, a threat to the community. And a sister to Yè. Jiànyǔ sighed. "We have to tell them," he said. "Put a stop to the sky-burials."

"Héng will never allow it," Téngfēi said.

"We'll see about that," Jiànyǔ replied.

Sun Phase Five

The Metalmark's long white hair, tips smeared with ink, blew in the breeze as he lay on the edge of the branch, peering downwards. He was holding one of his little black eyes to a seed husk. A raindrop wobbled underneath.

"What do you see?" Téngfēi asked.

"We've got another one," the Metalmark said. "They're gathering near the Pavilion."

"Let me see," Jiànyǔ said. The Metalmark handed him the seed. Jiànyǔ put it to his eye and looked down. The raindrop magnified the view. He could make out little bodies sitting in rows near the Cenotaph. The Priest, a mere smudge of white, was crawling up to the northernmost leaf. "It's time," Jiànyǔ said.

"Are you sure about this?" Téngfēi asked, as he finished strapping Jiànyǔ, Yè and Qiū's cocoon to the Sunbird's back.

"Thank you," Yè said. "Thank you for everything, but Jiànyǔ's right. We can't let this go on."

Téngfēi swung his head, slapping the Sunbird's tail with his stalks. Its wings thundered and it rose into the air with a shrill call.

Jiànyǔ groaned.

Yè laughed. "Got to get used to flying if you're going to be a Luna Moth."

"I'm never eating again," Jiànyǔ moaned.

The Sunbird swooped down through the canopy, branches flashing by. Jiànyǔ gritted his jaw as greens and browns blurred past.

They flew in low over the Cenotaph and landed almost on top of the Priest, who fell backwards in a mass of tangled white hair and stared up, jaws gaping.

Jiànyǔ saw Héng and his Administrators in the front row shrink back. Red Stingers, spines spread and primed, rushed forwards to guard the congregation.

Yè clambered off the Sunbird's back and helped Jiànyǔ down. He winced as his bandaged abdomen rested on the leaf. Together, they unfastened Qiū's cocoon and carried her towards the centre of the Gathering Place.

The crowd gasped.

The Sunbird picked a bright-red berry from the base of the Cenotaph, gulped it down and flew off.

"What is the meaning of this?" Héng shouted.

"Everyone," Yè called, "we've got something to tell you."

"Don't listen to these heretics," the Priest cried.

"Arrest them!" Héng ordered.

The Stingers edged forward, spines pointed ahead, venom dripping from their tips. But the crowd surged past the guards, little pre-shedders on the backs of older caterpillars; Weavers, Metalmarks and Dew Mouths huddled around Jiànyǔ and Yè. The Stingers, uncertain, looked around and had to retract their spines before they stung someone by accident.

Jiànyǔ recognised the little iridescent Silk Weaver from Yè's class atop his mother's back.

"What do you want to tell us, Miss?" he asked.

Jiànyǔ and Yè shared a look. Jiànyǔ took a deep breath and began. He recounted how they'd found the writing on Qiū's cocoon. Their journey up the Tree, the mantis attack, which drew gasps and moans, as he pointed to his green-soaked bandages.

Yè joined in, telling of her time with Téngfēi and how the Myriad had tamed the Sunbird. What he had told her.

The crowd was silent.

"So you see," Jiànyǔ said, gesturing to Qiū's cocoon with a foreleg, "pupation isn't death and the Moths aren't parasites laying their eggs in us – they *are* us."

Yè passed around the silk cloth, painted faithfully with Qiū's markings, as they would be translated onto her wings. "The Puss

Mouth – I mean Puss Moth – he does this for each of them," she said. "All your loved ones, taken by the Sunbird, have been charted by the Myriad."

Murmurs ran around the crowd, growing into shouts and cries.

The Undertaker, in his place over on the eastern side of the leaf, shook his head, black bristles quivering. An assistant patted one of his shoulders gently.

Some once-shedders, skulking at the back, started to chew on the leaves of the Gathering Place.

"Sacrilege!" the Priest yelled.

"Do not hasten your –" Héng began, but the crowd swarmed over him. Weavers tied his forelegs with silk threads and wrapped a noose around his neck. The Priest backed away, uttering fragments from the *Jueju of Life*, but they tied him up too, and gagged him. The pair were dragged past the Cenotaph towards the edge of the Gathering Place.

"No, stop!" Jiànyǔ cried. "They didn't know what they were doing." But it was no use; the crowd ignored him.

The cocoon began twitching.

"Everyone, look," Yè shouted, pointing at the cocoon.

It trembled and a split ran down its side. Something started to emerge, unfurl, and uncrease.

The crowd fell silent.

The once-shedders stopped chewing.

Héng and the Priest stopped struggling.

Giant wings flapped in the sunlight. They were a soft, velvet green, framed by pink and orange. The tails were thin and long, growing redder and ending in gold tips.

Qiū flapped her wings. A pattern of pink spots spiralled towards the abdomen. The same pattern as in the painting.

Yè called out, "Qiū, Qiū, it's Yè, your sister."

Qiū flapped harder and lifted into the air. She fluttered all around the crowd, over the eastern leaf, to the south, the west, the north, and hovered over Yè, her feather-like antennae quivering.

Then she rose higher and flew away.

Notes on Contributors

Jenn Ashworth's first novel, *A Kind of Intimacy*, was published in 2009 and won a Betty Trask Award. On the publication of her second, *Cold Light* (Sceptre, 2011), she was featured on the BBC's *The Culture Show* as one of the UK's twelve best new writers. Her third novel, *The Friday Gospels*, was published in 2013, and her fourth and most recent, *Fell*, in 2016 (both Sceptre). Jenn lives in Lancashire and teaches creative writing at Lancaster University.

Alan Beard is a short-story writer with two collections: *Taking Doreen Out of the Sky* (Picador, 1999, also available on Kindle) and *You Don't Have to Say* (Tindal Street Press, 2010). He has won the Tom-Gallon Trust Award for best short story, and his work has featured in many magazines and anthologies, including *Critical Quarterly*, *Malahat Review*, *The London Magazine*, *Telling Stories Volume 3*, *Best Short Stories 1991* and *Best British Short Stories 2011*, as well as on BBC Radio 4. He has been a member of the Tindal Street Fiction Group for over thirty years.

Julia Bell is a writer and Course Director of the Creative Writing MA at Birkbeck. She is the author of three novels – most recently, *The Dark Light* (Macmillan, 2015) – and co-editor of *The Creative Writing Coursebook* (Macmillan, 2001) as well as three volumes of short stories, the latest being *The Sea in Birmingham* (Tindal Street

Fiction Group, 2013). She also takes photographs and writes poetry, short stories, occasional essays and journalism.

Dane Buckley has an MA in creative writing from Birkbeck. He has read his stories at MIRLive, had work performed at Liars' League, been an editor for Issue 9 of *The Mechanics' Institute Review*, and written for *Gay Times*. He recently won a place on Escalator 2017, a talent development scheme run by Writers' Centre Norwich; he is being mentored by Tahmima Anam. A child of emigrants, Dane writes about the resilience, charm, humour and tragedy of those on the move. He works at the London Irish Centre and is currently writing his debut novel. "The Last Empress of Calcutta" is his first printed publication. @daneacle

Madeline Cross graduated from the Birkbeck Creative Writing MA in 2015 and was one of the editors for *The Mechanics' Institute Review* Issue 13. She is currently based in Edinburgh and is working on her first collection of short stories. Her stories have previously been published in *MIR12*, *Rattle Tales*, *Pea River Journal*, *Structo* and *The Honest Ulsterman*.

Sarah Evans has had over a hundred stories published in anthologies, magazines and online. Fiction prizes won include: Words and Women, Winston Fletcher, Stratford Literary Festival, Glass Woman and Rubery. Other publishing outlets include: the Bridport Prize, Unthank Books, *Riptide*, *Shooter* and *Best New Writing*. She has also had work performed in London, Hong Kong and New York.

Charlie Fish is a popular short-story writer and screenwriter. His stories have been published in several countries and inspired dozens of short film adaptations. Since 1996, he has edited www.fictionontheweb.co.uk, the longest-running short-story site on the Web. He was born in Mount Kisco, New York in 1980, and now lives in South London with his wife and daughters. "The Cut" is the third of his stories to appear in *The Mechanics' Institute Review*.

Gilli Fryzer is a current creative writing PhD student at work on a contemporary novel with some good old-fashioned spells and curses stirred in. Gilli only started writing fiction in 2012 when she stumbled across the MA Creative Writing course at Birkbeck while studying something completely different. Since then, her short stories and poetry have been published by *The Mechanics' Institute Review* Issue 12, *EarthLines*, the Word Factory, and *Litro*, as well as performed live at various venues. Her short story "The Basket Weaver's Tale" was one of the prize-winners in the 2015 Word Factory/Neil Gaiman competition to write a modern fable.

Ellen Hardy is a student on the Birkbeck MA Creative Writing 2016/18. As an editor at *Time Out* she lived and worked in London, Paris and Beirut, and her journalism and reviews have been published in *New York Magazine*, the *Sunday Times*, *Delayed Gratification*, *Fire & Knives*, *Brownbook* and others. She is currently based in Oxfordshire, working as a digital-content strategist communicating sustainable agriculture research to farmers. Her main work in progress is a historical novel retelling the story of a little-known seventeenth-century suicide.

Tom Heaton is a writer and videogame designer. His stories have appeared or are forthcoming in *Ambit*, *Cōnfingō* and *Dream Catcher* and have been performed at Liars' League events. He is working on his first novel.

Sarah Hegarty studied Mandarin at Leeds University and worked as a journalist before taking an MA in creative writing at Chichester University. Her short fiction has been published by Cinnamon Press, *Mslexia*, *Hysteria 2*, the *Momaya Annual Review*,

Bridge House and online. Her first novel, *The Ash Zone*, won the 2011 Yeovil Literary Prize. She is working on her second novel, *Under a Different Sky*, which won the 2014 Yeovil Literary Prize and was shortlisted for the inaugural Bridport First Novel Award. Follow her on Twitter @SarahHegarty1 www.sarahhegarty.co.uk.

Jo Holloway is from Hertfordshire. She moved to London when she was eighteen, where she studied history at Queen Mary University of London. Jo went on to become a history teacher in Camden, Tower Hamlets and, currently, Newham. She is also a copywriter of educational resources. She has just completed the MA in creative writing at Birkbeck. Her short story "The Night Shift" was published on MIROnline in 2016 and she is now working on her first novel.

Stephanie Hutton is a writer and clinical psychologist in Staffordshire, UK. Her short-form work has been published online and in print. She has been placed in competitions including National Flash-Fiction Day, shortlisted for the Brighton Prize for flash fiction, and was highly commended in the InkTears Short Story Contest. Stephanie was selected for the Writing West Midlands 2017/18 Room 204 Writer Development Programme for emerging writers.

Ruth Ivo is a writer from North-West London. With a background in performance, she has worked at various times as a cabaret artist, blues singer and scarer of children on a Blackpool ghost train. She is also a creative producer and director working across a wide range of disciplines. She lives in Brixton and is currently studying for an MA in creative writing at Birkbeck.

Grace Jacobson lives in Tulse Hill with her three children. "Take Me Out Tonight" is her first published short story, although she's written features for *The Times* and the *Guardian*. Right now, she's exploring female desire, motherhood, sexuality, the tyranny of masculinity, addiction and obsession through her work. She'd love to spend an evening with the photographer Nan Goldin.

Keith Jarrett lives and works in London. Poet and fiction writer, he is a former London and UK Poetry Slam champion and has performed at the World Cup Poetry Slam, the Rio International Poetry Slam, and festivals in Warsaw and Bilbao. His debut poetry pamphlet, *Selah* (Burning Eye Books), was released in 2017, and his short stories have been published in *The Mechanics' Institute Review* Issue 5, *Tell Tales* Volume 4 and *Boys & Girls*. His monologue *Safest Spot in Town* was performed at the Old Vic and broadcast on BBC Four as part of its *Queers* series in the summer of 2017. Keith is working on his first novel – partly in verse – which seems to be about a boy with a God complex on the run from the influence of a Pentecostal church.

Elinor Johns was born in South Wales. She was a teacher for twenty years, reaching dizzy heights of responsibility as Head of Sixth Form, until giving it up to spend more time out running with her dog. She has read her work at the Literary Kitchen Festival, BBK Writers Room and MIRLive, and has had non-fiction published on MIROnline. Elinor has just finished the MA in creative writing at Birkbeck, and lives in Hertfordshire with her family.

Amy J. Kirkwood writes primarily young adult fiction and is represented by Charlotte Maddox at Tibor Jones, where she is part of the Young Adult Studio. She is currently editing the manuscript for her first novel, *Blazers*, which received a special commendation in the 2017 Pageturner Prize. She has also recently been shortlisted for The Short Story's quarterly Flash Fiction competition and was longlisted for the 2016 Bath Short Story Award. Amy graduated with Distinction from her MA in creative writing at Birkbeck in 2016. She lives in London and can be found on twitter at @amyjkirkwood.

Kev Pick hails from the North East where he grew up reading a lot of horror fiction and watching terrible movies on VHS. He enjoyed a career as a writer and producer for radio, magazines and film, even winning a few industry awards. He spent some time as a musician and a painter, but has now returned to his first love of writing and dedicated himself to fiction. Kev currently lives in Brighton and is working on a novel.

Anna Pook is from South London. From 2009 to 2014, she was the resident creative writing instructor at the Paris bookshop Shakespeare and Company. She received an MA in prose fiction from the University of East Anglia, where she was the 2014/15 recipient of the Man Booker Scholarship. She is working on her debut novel.

Reshma Ruia is the author of *Something Black in the Lentil Soup* (BlackAmber Books, 2003), described in the *Sunday Times* as "a gem of straight-faced comedy". Her second novel, *A Mouthful of Silence*, was shortlisted for the 2014 SI Leeds Literary Prize for unpublished manuscripts by Black and Asian female writers. Her short stories and poetry have appeared in various international anthologies and magazines and also commissioned for Radio 4. She is the co-founder of The Whole Kahani, a collective of British writers of South Asian origin. Born in India, but brought up in Italy, Reshma's narrative portrays the inherent preoccupations of those who possess multiple senses of belonging.

Leila Segal was born in London, of Polish, Lithuanian and Romanian descent. Her debut short-story collection, *Breathe: Stories from Cuba* (lubin & kleyner, 2016), was funded by Arts Council England, and originates in the time she spent living in Havana and Cuba's rural far west. Her stories have been published in anthologies and journals including *Wasafiri*, *Generations Literary Journal*, *The London Magazine*, *Papeles de la Mancuspia*, *Litro*, *The Lonely Crowd*, and *Ink, Sweat & Tears*. Leila trained as a barrister before going on to work as a legal editor and journalist for several years, and since then has used writing and photography in community advocacy projects, such as Change The Picture (2007), the Jaffa Photography Project (2008), and Voice of Freedom (2010 to the present).

Sogol Sur was born in 1988 in Tehran. She is a London-based performance poet and the author of the poetry collection *Sorrows of the Sun*. Both her creative and academic writing explore themes of queerness and hybridity. She is now undertaking her doctorate in creative writing at Birkbeck, University of London, whilst finishing her first collection of short stories.

Touted in the *Independent* as "a name to watch", **Gemma Weekes** is critically acclaimed author of *Love Me* (Chatto & Windus). Her poetry and fiction have appeared in several anthologies and literary journals including *IC3: The Penguin Book of New Black Writing in Britain* and *Kin* by Serpent's Tail. Passionate about the possibilities of interdisciplinary work, she is also an established performance/spoken-word artist and musicmaker who has performed nationally and internationally. She is currently working on a live literature/art piece entitled *Who Murked Basquiat* with accompanying chapbook/EP, her second novel, and raising her witty and wise tween-aged son.

Bridget Westaway lives in Lewes, East Sussex. She has worked as a teacher of English as a foreign language and English for speakers of other languages. She has a UEA *Guardian* diploma in creative writing and continues to meet regularly with the writing group that formed out of the course. She is currently working on a novel.

Katie Winfield is a writer based in London. Having grown up in a coastal town in South Wales, she went on to study English literature at Oxford University. Recently, while teaching English in a London academy, she completed the Master's in creative writing at Birkbeck and has since won the Literary Kitchen Festival flash fiction competition and been shortlisted for the Bridport Prize. She is currently working on her first novel.

James Wise has been writing most of his life, with poems published in local Oxford anthologies *Hidden Treasures* and *Island City*, alongside Tom Paulin, Paul Muldoon and Helen Kidd. He has a BA in English and publishing from Oxford Brookes, and an MA in creative writing from Birkbeck. James has performed at Hackney's popular There Goes the Neighbourhood spoken-word event, was an editor for Issue 13 of *The Mechanics' Institute Review*, and his story "A Jailor" was published by MIROnline in 2016.